Stitching a New Tomorrow

Colleen Marshall

Published by Colleen Marshall, 2024.

This is a work of fiction. Similarities to real people, places, or events are entirely coincidental.

STITCHING A NEW TOMORROW

First edition. October 5, 2024.

Copyright © 2024 Colleen Marshall.

ISBN: 979-8227021410

Written by Colleen Marshall.

Chapter 1: The Fabric of My Dreams

The hum of the sewing machine fills the room, a rhythmic melody that resonates within the chaotic tapestry of my thoughts. I stand amidst a riot of colors, bolts of fabric cascading around me like a vibrant waterfall frozen in time. The walls are lined with shelves brimming with spools of thread in every hue imaginable, the stark whites and brilliant reds whispering secrets of potential and possibility. It's here, in my aunt's petite boutique, nestled in the heart of Rivertown, that I've crafted a sanctuary—a refuge from the relentless waves of self-doubt that crash against the shores of my ambition.

My fingers glide over the soft cotton, the texture an invitation to create, to express the visions swirling in my mind. Each thread, each seam holds a fragment of my aspirations, but I grapple with the gnawing fear that my creations might never see the light of day beyond this cramped sanctuary. I can almost hear my mother's voice echoing in my mind, her gentle admonitions reminding me that dreams are only as strong as the courage to pursue them. But courage feels like an elusive phantom, tantalizingly close yet just beyond my grasp.

"Hey, do you think you could help me with these?" Emma's voice slices through my reverie, rich with the vibrant energy that draws people in like moths to a flame. She stands at the entrance, arms piled high with fabric swatches, her wild curls bouncing with each movement. I can't help but smile; her enthusiasm is infectious, a balm to my frayed nerves.

"Sure! What are you working on?" I ask, my curiosity piqued as I watch her navigate the sea of textiles. Emma has always been my creative counterpart, a relentless dreamer who effortlessly weaves her imagination into everything she touches.

"I'm trying to put together something that screams 'fun summer picnic,'" she explains, spreading the swatches across the worktable, where sunlight spills through the window like liquid gold. "I was thinking a mix of pastels and florals, maybe with some ruffles?"

I nod, already envisioning the final look in my mind. "Ruffles would be perfect," I reply, my heart swelling with excitement. "They'll add a playful touch. Maybe we could use the mint green for the base and add the lavender floral pattern as an overlay?"

As we dive into the project, the air thickens with creativity, each decision layered with laughter and shared visions. For those fleeting moments, my anxieties dissolve, leaving only the joy of creation. The sun dances on the fabric, casting patterns of light that flicker like dreams waiting to be realized. Emma's laughter mingles with the hum of the sewing machine, creating a symphony of friendship and artistry.

But as the afternoon sun sinks lower, casting long shadows in the room, the specter of the Rivertown Fashion Gala looms in the back of my mind like a storm cloud on the horizon. Emma is convinced I should present my designs, to step into the spotlight I've so carefully avoided. The idea sends chills racing down my spine. What if my work is met with disinterest? What if I pour my heart into the fabric only to have it met with cold, judgmental stares?

"Come on, Mia," Emma nudges, her voice teasing yet earnest. "You have to do it! This is your moment! Just think—your designs could be on display for everyone to see! You'll finally show them what you're made of!"

I bite my lip, my heart thumping against my ribs like a caged bird. "I don't know, Em. What if they don't like it? What if I fail?"

"Failure is just a stepping stone," she replies, her eyes sparkling with determination. "Besides, what's the worst that could happen? You get a little critique? You'll learn and come back even stronger! Plus, I'll be right there with you!"

Her unwavering support is both a comfort and a pressure, igniting a fire within me that fights against the overwhelming waves of doubt. In that moment, I can almost envision my creations taking center stage, shimmering under the bright lights, the audience captivated by the stories I've woven into each piece. The thought is exhilarating, yet terrifying, a double-edged sword that threatens to slice through the fabric of my self-assurance.

As the days slip away, the pressure mounts. I can feel it in the way my heart races at night, in the restless dreams that flit through my mind—visions of runways and applause, of shadows morphing into critics lurking just out of sight. With each stitch I complete, I wrestle with the duality of hope and despair, crafting garments that feel like extensions of my very soul. Yet, with every thread that passes through my fingers, I can't shake the feeling that I'm weaving my own downfall.

Emma, ever the optimist, pushes me to embrace my fears, urging me to step outside the narrow confines of my self-doubt. "You can't let fear dictate your life, Mia," she insists, her voice steady as she helps me pin a dress for the gala. "You have a talent that deserves to be seen. Just think of all the people who will be inspired by your work!"

Her words echo in my mind, a gentle nudge urging me toward the precipice of possibility. And yet, as the day of the gala approaches, a part of me clings to the safety of the known, the warm embrace of my aunt's boutique, where dreams feel tangible yet safely tucked away. The battle between fear and ambition rages on, a relentless storm brewing within as I grapple with the fragility of my dreams.

In the quiet moments, I find solace in the threads, each one a lifeline to the hope that perhaps, just perhaps, I am capable of more than I've ever dared to believe. The fabric begins to take shape, but so too does my resolve. With each stitch, I am slowly piecing together not just a collection, but the courage to show the world who I truly am.

The day of the Rivertown Fashion Gala dawns, cloaked in a veil of anticipation and self-doubt. I wake to the soft chirping of birds outside my window, their cheerful melodies contrasting sharply with the tempest swirling within me. Sunlight spills into my room, illuminating the chaos of my designs strewn across every surface—a riot of colors, textures, and aspirations waiting to be transformed into something magical. My heart races as I take in the sight of it all, each piece a fragile promise, each garment a step toward the unknown.

I dress carefully, the fabric of my chosen outfit—a flowing, ivory dress dotted with delicate embroidered flowers—feeling like a second skin. As I pull the garment over my head, it cradles me with its familiar comfort, wrapping me in the illusion of confidence. I style my hair into loose waves, each strand cascading down my shoulders like a waterfall of hope, and dab on a hint of lavender perfume, a scent that makes me feel as though I could conquer the world, or at least the gala.

Emma arrives, her exuberance bursting through the door like the summer sun. "You look stunning!" she exclaims, eyes wide with admiration. Her outfit—a bold, cherry-red dress that hugs her figure—matches the fire of her personality, igniting a spark of excitement in me. We embrace, the warmth of her enthusiasm grounding me amidst the swirling uncertainties.

"Are you ready for this?" she asks, her voice tinged with both excitement and a hint of nervousness. I nod, though my stomach twists in knots. It's the moment of truth—the culmination of countless hours spent toiling over fabric and thread, each piece a reflection of my innermost self.

We make our way to the venue, the air thick with the scent of freshly cut flowers and the distant sound of laughter echoing from within the grand hall. As we step inside, I am enveloped in a kaleidoscope of colors, the atmosphere electric with energy. Elegant chandeliers hang overhead, casting a warm glow that dances across the sea of well-dressed attendees milling about. The laughter and chatter of excited voices create a symphony of social connection, while I stand on the periphery, a tiny island in a vast ocean.

Emma drags me deeper into the crowd, her confidence like a lifeline. "Come on! Let's find our spot," she encourages, weaving through clusters of people who are absorbed in conversation, their faces radiant with the thrill of the evening. I try to absorb the vibrant ambiance—the elaborate table settings adorned with glimmering candles and exquisite floral arrangements—but my focus keeps drifting back to the deepening pit of anxiety in my stomach.

"Do you see it?" Emma nudges me, pointing toward a raised platform where a makeshift runway stretches across the room, adorned with lights that twinkle like stars. "That's where your designs will shine!"

The sight sends a wave of dread washing over me. "What if they don't like it? What if I'm just... not enough?" I murmur, my voice barely rising above the laughter that envelops us.

"Mia," Emma says, her tone serious now, "this is your chance to show everyone who you are. You're more than enough. You're brilliant." Her unwavering belief in me, like a beacon in the dark, stirs something deep within, urging me to rise above the fears that have kept me bound in a cocoon of uncertainty.

With a deep breath, I steal a glance around the room, letting my eyes wander over the sea of faces. Some are familiar, others strangers, all absorbed in their own moments of anticipation and joy. The air crackles with possibility, and as I draw in the scents of perfume mingling with the delicate aroma of hors d'oeuvres being served, I can almost taste the sweetness of dreams waiting to be realized.

"Look!" Emma gestures toward a familiar figure across the room. My heart skips a beat as I spot Miss Margaret, the local fashionista and the gala's esteemed judge. Clad in a sleek black gown, her presence commands attention. The very woman whose opinions could either elevate my dreams to dizzying heights or cast them into the abyss. I swallow hard, the weight of her gaze feeling like an impending storm.

"Just focus on your creations," Emma reassures me, squeezing my hand tightly. "We're here to celebrate you, not just survive the night."

Before I can respond, the gala's host steps onto the platform, his voice cutting through the cacophony with a warmth that feels inviting. "Welcome, everyone, to the Rivertown Fashion Gala! Tonight, we celebrate not only the art of fashion but the dreams that fuel it."

I glance at Emma, our eyes wide, both feeling the pulse of excitement throbbing through the crowd. The lights dim, and a hush falls over the room, creating an intimate cocoon around us. The first model steps onto the runway, draped in a flowing gown that billows like clouds, evoking gasps of admiration. My breath catches as I watch each design come to life, fabric transformed into art that whispers stories of passion and perseverance.

As the show unfolds, I am transported into a world of vibrant hues and intricate designs, each piece an expression of the designer's heart and soul. A part of me yearns to leap onto that stage, to showcase my creations, while another part quakes with fear. I steal glances at Emma, who watches with rapt attention, her eyes glimmering with hope and pride. She whispers encouraging words, but the thunderous applause that erupts after each model leaves me wondering if my voice could ever be heard in such a vibrant chorus.

And then it happens—the moment I've been both dreading and longing for. The host announces, "And now, we present the local talent—the designs of Mia Harrington!"

Time seems to freeze as my heart races, a million thoughts cascading through my mind like a rushing river. Emma gives my hand a squeeze, her smile reassuring, but the weight of expectation presses down on me. I feel like a tightrope walker, balancing precariously between fear and ambition. My name rings out in the air, and I can't shake the feeling that I'm standing on the edge of a precipice, ready to leap into the unknown.

Taking a deep breath, I step toward the platform, the fabric of my dreams billowing behind me. Each step feels like a small rebellion against the doubt that has held me captive for far too long. The lights shine bright, illuminating my creations, and for the first time, I don't just see fabric—I see potential. With every heartbeat, I embrace the risk, the vulnerability, and in that fleeting moment, I choose to believe that my dreams are worth the leap.

The stage beckons like a siren, calling to me with promises of dreams realized and fears confronted. As I step onto the runway, the light washes over me, illuminating the delicate details of my creations that I had poured my heart into over sleepless nights. The fabric feels alive under the spotlight, shimmering with the stories of resilience and creativity stitched into every seam. A rush of exhilaration mingles with an undercurrent of apprehension, setting my nerves aflame as I glance out into the crowd, their faces a blur of anticipation and intrigue.

My first model, a young woman with an air of confidence, strides down the runway in a dress crafted from layers of soft, flowing silk. The fabric glides with her movements, catching the light like liquid silver. As she twirls, the audience erupts in applause, the sound reverberating through my chest like a heartbeat echoing back my own hopes and dreams. My creations dance before me, breathing life into the fantasies I once harbored in solitude.

With each model that steps onto the platform, I feel my fears dissipating, replaced by an overwhelming sense of belonging. The applause becomes a symphony, an affirmation that my designs resonate with others, echoing the very dreams I struggled to articulate. The vibrant colors and intricate patterns speak of summer picnics, garden soirées, and whispered secrets under starlit skies, each piece an invitation to step into a story.

Then, it's my turn. The moment arrives with a tidal wave of emotion crashing over me, nearly drowning me in a sea of anticipation. As I watch the model walk forward, draped in a delicate, pastel gown adorned with hand-stitched flowers, my breath catches in my throat. The fabric sways with an ethereal grace, capturing the very essence of my vision—a celebration of femininity and strength.

The crowd leans in, captivated, and I can feel their energy intertwining with my own. The soft gasps, the murmurs of approval, the gentle applause; it's all a melody that fuels my spirit. I step forward, my heart pounding in sync with the rhythmic beats of the music filling the room. My fingers brush against the hem of the gown as the model turns to showcase the intricate details that adorn the back, and in that moment, I am overcome with pride. Each stitch, each floral embroidery tells the world that I am here—not just as a designer, but as a storyteller eager to share my tales.

As the final model strides down the runway in a bold, statement piece that challenges conventionality—a dress with asymmetrical cuts and unexpected bursts of color—I see Miss Margaret nodding approvingly from her seat. My heart flutters, and the realization that my work might actually resonate with someone as discerning as her sends a rush of adrenaline coursing through me.

When the final applause erupts, a crescendo that sweeps through the room like a summer storm, I find myself grinning from ear to ear. I take a step back, allowing the moment to wash over me, savoring the thrill of exposure, of vulnerability laid bare. Emma joins me at the edge of the stage, her eyes shining with pride, her cheeks flushed from excitement.

"You did it! You were incredible!" she squeals, pulling me into a jubilant embrace that nearly topples us both. The weight of fear that once clung to my shoulders lifts, replaced by an intoxicating sense of possibility. The dreams I had tucked away, like delicate treasures hidden in the corners of my mind, suddenly feel within reach, no longer reserved for fantasies but instead ready to be woven into reality.

As I step off the stage, a whirlwind of emotions swirls within me. The crowd buzzes with excitement, conversations igniting around me like fireflies in the night. I'm engulfed in a torrent of praise from familiar faces and strangers alike, each word a tiny affirmation that I belong here, in this vibrant world of fashion and creativity. But amidst the excitement, I can't shake the thrill of uncertainty that hangs in the air like the scent of cotton candy—a reminder that every dream comes with its share of risks.

"Let's celebrate!" Emma declares, her enthusiasm infectious as she pulls me toward the refreshment table laden with delectable hors d'oeuvres and sparkling drinks. The atmosphere buzzes with chatter, laughter, and the clinking of glasses as people toast to one another's successes. I feel a sense of belonging wash over me, the camaraderie of creative souls mingling in this vibrant space.

As I sip on a sparkling lemonade garnished with fresh mint, I catch a glimpse of Miss Margaret across the room, her sharp gaze scanning the crowd. My heart races with both excitement and apprehension. I had imagined this moment countless times—what it would be like to connect with someone whose opinion could shape my career. Gathering my courage, I weave through the crowd, each step feeling heavier with anticipation.

"Miss Margaret," I finally manage to say, my voice steady despite the whirlwind of nerves dancing in my stomach. She turns to me, a knowing smile playing on her lips.

"Mia Harrington," she acknowledges, her tone warm yet authoritative. "Your collection was refreshing. You have a unique voice."

"Thank you," I reply, feeling my cheeks flush with a mix of pride and disbelief. "I've always dreamed of sharing my designs, and tonight felt like... well, a dream come true."

She studies me for a moment, her expression thoughtful. "Dreams are important, but don't forget to cultivate them with action. You've shown talent tonight, but true artistry requires persistence."

Her words linger in the air, a gentle challenge wrapped in encouragement. I nod, taking in her advice like a precious gem.

As the evening progresses, I find myself swept into conversations that sparkle with inspiration and ideas. Designers share their stories, their struggles, and triumphs, weaving a tapestry of dreams that resonates with my own. Each exchange feels like a thread added to my journey, creating connections that promise to blossom into something beautiful.

Amidst the revelry, I glance back at the stage, now empty but still pulsing with the energy of the show. In that moment, I realize that the gala is just the beginning. The world of fashion is vast, filled with myriad opportunities waiting to be explored. And though the fear of failure still lingers at the edges of my consciousness, it no longer holds the same power over me.

With a heart full of hope and determination, I resolve to embrace the unknown. I will chase my dreams not just through fabric and thread but through each experience that comes my way. The road ahead may be fraught with challenges, but with every stitch, every creation, I am carving a path toward the life I envision—a life bursting with creativity, resilience, and unabashed passion.

As I laugh with Emma, our spirits buoyed by the celebration, I know that this night will forever mark a turning point in my journey. The fabric of my dreams has begun to unfurl, woven intricately into the tapestry of my life, and I'm ready to step boldly into whatever comes next.

Chapter 2: A Twisted Thread

The grandeur of the Rivertown Fashion Gala unfolded before me like a dream caught in the shimmering haze of chandelier crystals, each light flickering like a heartbeat in the pulsating atmosphere. As I stepped into the expansive hall, the scent of polished wood and fresh blooms wrapped around me like an embrace. My fingertips tingled with anticipation, a silent promise that this evening would be the culmination of sleepless nights spent stitching fabric and sketching dreams onto paper.

I paused for a moment to soak it all in—the intoxicating blend of excitement and anxiety swirling within me. The walls were draped in deep emerald satin, complementing the gleaming silver accents that reflected the laughter and chatter of elegantly dressed guests. Each corner of the hall burst with life, adorned with artfully arranged bouquets of peonies and dahlias, their vibrant hues illuminating the otherwise muted palette of the evening.

The sound of heels clicking against the marble floor created a rhythm that matched the thrumming of my heart, a symphony of glamour and ambition. As I maneuvered through clusters of designers and socialites, my mind danced between the intoxicating energy of the gala and the anxious flutter of my nerves. I found my designated display area, a modest space compared to the grandiose showcases of the established designers surrounding me. My collection—a blend of bold patterns and soft fabrics—represented everything I aspired to be: vibrant, daring, and unapologetically myself.

I meticulously arranged my designs, each piece a labor of love that echoed the late nights spent in my cramped apartment, the sound of my sewing machine humming a lullaby as I poured my heart into every stitch. My eyes gleamed with pride as I adjusted the final dress, a kaleidoscope of colors that seemed to sing against the backdrop of the gala's more muted tones. With each twirl of fabric, I imagined the faces of those who would wear my creations, their laughter mingling with the elegance of the evening.

Just as I stepped back to admire my handiwork, I felt the smooth stem of a wine glass slip through my fingers, the contents a vibrant crimson that spread like wildfire across the pristine white tablecloth of a nearby designer's display. Time slowed as I watched the red liquid bloom in all its disastrous glory, splattering against the carefully curated pieces, their elegance now marred by my clumsiness.

Mortified, I turned to the nearby designer, my heart sinking as I registered the sharp glare directed my way. It belonged to Blake Hart, the head designer of Hart & Co., his reputation a well-known force in the fashion industry, a tempest of creativity wrapped in an undeniably arrogant charm. His piercing blue eyes met mine, a storm swirling within them, and for a fleeting moment, the chaos of the gala faded into the background.

"I'm so sorry," I stammered, rushing to the display to grab napkins, my cheeks burning with embarrassment. The air around us crackled, charged with an intensity that felt both electrifying and terrifying. As I frantically dabbed at the stain, I could feel Blake's presence looming close, an enigmatic force that demanded attention. "I didn't mean to—"

His curt apology cut through my flurry of words, his tone cool and measured, yet laced with an undeniable sharpness. "It happens," he replied, his gaze unwavering as he assessed the damage. Beneath his polished exterior, I sensed a current of intrigue, as if he found my predicament amusing rather than infuriating.

I tried to focus on the task at hand, my fingers trembling as I attempted to mitigate the damage. But the heat of his stare ignited a flutter of something I couldn't quite define—a challenge wrapped in curiosity that stirred within me, urging me to rise above my embarrassment. "I really am sorry. This isn't exactly how I envisioned my evening," I admitted, glancing up to meet his gaze.

He chuckled softly, the sound warm against the backdrop of the gala's clamor, and for a moment, the tension between us morphed into an unspoken understanding. "Neither did I, but perhaps it's a sign of the unpredictability this industry thrives on." His voice was smooth, like honey poured over velvet, and I found myself captivated despite my initial trepidation.

Just as the words hung in the air, the chaos around us swirled on, laughter echoing off the walls, a celebration of dreams and aspirations. I stood, wine-soaked napkin in hand, desperately searching for the right thing to say, some clever retort that might balance the scales of embarrassment with a sliver of charm. But as I watched Blake, the king of this glittering realm, I felt small and insignificant, a mere whisper in a symphony of voices.

"Maybe you should take a lesson from this moment," he continued, a teasing glint in his eye. "Life's imperfections are often more interesting than the polished façade we put on display." His words, laden with wisdom, resonated deep within me, challenging the very foundation of my aspirations.

It was as if the air between us thickened, a taut string ready to snap, and I realized then that this wasn't just about spilled wine and stained cloth. It was about seizing the moment, about the audacity to embrace the unexpected twists that life threw our way. My heart raced, fueled not only by embarrassment but by the thrill of standing before someone who might just see me beyond my creations, someone who might challenge me to be more than I ever thought possible.

As I caught his gaze again, I felt a spark—a tiny flame igniting in the depths of my being, whispering secrets of ambition and dreams yet to be realized. In that crowded hall, amidst the cacophony of laughter and chatter, I stood on the precipice of something both thrilling and terrifying, a thread of destiny weaving itself between us, binding our fates in a way I could hardly comprehend.

The murmur of voices and the soft clinking of glasses surrounded me like a warm blanket, but my heart continued to race, caught in the exhilarating chaos of the gala. I felt as though I were floating, suspended between embarrassment and something that felt dangerously close to exhilaration. The vibrant colors of my designs swirled around me, each fabric an echo of my determination, yet my thoughts kept returning to Blake Hart—his presence felt like a gravitational pull, drawing my attention against all reason.

As I hurriedly dabbed at the wine-stained tablecloth, I could sense the subtle tension between us. His gaze lingered, a mix of amusement and something deeper that flickered in those piercing blue depths. It was unsettling yet thrilling, like standing on the edge of a high dive, heart pounding as I stared into the depths below. "You know," he said, tilting his head slightly as he studied my efforts, "sometimes the best designs emerge from chaos. A little bit of mess can spark the most creative ideas."

I paused, the cloth in my hands becoming momentarily weightless as I absorbed his words. Could he be serious? The thought of transforming this blunder into something artistic felt almost ridiculous. "You might be right," I replied, attempting to inject a hint of humor into my voice, "but I'd prefer my artistry without the risk of a stain becoming a permanent fixture in the fashion world."

Blake chuckled softly, the sound rich and inviting, enveloping me in an unexpected warmth. "Every designer has a horror story to tell. Consider this your initiation." His smirk held an edge, one that dared me to embrace the moment rather than shy away from it. Perhaps I could salvage this evening, turn it into an opportunity to make a name for myself—not just as another fledgling designer but as someone bold enough to rise above her mistakes.

With a newfound resolve, I straightened my posture, allowing the remnants of my embarrassment to melt away like the last rays of sun at dusk. "Challenge accepted," I declared, an unexpected grin spreading across my face as I met his gaze head-on. I grabbed the last few napkins and hastily mopped up the remaining traces of wine. I could feel his eyes upon me, an intensity that made my skin tingle and my heart quicken.

"Now that's the spirit," he said, a spark of interest flickering in his expression. "Let's see what you're really made of." I felt my cheeks flush, a mix of gratitude and something more intoxicating. There was an undeniable chemistry crackling between us, a mutual recognition of ambition and vulnerability layered beneath the surface.

As I gathered my composure, I couldn't help but notice the vibrant array of people around us—each one dressed to the nines, their outfits a kaleidoscope of textures and hues. A stunning woman in a form-fitting emerald gown strutted past, her smile dazzling, but it was the artistry behind her ensemble that truly captivated me. The interplay of silk and lace was both daring and delicate, a balance I longed to achieve in my own designs.

"Are you ready to unveil your collection?" Blake asked, drawing me from my thoughts. The warmth of his presence steadied my fluttering heart. I nodded, glancing toward my display, where my creations stood proudly, colors singing against the backdrop of the gala's opulence. "Then let's get you some attention," he said, his confidence infectious as he gestured toward the crowd.

Before I could voice my doubts, he took my hand, leading me through the throngs of stylish attendees. His grip was firm, reassuring, as though he believed in me more than I did. As we approached a group of well-known fashion influencers, I could feel the weight of their gazes, appraising me with the keen eyes of those who had seen it all.

"Ladies and gentlemen," Blake announced, a flourish of charm accompanying his words. "I'd like to introduce you to an emerging talent in our midst. This is Ava James, and her collection embodies everything we love about innovation in fashion." I stood frozen, disbelief mingling with the thrill of being recognized. Their attention felt like a spotlight, illuminating my insecurities while simultaneously urging me to step forward.

"Let me show you what she's created," he continued, effortlessly guiding the conversation as if it were an art form in itself. As I shared the inspiration behind my collection—a fusion of urban grit and ethereal elegance—Blake's presence bolstered my confidence, his subtle nods encouraging me to lean into my passion.

The attendees leaned in, their expressions shifting from polite interest to genuine intrigue. I recounted the nights spent in my tiny apartment, sketching by the light of a single bulb, my dreams weaving into the fabric of my reality. I spoke of the vibrant streets of Rivertown, how the murals and graffiti had inspired bold colors and daring patterns in my designs. My words flowed freely, each one carrying the weight of my hopes and dreams, no longer restrained by the fear of failure.

"Fascinating!" exclaimed a chic woman adorned in a cascading gown of silver sequins. "You really capture the essence of the city in your work." Her words were a balm to my anxious spirit, igniting a fire within me that I hadn't realized existed.

Blake's gaze held mine, a silent connection forming between us, one that spoke of uncharted territories and ambitions yet to be fulfilled. It was exhilarating to stand on the precipice of something larger than myself, to know that in this moment, I was more than just the girl who spilled wine. I was a designer, an artist, a creator.

As the night unfolded, I found myself mingling more freely, buoyed by the positive feedback and Blake's unwavering support. The laughter and chatter flowed like a river, and the once-daunting atmosphere transformed into an intoxicating blend of camaraderie and creative possibility. With each passing moment, I felt the boundaries of my former self begin to dissolve, revealing a more vibrant version of who I was meant to be.

And through it all, Blake remained a constant presence, his piercing blue eyes always finding mine, a shared spark of ambition igniting in the space between us. The gala had morphed into a dance of aspirations and dreams, and with every step I took, I began to envision a future woven from the threads of this very night—one marked by challenges, yes, but also by triumphs and the intoxicating promise of what lay ahead.

The evening unfolded like a tightly woven tapestry, each thread shimmering with possibility and adventure. As the laughter and lively chatter enveloped me, I felt the intoxicating rush of the crowd, drawing me into their world—a world where dreams and designs collided, creating something spectacular. With Blake by my side, I ventured deeper into the gala, the vibrant energy sparking new ideas that danced in the recesses of my mind like playful wisps of smoke.

As we navigated the throng of socialites and industry veterans, I couldn't help but steal glances at Blake. His effortless charm was captivating, a magnetic force that drew people to him, yet his piercing gaze lingered on me in a way that made my heart stutter. He exuded confidence, dressed in a tailored suit that accentuated his tall, athletic frame, the fabric gleaming under the twinkling lights. The way he moved—self-assured yet purposeful—made me both anxious and exhilarated, as if I were riding a rollercoaster that spiraled higher with each passing moment.

"Tell me more about your collection," Blake prompted, his voice low and encouraging. We had slipped away from the crowd, the noise fading into a gentle hum as we found a quieter corner adorned with oversized floral arrangements and twinkling fairy lights. I could hear the distant strains of music, a melody that wove itself into the very fabric of the evening, creating a magical atmosphere.

I took a deep breath, summoning my courage. "My collection is inspired by the contrasts of urban life," I began, my hands gesturing animatedly as I spoke. "I wanted to capture the raw energy of the city, the way the mundane can transform into something beautiful. Each piece reflects a different aspect of that duality—hard edges softened by flowing fabrics, vibrant colors set against monochrome backgrounds."

Blake nodded, his eyes focused intently on mine, making me feel as if I were the only person in the room. "That's a fascinating approach," he said, a hint of admiration in his tone. "Fashion is about storytelling, and it seems you have a compelling narrative to share. What's your favorite piece?"

A smile crept onto my face as I thought of my favorite dress, a sweeping creation of deep burgundy and rich gold, inspired by the sunsets I often watched from my apartment balcony. "It's this one," I replied, my enthusiasm bubbling over. "I call it 'Urban Sunset.' It features layers that mimic the changing colors of the sky—starting with dark hues at the bottom, fading into warm golds and reds near the neckline. It's meant to evoke that feeling of hope when day transitions into night."

He leaned closer, his interest palpable. "I'd love to see it. Have you brought it with you?"

"I have!" I exclaimed, my heart racing with excitement. I gestured toward the display, where my designs gleamed under the soft light. "I can show you! Just a moment."

As I made my way back to the display, I felt a swell of pride that almost eclipsed the earlier embarrassment. I retrieved the dress, carefully unwrapping it from its protective covering and allowing it to cascade into view. The fabric caught the light, revealing a play of colors that shimmered like a living canvas.

Blake's expression transformed, his eyes widening with appreciation as he took in the sight. "Wow," he murmured, reaching out to touch the fabric lightly, as if afraid to disturb its beauty. "This is stunning, Ava. You've captured something extraordinary here."

The thrill of his praise sent warmth coursing through me, a validation I had long sought in a world that often felt intimidating and unforgiving. "Thank you," I replied, my voice barely above a whisper, overwhelmed by the unexpected swell of emotion. "It means a lot to hear that from you."

"Don't sell yourself short. You have real talent," he said, his gaze unwavering. "You should be proud of this work. It's not just clothing; it's art."

In that moment, I felt a shift within myself, as if a door I hadn't realized was locked had swung open. Blake's words ignited a flame of determination, stirring a deeper ambition that whispered of greater things yet to come. I realized that this evening was not merely an event; it was an opportunity—an invitation to carve my name into the tapestry of the fashion world.

Just as I was about to express my gratitude, the atmosphere around us shifted. A group of designers, their faces marked with envy and thinly veiled disdain, approached with the kind of confidence that spoke of years spent in the limelight. Among them was Elise Carrington, a rival designer known for her cutting-edge aesthetics and ruthless ambition. She wore a dress that looked like it had been stolen straight from the pages of a high-fashion magazine, its intricate beading sparkling like shards of glass.

"Well, well, if it isn't the fresh talent making waves," Elise drawled, her voice dripping with sarcasm. "What a lovely display you have here, Ava. Quite brave of you to showcase such... unconventional choices."

I could feel the tension rising like steam from a boiling pot. "Thanks," I replied, forcing a smile as I felt Blake's presence beside me, a steady anchor amidst the tempest.

Elise's gaze flicked to Blake, and the corners of her lips turned up slightly, a predatory glint flashing in her eyes. "Blake, darling, I see you've taken a shine to the new girl. Are you trying to elevate her into the limelight, or are you merely enjoying the novelty?"

I held my breath, the air thick with anticipation. The implications of her words hung heavily in the air, weaving a web of unspoken rivalry.

"Maybe both," Blake replied smoothly, his tone unwavering as he stepped slightly closer to me, shielding me from Elise's condescension. "Ava has talent that deserves recognition, unlike some who rely solely on their reputation."

The spark of admiration ignited into a flame, filling me with a mix of gratitude and unexpected courage. It was as if he was not just defending my work but also asserting my place in this world—my right to belong among the titans of fashion.

Elise's smile faltered momentarily, and I seized the moment to speak. "Fashion is about evolution," I said, my voice steadying. "It's about daring to be different and embracing that uniqueness. If that makes me unconventional, then I wear that label proudly."

A collective gasp echoed around us, and for an instant, the cacophony of the gala faded into the background. My heart pounded in my chest, emboldened by the surprising swell of confidence surging through me. I stood tall, feeling the energy shift as the crowd acknowledged my words, a mix of surprise and respect glimmering in their eyes.

Elise opened her mouth, perhaps to retort, but Blake interjected smoothly, "It seems we're all here to celebrate creativity and passion, aren't we? Let's keep the spirit of the evening alive." He turned to me, a playful grin breaking across his features. "How about we showcase that remarkable dress of yours on the runway?"

The suggestion hung in the air, thick with excitement and trepidation. A runway show? My heart raced, the weight of his words igniting a cascade of emotions—thrill, anxiety, and a fierce determination to seize this moment.

"Are you serious?" I stammered, barely able to wrap my head around the opportunity presented.

"Absolutely," Blake replied, his gaze unwavering, a light of mischief dancing in his blue eyes. "If anyone deserves a chance to shine tonight, it's you."

As the gala continued to buzz with life, I felt a rush of clarity surge through me, the moment crystallizing into something significant. I was ready to embrace this whirlwind, to step into the light and show the world the essence of who I was. No longer just a girl with dreams caught in the shadows, I was about to become a force to be reckoned with. With Blake by my side and the vibrant energy of the evening propelling me forward, I felt invincible.

The stage was set, not just for my designs but for my story—woven from the threads of ambition, creativity, and resilience. And I was ready to weave it into something extraordinary.

Chapter 3: Stitches and Sparks

The scent of fresh fabric swirled around me like an inviting hug as I entered our weekly sewing meet-up. The room was alive with vibrant colors and soft laughter, a sanctuary crafted from spools of thread and rolls of fabric. Every corner of the space buzzed with creativity, yet I felt like a clumsy butterfly trying to find my way out of a flower-filled garden. My fingers grazed over the bolts of cotton, their textures whispering tales of potential creations yet to be born. Emma, always the beacon of enthusiasm, had already set up her workstation in the far corner, surrounded by a riot of patterns that clashed yet harmonized in their chaos.

"Hey! You made it!" she chirped, her eyes sparkling with that infectious energy I could never quite match.

I nodded, forcing a smile, though my thoughts were miles away—lost in the aura of Blake. Each encounter with him left me a little more breathless and a lot more confused. The confidence he exuded was like a dazzling light that drew me in, yet beneath that surface shimmer lurked shadows I was desperate to understand. He was an enigma wrapped in denim and charm, his laughter echoing in my mind long after he'd walked away.

Emma didn't miss a beat, picking up on my distracted state. "What's going on in that head of yours? You've been quieter than a mouse in a cheese shop."

I sighed, dropping onto the stool beside her. "It's Blake. I just can't shake the feeling that there's something more to him, you know? He has this way of making me feel alive, yet all I can think about are the walls he puts up."

"Maybe you should just ask him about it. Go for it!" she said, her enthusiasm practically radiating from her. "Or, we could crash that Hart & Co. event next week. It could be the perfect opportunity to get to know him better—and learn about the industry while we're at it."

The idea danced on the fringes of my mind, a mix of excitement and dread. Hart & Co. was known for their high-profile events, a confluence of industry veterans and aspirants, a sea of creativity where everyone was either pitching their dreams or showcasing their successes. It could be a chance to dive deeper into the world I adored, yet it was also a plunge into an unknown realm where Blake would likely be surrounded by admirers, his laughter echoing against the walls while I blended into the background.

"What if he doesn't want to see me?" I murmured, tracing the floral print on the fabric in front of me, letting my fingers dance over the petals as if they could lead me to answers.

"Or maybe he's just waiting for you to make a move," Emma suggested, her voice a teasing whisper, "You've got to give him a chance to surprise you."

Her words settled in my mind, a gentle nudge toward something I wasn't quite ready to confront. Yet, as I watched Emma cut her fabric with surgical precision, I felt the stirrings of ambition flickering within me. Maybe it was time to gather my courage, to rip the seams of doubt that held me back and sew new patterns of hope.

As the afternoon wore on, I found myself embroiled in a flurry of creativity, channeling my swirling emotions into the fabric before me. The humming of machines and the soft murmur of conversation created a backdrop that seemed to fuel my fervor. I was stitching not just fabric, but my very essence into each seam, pouring my heart into a vibrant quilt of possibilities.

Yet, even as I found solace in my craft, the thought of Blake lingered like an elusive thread, just out of reach. Would I find the right words? Would he even want to listen? My fingers worked on autopilot, crafting delicate flowers from scraps, each petal a representation of my tangled emotions.

Later, as the sun dipped low, casting a warm, golden hue over the room, Emma clapped her hands together, breaking my reverie. "Okay, let's pack up! We need to come up with a game plan for Hart & Co. before next week."

Her excitement was contagious, a gentle tide pulling me toward the shore of resolve. Maybe this was what I needed—an adventure that could not only lead me closer to Blake but could also deepen my understanding of this world I loved.

As we walked out, the crisp autumn air greeted us, carrying the scent of fallen leaves and woodsmoke. The sunset painted the sky in shades of pink and orange, a kaleidoscope of colors that mirrored the ones I'd seen in the fabric swatches earlier.

Emma turned to me, a mischievous grin on her face. "So, what's the plan? You're going to swoop in and catch him off guard, right? Or are you thinking something more subtle, like an accidental bump into him while holding a tray of hors d'oeuvres?"

I laughed, the tension easing from my shoulders as we strolled down the street, the glow of the town's streetlamps beginning to flicker on. "Maybe a bit of both? Who knows, perhaps I'll reveal my secret weapon: an irresistible charm that just happens to catch him off guard."

"Or you could trip over your own feet," she teased, elbowing me gently.

We shared a laugh, and for the first time since that day at the café, I felt a spark of excitement. Maybe this unexpected detour into the world of fabrics and thread would unravel not just my creations but also the mystery that was Blake. And perhaps, just perhaps, I could weave a story of my own amidst the stitches and sparks of this new chapter.

The week drifted by with an odd mix of anticipation and dread, each day blurring into the next like the soft strokes of a painter's brush on canvas. The looming Hart & Co. event felt like a ship anchored in the harbor of my mind, the thought of it both thrilling and terrifying. I often caught myself staring out the window, watching leaves spiral and tumble from the trees, their descent a reminder that change was inevitable. Change, however, was often accompanied by a tremor of uncertainty. As I sat in my small, sunlit living room surrounded by spools of thread and fabric swatches, I could hear Emma's voice resonating in my head, urging me to seize the day.

"Just think of it as an adventure!" she had said with that dazzling grin. "A chance to learn something new and meet interesting people. Plus, if Blake is there, you'll finally get to know him better!"

But what if I completely flubbed it? What if I stood there like a deer caught in headlights, unable to form coherent thoughts in his presence? The very idea sent butterflies fluttering chaotically in my stomach.

I looked at the small stack of fabric beside me, each piece a vibrant hue—reds, blues, yellows—each one carrying its own story, waiting for me to transform it into something beautiful. The irony wasn't lost on me; I had the tools to create magic, yet I felt utterly paralyzed by the thought of a mere conversation.

In an effort to drown out my anxious thoughts, I threw myself into my work, meticulously cutting and stitching a patchwork quilt that spoke of autumn—rich oranges and browns stitched together to create a landscape of warmth. I allowed the rhythmic sound of my sewing machine to lull me into a creative trance, letting my mind wander through all the "what ifs" of the upcoming event. What if I approached him confidently? What if he smiled at me like he had before? Or worse, what if he didn't remember me at all?

The day of the event arrived, draped in a soft blanket of twilight that whispered of excitement and possibility. I slipped into a deep emerald dress that hugged my curves just right, the color reminiscent of the evergreens that lined the outskirts of town. As I stared at my reflection, I felt a flicker of hope light within me—a reminder that I was not just a bundle of nerves but a woman ready to embrace whatever came next. I swept my hair into a loose bun, letting a few tendrils escape to frame my face, and added a pair of dainty earrings that sparkled under the dim glow of my living room light.

Emma arrived punctually, her enthusiasm spilling over like champagne. "You look stunning! Are you ready to conquer the world?" she beamed, and in that moment, I felt the tides shift in my favor.

"Ready as I'll ever be," I replied, though my heart raced like a runaway train. We hopped into her car, the air inside thick with anticipation and a hint of nervous laughter.

The Hart & Co. event unfolded like a scene from a glamorous movie. The venue was an old, restored warehouse, its industrial charm softened by twinkling fairy lights that crisscrossed overhead, illuminating the eclectic mix of people milling about. I could see established designers, budding creators, and everyone in between, each lost in their worlds of fabric and ambition.

The murmur of conversations swirled around me like the sweet scent of freshly brewed coffee mingling with hints of burnt sugar from a nearby dessert table. Emma tugged me along, her excitement bubbling over as she introduced me to various attendees, each handshake a brief exchange of dreams and aspirations. Yet, amidst the animated chatter, I felt a gentle pull, a gravitational force urging me toward the center of the room where Blake stood.

He was engaged in conversation, his tall frame relaxed yet commanding, his laughter rich and inviting, like a warm fireplace on a chilly night. I watched him with a mix of admiration and anxiety, feeling as though I were observing a comet from afar, too afraid to reach out and touch it.

"What are you waiting for?" Emma nudged me, her eyes glinting with mischief. "Go say hello!"

I hesitated, my heart pounding in my chest like a drum, but her encouragement spurred me into action. With a deep breath, I stepped forward, weaving through the crowd until I found myself standing just a breath away from him.

"Blake," I managed, my voice steadying itself like a ship finding its course in turbulent waters.

He turned, those captivating blue eyes locking onto mine, and for a moment, time felt suspended. "Hey! I didn't think I'd see you here," he said, that signature grin spreading across his face, illuminating the space around us.

"I almost didn't come," I admitted, the truth spilling out more easily than I anticipated. "But Emma convinced me it would be fun."

"Good call," he replied, his voice smooth like honey, drawing me in further. "What do you think of the event so far?"

"It's amazing! So many talented people in one place—it's like a dream." My nervousness began to melt away, replaced by the warmth of his presence. We exchanged ideas and stories about our sewing projects, the conversation flowing more naturally than I could have ever hoped.

As we chatted, I found myself laughing at his playful banter, the connection between us growing like a well-tended garden. I shared snippets of my experiences and aspirations, watching his expression shift from intrigue to genuine interest. Each word we exchanged unraveled the complexities of his aloofness, revealing a man who, despite the confident exterior, harbored dreams and vulnerabilities of his own.

Just then, a loud announcement broke through our conversation, calling attention to a featured designer ready to showcase their latest collection. Blake gestured toward the stage, and we made our way to the front, the energy in the room crackling like static electricity.

As the lights dimmed, I glanced at Blake, our shoulders brushing against one another in the crowd. The electric connection surged between us, a promise of something extraordinary lingering in the air. The designer began unveiling a series of stunning garments, each piece telling a story woven into its very fabric, yet all I could think about was the spark that ignited between Blake and me, a tapestry of emotions beginning to stitch itself together, filling the voids of uncertainty that had lingered in my heart.

With every passing moment, I felt as if I were no longer just a spectator in this vibrant world of creativity; I was part of it, woven into the very fabric of the night, entwined in the magic that Blake brought with him. The night unfolded, each moment a thread in the tapestry of my life, leading me deeper into a narrative I was beginning to understand.

The designer's collection unfolded like a well-constructed narrative, each garment narrating a chapter filled with rich textures and vibrant colors. The audience was enraptured, their collective breath caught as a model floated down the runway in a gown that sparkled like starlight, each bead reflecting the soft glow of the overhead lights. I felt an electric pulse in the air, a blend of excitement and artistry that resonated within me. As I leaned closer to Blake, my heart danced in tandem with the rhythm of the show, the fabric of my insecurities slowly unraveling.

"What do you think?" I asked, my voice barely above a whisper, captivated by the stunning display before us.

Blake's gaze flicked toward me, a smile playing at the corners of his mouth. "It's brilliant, isn't it? The way each piece tells a story? I love how they're not just clothes but an expression of identity." His eyes sparkled with genuine enthusiasm, illuminating the dimness of the room.

"Exactly!" I replied, my heart swelling at the realization that our thoughts aligned in this shared passion. "It's like each outfit breathes life into the wearer. It's poetry stitched into fabric."

Blake chuckled, and the sound vibrated through the air like a soothing melody. "I've never heard fashion described quite like that. I like it. Maybe I should have you write my next press release."

His teasing tone sent a flutter through my chest, igniting something within me that I couldn't quite place. The laughter we shared felt like a delicate thread weaving us closer, stitching our experiences together in the vast tapestry of this night. As the show continued, I found myself stealing glances at him, marveling at the way his passion painted his expressions, the sharp lines of his jaw softening with every exclamation.

When the final model twirled off the runway, applause erupted like a summer storm, filling the air with palpable excitement. The atmosphere buzzed, and Blake turned to me, his eyes bright with anticipation. "What do you say we go grab a drink and talk more about our favorite pieces?"

A surge of adrenaline coursed through me. "Absolutely," I replied, fighting to keep my voice steady. I hoped my smile didn't betray the whirlwind of emotions I felt inside.

As we navigated through the throngs of attendees, I noticed how Blake moved with effortless grace, as if the crowd parted for him without effort. His presence commanded attention, and I wondered if people felt the same pull toward him that I did, as if he were a magnet drawing them in. When we reached the bar, I watched him order drinks with a casual charm that seemed to put everyone at ease. The bartender laughed at one of his jokes, and I felt a swell of pride knowing I was sharing this moment with someone so captivating.

With drinks in hand, we settled into a quieter corner, an oasis away from the pulsating crowd. The lights dimmed slightly, casting a soft glow around us, and the low hum of music enveloped our conversation.

"So, tell me more about yourself," Blake said, leaning back with an easy confidence that was both inviting and intimidating. "What brought you into the world of sewing?"

I took a sip of my drink, the sweetness mixing with the nervous energy thrumming in my veins. "I've always found comfort in creating something from nothing. There's a kind of magic in transforming a flat piece of fabric into something that tells a story—something that can be worn, shared, cherished."

He listened intently, nodding as if each word I spoke resonated within him. "That's beautifully said. It's almost like you're a storyteller, weaving your tales into every stitch. I admire that."

His compliment wrapped around me like a warm blanket, and I felt a flush creep up my cheeks. "Thank you. It's something I've always loved. But it's also scary, you know? Putting your heart out there for everyone to see. There's always a fear of judgment."

"Trust me, I understand that fear. This industry can be unforgiving," he said, his voice softening, revealing a hint of vulnerability. "But I think it's important to embrace the risk. After all, the best stories are often the ones that make us feel something."

His words lingered in the air, a delicate dance between our shared experiences and dreams. I found myself leaning in closer, captivated by the earnestness in his gaze. "What about you? What drew you into fashion?"

Blake paused, his expression shifting as if he were unearthing a cherished memory. "It's a long story, really. I grew up surrounded by it. My grandmother was a seamstress, and she taught me the basics when I was just a kid. She had this incredible ability to breathe life into fabric, and I always wanted to understand that magic."

"Sounds like she was your inspiration," I remarked, my heart swelling at the thought of a nurturing figure guiding him.

"Absolutely," he nodded, a fond smile gracing his lips. "But it wasn't until I went to college that I realized I wanted to do more than just create. I wanted to help others tell their stories through their work, to showcase their artistry to the world."

His passion was contagious, and I found myself drawn deeper into the conversation, the barriers of my initial nerves crumbling with every shared story. We laughed over our creative mishaps, bonded over late-night sewing sessions fueled by caffeine and ambition, and by the time the clock ticked toward midnight, the world outside felt miles away.

As we shared a moment of comfortable silence, a sudden thought struck me. "Do you ever feel like the industry can stifle creativity? With all the trends and pressures, it can be overwhelming."

Blake sighed, his expression shifting to one of thoughtful reflection. "It can be, but I think it's about finding your own voice within the noise. For me, it's essential to stay true to what inspires you. Otherwise, you risk losing the essence of who you are."

His sincerity resonated within me, echoing the struggles I faced in my own journey. "That's so true. It's easy to get caught up in what everyone else is doing, especially when you're just starting."

Blake leaned closer, his eyes locked onto mine, the intensity of his gaze making my heart race. "You have a voice. You just have to trust it. I've seen the way you create, and it's beautiful. Don't let anyone dim that light."

The warmth of his words wrapped around me, a soothing balm for my insecurities. At that moment, the noise of the event faded into the background, leaving just us in a cocoon of understanding. I felt a flicker of courage ignite within me, daring me to step outside the comfort of my own hesitations.

As the night wore on, I realized that this moment—this connection with Blake—was not merely a fleeting spark but a fire that had the potential to grow. It was a chance to step into a world

I loved while embracing the unknown, a blend of passion and uncertainty that made life vibrant and alive.

Finally, as the crowd began to thin and the energy in the room shifted toward winding down, Blake and I stood outside the venue, the cool night air wrapping around us like a soft whisper. The stars overhead twinkled with a promise of dreams yet to be fulfilled, and I felt a surge of hope within me.

"Thank you for tonight," I said, my voice steady despite the fluttering excitement inside. "It's been one of the best nights of my life."

Blake turned to me, his expression softening, and I could see a hint of something deeper flickering in his eyes. "I feel the same way. I'm really glad you came."

As we exchanged goodbyes, I felt a sense of warmth blossoming in my chest, a thread of connection that intertwined our stories in a way I hadn't anticipated. Walking away, I couldn't shake the feeling that this was just the beginning—a tapestry of moments, adventures, and revelations waiting to unfold.

In that vibrant world of fabrics, dreams, and newfound connections, I realized I was ready to embrace the journey ahead, to stitch together the threads of my life into something uniquely my own.

Chapter 4: The Unraveling

The lights of the Hart & Co. event flickered with a warm glow, a dazzling symphony of gold and cream that draped the expansive ballroom in an air of luxury. Crystal chandeliers hung like celestial bodies, their prisms casting playful shadows across the marble floor, where elegantly dressed guests floated in a sea of silk and satin. Laughter intertwined with the clinking of champagne flutes, creating a melody of sophistication that seemed to echo off the high ceilings. The scent of exotic perfumes wafted through the air, each note a whisper of ambition and artistry, mingling with the tantalizing aroma of gourmet hors d'oeuvres being expertly passed around by servers in crisp black suits.

I stepped into this world of glamour, feeling like a moth drawn to a flame, though my wings were slightly singed from the mere act of entering. As I navigated through clusters of luminaries, I felt an inexplicable mix of excitement and trepidation thrumming through me. My heart beat in sync with the music that enveloped the space, and every breath I took seemed heavy with the weight of my aspirations. I'd come to make a mark, to forge connections that could lead me into the realm of fashion I'd long dreamt about, yet the shimmering façade felt impenetrable.

Among the sea of polished faces, I spotted Blake, a beacon of charisma that seemed to draw in admirers like moths to a flame. He stood confidently, his tall frame draped in a tailored suit that accentuated his athletic build, the fabric hugging his shoulders just right. His tousled hair framed a face that boasted sharp features and deep-set eyes, the kind that could ignite fires or extinguish them with a single glance. As he laughed—his voice a rich, velvety baritone that rolled through the crowd—I felt an involuntary flutter in my stomach. I tightened my grip on the clutch that rested at my side, steadying myself against the current of ambition and desire surging within.

Gathering my courage like a cloak around my shoulders, I made my way through the labyrinth of fashion elites, each conversation buzzing with insider knowledge and the latest trends. My mind raced as I rehearsed my approach, fighting off the anxious doubts that whispered I didn't belong here. I could feel the fabric of my outfit clinging to me, a vibrant orange dress that I had painstakingly chosen for its ability to command attention. It wasn't merely clothing; it was an extension of who I was—a proclamation of my passion for fashion.

As I reached Blake's circle, I could hear snippets of their conversation—declarations of superiority about the latest runway trends, critiques dripping with the sweetness of disdain. "Fashion is nothing without a story," I heard him say, his voice steady and authoritative. In that moment, I felt the air shift; my heart thrummed with indignation. I wanted to yell, to scream, to shatter the preconceived notions about fashion being mere threads and fabrics. But I swallowed my instinct and stepped forward instead, my voice trembling slightly but determined.

"Isn't fashion a canvas for expression?" I interjected, surprising even myself with the strength of my tone. All eyes turned toward me, a kaleidoscope of disbelief and curiosity painting their expressions. "A chance to tell a story that transcends the boundaries of words?" I felt the collective energy of the room shift, the murmurs weaving through the air like a melody. Blake's gaze locked onto mine, an arch of his brow inviting me to elaborate, a challenge twinkling in his eyes.

"I mean, look at this event!" I gestured around, my hands dancing through the air. "Every piece of clothing worn tonight tells us something about the person beneath it. It's an art form, an emotion. You can't simply dismiss it as superficial." I caught my breath, my pulse racing as I continued. "It's about identity, transformation, and the courage to wear your truth. It's deeply personal."

Blake leaned back slightly, a smirk tugging at the corners of his mouth, and the flicker of admiration I'd glimpsed earlier danced within the depths of his eyes. "A bold perspective," he replied, his voice smooth like honey. "But don't you think that the obsession with the surface can overshadow the art itself?"

Our banter ignited a spark in the crowded room, the tension building like a thick fog. "Isn't that the beauty of it?" I countered, feeling emboldened by his scrutiny. "The surface is a reflection of the deeper story. And sometimes, it's the surface that pulls you in, that makes you want to know more. Why shouldn't we revel in both the art and the allure?"

His gaze softened, the skepticism giving way to something warmer, a hint of respect shimmering like the reflections of the chandeliers. "You make a valid point," he conceded, leaning closer, the air between us crackling with an undeniable chemistry. "But tell me—what's your story? Why are you here?"

The question hung between us like a delicate thread, and suddenly, I felt raw, exposed. "I want to make a mark in this industry," I admitted, my voice barely above a whisper. "To create pieces that resonate with others, to bring forth stories that haven't been told." The words poured out, unfiltered and honest, weaving a narrative of ambition and hope. "I want to be more than just a face in the crowd."

In that moment, the cacophony of voices faded into the background, leaving just the two of us suspended in this shared vulnerability. I could see the wheels turning in his mind, the initial icy charm thawing into something more genuine, perhaps even intrigued. It was in that fleeting exchange that I realized, amidst the glitz and glamour, I wasn't merely trying to crash an event; I was forging a connection, a bridge between my dreams and the man who stood as a pillar in the very world I aspired to conquer.

The laughter around us transformed into a distant hum, a low thrumming that faded as Blake and I remained suspended in our own little world. His expression softened, the playful skepticism melting away as genuine curiosity took root. I could feel the weight of his gaze, a warm tide that pushed and pulled at my insides, both thrilling and unnerving. In that instant, the grand ballroom of Hart & Co. felt less like a showcase of fashion and more like an intimate stage where two souls had stepped into the spotlight.

"What kind of stories do you want to tell?" Blake's voice broke through the charged silence, pulling me from the depths of my thoughts. There was a newfound intensity in his eyes, and I found myself caught in the gravity of that moment, the kaleidoscope of colors swirling around us blurring into a soft focus. My heart raced as I contemplated how to express the whirlwind of dreams and aspirations swirling within me.

"I want to create pieces that resonate with people on a personal level," I said, my voice steadying with each word. "Clothing that evokes memories, feelings—something that can transport them to another place or time." I paused, allowing my imagination to weave the intricate tapestry of my aspirations. "Imagine a dress that feels like summer evenings spent by the ocean, or a jacket that holds the warmth of a loved one's embrace. Fashion shouldn't just be worn; it should be lived."

Blake nodded, and I caught a flicker of something almost reverent in his expression. "That's a beautiful thought," he murmured, his voice softening. "But how do you intend to bridge the gap between your vision and this cutthroat industry?" The challenge lay there, wrapped in sincerity. I could see the puzzle pieces of his intrigue forming a clearer picture, and I felt emboldened.

"I'm not looking to play the game by their rules," I declared, the words flowing freely. "I want to redefine the parameters of success. The industry often elevates the superficial—who wears what and when—but I believe the true essence of fashion lies in its ability to connect us." I gestured emphatically, my excitement spilling over. "We've all worn something that made us feel invincible or brought back a flood of memories. That's what I want to tap into."

His brow furrowed slightly, as though he were piecing together a riddle that only I had the key to solve. "You make it sound easy," he said, a hint of skepticism creeping back into his tone. "But passion alone isn't enough. What are your plans? How do you start?"

I took a breath, feeling the weight of the moment settling around us. "I'm working on a collection inspired by personal stories—people's journeys, their struggles, and triumphs. I want to interview them, understand their narratives, and translate those into fabric." My heart swelled with pride as I articulated my vision. "I want my designs to carry a legacy, not just a label."

Blake regarded me with newfound intensity, as if seeing me for the first time. "That's ambitious," he replied slowly, his tone revealing an appreciation I had not anticipated. "And a bit risky, don't you think? The fashion world loves trends, not stories."

A playful smile crept onto my lips, my wry humor breaking through the earnestness of our conversation. "Ah, but trends are like fast fashion—they come and go. Stories, however, linger in the hearts of those who carry them." My voice danced with certainty, each syllable imbued with the conviction that had guided me through countless late-night sketches and caffeine-fueled brainstorming sessions.

Blake chuckled, and the sound was rich and inviting. "You certainly have a way with words. I'll give you that." He leaned back, crossing his arms over his chest, the playful challenge evident in his demeanor. "So, what's stopping you? Why not take the plunge now?"

I hesitated, the question striking a nerve. A storm of insecurities swirled beneath the surface, and for a brief moment, I could feel the familiar chill of self-doubt creeping in. "I guess... it's fear," I confessed, my voice barely above a whisper. "Fear of failing, of being ridiculed by those who seem to have it all figured out."

Blake's expression shifted, a subtle shift that revealed a vulnerability I hadn't expected. "We all fear something, even those at the top." He paused, as if choosing his words carefully. "But the only way to make your mark is to step out of the shadows and take risks. You never know what you might create if you let go of that fear."

The sincerity of his words lingered in the air, a breath of hope that filled the space between us. I felt a swell of admiration for him, not just for his success in the industry but for this unexpected glimpse into his character. Beneath the polished exterior lay a depth that intrigued me, and I found myself wanting to know more about the man behind the icy charm.

As our conversation meandered, we navigated the layers of our lives like seasoned explorers. Blake spoke of his own journey, the sacrifices he had made to carve a path in an unforgiving industry. "It's not always as glamorous as it appears," he admitted, his voice low and contemplative. "There are days when I doubt everything, when the weight of expectations feels suffocating. But you learn to push through, to find the glimmers of joy that remind you why you started."

I found myself captivated, hanging on every word as if they were threads woven into the fabric of my own aspirations. The realization struck me like a bolt of lightning: perhaps this connection was more than just a chance encounter. Here we were, two dreamers exchanging fragments of our souls amid the chaos of an opulent ballroom, and the thought both thrilled and terrified me.

As the evening unfolded around us, the laughter and chatter of the crowd faded into a gentle backdrop, an orchestra playing for an audience that didn't exist. I was fully present, immersed in the warmth of his gaze, the sincerity of his words. The energy between us pulsed with the promise of something new—an electric charge that whispered of possibilities and untold stories yet to unfold. I felt like a butterfly poised to break free from its cocoon, my dreams fluttering just beyond the horizon.

"Would you be willing to help me?" I asked, the words slipping out before I could second-guess myself. "I mean, your insight could be invaluable. I'd love your perspective on my collection."

Blake's eyebrows raised in surprise, but there was a flicker of excitement in his expression. "You want my help?" he asked, as though the idea both intrigued and amused him. "Now that's a bold move."

"It may be," I replied, a confident grin spreading across my face. "But I think we could create something beautiful together."

The invitation hung in the air, a fragile thread of hope weaving between us, and I felt a surge of exhilaration as I envisioned the possibilities. The evening may have begun as a daunting endeavor, but it was transforming into something unexpected—a partnership, perhaps, or maybe the start of a beautiful friendship built on shared passions and dreams. Whatever it was, I couldn't wait to see where this new connection would lead us, one captivating thread at a time.

As I extended my invitation, the moment seemed suspended in time, the vibrant world around us fading into a soft blur. Blake regarded me with a blend of surprise and intrigue, the flickering lights casting playful shadows across his face. I could sense the wheels turning in his mind, weighing the implications of my bold proposal. My heart raced as I watched him absorb my words, my dreams hanging in the balance like the delicate threads of a tapestry waiting to be woven.

"You want me to help you?" He leaned in, the casualness of his tone belied by the intensity in his eyes. "With your collection? You realize this isn't just some little project, right? It's a commitment." His voice dripped with a challenge, yet I could detect a hint of excitement nestled within the skepticism.

"I'm well aware," I replied, my resolve solidifying as I met his gaze. "But I'm not looking for a fairy tale. I want raw, honest feedback, and if I'm going to brave this world, I need someone who knows the ropes." The urgency of my words echoed the determination that had propelled me to crash this high-profile event in the first place.

He studied me, as if trying to gauge whether I was merely another naive dreamer or someone genuinely worthy of his time. I could see the corners of his mouth twitching as if he was on the verge of a smile, and I felt a rush of hope. "Alright," he finally said, his voice low and deliberate. "But know this: I don't sugarcoat anything. If I think something's off, I'll tell you."

A grin broke across my face, relief flooding through me. "That's exactly what I need," I said, my heart swelling with gratitude. "I want the truth, even if it stings."

With that, we struck an unspoken deal, and just like that, a connection formed in the flickering lights of that lavish ballroom, a partnership that danced on the precipice of uncertainty and potential. The night unfolded around us, the music pulsing like a heartbeat, but all I could focus on was Blake's presence beside me, the electricity sparking with every word exchanged.

As the evening wore on, we continued to engage in a lively back-and-forth, the barriers of formalities dissolving with every shared laugh. He challenged my ideas, each critique wrapped in playful banter that ignited my passion even further. "You say you want to tell stories through your designs, but what's your story?" he pressed, his voice both curious and teasing. "Are you even sure what that is yet?"

I paused, feeling a knot tighten in my stomach. "I guess I'm still figuring that out," I admitted, the vulnerability catching in my throat. "Growing up, I was always the one in the background, observing rather than participating. But I've realized that the stories

I want to tell are rooted in my own experiences—my struggles, my hopes, and even my failures." I took a breath, the words tumbling out with unexpected ease. "Fashion is my way of taking control, of expressing who I am and who I want to be."

Blake nodded, his expression softening as he absorbed my honesty. "That's a good start," he replied, his voice sincere. "But you need to dig deeper. Don't just scratch the surface. What truly drives you?"

His question hung in the air, and I could feel the wheels turning in my mind, unearthing memories I had long tucked away. "I grew up in a small town where dreams felt like luxuries. I watched people settle for mediocrity because they were afraid to reach for more." My voice trembled slightly, but I pressed on. "I never wanted that for myself. I want to break the mold, to inspire others to chase their passions unapologetically."

The earnestness in my voice seemed to resonate with him. Blake's demeanor shifted, the teasing lightness of our conversation giving way to something deeper. "Then you need to own that," he said, his tone steady and firm. "Make it your foundation. Your story should pulse through every piece you create. It should be unshakeable."

A wave of determination surged through me as I absorbed his words. This was more than just about clothing; it was about authenticity and resilience. In that opulent ballroom, among the swirling conversations and glimmering lights, I felt the seeds of my dreams begin to take root, nourished by the connection we had formed.

As we continued to discuss ideas, Blake shared his own experiences in the industry, weaving in anecdotes that were equal parts cautionary tales and inspiration. "I've seen talented designers crumble under the pressure," he admitted, a hint of sadness in his voice. "They forget why they started and lose themselves in the chase for validation. Don't let that happen to you."

I listened intently, absorbing every word. The more he spoke, the more I realized how much I wanted to be part of this world, not just as a bystander but as a vital player, carving out my own niche. It was exhilarating and terrifying all at once, and I couldn't shake the feeling that this moment was pivotal.

Hours melted away in the swirl of laughter and deep conversations, and before long, the event began to wind down. Guests started to trickle out, their glamorous silhouettes fading into the night, but Blake and I remained, lost in our own world.

As the last of the crowd dispersed, he turned to me, a genuine smile breaking through his once-cool demeanor. "So, what's next for you?" he asked, his tone light but filled with genuine curiosity.

"I'll start gathering stories, interviewing people, and sketching designs that reflect their journeys," I said, the fire within me rekindled. "I want to create a collection that not only showcases my vision but also honors the lives of those who inspire me."

Blake's smile widened, and I felt a rush of warmth, a thrill that sent a shiver down my spine. "That's the spirit. And if you need someone to bounce ideas off or critique those designs, you know where to find me."

The offer hung between us, rich with promise and possibility. My heart swelled with gratitude, not just for his willingness to help but for the unexpected camaraderie we had forged amidst the glitz and glamour.

As we made our way toward the exit, the crisp night air wrapped around us like a comforting blanket. The city sparkled beyond the venue, the lights twinkling like stars scattered across the sky. I felt a sense of exhilaration coursing through my veins, a feeling of being on the precipice of something monumental.

"Hey, can I ask you something?" I said, breaking the comfortable silence as we stepped onto the sidewalk.

"Of course," he replied, turning to face me, his expression inviting.

"What's your story?" I asked, a spark of curiosity igniting within me. "What drives you in this chaotic world of fashion?"

Blake paused, his brow furrowing slightly as if considering how much to reveal. "That's a complex question," he finally replied, a hint of vulnerability slipping through his confident façade. "But in essence, I want to create pieces that challenge the norms, that push boundaries. I want to be part of the conversation that reshapes the industry."

The sincerity in his words resonated deeply with me, and I couldn't help but admire the fire behind them. "You're already doing that," I said softly, and for a moment, the world around us faded into nothingness, leaving just the two of us under the shimmering night sky.

In that fleeting moment, I felt a connection that transcended the superficial glamour surrounding us—a bond forged through shared passions and dreams. The journey ahead loomed large and daunting, but with Blake by my side, the path felt a little less intimidating and a lot more exciting. Together, we were poised to weave a tapestry of stories that would echo in the fabric of our lives, one stitch at a time.

Chapter 5: Tangles and Tension

The sun hung low in the sky, casting long shadows across the cobblestone streets of Rivertown, where the old buildings leaned together like gossiping friends. Each brick, with its own story, spoke to the quiet vibrancy of this town—a blend of rustling leaves, distant laughter, and the scent of fresh coffee wafting from the café on the corner. I strolled past the familiar storefronts, my mind racing with the impending Rivertown Fashion Week, which loomed like a storm cloud overhead. My fingers brushed the smooth fabric of my sketchbook tucked under my arm, the pages filled with ideas that seemed to evaporate into thin air whenever I needed them most.

With each step, I felt a sense of disquiet, a gentle but persistent tugging at my heart, reminding me of Blake. His presence was as undeniable as the midday sun, and I could no longer ignore the spark he ignited in me. Our encounters had shifted from the awkward silence of strangers to a tapestry of teasing exchanges and reluctant camaraderie. Beneath his sarcasm, I sensed an ember of vulnerability, flickering just beneath the surface, begging to be acknowledged.

I paused outside the café, captivated by the vibrant display of pastries, their glossy surfaces beckoning me closer. The sound of laughter filtered through the open door, and for a fleeting moment, I envisioned myself inside, sharing a table with Blake, the warmth of camaraderie radiating between us. But with the weight of deadlines pressing down like an iron shroud, I turned away, dismissing the impulse. Perhaps another day, I thought, allowing myself a soft sigh as I headed towards the design studio, the air heavy with expectation.

Inside the studio, the chaos was palpable. Fabrics lay strewn across every surface, vibrant swatches of color colliding like paint on a palette. My colleagues flitted about like hummingbirds, buzzing with energy as they crafted their own masterpieces. Yet, amidst the vibrant chaos, I felt like a muted note in an otherwise harmonious symphony. The looming Fashion Week was an artist's dream and nightmare intertwined, a showcase of creativity battling against the demands of reality. I wanted to dive in, to lose myself in my designs, but instead, I felt stuck, marooned on an island of indecision.

In a moment of frustration, I reached for my phone, scrolling through contacts until Blake's name caught my eye. An impulsive thought flared within me—why not ask for his input? My mind played back the memory of our recent banter, his sharp wit laced with an underlying kindness. Swallowing my pride, I sent him a quick message, words tumbling out as I laid bare my struggles, not expecting much in return.

Surprisingly, a response buzzed back almost instantly. "What's the worst that could happen? You might actually get something done." A smile crept across my lips, the lightheartedness of his words somehow lifting the weight pressing on my chest. We agreed to meet at the park, a quaint little nook where blooming cherry blossom trees showered the ground in pink petals, creating a picturesque scene that felt stolen from a postcard.

When I arrived, I found Blake leaning against a weathered bench, arms crossed and a slight frown etched on his handsome face, the golden rays of the sun highlighting the angles of his jaw. He looked like he had stepped out of a different era, a rugged figure amid the delicate beauty surrounding him. The contrast made my heart flutter—a strange mix of attraction and apprehension.

"Thought you'd bail," he said, his tone teasing but his eyes flickering with something deeper, something I couldn't quite place.

"I wouldn't miss the chance to gain some of your wisdom," I shot back, a grin breaking the tension. He chuckled, the sound low and genuine, stirring something within me.

As we settled on the bench, I spread out my sketches between us, each one a glimpse into the chaotic world in my mind. Blake leaned in, examining the designs with a critical eye, the sunlight catching the strands of hair that fell across his forehead. "You know, you have talent," he said, surprising me with his sincerity. "But these," he gestured to a particularly frilly design, "are too much. Less is more, especially when you want to stand out."

I stared at the design, biting my lip. It was a look I loved, but his honesty was refreshing. "So, what do you suggest?"

And just like that, we began to collaborate. He tossed out ideas, his style blending unexpectedly well with mine, creating a tapestry of creativity that was thrilling. We talked, laughed, and debated the merits of ruffles versus sleek lines, our banter igniting sparks of inspiration that had lain dormant for too long.

But the air around us shifted, an electric tension weaving itself into our interactions. Every accidental brush of shoulders sent a shiver down my spine, and the playful glances we exchanged hinted at something unspoken—a yearning that threatened to spill over into chaos. I felt my heart race as I caught him staring, his expression unreadable, the world around us fading into a blur.

Hours melted away in the warm embrace of the afternoon sun, and as the shadows grew longer, I found myself reluctant to part ways. Our collaboration was exhilarating, but it was also a jigsaw puzzle of feelings I had yet to sort through. The camaraderie was intoxicating, but the undercurrents left me breathless, tangled in emotions I couldn't decipher.

Blake packed up my sketches, his fingers brushing against mine—a fleeting touch that lingered long after we had parted. As I walked home, the streets of Rivertown shimmered with possibility, each step a reminder of the connections woven between us. There was chaos, yes, but within it lay the promise of something more—something that could either uplift or unravel me entirely.

The streets of Rivertown transformed as dusk draped its velvet cloak over the town, casting a soft glow that wrapped around the buildings like an embrace. The air turned crisp, sending a gentle shiver through me as I strolled back from the studio, my mind still buzzing with the electric energy of my day with Blake. The designs we had sketched together danced in my thoughts, an intricate ballet of fabric and color that felt more alive than anything I had conjured up in months.

As I walked, I replayed our conversation, his teasing remarks and honest critiques swirling together, creating a peculiar blend of admiration and attraction that made my cheeks warm. His laughter echoed in my ears, and I found myself wishing I could bottle that feeling—the way he leaned in, his eyes sparkling with mischief, as if sharing a delicious secret that only we understood. Each moment felt charged, a flurry of emotions threading through the fabric of my reality, blurring the lines between collaboration and something much deeper.

Once home, the familiar scent of jasmine from the flowers outside wafted through the window, mingling with the faint aroma of my half-finished dinner—some uninspired pasta left untouched on the stove. I dropped my bag on the floor and shuffled into the kitchen, a tired smile creeping across my face. The walls of my apartment were a canvas of my life, adorned with sketches and photos that chronicled my journey. Each piece told a story, but lately, they felt static, almost like ghosts of what I once imagined my dreams to be.

With a huff, I slid into a chair at my small dining table, the wood cool against my fingers as I picked up a fork, pushing the pasta around in its bowl as if it might spring to life with inspiration. My phone chimed on the table, the screen lighting up with a new message from Blake. A jolt of excitement surged through me. It was a simple line: "Hey, what do you think of the idea of adding more layers? We could really create something fresh."

My heart raced as I considered his words. Layers—both in fashion and in life—could signify so much. My own feelings toward

Blake were an intricate tapestry, rich with textures and complexities I had yet to unravel. I typed a quick response, a playful jab about his newfound fashion wisdom, but I couldn't shake the weight of what lay beneath our exchanges. This collaboration was more than just work; it felt like an invitation to delve deeper into the tangled emotions that simmered just below the surface.

Days turned into a blur as our meetings became a routine. We found ourselves tucked away in coffee shops, the hum of the espresso machines blending with our discussions, ideas swirling like steam rising from our cups. The air crackled with creativity, but there was also an undercurrent of tension that made my pulse quicken. Each time our knees brushed beneath the table, or he leaned in closer to examine my sketches, it felt like stepping closer to an edge—wonderful, terrifying, and exhilarating all at once.

On one particularly crisp evening, as the sun dipped behind the horizon and painted the sky in hues of orange and purple, I arrived at our usual spot, my heart racing in anticipation. Blake was already there, his back to me, hands shoved deep into the pockets of his worn denim jacket. He turned at the sound of my footsteps, a slow smile unfurling across his face that sent butterflies fluttering wildly in my stomach.

"You're late," he teased, tilting his head, a playful smirk dancing on his lips. "I thought you got lost in your thoughts."

"Just making sure I had something worth sharing," I shot back, and as I settled across from him, I could feel the charged energy crackling between us.

With the weight of our upcoming showcase looming over us, we poured ourselves into the work, dissecting every detail of our designs. He suggested a bold approach, layering textures and colors that I hadn't considered before. It was exciting, thrilling, and terrifying. Each idea he proposed seemed to peel back another layer of his personality, revealing glimpses of the man behind the bravado. I caught sight of the passion that ignited his words, the fierce determination that mirrored my own insecurities and aspirations.

As we discussed, a question nagged at the back of my mind, something I had yet to voice. "What made you want to get involved in fashion?" I asked, curiosity threading through my words as I leaned in, studying his expression.

Blake hesitated, the lighthearted banter momentarily fading. "It's a long story," he finally said, his tone shifting, revealing the more profound intricacies of his character. "I grew up watching my mom struggle to make a name for herself in the industry. She was talented but faced so many obstacles. I wanted to prove to her that talent could shine through if given the right push."

His vulnerability took me by surprise. Beneath the biting sarcasm and gruff exterior lay a heart that beat with fierce loyalty and love. I could see the fire in his eyes, a determination to forge a path not just for himself but for those who had fought so hard to be recognized. My respect for him deepened, weaving another thread into the fabric of my feelings.

The conversation flowed, with moments of laughter punctuating the deeper exchanges. We lost ourselves in a bubble, the world outside fading into a distant hum. Yet, as the evening deepened, the flickering candle on our table cast long shadows, and the reality of our lives outside this cozy haven loomed large.

Eventually, the hour grew late, and reluctantly, we packed our sketches, the air between us thick with unspoken words. As I rose to leave, a lingering question danced in my mind, teasing at the edges of my thoughts.

"Blake," I began, my voice trembling slightly as I turned to face him. "What happens when Fashion Week is over?"

He looked up, surprise etched on his face, but it was quickly replaced with a knowing expression. "We'll figure it out," he said, his voice steady yet soft, as if he understood the complexity of what I was asking.

As I stepped out into the cool night air, the stars overhead twinkled like distant promises. A mix of anticipation and uncertainty coursed through me. With every encounter, the lines between friendship and something deeper blurred, leaving me feeling exhilarated yet anxious. I had willingly stepped into a chaotic whirl of creativity and emotion, where the stakes felt impossibly high, and the risks loomed larger than ever before.

The air crackled with excitement as Rivertown Fashion Week drew nearer, an electric buzz that coursed through the streets and found its way into my very bones. Each day unfolded with a kaleidoscope of colors and textures, the anticipation palpable as the town transformed into a vibrant tapestry of creativity. Banners fluttered from storefronts, showcasing the promise of artistry and expression that would soon spill onto the runways. Yet, for all the exhilaration that surrounded me, my heart felt like an unsteady drum, each beat a reminder of the uncertainties that lay ahead.

Blake and I found ourselves tangled in a whirlwind of late-night brainstorming sessions and early morning coffee runs, our collaboration blossoming amid laughter and the occasional shared sigh of frustration. With each meeting, we ventured deeper into the world we were crafting together, building something that felt entirely new—a fusion of our distinct styles and ideas, yet completely in harmony. It was intoxicating, a dance of creative minds that thrummed with energy, yet beneath it lay a tension that sent ripples of anticipation through me.

One evening, as the sun dipped below the horizon, painting the sky in strokes of fiery orange and dusky lavender, we met at our usual spot—a quaint little bistro tucked away on a side street. The scent of freshly baked bread mingled with the aroma of espresso, wrapping around us like a warm hug as we settled into our seats outside, the twinkling fairy lights above casting a magical glow over our table. I watched Blake as he sketched, his brow furrowed in concentration, the pencil moving deftly across the page. There was a fierceness to him in these moments, a fierce passion that made me want to unravel the mysteries locked behind his guarded gaze.

"Okay, so what about incorporating a theme?" I ventured, leaning forward, excitement bubbling within me. "Something that captures the essence of Rivertown—maybe the river itself?"

Blake paused, his pencil hovering just above the page, and then he looked up, a spark of interest lighting his eyes. "Water can symbolize fluidity, adaptability. It's beautiful. I like it."

The warmth of his praise washed over me like a gentle tide. "And we could use materials that mimic water's movement—flowy fabrics, translucent layers..." I could feel the energy between us morphing into something palpable, our ideas swirling together like eddies in a stream.

"Yes, and colors that echo the river—blues and greens, maybe some silver accents." He grinned, the corners of his mouth lifting in a way that made my heart leap. In that moment, I saw not just a collaborator but someone who shared my vision, who understood the depths of what I was trying to achieve.

As the evening wore on, we lost ourselves in sketches and discussions, the outside world fading into a backdrop of soft music and laughter. But beneath the creative spark, I sensed the currents of something more—a connection that had deepened beyond our designs. Every brush of our fingers, every lingering glance became imbued with a weight that made it difficult to breathe. I had thought collaboration would bind us, but it was also fraying the edges of my heart.

The pressure of the upcoming showcase hung over us like a looming storm, yet it was this very chaos that thrust us into unexpected moments of intimacy. The closer we got to the date, the more tangled our emotions became.

One particularly late night, as we poured over the final touches of our collection, exhaustion began to creep in. The flickering overhead lights cast shadows that danced around the studio, and I stifled a yawn, leaning back in my chair. "We might need to call it a night soon," I suggested, glancing at Blake, who seemed lost in thought, his eyes distant yet sparkling.

He looked up, and the intensity in his gaze sent a shiver down my spine. "Or we could grab some coffee and keep pushing through." His voice was low, coaxing.

"Isn't that the very definition of insanity?" I teased, but the thrill of the idea stirred something within me. There was an allure to the chaos, the way it wrapped around us like a cocoon, isolating us from the outside world.

With a shared understanding, we ventured out into the cool night, the air fresh and crisp, invigorating. The streets were quiet, our laughter echoing against the cobblestones as we walked to the nearby café that remained open late, the glow of its neon sign inviting us inside.

As we settled into a booth, I leaned across the table, a playful challenge dancing in my eyes. "Alright, let's talk strategy. How do we make our collection stand out?"

Blake chuckled, running a hand through his tousled hair. "We've got the designs, the theme... now we need a killer presentation. Something that will blow everyone away."

"Like a dramatic entrance?" I suggested, excitement thrumming through me.

He grinned, his eyes sparkling with mischief. "Exactly. Maybe we can have the models walk in, the music crescendoing, and the lighting shifting to mimic water flowing. We can create an experience."

The vision unfolded before us like a movie, each idea layering upon the last until it became a magnificent tapestry of sound, light, and movement. As we brainstormed, I couldn't help but steal glances at him, the way his passion ignited with each idea only intensified the longing that flickered within me.

Hours slipped away unnoticed, the café beginning to empty as we remained enveloped in our own world. Yet as I watched Blake speak, I couldn't shake the feeling that we were walking a tightrope, balancing between a shared creative spark and something that threatened to unravel the very fabric of our partnership.

Finally, as the café began to dim the lights for closing, we decided to head back. The air was cool, our breath misting in front of us like whispers of unspoken words. As we walked side by side, the silence became a comfortable companion, filled with the weight of everything left unsaid.

When we reached the studio, I hesitated at the door, the thrill of the evening still tingling in my fingertips. "Thanks for tonight, Blake. I didn't realize how much I needed this."

He turned, his expression softening. "Me too. Sometimes I forget how good it feels to create with someone else." The sincerity in his voice struck a chord deep within me, a bittersweet melody that resonated through my heart.

Before I could process my next move, he stepped closer, the warmth of his body radiating toward me, creating an electric connection that hummed in the air between us. "Maybe we should... you know, take a moment to acknowledge this," he said, his voice low and inviting.

My breath caught in my throat, and I could feel the world narrowing down to just the two of us. In that charged moment, I understood that this wasn't just about the fashion show anymore. It was about us—two tangled souls navigating the waters of creativity, vulnerability, and uncharted emotions. The urge to lean in, to close the distance, was overwhelming. But the weight of uncertainty loomed like a shadow over us, threatening to pull us under.

Instead, I took a step back, my heart pounding in my chest. "Let's focus on the collection first," I suggested, though I could hear the unsteady tremor in my voice. "We can figure out everything else later."

Blake nodded, the flicker of disappointment crossing his face momentarily before he masked it with a playful grin. "Alright, later it is. But just know, I'm not giving up that easily."

As I slipped out into the night, the cool air greeted me like a long-lost friend, but the warmth of our encounter lingered, wrapping around my heart like an intricate design—beautiful, complicated, and utterly undeniable. The stakes were higher now, and as I stepped into the vibrant pulse of Rivertown, I couldn't shake the feeling that the real chaos was only just beginning.

Chapter 6: Threads of Discontent

The sunlight streamed through the expansive windows of the studio, flooding the space with a warm, golden hue that caught the dust motes dancing lazily in the air. My workspace was a cacophony of swatches, sketches, and scattered remnants of ideas half-formed and half-forgotten. Each piece of fabric whispered stories of ambition, heartache, and a fierce desire to create something that could transcend the mundane. This was my sanctuary, a vibrant realm where the fabric of dreams intertwined with the stitches of reality. Yet, today, the sanctuary felt more like a battleground.

Blake strode in, all sharp angles and fierce determination, his presence commanding the room as if he owned it. The air between us crackled with a tension that was both electric and infuriating. I couldn't quite put my finger on whether it was his meticulousness or the way he carried himself with an air of unyielding confidence that rubbed me the wrong way. Perhaps it was the perfect way he draped himself in the latest designer threads, as if he were some sort of fashion oracle, coming to bestow wisdom upon the unworthy. I rolled my eyes but couldn't suppress the fluttering in my chest, a response I loathed to admit even to myself.

"What do you think of this?" I asked, gesturing toward a vibrant array of fabrics. A kaleidoscope of colors and textures lay sprawled across the table, each piece more captivating than the last. There was a sumptuous emerald silk that felt like liquid dreams and a textured, rough-hewn linen that spoke of rustic elegance. I was excited to unveil my vision, the fusion of elegance and rebellion that had been swirling in my mind like a tempest.

Blake leaned in, his brow furrowing as he scrutinized my selections. "These are bold choices," he remarked, his tone oscillating between admiration and critique. "But they don't speak to the elegance we're aiming for this season."

I could feel my patience wearing thin, frayed at the edges like a well-loved quilt. "And what's wrong with a little boldness?" I shot back, my voice sharper than intended. "Fashion is about pushing boundaries, about embracing what makes us uncomfortable. This collection should scream authenticity, not whisper conformity."

A flicker of surprise crossed his face, followed by a flash of something deeper—maybe respect or curiosity, but it vanished as quickly as it appeared. "You're right, but there's a fine line between bold and chaotic," he replied, his gaze steady and unyielding. "We can't risk losing our audience."

"Losing our audience?" I echoed, incredulity rising in my throat like bile. "It's not about them; it's about us! About what we want to say with our designs." I took a deep breath, inhaling the fabric fumes that filled the air, trying to calm the storm brewing within me. "We have a chance to make a statement here, Blake."

The brief silence that followed was pregnant with tension. I could see the gears turning in his mind, a mix of admiration for my passion and an unwillingness to let go of his own vision. Yet, beneath that stony facade, a strange chemistry simmered, igniting sparks with each heated exchange. There was a thrill in our arguments, an energy that made me question whether this collaboration would spark creativity or set us ablaze in a frenzy of conflict.

Just as I felt we were on the cusp of a breakthrough—or a breakdown—a notification pinged on my phone, slicing through the intensity of our conversation. I glanced at the screen, my heart plummeting as if it had been yanked from my chest. My designs, the very essence of my soul stitched into each sketch, had been pilfered. A rival designer had taken my work, twisting it into something that felt like a cruel mockery of my dreams.

I could hardly breathe, the air suddenly thick with dread. "Blake," I murmured, my voice trembling as I shared the news. "They've stolen my designs."

The expression on his face morphed from curiosity to concern in a heartbeat, but it wasn't the comforting reaction I had hoped for. Instead, it seemed to ignite a competitive fire within him. "We have to respond strategically," he said, his eyes narrowing as he shifted into problem-solving mode. "This could turn the tide for us."

I blinked, confusion swirling in my mind like the scattered threads across the studio floor. "Strategically?" I repeated, incredulity mixing with anger. "These are my creations, Blake! It's not just about strategy; it's about integrity and respect for what we've worked so hard to build."

He waved a dismissive hand, and I could see the gears in his mind whirring faster than I could keep up. "I get that. But in this industry, it's not just about the designs; it's about the perception. We can't let them overshadow us."

Frustration welled within me like an unrelenting tide. Was he truly unable to see the gravity of what had happened? My heart felt heavy, caught between the disappointment of losing my art and the bewildering pull I felt toward him. I had expected a confidant, a partner who would share in my pain, not someone who viewed it as just another battle in the relentless war of fashion. The very essence of what I had poured into those designs—the late nights, the fervent sketches, the countless revisions—seemed to be slipping away, reduced to mere strategy in his eyes.

As I watched Blake delve deeper into the fray of his ambitions, a chill gripped my heart. Could I trust him, not just with my designs, but with my vulnerability? With the fragments of my heart that now lay bare, exposed to the merciless winds of competition? In that moment, the air grew thick with uncertainty, a fragile thread pulling taut between us, threatening to snap at any moment. The vibrant world I had built around me began to feel like a cage, each color fading as doubt crept in, leaving only a stark reminder of the delicate balance between creativity and chaos.

The air in the studio felt heavy, as if the very walls were closing in on me, amplifying my confusion and frustration. The fluorescent lights flickered above, casting a harsh glow on the mess of sketches strewn across the table, their vibrant colors now dulled by despair. I stared at my creations, each one a snapshot of my dreams, my aspirations, and my heart laid bare. They had been so full of life, and now they felt like ghosts haunting the edges of my mind.

Blake stood across from me, his expression a mixture of determination and distraction as he clutched his phone, scrolling furiously, likely searching for any morsel of information to twist this situation to our advantage. I wanted to scream, to shake him out of this relentless pursuit for strategy and tactics, to make him understand that this was more than just a business move. My designs were extensions of myself, living entities that had been birthed through countless sleepless nights and fervent daydreams.

"What are you thinking?" I blurted, frustration spilling out like a broken dam. "Do you even care that someone has taken what was ours? What I worked so hard for?"

He looked up, the storm of thoughts momentarily dissipating from his gaze. "Of course I care. But we need to focus on how we can turn this into an opportunity. If they're stealing your work, that means they see value in it, and that's a good sign for us."

I clenched my fists, fighting against the tide of emotion that threatened to drown me. "A good sign? Blake, they're not just 'seeing value.' They're stealing my soul!" My voice broke on the last word, and the realization that I was about to cry in front of him made my heart race with embarrassment.

Blake's brow furrowed, and I could see a flicker of genuine concern in his eyes. "Hey," he said softly, his authoritative demeanor momentarily softening. "I didn't mean to downplay your feelings. I just... I'm trying to figure out how to help us move forward."

His sincerity washed over me like a cool breeze, grounding me in the moment. The sharp edges of my frustration began to dull, replaced by a new wave of vulnerability. "I don't want to just move forward," I admitted, my voice trembling. "I want my designs back. I want what's rightfully mine."

A pause hung between us, thick with unspoken truths. In that moment, I saw him—not just as the competitive whirlwind he usually presented but as a man caught in his own storm, trying to navigate a world that often felt like a relentless tide threatening to swallow him whole. Maybe he was more than just a rival in this chaotic dance of creation.

"We can fight back," Blake finally said, the fire in his eyes rekindling. "Let's craft a collection that embodies your original vision but adds our twist. We'll show them what you're truly capable of."

I regarded him warily, the remnants of my earlier frustration still bubbling beneath the surface. "And what if it flops? What if they take this new collection too? What if they twist it again?"

"Then we create something even better. Something they could never dream of stealing," he replied, his confidence slowly rekindling my own spark. "Let's make them wish they hadn't crossed you."

As I considered his words, a part of me yearned for the strength he projected. It was intoxicating, this idea that we could rise from the ashes together, reborn like a phoenix. But another part of me—a nagging whisper of self-doubt—wondered if I could truly rely on him. Could I let him into my world, into my heart, and still protect the fragile remnants of my dreams?

That night, I lay in bed, staring at the ceiling, my mind a whirlpool of thoughts and emotions. The streetlights cast long shadows across my room, flickering like the doubts that danced in my mind. I thought about the way Blake's eyes lit up when he discussed designs, how he moved with an energy that felt almost magnetic. It was maddening to think that amidst the chaos of our collaboration, there was something more—something that made my heart race in ways I had never expected.

With a sigh, I rolled onto my side, pulling the blankets tighter around me. The familiar comfort of my quilt enveloped me like a warm hug, but the comfort faded as images of the stolen designs invaded my thoughts. I could almost see the rival designer's smug expression as he paraded my creations like trophies.

Morning broke with a reluctant sun peeking through the curtains, bathing my room in a soft, golden light. As I prepared for the day, I steeled myself for the meeting ahead. Blake had suggested we brainstorm new ideas for the collection, and I knew it was time to step into that arena, to reclaim my power.

The studio buzzed with a frenetic energy as we set up for our brainstorming session. I could feel the tension from last night still lingering in the air, crackling with possibility. Blake arrived early, his hair slightly tousled, an expression of determination etched across his face.

"Ready to shake the world?" he asked, his tone light, yet serious.

I couldn't help but smile at his enthusiasm, the nerves in my stomach beginning to settle. "Ready as I'll ever be."

We spread out swatches of fabric across the table, vibrant hues of ruby and sapphire mingling with muted earth tones, creating a tapestry of endless possibilities. As we began to discuss ideas, our synergy transformed the room. I watched as Blake sketched out designs, his fingers dancing across the paper with an artist's grace. It was mesmerizing, the way he could take my raw concepts and elevate them into something spectacular.

"Imagine this," he said, holding up a rough draft of a dress that combined elements of my original designs with his sharp lines and bold silhouettes. "This could be our statement piece, a fusion of elegance and audacity."

As I looked at the sketch, my heart fluttered. There was something about his vision that resonated with me, igniting the flicker of hope I thought had been extinguished. "It's incredible," I breathed, warmth flooding through me.

Blake grinned, his eyes lighting up as he caught the spark of inspiration radiating from me. "We can do this. We'll take the fashion world by storm."

With each passing moment, the creative energy between us grew stronger, filling the studio with a palpable sense of hope. The worries of betrayal and competition began to fade, replaced by a burgeoning camaraderie that felt both exhilarating and terrifying. As we dove deeper into our designs, I couldn't shake the feeling that this collaboration might not only reclaim my designs but also uncover something deeper between us, something worth fighting for.

Yet, as the day unfolded, I couldn't help but glance at Blake, still wrestling with the lingering doubt that had taken root in my heart. In the swirling chaos of fabric and dreams, could I trust him—not only with my vision but with the fragile pieces of myself that I had been so careful to guard?

As the sun dipped low, casting a golden hue across the cityscape, the studio transformed into a sanctuary of creation, illuminated by the warm glow that filtered through the vast windows. We had settled into a rhythm, our creative energies flowing like a symphony, each note echoing the laughter and light-hearted banter that punctuated our discussions. Every moment felt electric, as if the very air hummed with the potential of what we were building together.

Blake stood at one end of the long, polished table, sketching furiously while I spread out swatches like a painter preparing a canvas. The vibrant textiles shimmered in the late afternoon light, and I could hardly contain the excitement bubbling within me. Each piece we selected sparked another idea, another burst of inspiration that sent us spiraling deeper into our collaborative vision.

"Imagine this—" I began, holding up a deep burgundy satin, "—paired with that lace overlay you love. It would give this collection a touch of vintage charm while maintaining that edgy twist we're going for."

Blake paused, his pencil hovering over the paper as he considered my suggestion. "And we can layer in those sharp cuts you mentioned earlier. The contrast could really make a statement." He grinned, and I could feel my heart do a little flip. There was something intoxicating about the way we bounced ideas off each other, each thought propelling us forward into uncharted territory.

The air grew thick with creativity, and I reveled in the newfound connection between us, a delicate balance of friendship and collaboration that felt almost like magic. For the first time since the theft of my designs, the clouds of doubt began to disperse, revealing a silver lining I had almost forgotten existed.

"Okay," I said, determination fueling my words. "Let's create a piece that pays homage to what was taken but elevates it. We can show them that nothing can dim our light."

Blake nodded, his expression serious yet excited. "We'll take what they think they've stolen and turn it into something they could never dream of replicating." His intensity ignited a fire within me, and together, we crafted our battle plan—a declaration of resilience wrapped in fabric and thread.

As the evening deepened, the studio pulsed with life. I lost track of time, caught up in the joy of creation. Blake was infectious in his enthusiasm, a whirlwind of ideas and laughter that wrapped around me like a warm embrace. We were two artists dancing in harmony, crafting a collection that felt not just like a response to a theft but like a declaration of our presence in a world that often tried to silence individuality.

But as the hours slipped away, and our sketches began to fill the boards around us, a gnawing uncertainty crept back in, weaving through the strands of our collaboration like a dark thread in an otherwise vibrant tapestry. I watched Blake intently, noticing the way he seemed to lose himself in thought, his brows knitting together as he pondered our designs. The weight of his ambition was evident, and I couldn't help but wonder where I fit into that equation.

"Blake," I said, a hint of hesitation in my voice. "What if we actually pull this off? What if we become successful?"

He turned to me, his eyes gleaming with passion. "Then we'll have done something incredible, something that challenges the status quo. But I want to be clear: this isn't just about the success, it's about the art. It's about making our mark."

A smile spread across my face, and for a moment, I was swept up in the whirlwind of his dreams. Yet, lurking beneath that exhilaration was a seed of doubt that whispered of betrayal. I couldn't shake the feeling that in this volatile industry, where friendships could shift like the winds, the stakes were higher than ever. Could I trust him with not just my designs but the very essence of who I was becoming?

That night, I lay awake, replaying our conversations like a film loop in my mind. I could hear his laughter, the way he challenged me, pushed me to see beyond my initial visions. There was a chemistry between us that was both exhilarating and terrifying, a tension that crackled like static electricity whenever we were near one another. Yet, the ever-present worry lingered—was I truly safe in this partnership, or would the moment my back was turned, he betray me like the rival designer who had stolen my heart?

The next day dawned with a renewed sense of purpose, and we plunged headfirst into the whirlwind of our upcoming fashion show. The studio became our playground, a vibrant hub of activity filled with laughter, late-night brainstorming sessions, and the intoxicating scent of fresh fabric mingling with the musky aroma of coffee. Our designs began to take shape, each piece a testament to our resilience—a collection born from the ashes of theft, transformed into something extraordinary.

As we draped the final garment on a mannequin, I stepped back, a gasp escaping my lips. The gown shimmered under the studio lights, a breathtaking blend of elegance and boldness that embodied everything we had worked for. My heart swelled with pride, the worry momentarily eclipsed by the beauty of our creation.

"Can you believe we did this?" I said, my voice barely above a whisper as I admired our handiwork.

Blake stood beside me, his gaze fixed on the gown, a mix of awe and satisfaction etched on his features. "We didn't just do this; we redefined what it means to collaborate. This is our story now."

And in that moment, the doubts that had clung to me like shadows began to fade. I could feel the threads of trust weaving between us, a delicate tapestry of shared ambition and creativity. The fashion world, with all its fierce competition and heartache, became a backdrop to our journey rather than a battleground.

As the day of the fashion show approached, the energy in the studio reached a fever pitch. Friends, family, and industry insiders buzzed with anticipation, their excitement palpable as we prepared to unveil our collection to the world. I felt a mixture of exhilaration and anxiety coursing through me, a rush that echoed the heartbeat of the city outside.

On the day of the show, the venue was ablaze with lights and the hum of eager voices. I stood backstage, surrounded by models in our creations, my heart racing in sync with the pounding music that reverberated through the walls. Blake appeared beside me, his presence both grounding and electrifying.

"Are you ready?" he asked, his eyes bright with adrenaline.

"As ready as I'll ever be," I replied, a smile breaking through the tension.

The curtain rose, and as the first model stepped onto the runway, I held my breath. Each silhouette glided forward, the vibrant colors and innovative designs weaving a narrative that was unmistakably ours. The crowd gasped and clapped, the energy surging like a tidal wave, and I felt tears prick at the corners of my eyes.

With each passing model, I glanced at Blake, catching his eye and exchanging smiles that held unspoken promises of trust and camaraderie. It was a beautiful dance we were performing—not just with fabric but with our hearts. We had taken a risk, but here, in this moment, it felt entirely worth it.

As the final model took her turn, adorned in the show-stopping gown, the applause thundered through the venue, washing over us like a warm tide. It was a symphony of approval, a testament to our hard work, our late nights, and the soul we had poured into every stitch.

And in that exhilarating moment, amidst the chaos and the accolades, I realized that while the fashion world was fierce and ever-changing, the bond we had forged—full of respect and creativity—was the foundation upon which I wanted to build my future. Trusting Blake didn't feel like a gamble anymore; it felt like the beginning of a new chapter, one I was eager to write alongside him.

Chapter 7: The Stitches that Bind

The fabric of the city buzzed with life, an electric hum woven into the very streets where dreams and regrets mingled like the petals of spring flowers. I stood in my studio, a quaint nook nestled between an old bookstore and a coffee shop that smelled of roasted beans and sugar. The sun filtered through the tall windows, casting a soft glow on my latest designs, each piece a patchwork of my heart and spirit. My hands, still trembling from the tremors of self-doubt, worked tirelessly, threading together memories, desires, and the occasional tear.

It wasn't easy, this act of creation. It demanded that I excavate the depths of my soul, unearthing fragments of my past that I had tucked away under layers of fabric and ambition. Each stitch was a declaration, a proclamation that I would not be defined by my failures but rather by my relentless pursuit of beauty in the chaos. I could feel Emma's spirit beside me, her unwavering support a warm embrace that kept the shadows at bay. She had a knack for knowing just when to pop in with a cup of herbal tea or a cheeky comment that made me laugh when the weight of the world threatened to crush my creativity.

As the days blurred into nights, I poured my heart into this collection, each piece imbued with the essence of my journey. A soft, lavender silk dress echoed the innocence of my childhood summers, while a structured black jacket encapsulated the fierce determination that had grown from my struggles. I wanted this collection to tell a story—not just mine, but that of anyone who dared to weave their own narrative against the harsh backdrop of expectations and norms. I longed to create garments that would make people feel seen, beautiful, and empowered.

Then came the day when Blake Hart, the enigmatic founder of Hart & Co., offered to showcase my designs at one of his high-profile events. My heart raced at the thought. A million thoughts tumbled through my mind: gratitude, excitement, and an insidious thread of fear that snaked through my veins. Blake was a force of nature, his presence commanding and magnetic. I had heard whispers about him—the untamed genius who turned the fashion world on its head but still wrestled with the demons of his past. The opportunity was a shimmering jewel in the rough landscape of my life, but it came with the fear of exposing myself to a scrutiny I wasn't sure I could withstand.

Meeting Blake was nothing short of an electric jolt. When he stepped into my studio for the first time, the air crackled with unspoken possibilities. He wore a tailored jacket that hinted at his impeccable taste, but his eyes—deep, stormy blue—told a different story. They held an intensity that captivated and unnerved me all at once. As we exchanged pleasantries, I found myself lost in his gaze, the world outside fading into a mere background hum. The way he looked at me, like I was an unsolved puzzle, ignited a fire of ambition within me that I had thought extinguished.

The initial meetings were a delicate dance. We discussed fabrics, colors, and inspirations, our conversations laced with a chemistry that felt both exhilarating and dangerous. Blake shared snippets of his life, stories layered with laughter and shadows, tales of family expectations that loomed large over him, stifling his creative spirit. The pressures of his upbringing hung like a low-hanging fog, obscuring the path he longed to carve for himself. In those moments, he transformed from the untouchable mogul into a man grappling with vulnerability, and I found myself drawn to him like a moth to a flame.

I began to peel back the layers of his guarded heart, discovering the rawness behind his confident façade. There were moments when he would let his guard down—brief glimmers of a boy who once dared to dream, marred by heartbreak and disappointments. It was in those shared silences, punctuated by the distant sounds of the city—the laughter of children playing in the park across the street, the melodic hum of a guitar strumming nearby—that I realized we were connected by a common thread of ambition and vulnerability.

Working side by side, we wove our dreams together, his meticulous eye for detail complementing my bold designs. The studio became our sanctuary, a cocoon where we could explore creativity without the weight of the outside world. I discovered a profound joy in watching him sketch ideas, his hands moving with an elegance that mirrored his thoughts. Each line he drew was like a heartbeat, a pulse of inspiration that surged through me, compelling me to create with the same fervor.

As the date of the showcase approached, anticipation coiled around my stomach like a tightly wound spring. Would I be able to present my designs without crumbling under the weight of my insecurities? Would Blake be as impressed with my creations as I hoped? I questioned my every decision, the fear of failure looming large, but as I poured my heart into the final touches, I felt a burgeoning sense of pride. This collection was not merely fabric and thread; it was a tapestry of resilience, stitched together with hopes and dreams that could no longer be silenced.

The day of the event dawned, and I stood before the mirror, the soft fabric of my dress brushing against my skin like a gentle whisper of encouragement. I felt the echoes of my journey resonate within me, an unwavering belief that I was meant to take this step. With Emma by my side, offering her unwavering support, I took a deep breath and stepped out into a world that awaited my story, a world where every stitch would reveal the strength that bound us all together.

The venue for the showcase was a historic theater nestled within the bustling streets of downtown, a place where laughter and dreams had long danced in the shadows of its gilded arches. It was a building steeped in the echoes of glamorous evenings, the kind of space that felt alive with possibility. As I stepped into the grand foyer, adorned with shimmering chandeliers and intricate moldings, a thrill of anxiety and exhilaration raced through me. Each heartbeat resonated in my chest, a reminder of the stakes I had willingly chosen to embrace.

Emma flitted beside me, her infectious energy a grounding force against my swirling thoughts. Her dress, a vibrant splash of color that mirrored her personality, turned heads as we made our way through the throngs of guests arriving for the event. She leaned in close, whispering a quick reassurance that settled like a warm blanket around my shoulders. "You've poured your soul into this. Just let them see you." With her encouragement, I felt a flicker of confidence ignite within, urging me to embrace the night ahead.

Blake appeared moments later, cutting through the crowd like a comet streaking across the night sky. His presence commanded attention, a magnetic pull that drew the eyes of everyone in the room. He wore a deep navy suit that accentuated the angular lines of his figure, each crease in the fabric a testament to his meticulous nature. The way he moved through the crowd was both graceful and authoritative, and as our eyes met, a rush of warmth surged through me. It was a simple gaze, yet it spoke volumes, bridging the distance between us like an unbreakable thread.

"Are you ready for this?" he asked, his voice low and smooth, wrapping around me like silk. There was a softness behind his bravado, a vulnerability that hinted at the man beneath the polished surface. I nodded, the flutter of nerves still dancing in my stomach but tempered by a sense of purpose. Together, we stood on the precipice of something monumental.

The atmosphere was electric as guests mingled, their laughter and chatter creating a tapestry of sound that enveloped the theater. The walls, adorned with velvet drapes and golden accents, seemed to

STITCHING A NEW TOMORROW　　　　　　71

breathe in the excitement, every corner reflecting the anticipation of the evening. I took a moment to absorb it all—the vibrant energy, the shimmering lights, the promise of new beginnings that hung in the air like the scent of fresh blooms in spring.

As we moved toward the stage, I caught glimpses of the models who would showcase my collection, each of them embodying the spirit of the designs I had poured my heart into. They glided effortlessly, the fabric cascading around them like whispers of dreams yet to be fulfilled. I marveled at how they seemed to embody the very essence of my journey, their poised elegance a reflection of the strength I had discovered within myself.

Blake stood beside me, a pillar of calm amidst the storm of emotions swirling within me. As the lights dimmed, and the murmurs of the crowd hushed, I felt a palpable shift in the room. The spotlight illuminated the stage, and my heart raced with both dread and exhilaration. This was my moment, a culmination of late nights and whispered fears, a celebration of everything I had fought to create.

As the first model stepped onto the stage, clad in a flowing lavender gown that seemed to ripple like the surface of a tranquil lake, I held my breath. With each stride, she transformed into a vessel for my story, her presence a living testament to my struggles and triumphs. The audience erupted into applause, a cascade of sound that washed over me like a tide of affirmation. In that instant, I felt a shift, an awakening of sorts. I was not merely a designer but a storyteller, weaving my narrative into the fabric of the world around me.

Blake's eyes were fixed on me, a blend of pride and admiration shining through the depths of his stormy gaze. He leaned in, his voice a low murmur as he whispered, "They're loving it." A rush of warmth spread through me at his words, igniting a fire of ambition that surged through my veins. I could feel the threads of our shared experiences binding us closer, and in that moment, the distance between us began to dissolve.

The showcase unfolded like a beautifully choreographed dance, each model stepping into the spotlight, showcasing my designs as if unveiling the very essence of my soul. A structured black jacket glided across the stage, its sharp lines juxtaposed with the softness of a flowing skirt, a nod to the duality of strength and vulnerability. As the final model twirled, the audience erupted into applause, the sound reverberating within the grand hall like a symphony of acceptance.

The show concluded, leaving me breathless, standing amidst a whirlwind of excitement and applause. Emma rushed to my side, her face alight with joy. "You did it! You were incredible!" she beamed, wrapping her arms around me in an embrace that felt like home.

But amidst the celebration, I felt Blake's presence lingering nearby, his gaze contemplative as he absorbed the atmosphere. I watched him, curiosity tugging at my heartstrings, longing to understand the depths of his thoughts. It was in the quiet moments that I saw the shadows in his eyes—the remnants of past struggles, the burdens he still carried.

As the crowd began to disperse, I found myself drawn to him, needing to bridge the space that lingered between us. "What did you think?" I asked, my voice barely above a whisper, laden with vulnerability.

He turned to me, a flicker of surprise crossing his face. "I think you have an extraordinary gift," he replied, sincerity lacing his words. "You've created something beautiful, and it speaks volumes about who you are."

In that moment, I felt an unspoken connection, an understanding that transcended the glitz and glamour of the evening. We were two souls intertwined in a world that often demanded we suppress our true selves. I saw in Blake the same ambition that burned within me, a desire to carve out our identities in a landscape that often felt unforgiving.

As we stood there, surrounded by the remnants of the event—discarded drink glasses, the remnants of laughter and applause—I realized that this night was more than just a showcase of designs; it was a celebration of resilience, of stories stitched together by the threads of our experiences. And in that realization, I felt an unfamiliar warmth blossom within me, a sense of belonging to something greater than myself.

In the midst of our shared vulnerability, I knew that our paths were intertwined, a delicate tapestry of ambition and heart. I took a breath, feeling the weight of the world shifting as I stepped closer to Blake. The night was still young, and in that moment, possibilities unfurled like petals opening to the sun, beckoning us to explore what lay ahead.

The post-show buzz enveloped me like a warm embrace, yet I was acutely aware of the whirlwind of emotions swirling just beneath the surface. Emma was effervescent, her laughter ringing out like chimes in the evening breeze as she celebrated my triumph, but my gaze often drifted toward Blake, whose intensity remained captivating. As guests mingled, I caught snippets of conversations—praises for my designs, speculation about the future of Hart & Co., and a dash of envy that always seemed to follow success. But it was Blake's steady presence that anchored me, a constant amidst the rising tide of excitement and pressure.

With the show behind us, we retreated to a quieter corner of the theater, where the ornate architecture was momentarily forgotten amid the afterglow of the event. I leaned against a plush velvet cushion, feeling the texture of the fabric seep into my very being. Blake stood nearby, watching the scene unfold with an inscrutable expression. "You did something remarkable tonight," he said, breaking the silence that had settled between us. The way he said it made my skin prickle, a compliment layered with the weight of unspoken admiration.

"Thank you," I replied, my voice softer than I intended. The truth was, I hadn't just shown my work—I had revealed a part of myself that I had hidden for too long. "It feels surreal. Almost too good to be true."

Blake nodded, his stormy eyes reflecting a shared understanding that seemed to pulse in the air between us. "In this industry, moments like that are rare," he said. "But it's what you do next that defines your journey." His words lingered in the air, resonating with the truth I craved. I wanted more than this moment; I yearned for a future where my dreams were no longer just aspirations but tangible realities.

As the evening wore on, the theater began to empty, leaving behind a trail of glittering memories in the form of crumpled napkins, half-finished drinks, and discarded programs. The laughter faded, but my heart was still racing with the thrill of the night. Emma and I stood together, clutching each other's hands, reveling in the aftermath of our triumphs.

But in the depths of my heart, a new fear began to take root. What if this was it? What if I couldn't replicate the magic of tonight? I glanced at Blake, who was engrossed in conversation with a few influential guests, his charisma effortlessly drawing them in. The way he navigated the crowd was mesmerizing, yet I couldn't help but feel the distance of our worlds. Could I bridge the gap between my aspirations and his established presence in the industry?

When Blake finally turned back to me, he caught the flicker of doubt that crossed my face. "Hey," he said, stepping closer, the warmth of his presence a comforting balm. "You've got this. You're not just a designer; you're a storyteller. And tonight, you wrote a captivating chapter."

"Do you really think so?" I asked, the vulnerability in my voice betraying the confidence I wanted to project. He studied me for a moment, as if deciphering the depths of my uncertainty.

"I know so," he replied, his voice firm, with a sincerity that resonated deep within me. "You just need to keep telling your story. There's so much more to explore."

His words were a lifeline, anchoring me amidst the swirling chaos of my thoughts. Yet as we spoke, I couldn't shake the feeling that Blake held secrets of his own, threads of his past woven into the fabric of his present. He was an enigma, and the more I learned about him, the more I wanted to delve deeper into the complexities that lay beneath his polished exterior.

The days following the showcase passed in a blur of activity. I spent countless hours in my studio, pouring my thoughts into new designs inspired by the connections I was forging. Emma remained my steadfast partner in creativity, offering insights that sparked my imagination. "You know," she mused one afternoon, as we worked side by side, "your designs have a certain spirit. They're alive, like they're breathing."

I smiled at her words, feeling the warmth of encouragement wrap around me. "I want them to feel that way. Every stitch is a heartbeat, a reflection of the journey that brought me here."

As I stitched and cut, the memories of my past intertwined with the dreams I was building. Each piece felt like a chapter unfolding, revealing the depths of my journey. I created a gown that draped like a waterfall, shimmering with hues that echoed the sunsets of my childhood, while another piece was stark and minimalistic, a bold declaration of strength. The studio was alive with colors and fabrics, each element a testament to my growth.

Blake became a constant presence in my life, often dropping by to check on my progress. We shared laughter and stories, our conversations flowing effortlessly from design techniques to the emotional weight of our respective journeys. I discovered more about his past—how the expectations of his family had shaped him into the man he was today. He spoke of the pressure to conform, to achieve success in a world that often valued image over authenticity.

"Sometimes," he confided one evening as we huddled over sketches, "I feel like I'm running from a shadow. My family has this image of success, and I've spent so long trying to break free." His vulnerability was palpable, and I felt a kinship forming, a bond forged in the fires of our struggles. "But then I met you, and it made me question everything I thought I knew about my path."

His admission hung in the air between us, a shared understanding of the complexities of ambition and identity. I reached out, my fingers brushing against his, a fleeting connection that sent a jolt of electricity through me. "Maybe we're both searching for something," I said softly, my heart racing at the closeness of our bodies. "A way to be seen for who we truly are."

He looked at me, his eyes holding a mixture of intensity and tenderness, and in that moment, I felt a thread of connection binding us even tighter. It was a thread spun from shared dreams, hopes, and vulnerabilities, and I knew we were on the precipice of something profound.

As the days turned into weeks, anticipation built for the next Hart & Co. event—a showcase that would highlight not just my designs but also the essence of our creative partnership. Each fitting felt like an unveiling of our collective narrative, as we merged our visions into something greater than ourselves. Blake's presence brought a new energy to my work, pushing me to explore depths I had yet to touch.

And as the night of the event approached, the realization struck me that this was not just a showcase of clothing—it was a manifestation of our intertwined journeys, a celebration of resilience, creativity, and the strength that arises from vulnerability.

Underneath the twinkling stars and the vibrant lights of the city, I felt a surge of hope—an exhilarating promise that no matter how tumultuous the road ahead, I had found a partner to share it with. Together, we were weaving a tapestry of dreams that transcended our pasts, stitching together a narrative rich with ambition, connection, and the courage to embrace our true selves.

Chapter 8: Unraveling Truths

The day dawned with an electric pulse, the sun spilling golden light across the streets of New York City, a kaleidoscope of hope and chaos, each corner thrumming with the energy of impending possibilities. I stood at the entrance of Hart & Co., my heart a captive bird fluttering wildly against the confines of my ribcage. The building loomed above me, an architectural marvel of steel and glass that shimmered like an unclaimed treasure. This was it—the moment I had envisioned for years, the culmination of countless hours spent sewing sequins under dim lights and sketching wild, vivid designs that lived only in my imagination.

Inside, the atmosphere crackled with anticipation. The runway stretched before me like a tightrope, a gleaming strip that promised both triumph and terror. Each step echoed the sound of my racing heartbeat, a rhythm that seemed to sync with the pulsating music reverberating through the walls. As I navigated through throngs of stylists, models, and influencers, I caught fleeting glimpses of their sleek silhouettes and designer outfits. The air smelled of expensive perfume mixed with the faint trace of freshly brewed coffee, a heady concoction that made my stomach twist.

In a flurry of activity, I moved through the backstage area, a chaotic realm adorned with mirrors and makeup artists frantically applying the final touches to the models. Each gown hung on its designated rack, swaying gently like whispers of dreams just waiting to be set free. I couldn't help but marvel at the colors and textures before me—daring reds, soft pastels, and deep, enigmatic blues, each fabric telling its own story, waiting to unfold. My designs, the essence of my soul stitched into every seam, sparkled under the harsh backstage lights, a riot of creativity waiting to take center stage.

As the show began, the lights dimmed, and a hush fell over the audience, transforming the buzzing excitement into a palpable tension. I held my breath, my fingers brushing against the fabric of my own creation, a gown that flowed like liquid moonlight, adorned with intricate beadwork that captured the glimmer of the spotlights. I watched from the wings as the first model stepped onto the runway, the crowd's collective gasp sending shivers down my spine.

With each passing look, the audience responded with admiration, their applause a tidal wave of affirmation that threatened to drown my insecurities. But then, amidst the sea of faces, a sharp recognition sliced through my exhilaration. I caught a glimpse of a familiar figure nestled among the spectators, a woman with an air of elegance that was undeniably my mother. The sight of her stirred a tempest of emotions within me, dredging up years of unspoken disapproval and the shadows of our estrangement.

Her presence felt like a spotlight turned harshly on me, illuminating not only my designs but also the painful fractures in our relationship. I hadn't expected her to attend, to bear witness to my ascent into a world she had once scorned. I could feel the weight of her gaze, heavy and judgmental, and suddenly the vibrant world around me dulled into shades of gray. The music played on, but it became a distant hum as my mind spiraled back to the last time we had spoken—the bitter words exchanged like daggers, the silence that followed, a chasm too wide to bridge.

Blake's voice broke through my reverie, a soothing balm in the midst of my turmoil. "You're doing amazing," he said, his eyes warm and steady as he stood beside me, a reassuring presence in this whirlwind of glamour and dread. I stole a glance at him, his handsome features framed by tousled hair, a contrast to the polished individuals surrounding us. In that moment, he felt like my anchor, grounding me in a reality that threatened to slip through my fingers.

"Do you think she'll understand?" I whispered, a tremor of vulnerability creeping into my voice. The question hung between us, heavy with the weight of years spent trying to earn my mother's approval.

Blake turned his gaze to the audience, his expression contemplative. "Understanding doesn't always come easy, especially not with family. But what you're doing here, it's for you. You've fought for this, and it's beautiful." His words enveloped me like a warm embrace, infusing a flicker of courage into my heart.

As the show continued, I focused on the models gliding down the runway, showcasing my creations with grace and poise. Each step they took felt like a defiance against the doubts that had once paralyzed me. I could hear the murmurs of appreciation from the crowd, feel the excitement crackling like static electricity in the air. My dreams, once confined to the pages of a sketchbook, were now unfurling like the petals of a flower, vibrant and alive.

But no matter how captivating the spectacle, my thoughts drifted back to my mother. I imagined the conversations we never had, the laughter that faded into silence, and the dreams I had chased in solitude. The ache of longing intermingled with the exhilaration of success, creating a bittersweet symphony that played on repeat in my mind. What would it take to break through the wall of disappointment she had built around herself?

As the final model took her turn down the runway, draped in a gown that captured the essence of my artistic vision, I felt a rush of exhilaration mixed with dread. This was my moment—a moment that should have felt complete, yet a part of me remained entangled in the fear of rejection. I glanced back at Blake, who was watching me intently, his encouragement buoying me even as my heart sank under the weight of my mother's gaze.

And then it happened. In the midst of the applause and the flashing cameras, I caught her expression. It wasn't one of disdain; instead, there was a flicker of something else—curiosity, perhaps, or maybe a glimmer of understanding. It was enough to send a surge of hope through my veins, a whispered promise that maybe, just maybe, this was the beginning of something new.

The applause faded into a hushed murmur, a gentle tide pulling back after the storm of excitement. I stood backstage, the chaos of the runway still echoing in my ears, while the world around me transformed into a blur of sequins and whispers. As the last model turned and waved, I felt a mix of triumph and trepidation swelling within me. My heart raced not just from the adrenaline of the show, but also from the sheer weight of my mother's presence, a figure whose approval I had long yearned for yet never managed to capture.

Blake leaned in closer, his voice barely a whisper amidst the cacophony of chatter and camera clicks. "You were incredible out there. They loved it." His eyes sparkled with genuine pride, his admiration wrapping around me like a favorite blanket on a cold night. I nodded, a smile forming on my lips, but it felt heavy—weighted by the glances I dared to steal toward the audience.

My mother was still there, a silhouette in the throng, her expression unreadable, cloaked in the shadows of the auditorium. I could only imagine the thoughts swirling behind her composed facade—thoughts of disappointment or perhaps a flicker of curiosity, just as I had hoped. The years of conflict flooded back to me, vivid and raw, each memory sharp enough to sting. The harsh words exchanged in the heat of arguments felt fresh, as though they had just been spoken.

As the crowd began to disperse, my heart quickened. The thought of approaching her felt both electrifying and terrifying, a paradox that made my palms sweat. What would I say? How would I bridge the chasm between us? Blake sensed my hesitation, his hand resting reassuringly on my shoulder, a gesture that steadied me. "Do you want to talk to her?" he asked, his voice low and encouraging.

"Yes, but..." I trailed off, my thoughts scattering like leaves in a brisk autumn wind. "What if she just sees me as the daughter who defied her?" The vulnerability in my voice startled me. I had been strong, resilient even, but this was a different kind of strength—one that required the courage to confront my fears head-on.

Blake squeezed my shoulder, a silent promise of support. "You're not that girl anymore. You're a force. Go show her."

With a deep breath, I took a step toward the crowd, Blake beside me like a steadfast lighthouse guiding me through the storm. Each footfall echoed in my mind, reverberating with uncertainty. As I approached the edge of the crowd, I scanned the sea of faces, each one a different story, a different life. And then there she was, framed in the warm glow of the exit lights, my mother—the woman whose expectations had shaped so much of my identity, yet had also shackled me in a way I could never articulate.

Her hair, a cascade of silvery strands, framed her face elegantly, but I could see the tension in her jaw, the tightness around her eyes. I was close enough to see the subtle flicker of surprise that crossed her features as I approached. The world around us blurred, sounds fading into an insignificant hum, and all that remained was the space between us, thick with unspoken words and unresolved emotions.

"Mom," I said, my voice breaking slightly as I stepped into her line of sight.

She blinked, as if awakening from a trance, and for a moment, I felt suspended in time, the air heavy with anticipation. "I didn't expect to see you here," she replied, her tone measured, yet tinged with an unmistakable edge.

"I know," I said, my heart racing. "But I hoped you would come."

The silence that followed was deafening, a chasm filled with all the things we had never said. I could feel Blake's presence at my side, a silent witness to this moment of reckoning.

Her gaze softened slightly as she took in my appearance, the gown that clung to my frame like a second skin, the confidence that radiated from me in waves. "You've done well for yourself," she conceded, a hint of something almost resembling pride flickering in her eyes.

"Thank you," I replied, a warmth blooming in my chest. "I've been working really hard."

"I see that," she said, her voice a little steadier. "But why this? Why fashion?" The question hung in the air, heavy with implication.

I took a breath, choosing my words carefully. "Because it makes me feel alive. Because creating something beautiful is what I've always wanted." I paused, gathering my thoughts, my heart pounding as I ventured deeper into the conversation. "I wanted to show you that I can be happy doing this. That it matters to me."

The moment felt fragile, like glass poised to shatter. Her expression shifted, caught between recognition and restraint. "I just wanted what was best for you," she said softly, the edge of reproach in her tone dulled by uncertainty. "I never thought... well, I never believed you could make a living in a world like this."

A cascade of emotions washed over me—understanding, anger, and the sharp sting of past grievances. "I get that. But it's my life, Mom. I need to chase my dreams, even if they're not what you envisioned."

The air crackled with unspoken feelings, a tension that was both foreign and familiar. I searched her face for any sign of what lay beneath the surface, any hint that she might finally understand. "Can't we at least try to talk about it? Try to understand each other?"

For a moment, she was quiet, her gaze fixed on me as if trying to peel back the layers of time and misunderstanding that had woven a thick barrier between us. "Maybe," she whispered, the word carrying the weight of a thousand possibilities.

The room began to fill again with the remnants of celebration—the clinking of glasses, laughter rising like bubbles in the air, all the vibrant chaos I had almost forgotten in this moment of connection. But here we stood, two women on the precipice of a new beginning, ready to confront the past and perhaps, if we dared, forge a new path forward.

In that delicate moment, I felt a shift, a gentle loosening of the hold my mother's disapproval had long had over me. The air felt lighter, infused with the hope that we might finally begin to understand one another, that perhaps, in this journey toward our dreams, we could find a way back to each other.

The moment stretched between us like a gossamer thread, fragile yet impossibly resilient. My mother's gaze bore into mine, a blend of apprehension and curiosity that was both familiar and disconcerting. The applause from the audience still resonated, but it felt like an echo of a distant world. Here, in the soft glow of the backstage lights, we stood alone amidst the remnants of a bustling celebration, as if the rest of the universe had faded into nothingness, leaving just the two of us to navigate this delicate terrain.

"Can we sit down?" I suggested, gesturing to a row of empty chairs lined against the wall. She hesitated for just a moment before nodding, a silent concession that signaled the possibility of a conversation that had long been overdue. As we settled into our seats, the clamor of the crowd began to recede, and the weight of our shared silence enveloped us.

"I watched the show," she said finally, her voice almost tentative, as if each word required careful consideration. "You've come so far."

"Thanks," I replied, my heart fluttering at her acknowledgment. "It's taken a lot of hard work, and I'm still learning every day. But I love it."

Her brow furrowed slightly, and I could see the gears turning in her mind, processing what I had said. "You always were talented, even as a child. I just... I worried about you. The fashion industry can be unforgiving."

"Mom," I interrupted, my voice steady yet gentle, "it's unforgiving, yes. But it's also beautiful and filled with opportunity. I can't let fear dictate my dreams anymore."

The tension in her posture softened just a fraction, the lines around her mouth easing as she regarded me with a mix of surprise and something akin to hope. "I wish I could have seen that sooner," she admitted, her voice barely above a whisper. "I didn't understand how much it meant to you."

"Neither did I," I confessed, the admission tasting bittersweet on my tongue. "For so long, I thought I needed to prove myself to you. I thought if I could just be what you wanted, everything would be okay. But I lost sight of who I was in the process."

We sat in a silence that felt heavier than before, a profound understanding weaving through the air between us. I could see the shimmer of unshed tears in her eyes, reflections of years filled with both love and disappointment. It was a delicate balance, one I had felt on countless occasions but had never fully articulated.

"Do you remember when I made that dress for the school talent show?" I asked suddenly, the memory tumbling forth like a long-buried treasure. "The one that fell apart on stage? I was so embarrassed, but you encouraged me to keep going. You said that every failure was a stepping stone."

A soft smile crept onto her face, the corners of her lips lifting as she nodded. "You were always so determined, even then. I admired that."

"And I wanted you to be proud," I added, feeling the weight of those words settle between us. "I still do, but I can't live for your approval anymore."

Her expression shifted, a flicker of comprehension breaking through. "I never wanted to hold you back. I was scared, I guess. Scared that the world would hurt you, and that I couldn't protect you."

The truth of her words hung in the air like a fragile truce. "We both need to let go of the past, don't we?" I suggested, my heart pounding with the vulnerability of it all. "To find a way forward."

"Yes," she replied, her voice steadier now. "I want that too. I don't want to lose you."

The resolve in her words wrapped around me, warm and reassuring. I took a deep breath, my mind racing with possibilities. This was a new beginning, a chance to redefine our relationship on our own terms. "Then let's take it one step at a time. I'd love to share this journey with you, if you're willing."

Her gaze met mine, an unspoken agreement passing between us. For the first time in years, I felt a flicker of optimism igniting in the depths of my heart. The show had been just the beginning; perhaps this conversation could be the foundation for something more meaningful.

As we talked, the world outside continued its dance, oblivious to the profound shift taking place in this small corner of Hart & Co. With every shared memory and hesitant laugh, I could feel the distance between us shrinking, the walls we had built crumbling into dust. The noise of the celebration faded into a mere backdrop, a gentle reminder of the beauty and chaos that lay ahead.

When we finally stepped out of that intimate cocoon, the atmosphere buzzed with life, the energy electrifying. Critics mingled with models and photographers, the air thick with excitement and possibility. I felt a renewed sense of purpose, a realization that I was no longer alone in this journey. My mother's presence, once a source of anxiety, now felt like an anchor in the turbulent sea of the fashion world.

Blake appeared by my side, a knowing smile on his face. "How did it go?"

"Better than I expected," I replied, a surge of confidence coursing through me. "We're going to try to rebuild our relationship."

His eyes lit up, genuine happiness radiating from him. "That's amazing. I'm so proud of you."

As we made our way through the crowd, I felt the weight of uncertainty lifting, replaced by a sense of clarity. The conversations, the laughter, the flashes of cameras—it was all a testament to the world I had chosen, a world that was full of vibrant possibilities.

We paused at the edge of the crowd, the runway glowing behind us like a portal to the future. I watched the models mingling with critics, their laughter rising like a symphony, and I realized that I had a place here—a place to create, to inspire, and perhaps most importantly, to grow.

With my mother's tentative acceptance and Blake's unwavering support, I felt emboldened to chase my dreams without the shadows of doubt clouding my vision. The path ahead was still unwritten, but I was no longer afraid of the blank pages. With every step I took, I felt myself embracing not just my passion for fashion, but the love and connection that had always been lurking beneath the surface.

As we stood together, I could see the dawn of something beautiful—a future painted in shades of hope, laughter, and a shared understanding that would transform our lives in ways I had only dared to dream. The lights of Hart & Co. twinkled like stars, guiding me toward a new horizon where I would finally be free to create, to live, and to love without the chains of the past holding me back.

Chapter 9: The Fabric of Us

The air in the gallery was still heavy with the scent of fresh paint and polished wood, remnants of the showcase lingering like a dream half-remembered. The walls, adorned with a cacophony of color and emotion, whispered secrets only I could decipher. I stood in the center of it all, absorbing the aftermath of the night—the flurry of laughter, the clinking of glasses, the vibrant pulse of creativity. Each stroke of the artist's brush echoed the heartbeat of a city that thrived on aspiration and heartache, a symphony of ambition played against the backdrop of New York's skyline.

My hands trembled slightly, not from the chill of the early autumn evening seeping through the high windows, but from a rush of adrenaline still coursing through my veins. The anticipation had coiled around me like a silk ribbon, tightly wound, until it unraveled with the final applause. In that moment, I felt a mix of liberation and vulnerability, like standing atop the Empire State Building, gazing down at the world below—a dizzying freedom tinged with the fear of falling.

Blake's presence anchored me amidst the whirlwind of emotions. He had been there every step of the way, his laughter mingling with the sounds of the crowd, his warmth a steady flame against the cold reality of my self-doubt. It was remarkable how a single person could transform the mundane into the extraordinary, and Blake had a way of seeing beyond the surface. He grasped the intricacies of my designs, peeling back layers to reveal the heart of my vision, as though he could read the stories woven into the fabric of my creations.

Yet, standing there, amidst the remnants of our triumphant night, I grappled with a swirling storm of confusion. The professional walls that had defined our relationship had crumbled in the face of creativity, yet in their place rose an uncharted territory that felt both exhilarating and terrifying. Our connection had deepened, morphing from casual flirtation into something more profound, more personal. I could feel it in the way his eyes lingered on mine, in the hushed tones of our conversations, and the soft, unguarded moments we shared.

But love, I reminded myself, was not merely an idyllic tapestry sewn with hope and dreams; it was also a precarious gamble, one that required a brave heart and a readiness to embrace the unexpected. I had danced on the edge of that abyss before, only to recoil at the last moment, my heart encased in the iron-clad armor of fear. Would I dare to unravel the tightly knit strands of my heart and risk weaving them into this new relationship?

A soft laugh pulled me from my reverie, and I turned to find Blake watching me, an amused smile playing on his lips. The light from the gallery's chandeliers reflected in his eyes, making them gleam like the warm glow of autumn leaves caught in the sun. "You look like you're contemplating the meaning of life," he teased, stepping closer, his presence a heady mix of comfort and allure.

"Maybe I am," I replied, my voice playful yet laced with an undercurrent of seriousness. "Or maybe I'm just trying to decide what to do with the rest of my life."

He cocked his head, an endearing gesture that made my heart flutter. "Well, I hope that includes a certain tall guy who's been rooting for you since day one."

His gaze was earnest, piercing through my defenses and laying bare the hesitation I'd tried so hard to mask. It was a moment of vulnerability, both thrilling and frightening, the kind that could ignite a wildfire or extinguish it entirely.

"Blake, I—" My words faltered, tangled in the web of my emotions. I wanted to reach out, to bridge the gap between us that had shifted so dramatically, yet I was acutely aware of the potential for heartbreak. The prospect of opening myself up to him filled me with an intoxicating mix of hope and dread, much like the dizzying sensation of standing on the edge of a precipice.

"You don't have to say anything right now," he interjected gently, his voice a soothing balm. "Just know that I'm here. And whatever happens, I want to be a part of it."

His honesty wrapped around me like a comforting blanket, warding off the chill of doubt that threatened to seep into my bones. Maybe he was right; maybe I didn't have to rush into decisions or articulate every thought that flitted through my mind like a restless sparrow. Perhaps love was less about clarity and more about the willingness to explore the unknown together, one step at a time.

We lingered in the gallery, the soft murmurs of the remaining guests fading into a distant hum, creating a cocoon of intimacy just for us. The walls, adorned with vibrant artworks, bore witness to our tentative dance around vulnerability, the air thick with unspoken words and shared dreams. I could almost hear the fabric of our lives intertwining, threads of hope and uncertainty blending into a tapestry that was uniquely ours.

As I looked into Blake's eyes, I saw not just a partner in creativity but a companion ready to face whatever storms lay ahead. In that moment, I made a choice, a bold stitch in the fabric of our lives, to embrace the vulnerability that love demanded. I would take this leap, not with reckless abandon but with the measured courage that comes from knowing that life, like my designs, was an art form crafted with intention and heart.

And so, I took a breath, letting the weight of my fears drift away like leaves caught in the autumn breeze, ready to step into the warmth of the unknown, hand in hand with the man who saw the world through the same kaleidoscope of dreams.

The hum of the city outside the gallery pulsed like a heartbeat, a rhythm that echoed my own mingled emotions. The night had transformed, the vibrant energy of the showcase now giving way to the soothing embrace of twilight. Blake's presence wrapped around me, grounding me as we stepped onto the bustling streets of Manhattan. The air was cool and crisp, each breath filled with the promise of autumn—an invigorating mix of leaves, damp earth, and the distant aroma of roasted chestnuts from a vendor on the corner. It was the kind of evening that made the heart swell with possibility.

I turned to Blake, who walked beside me with an easy confidence, his hands casually tucked into his jacket pockets. The streetlights cast a warm glow, illuminating the soft angles of his face, making his dark hair gleam like polished wood. I admired the way he moved through the world, an effortless grace that belied the storm of creativity within him. With each step we took, the distance between us seemed to dissipate, replaced by an unspoken understanding that felt both comforting and exhilarating.

"What's next for you?" he asked, his voice smooth as the silk I had draped over my latest design. I felt the sincerity in his tone, a genuine curiosity that made my chest warm.

"Honestly? I'm still trying to figure that out," I replied, surprised at the honesty in my own voice. "I have a few ideas brewing, but I guess I'm waiting for the right spark. Something to ignite the passion again."

Blake nodded, a thoughtful look crossing his face. "Sometimes that spark comes when you least expect it. Or when you're busy thinking about something else entirely." He glanced at me, his blue eyes searching mine, as if trying to uncover the depths of my thoughts.

I chuckled lightly, half-heartedly pushing the worries from my mind. "You make it sound so easy. But sometimes it feels like I'm searching for that spark in a dark room, hoping to trip over something brilliant instead of falling flat on my face."

He laughed softly, the sound wrapping around us like a soft blanket, and I couldn't help but smile at how effortlessly he lightened the air between us. "Maybe the trick is to embrace the stumble. Falling can lead to something beautiful."

As we meandered through the crowded streets, I took in the vibrant nightlife that surrounded us—the laughter of friends gathered around tables, the clink of glasses at outdoor cafes, and the distant strains of music filtering from a bar down the block. It was a kaleidoscope of life, each fragment vibrant and alive, and it filled me with a sense of belonging I hadn't realized I craved.

"I think you might be onto something," I said, glancing sideways at Blake, feeling a surge of warmth wash over me. "Maybe I've been too focused on the destination rather than enjoying the journey. It's like I'm trying to fast-forward to the ending when I haven't even savored the beginning."

Blake's smile widened, and in that moment, I felt a shared recognition—a kindred spirit navigating the twists and turns of life, always yearning for more but sometimes forgetting to appreciate the moments that lead us there.

The streets grew quieter as we turned down a dimly lit alleyway, where the remnants of a street art mural danced against the brick wall. Bright colors clashed and harmonized in chaotic beauty, each stroke telling stories that words often failed to capture. I stopped, captivated by the vividness of it all, feeling a kinship with the art before me. It reminded me of my own designs—an explosion of color and pattern, a reflection of the complexities within me.

"Look at this," I said, my voice almost a whisper as I stepped closer, tracing a finger over the gritty surface. "It's so raw and unfiltered, just like life. It makes me think of the beauty in imperfection."

Blake stepped beside me, his shoulder brushing against mine. "You mean like how you stitched together that entire collection? Each piece has its flaws, but they're part of what makes them unique."

I turned to him, surprised at his insight. "You really think so?"

"Absolutely. I've seen how you pour your heart into every design. It's not just about making something pretty; it's about telling a story, embracing the chaos, and finding beauty in the unexpected."

His words wrapped around me like a warm embrace, igniting something deep within. I realized then that my journey in fashion mirrored my journey in life—both were a constant dance of creation, risk, and vulnerability. Each stitch I made was a reflection of my struggles and triumphs, each design a fragment of my identity sewn together with threads of courage and authenticity.

Blake shifted, a subtle movement that brought us closer. "You know, sometimes I think the best stories come from the messiest moments. It's when everything falls apart that we discover who we really are."

I felt a pang of resonance with his words. It was in the tumultuous moments that I had found my voice, where the chaos had shaped my artistry and forged my resolve. "You're right. It's easy to overlook the beauty in the struggle when you're caught up in it. But stepping back, I can see how every challenge has led me to this point."

He looked at me, his expression serious yet tender. "And I'm glad you're here, right now. I know we've been dancing around this thing between us, but I want you to know I'm all in. I want to see where this goes."

The sincerity in his voice sent a tremor of excitement through me, mingling with the fear that had kept me at bay. Here was the moment—the crossroads I had both dreaded and desired. I could either retreat into the safety of my carefully constructed walls or take a leap into the unknown, hand in hand with Blake, ready to embrace whatever awaited us on the other side.

My heart raced, and the city lights twinkled like stars against the night sky, illuminating the path ahead. I took a deep breath, feeling the weight of my fears lift like fog in the morning sun. "Then let's see where this leads us."

As we stood there, our worlds intertwining, I felt the threads of our lives beginning to weave a new tapestry—one that promised to be vibrant, chaotic, and beautifully imperfect, much like the city we inhabited. Together, we would embrace the journey, stepping boldly into the future, one stitch at a time.

The streets of Manhattan felt alive, every corner echoing with laughter and the soft murmur of conversations that danced through the cool night air. It was as if the city itself was celebrating my newfound resolution, each flickering streetlight casting a golden hue on the pavement, illuminating my path forward. Blake walked beside me, our shoulders brushing occasionally, a subtle reminder of the burgeoning connection we were both trying to navigate.

The sound of a saxophonist's melancholic tune wafted through the air, weaving through the chatter and laughter, drawing us toward a small square bustling with life. People gathered around tables draped in fairy lights, their animated voices blending into a soft hum of camaraderie. I could feel my heart quicken as the energy of the crowd enveloped us, amplifying the exhilaration of the moment.

"Shall we?" Blake gestured toward a table where an open seat awaited us. The flickering candles cast a warm glow, and I couldn't help but smile at the inviting ambiance. We settled into the wooden chairs, and I noticed the way he leaned in, an eager glint in his eyes, ready to delve deeper into this unpredictable adventure we had begun.

"Okay, Mr. All-In," I teased, leaning forward, resting my elbows on the table. "What's your plan for conquering the world of art and fashion?"

Blake chuckled, running a hand through his hair, his smile contagious. "Conquering the world sounds a bit ambitious, don't you think? But I do want to make my mark. I've been playing around with some concepts that blend different styles—art with fashion, making clothes that tell a story. But I'd love to hear more about your journey."

There it was, the glimmer of possibility in his eyes that mirrored my own dreams. "You know, I've always believed that fashion is more than just what we wear; it's a reflection of our identity, our experiences. Every piece tells a story, just like art."

As I spoke, I could see him hanging on to every word, his expression a mixture of fascination and admiration. It ignited something within me, a spark of creativity that had been flickering in the shadows for far too long. The conversation flowed naturally, weaving between our dreams and fears, creating a tapestry of our shared aspirations.

I reveled in the lightness of the moment, the way we could navigate serious topics with a wry sense of humor. "So, tell me," I said, "if you could dress any historical figure, who would it be and why?"

Blake leaned back, a thoughtful look crossing his face as he pondered. "Maybe someone unexpected, like Cleopatra. Imagine the intricate patterns and the sheer opulence of her gowns! It would be a challenge, but I bet there's a way to reinterpret that in a modern context."

I laughed, delighted by the vivid image he conjured. "And what would you do with her eyeliner? That's a bold statement to make in today's world!"

"Oh, definitely winged! But with a twist—maybe metallic colors or a more artistic flair," he replied, his enthusiasm infectious. The laughter flowed easily between us, like a familiar melody that lulled my anxiety into submission.

As the night wore on, we shared stories of our childhoods, dreams, and disappointments, each revelation bringing us closer. I felt an invisible thread binding us, something stronger than mere attraction—a shared understanding of the challenges we faced in our respective crafts. His passion for art mirrored my own, and the fear of vulnerability became less daunting in his presence.

The atmosphere shifted slightly as the saxophonist began to play a softer tune, enveloping us in a cocoon of intimacy. I found myself leaning closer, drawn to the warmth radiating from him. I could almost feel the heat of his breath on my skin as he spoke. "You know, it's refreshing to be able to talk about these things openly. Most people don't get the chaos behind the curtain."

"I know exactly what you mean," I confessed, my heart racing as I contemplated the next steps. "There's a fear that comes with exposing ourselves—what if we fail, or worse, what if we're misunderstood? But I think that's where the beauty lies, in the rawness of it all."

His gaze softened, a look of understanding passing between us. "Exactly. It's about being brave enough to show who we really are. And I admire that you've embraced that in your work."

Just as the conversation deepened, a familiar face emerged from the crowd, startling me. My heart sank as I recognized my mother, standing a few tables away, her expression a mix of curiosity and surprise. It was as if she had stepped out of a long-forgotten chapter of my life, her presence pulling me back into the complexities of our relationship.

"Speak of the devil," I murmured, feeling a knot tighten in my stomach. Blake followed my gaze, his brow furrowing slightly.

"Do you want me to introduce myself?" he offered, his voice a quiet strength against the wave of tension washing over me.

"No," I replied quickly, wanting to shield him from the storm I felt brewing. "I'll handle it."

As I stood to greet her, a flurry of emotions coursed through me—disappointment, resentment, but also a flicker of hope. Maybe this was another thread that needed weaving into the fabric of my life, a moment to confront the past. My mother was a complex woman, an artist in her own right, yet tangled in her expectations and unfulfilled dreams.

"Mom," I greeted, trying to keep my tone light, even as my heart raced. "What a surprise to see you here!"

She offered a hesitant smile, her gaze flickering between Blake and me. "I didn't expect to find you in such a lively place. I thought you'd be resting after your showcase."

"Couldn't resist the allure of the city," I replied, casting a glance back at Blake, who had fallen silent, observing our interaction with keen interest. "Mom, this is Blake. We've been working together."

Her eyes narrowed slightly, her protective instincts kicking in, I presumed. "Working together? In what capacity?"

I sensed Blake's discomfort, the tension thickening the air around us. "We've been collaborating on some designs," I explained carefully, hoping to navigate the conversation without triggering an avalanche of unspoken issues.

"I see," she replied, her tone now laced with an edge of judgment. "And how's that going for you, Blake?"

Blake, ever the diplomat, smiled warmly, ready to handle the challenge. "It's been an incredible experience. Mia has a talent that's truly remarkable."

As they exchanged pleasantries, I felt a swirl of apprehension tightening in my chest. The conversation danced awkwardly around us, each word laced with the tension of my unresolved feelings toward my mother. There was a depth of unspoken history between us that felt fragile, ready to shatter at the slightest provocation.

"Mom, can we talk?" I finally asked, my voice steadier than I felt. I could see the flicker of concern in Blake's eyes, and I wanted to reassure him, but my focus remained locked on my mother.

"Of course," she said, her smile faltering as I gestured toward a quieter corner of the square, away from the laughter and music. As we stepped away, I felt a mixture of dread and determination surge within me.

This was my moment—an opportunity to confront the tangled threads of our relationship and, perhaps, begin to weave a new pattern, one that acknowledged both our flaws and strengths. I knew it wouldn't be easy, but the weight of unspoken words hung heavily between us, begging to be released.

With Blake watching from a distance, I braced myself for the conversation that would unravel the complexities of our lives. The night was far from over, and as the city pulsed around us, I felt the threads of my life intertwining in unexpected ways, ready to embrace whatever came next.

Chapter 10: The Price of Fame

The sun had barely dipped below the horizon, painting the sky with the deep hues of twilight, when I found myself nestled in the vibrant chaos of downtown San Francisco. The air was thick with the mingling scents of street food, each cart a beacon of temptation—tacos sizzling on a grill, the sweet notes of caramelized onions, and the unmistakable warmth of freshly baked bread wafting through the streets. It was here, among the bustling throngs and the glittering lights, that my life had taken an unexpected turn, one I had once fantasized about but never truly believed would materialize.

As I made my way down Market Street, the weight of my recent success hung heavily around my shoulders, a shimmering cloak that both dazzled and suffocated. Each step echoed with the pulse of the city, the rhythmic beat almost matching the rapid thumping of my heart. My designs had caught fire, igniting a frenzy of interest that swept me into an unforgiving spotlight. A barrage of notifications greeted me on my phone, each ping a reminder of the demands and expectations now draped around my neck like an albatross. Collaborations flooded in, some from established names in the industry, others from hopeful newcomers whose sincerity tugged at my heartstrings. Yet, amid the excitement, a cloud of anxiety loomed, casting shadows over my once-simple dream.

With every interview I accepted, every photo shoot I reluctantly participated in, the thrill I felt began to fray at the edges. I had envisioned a world where creativity reigned, where my designs would tell stories, evoke emotions, and transform lives. But instead, I found myself drowning in a sea of questions. Was I truly ready for this? Did I have the stamina to keep up with the demands of an industry that was as cutthroat as it was exhilarating? And there was Blake, my fierce and ambitious partner, whose relentless drive mirrored my own. Initially, we had been a perfect pair, each pushing the other toward greater heights, but lately, I sensed a shift. The camaraderie we had nurtured was becoming overshadowed by an insatiable need for recognition that threatened to unravel our partnership.

Late nights became my refuge, each brainstorming session with Emma a sanctuary from the whirlwind outside. Emma, with her electric laughter and contagious enthusiasm, had a gift for turning my fears into ideas. We'd spread out my sketches across her dining room table, a riot of colors and patterns that reflected the chaotic beauty of our lives. The warm glow of the overhead lamp cast gentle shadows on our faces as we sipped coffee, the rich aroma mingling with the sweetness of freshly baked pastries. In those moments, I could almost forget the relentless noise of social media and the pressure to constantly produce. We were just two friends weaving dreams out of fabric and thread, each conversation a step further into the world I wanted to create.

But just as I felt myself regaining my footing, the specter of doubt slithered back into my mind. I watched Blake during those nights, his brow furrowed in concentration, his hands dancing over sketches that rivaled my own. He was an artist in his own right, yet the competition between us felt like a silent predator, creeping ever closer. I admired his passion, the way he dissected trends with surgical precision, yet there was an unsettling sense of urgency in his work, a desperation to eclipse my newfound fame. The more we collaborated, the more I questioned whether we could balance ambition and friendship without losing ourselves in the process.

It was during one particularly late night, surrounded by sketches and coffee mugs, that the tension bubbled over. We had been discussing a project that could potentially catapult us into the stratosphere of the fashion world, a collection that would blend our unique styles into something groundbreaking. The excitement crackled in the air, but as I shared my ideas, Blake's expression hardened.

"Why do you keep holding back?" he snapped, frustration bubbling just beneath the surface. "You have the talent, but you're afraid to take risks. This is our moment! You need to step up."

I felt my heart sink, a heavy stone lodged in my chest. "I'm not holding back," I replied, my voice trembling. "I just want to ensure we don't lose sight of what makes us, us. This isn't just about fame for me, Blake. It's about creating something meaningful."

His eyes narrowed, and the room fell into an uncomfortable silence. The vibrant sketches around us felt like judgmental spectators to our exchange. I yearned to reach out, to bridge the chasm that seemed to widen with each passing moment, but the words lodged in my throat like an unwelcome intruder.

Days turned into weeks, the pressure mounting like a coiled spring ready to snap. The more success I tasted, the more I questioned its worth. I often found myself wandering the streets of San Francisco, seeking solace in the familiar yet always unpredictable cityscape. The iconic Golden Gate Bridge loomed in the distance, a colossal silhouette against the night sky, a symbol of both aspiration and isolation.

Standing on the edge of the bay, I watched the waves dance against the rocks, their rhythmic ebb and flow a reminder that everything—fame, friendship, dreams—was fleeting. The stars flickered above, each one a reminder of the hopes I held tightly, yet beneath the brilliance lay the cold truth of my uncertainty. Fame had its price, and I was beginning to realize that the cost might be more than I was willing to pay.

In the depths of that night, as I breathed in the salty air, I pondered what it meant to be seen, truly seen, in a world that thrived on superficiality. Was I merely a reflection of the glamour and glitz that surrounded me, or could I carve out a space where authenticity flourished? The answer felt elusive, a mirage shimmering just beyond my reach, yet it urged me to continue searching, to find my voice amid the cacophony.

The glimmer of the cityscape felt both enchanting and suffocating, like a beautiful dress that was just a size too small. The tall buildings loomed above me, casting long shadows that danced in the fading light, reminiscent of giants whispering secrets I could barely grasp. Each day felt like an intricate tapestry woven from threads of excitement and trepidation. I often found myself navigating a maze of pop-up shops and vibrant murals that adorned the walls of Mission District, the artistry offering a colorful reprieve from the monochrome worries that often plagued me. Yet, amidst the vibrancy, I was beginning to feel like an imposter in my own life.

One evening, with the promise of an unyielding fog wrapping the city in a blanket of mystery, I joined Emma at a local art gallery showcasing young talent. The gallery buzzed with anticipation, the walls adorned with canvases that screamed rebellion, love, and heartache. Emma's eyes sparkled with enthusiasm as she guided me through the exhibits, each piece a testament to someone's raw experience, much like the designs I had begun to produce. I marveled at the courage it took for these artists to bare their souls, each brushstroke a daring proclamation of existence. I wished I could channel that same bravery into my work, yet I found myself retreating further into my shell.

As we wandered through the gallery, the dim lighting illuminating our path, I noticed a group gathered around a particularly striking piece—a vibrant explosion of color that seemed to pulse with life. "This reminds me of your latest collection," Emma remarked, nudging me with her elbow, her voice filled with genuine admiration. I looked closely at the piece, a chaotic blend of emotions that echoed the turmoil I felt inside. "Maybe," I murmured, my self-doubt creeping in like the fog outside. "But what if it's not enough?"

"Enough?" Emma chuckled, her laughter warm and inviting. "There's no such thing. Art isn't about being enough; it's about being true. Your voice is what makes your work resonate." I wished I could believe her, but the weight of expectations loomed large, threatening to crush my spirit beneath its relentless pressure.

That night, as I lay in bed, the soft hum of the city outside my window lulled me into a restless sleep. I tossed and turned, my mind a kaleidoscope of unfinished sketches and unanswered emails. The fear of letting people down had transformed from a quiet whisper into a relentless scream, drowning out my creative instincts. I woke to the gray light of dawn filtering through my curtains, an all-too-familiar sense of dread settling in the pit of my stomach. It was another day of meetings and pitches, each one a chance to either shine or falter.

At a trendy café buzzing with the early morning crowd, I met Blake for our weekly brainstorming session. The atmosphere was electric, baristas crafting lattes with artful precision while the aroma of freshly baked pastries enveloped us like a comforting hug. Blake was already seated, his laptop open, the screen reflecting his determined gaze. His intensity was both inspiring and intimidating, a spark that often ignited my own creativity but could easily incinerate my confidence.

"Did you see the latest feedback from the fashion blog?" he asked, his eyes gleaming with excitement. "They love the direction we're headed! It's only a matter of time before we blow up." I tried to match his enthusiasm, but the nagging voice in my head cautioned against getting too caught up in the whirlwind of praise.

"Yeah, I saw," I replied, my tone hesitant. "But I'm worried about the next collection. What if we don't meet their expectations? What if it's not as groundbreaking?"

Blake leaned back in his chair, his expression shifting to one of frustration. "We're not here to play it safe. We have to push boundaries. If we don't take risks, we'll be forgotten." The conviction in his voice was palpable, a challenge thrown into the air like confetti. But with every risk he proposed, I felt a wave of anxiety crash over me. What if I faltered? What if the very things that made me unique became the reason I fell short?

As the day wore on, my thoughts drifted back to the gallery and the artists who had poured their souls onto the canvas. They had embraced vulnerability, wielding their paintbrushes like swords against conformity. Inspired, I spent the evening sketching, allowing my emotions to spill onto the paper without the constraints of expectation. The strokes were wild and free, a dance of colors that reflected my heart's tumultuous rhythm. In those moments, I found a fleeting sense of liberation, a reminder of why I had fallen in love with design in the first place.

Yet, that night, as I laid my sketches aside, the looming specter of doubt returned with a vengeance. I picked up my phone and scrolled through social media, each scroll feeling like an open wound. Pictures of my peers adorned with praise, their work celebrated while I stood in the shadows, trembling in uncertainty. The excitement of my earlier creative burst dimmed under the glaring light of comparison. I couldn't shake the feeling that I was running a race I hadn't signed up for, and with each step, I risked losing pieces of myself.

As the days turned into a blur of events and obligations, I often sought solace at the beach, where the crashing waves offered a symphony of reassurance. The salty breeze whipped through my hair, and for a moment, I allowed the chaos of my thoughts to fade, replaced by the simple beauty of the moment. Standing barefoot in the sand, the ocean stretched endlessly before me, a reminder of the vastness of life and possibility. I felt a flicker of hope—perhaps the journey was more important than the destination.

And then there was the day when everything shifted again. An unexpected email pinged into my inbox, the subject line promising an opportunity that could change everything. As I read through the details, my heart raced, hope igniting within me. A collaboration with a well-known designer known for championing emerging talent. The prospect was both exhilarating and terrifying, an invitation to step even further into the spotlight. Yet the exhilaration was tinged with the fear of failure—a chance to soar or to crash and burn.

I took a deep breath, the weight of the world lingering in the air around me. It was a moment of reckoning, an intersection of ambition and trepidation. Would I seize this chance and dive headfirst into the uncertainty? Or would I let the fear of what might go wrong keep me anchored to the shore, forever wondering what could have been? As the sun began to set, casting a golden hue over the ocean, I realized that perhaps the only true failure lay in not trying at all. With that thought clinging to my heart, I made a decision that would shape the course of my journey, ready to embrace the uncertainty of fame, creativity, and the adventures that awaited me.

The sun rose with a lazy grace, illuminating the Pacific horizon with its golden fingers, coaxing me out of the haze of restless dreams. I stood on my tiny balcony, a steaming cup of coffee cradled in my hands, watching the waves kiss the shore like an artist whispering tenderly to her canvas. Each swell brought with it a new rush of inspiration, but also a wave of anxiety that crashed over me just as fiercely. The morning air felt alive, and as the scents of salt and coffee intertwined, I sensed a shift within me—a quiet resolve beginning to take root.

That day marked the beginning of what felt like a turning point. I had finally decided to take the plunge into that collaboration, my heart racing at the thought of it. The designer's name danced on the tip of my tongue, a mixture of excitement and apprehension. Renowned for their avant-garde style and commitment to sustainability, this was an opportunity that many would kill for. Yet, in the solitude of my thoughts, I couldn't shake the feeling that this might lead me down a path I couldn't return from—a path laden with expectations that I wasn't sure I could meet.

As I arrived at the sleek, glass-walled studio, I was greeted by a whirlwind of activity. The air buzzed with energy, and the atmosphere felt charged, as if the very walls were imbued with creative tension. Designers and assistants darted around, their chatter punctuated by the sound of fabric scissors snipping through vibrant textiles. My heart raced as I stepped inside, the glint of polished concrete floors reflecting the chaos around me. I was struck by a mixture of awe and intimidation; this place was a shrine of creativity, each corner bursting with potential.

My new partner in this venture, Ava, a seasoned designer whose work I had admired from afar, welcomed me with a warm smile that instantly put me at ease. She had a reputation for her keen eye for detail and an uncanny ability to meld innovative concepts with commercial appeal. "I've seen your work, and I'm excited to see what we can create together," she said, her voice a blend of encouragement and enthusiasm that made me feel seen in a way I hadn't in weeks.

As we delved into discussions about themes and concepts, I found myself slowly unfurling, like a flower greeted by the sun after a long winter. Ava encouraged me to let go of my fears, to embrace the chaotic energy of creation rather than shrink from it. We tossed ideas back and forth, our laughter weaving through the fabric of our collaboration, reminding me of late-night brainstorming sessions with Emma. But as the day wore on and we began to put pen to paper, I felt the shadows of doubt creeping in again, whispering that I wasn't enough, that I couldn't measure up to her brilliance.

With every sketch we produced, I felt both exhilarated and drained. The ideas flowed like the waves outside, unpredictable and wild, but just as daunting. As the sun dipped lower in the sky, bathing the studio in a warm amber glow, I caught a glimpse of myself in the mirror—smudged eyeliner, frizzy hair, and a look of sheer determination mixed with vulnerability. This was who I was in this moment, a patchwork of imperfections and aspirations, yet I felt a flicker of pride within me, a realization that I belonged here.

That evening, as I navigated the fog-laden streets on my way home, my mind buzzed with new ideas and possibilities. The path ahead felt illuminated, no longer overshadowed by the specter of fear. The familiar streets of San Francisco, often bustling with tourists and locals alike, were quieter than usual, the damp air wrapping around me like a comforting embrace. I was almost home when I spotted a flicker of light in the distance, a small gallery nestled between two larger buildings, its windows aglow with creativity.

Drawn by the warmth spilling onto the sidewalk, I ventured inside, discovering an eclectic mix of art pieces that seemed to capture the very essence of the city—vibrant, unrefined, and full of life. I wandered from piece to piece, losing myself in the stories they told. Each brushstroke spoke to me, whispering the truth that had become increasingly elusive: art is not merely about perfection; it's about expression. It is about revealing one's self, imperfections and all.

The owner, an elderly woman with silver-streaked hair and an infectious smile, caught my eye. "Art is a reflection of life, dear," she said, her voice soft yet firm. "It's messy, chaotic, and sometimes heartbreaking, but therein lies its beauty." Her words lingered in my mind as I made my way home, settling into my thoughts like a beloved book dog-eared from countless readings.

The days that followed became a whirlwind of inspiration and collaboration, each moment steeped in the urgency of creation. Ava and I worked late into the night, sketching designs that pushed boundaries I hadn't even known existed. I watched in awe as she transformed our wild ideas into cohesive concepts, her expertise illuminating the path ahead. Yet, even as I felt my confidence blossoming, Blake's presence loomed large in my mind.

I noticed the distance between us widening, the shared laughter replaced by tension. Our late-night brainstorming sessions morphed into quiet standoffs, as he struggled to come to terms with my evolving role in the collaboration. I could see the competitive fire in his eyes; the ambition that had once united us now felt like a wedge driving us apart. It was as if he was watching from the sidelines, unwilling to acknowledge that I was carving my own path in a landscape that was rapidly changing.

One afternoon, as I poured over sketches, my phone buzzed with a familiar notification. Blake had tagged me in a post on social media, an unfiltered shot of us at one of our earlier events, his arm draped over my shoulder. The caption read: "Can't wait for what's next! Watch out world!" But the enthusiasm felt hollow, a stark contrast to the reality of our unspoken tension. I couldn't help but feel a pang of regret. What had happened to our unity, the joy of collaboration?

That night, I reached out to Emma, seeking her wisdom to navigate the emotional minefield I found myself in. We met at a cozy café, the scent of cinnamon and freshly brewed coffee enveloping us like a warm embrace. "It's like we're on two separate tracks, and I don't know how to bridge the gap," I confessed, stirring my drink absentmindedly.

Emma listened intently, her expression shifting from concern to understanding. "Sometimes, change brings out the worst in people," she said, her voice steady. "But it's important to remember that you're allowed to grow. Just because you're evolving doesn't mean he has to resent you for it. Have you talked to him about how you're feeling?"

"I'm afraid it'll shatter what's left of our friendship," I admitted, my heart heavy. "What if he feels betrayed?"

"You can't let fear dictate your path," she replied, her tone encouraging. "You both need to communicate. If he's your friend, he'll understand your journey, even if it's not the same as his."

Her words lingered long after we parted ways, settling into the corners of my mind. I knew she was right; the bonds we forged were fragile yet resilient, requiring maintenance and honesty. The next day, I resolved to approach Blake, hoping to confront the chasm that had formed between us.

As I walked into the studio, the atmosphere crackled with creativity, yet a tension hung in the air that felt palpable. Blake was hunched over a table, his fingers twitching restlessly over the fabric. "Hey, can we talk?" I ventured, my heart racing.

He looked up, surprise flickering in his eyes, but there was an edge to his expression, a protective barrier that I could sense between us. "Sure," he replied, but the coolness in his tone sent a shiver down my spine.

We moved to a quieter corner, and I took a deep breath, gathering my thoughts. "I've been feeling a lot of pressure lately," I began, my voice steadier than I felt. "With the collaboration and everything, it feels like there's this unspoken competition between us."

Blake's gaze softened for a moment, but the tension remained, a silent storm brewing just beneath the surface. "I guess I've been feeling that too," he admitted, running a hand through his hair. "I just... I don't want to lose what we had. It feels like you're moving on without me."

The vulnerability in his voice struck a chord deep within me, and I stepped closer. "You're not losing me, Blake. We're both evolving, and that's okay. I want to support you as much as I want to grow myself."

His eyes met mine, and for a moment, the distance between us seemed to shrink. "I guess I've been afraid of what this means for us," he murmured, the honesty in his voice a balm to my anxious heart.

"We can make this work," I urged, a sense of determination washing over me. "Let's push each other instead of pulling away. I need you as much as you need me."

Slowly, a smile crept across his face, and the tension began to dissipate like morning fog under the sun. "Okay," he said, his voice steadier now. "Let's do this together."

As we returned to our sketches, the collaborative energy surged back to life, infused with a newfound understanding. We were artists on a shared journey, our paths winding together even as they branched out in different directions.

In that moment, I realized that fame, though daunting, could be navigated with

Chapter 11: A Stitch in Time

The bell above the door tinkled softly as I stepped into the fabric shop, a sound that danced through the air, a sweet serenade welcoming me back to a sanctuary of creativity. The place was a patchwork of memories stitched together with threads of time. Light filtered through the dusty windows, illuminating the countless bolts of fabric that lined the walls, each one a tapestry of stories waiting to be told. The faint scent of cotton mingled with a hint of lavender, a relic of my grandmother's favorite potpourri, which hung like an invisible aura around the shop. It wrapped around me, suffusing the air with warmth, enveloping me in a cocoon of familiarity.

I walked through the narrow aisles, letting my fingers glide over the soft textures, the cool satin, the robust denim, and the delicate silk that craved attention. Each touch sent ripples of nostalgia through me, igniting memories of late-night sewing sessions, the hum of the sewing machine filling the air, and my grandmother's gentle guidance as I navigated my first designs. Those evenings, filled with laughter and the occasional seam ripper, had woven themselves into the fabric of my childhood, creating a rich backdrop against which my love for sewing flourished.

A gentle breeze wafted through the open window, rustling the fabric and stirring up a swirl of dust motes that danced like tiny stars. I made my way to the back of the shop, where the oldest treasures were kept. This section felt like a time capsule, each bolt and pattern a relic from a different era. It was here that I found the remnants of my grandmother's legacy. A small wooden box, weathered but sturdy, sat atop an old sewing machine, its lid slightly ajar. Inside, the fabric lay coiled like a slumbering serpent—delicate lace, tinged with soft hues of cream and ivory, threaded with a story that begged to be unraveled.

As I lifted the lace from the box, a flurry of memories engulfed me. I could almost hear my grandmother's voice, soft and melodic, recounting tales of her own youth, of elegant soirées and dances where women twirled in flowing gowns adorned with lace. This particular piece was special; it was the lace she had worn to her wedding, intricate and exquisite, each detail meticulously crafted. I could envision her, a young bride, her laughter echoing as she glided through the room, the lace whispering against her skin as she danced the night away.

I ran my fingers over the delicate patterns, feeling the gentle curves and sharp edges, a map of her life etched into the fabric. In that moment, the world outside faded away, leaving just me and this fragment of history. The weight of expectation that had clung to me like a shadow all week began to lift, replaced by a rekindled passion that bubbled up within me. Here was my grandmother, my guiding star, reminding me of the joy and love that had once inspired my craft. I was reminded that creating was not merely a means to an end, but a journey that blossomed from the heart, nourished by memories, and fueled by dreams.

I settled into a cozy corner of the shop, surrounded by an array of vibrant colors and patterns, letting the lace drape over my lap. It was time to breathe life into this moment. I opened my sketchbook, the familiar sound of the pages crackling under my fingertips, and began to draw. The lace inspired a vision—a dress that would embody the spirit of both my grandmother and my journey. Each stroke of the pencil felt like a step closer to rekindling my original spark, reminding me of the essence of my craft that I had strayed from.

I envisioned a flowing gown that danced with the wearer, the lace cascading like gentle waves, whispering secrets with each movement. I added delicate embellishments, imagining how they would catch the light, much like my grandmother's laughter had caught the eyes of those around her. The dress would be a tribute, a celebration of love and resilience, a reminder that beauty could emerge from the delicate balance of vulnerability and strength.

Lost in my thoughts, I barely noticed the time passing until the gentle chime of the bell above the door brought me back to reality. I looked up to see an elderly woman step inside, her silver hair glowing like spun silver under the sunlight. She looked around with a mixture of wonder and nostalgia, a soft smile blooming on her face as she approached the counter. I felt a rush of warmth as I recognized the familiar glint in her eyes—a shared passion for fabric and creation.

"Is this where dreams are stitched together?" she asked, her voice thick with the richness of memory.

I chuckled, drawn into her aura of warmth and wisdom. "It certainly feels like it. My grandmother used to say that every piece of fabric holds a story, waiting for someone to bring it to life."

She nodded, her gaze drifting toward the lace still resting on my lap. "That lace has a story of its own," she mused, her voice laced with reverence. "It's seen love, joy, and perhaps even a tear or two. Every thread woven with intention, a reflection of the soul of its maker."

In that moment, I felt a kinship, an understanding that transcended the years between us. Here, in this vintage fabric shop, I was not merely revisiting my past; I was forging connections that linked generations through the threads of creativity. The shop became a haven, a bridge between history and the future, and as I looked around, I saw not just fabric, but a tapestry of lives interwoven—a reminder that while trends may fade, true artistry, rooted in passion and heart, never goes out of style.

The elderly woman and I shared a moment of understanding, two souls adrift in the ocean of fabric and memories. She approached the counter, the weight of her shopping bag settling against her hip, the fabric within rustling like secrets waiting to be told. I watched as she rifled through her collection of swatches, her eyes lighting up with each find, and I couldn't help but smile. Her enthusiasm was contagious, rekindling the embers of my own passion that had felt dimmed by the pressures of modern life.

"Do you come here often?" I asked, intrigued by her air of familiarity with the shop, the way she navigated the aisles as if she were wandering through a garden of forgotten dreams.

"Oh, darling, I used to be here every week," she replied, her voice soft yet firm, like the warmest hug you could imagine. "Back when I was a young seamstress, I would scour this place for just the right fabric, dreaming of what I might create. Each piece was like a new adventure, a blank canvas begging for life."

I nodded, imagining her as a bright-eyed girl with frizzy hair and ink-stained fingers, poring over fabrics with the same fervor I felt now. "What was your favorite creation?"

Her eyes sparkled, lost in the past as she recalled her triumphs. "A dress for my daughter's wedding. It was a simple silhouette, but I lined the bodice with lace just like that one," she gestured to the delicate fabric draped over my lap. "Every stitch was sewn with love, and when she wore it, I could see all the dreams I had for her life reflected in the fabric."

A wave of warmth washed over me as I listened to her, the connection weaving between us like threads in a tapestry. "I think we often forget how much heart goes into what we create," I mused. "We get caught up in trends and expectations, and sometimes we lose sight of the joy it brings us."

"Exactly," she said, her voice tinged with nostalgia. "Fashion is fleeting, but the love behind each piece? That lasts forever."

With those words echoing in my mind, I set my sketchbook aside and turned my focus back to the lace. As I held it up, the sunlight filtering through the window illuminated its intricate patterns, casting delicate shadows on my lap like lace tattoos. I imagined transforming it into something beautiful—a dress that would evoke memories of my grandmother while capturing my own modern aesthetic. I could see it: flowing, graceful, with a hint of rebellion woven into the seams.

After chatting with the woman a while longer, I excused myself to explore the back of the shop again, feeling energized by our exchange. I brushed my fingers against the bolts of fabric, picking up remnants that spoke to me in whispers of color and texture. I let my intuition guide me, gathering a small selection—soft chambray for the bodice, a rich emerald silk for the skirt, and a hint of coral for the accents, creating a palette as vibrant as my own dreams.

In a flurry of excitement, I settled at a nearby cutting table, the surface worn but sturdy, with decades of creative energy embedded in its surface. I laid out the fabrics, allowing their colors to converse and mingle under the soft glow of the overhead lights. The idea of creating something meaningful was thrilling, and I felt a rush of inspiration surging through me, revitalizing my spirit.

With each cut, each measurement, I was not just fabricating a garment; I was stitching together my identity, piecing together fragments of my past, present, and future. I lost myself in the rhythm of it, finding solace in the mundane yet magical act of creation. The world outside faded, and time slipped through my fingers like the threads I was manipulating, each moment a reminder of the importance of following my heart.

As the sun dipped lower in the sky, casting long shadows across the shop, I heard the bell jingle again, this time accompanied by a flurry of laughter. A group of young women entered, their voices bright and jubilant, filling the space with a youthful energy. They fluttered from bolt to bolt, touching the fabric as if each one were a whisper of a potential adventure. I watched them, a smile playing at the corners of my lips.

One of them, a petite girl with wild curls and an infectious laugh, caught my eye. She paused in front of a bolt of vibrant floral print, her expression a mixture of delight and disbelief. "Can you believe this? It's like a garden exploded in here!"

The others gathered around, their enthusiasm contagious. I felt a pang of nostalgia—once upon a time, I was just like them, eager and bright-eyed, ready to take on the world with nothing but a sewing machine and a head full of dreams.

"Do you think it would make a good dress?" the girl asked, holding up the fabric as if it were a precious artifact.

"Absolutely," I chimed in, feeling an unexpected surge of mentorship rise within me. "You could create a lovely sundress with that, or even something a bit more daring. The possibilities are endless."

They turned toward me, surprise and excitement mingling in their gazes, their energy radiating like sunlight on a crisp morning. "Do you sew?" another girl asked, her eyes wide with curiosity.

I nodded, glancing at the lace now tucked safely beside me. "I do. In fact, I'm working on something right now," I said, gesturing to my spread of fabrics. "It's a dress inspired by my grandmother's lace."

Their eyes lit up with intrigue, and I felt a spark of connection ignite between us, an intergenerational link formed by the simple act of creating. They crowded around, asking questions, their laughter filling the space as they eagerly engaged in my process, each one offering their insights and ideas.

As I explained my vision for the dress, I found myself reveling in the energy of their enthusiasm. It was a reminder that inspiration knows no age, no boundary, and that creativity flourishes when shared. In this small vintage fabric shop, a new tapestry of connections was woven, blending the past with the present, creating a vibrant narrative that would carry forward into the future.

I watched as they scattered around the shop, each finding their own treasures, laughter and joy intertwining like the threads I cherished so deeply. In that moment, I realized that I was not just a designer or a creator; I was a part of something larger, a community of dreamers bound together by the fabric of life itself. And as I stitched my grandmother's legacy into my new creation, I felt a renewed sense of purpose—a commitment to embrace the beauty of every thread, every moment, and every connection that enriched my journey.

The vibrant laughter of the young women filled the shop like a symphony of joy, pulling me deeper into the moment. They flitted from fabric to fabric, their excitement contagious, reminding me of the days I spent here as a child, my imagination as boundless as the fabric surrounding me. One of the girls, with fiery red hair and an adventurous spirit, turned to me, her eyes sparkling with curiosity.

"What's your inspiration?" she asked, her voice bubbling with eagerness. "That lace looks incredible. I can practically see the dress in my mind already."

I felt a warmth in my chest, a blend of pride and nostalgia. "It belonged to my grandmother," I explained, my fingers brushing over the lace as if greeting an old friend. "She used it for her wedding dress, and I want to honor her spirit in my design. Something that captures both her elegance and my modern twist."

They crowded around me, their faces alight with wonder, hanging on my every word as I delved into the details of my vision. With each description, I noticed how their admiration ignited my own passion. I began to sketch out more ideas, encouraged by their enthusiasm as they chimed in with suggestions, each voice adding a note to our collective creative melody.

The petite girl with curls leaned in, her excitement palpable. "What if you added a high-low hem? It's super trendy right now, and it would let the lace flow beautifully in the wind!"

"Or maybe some subtle embroidery along the edges?" another chimed in, her hands mimicking delicate stitches in the air as she spoke.

As I took in their ideas, I could feel the fabric of my grandmother's legacy intertwining with new threads of inspiration, bridging generations and creating a narrative that transcended time. The atmosphere hummed with creativity; it was as if the very walls of the shop were cheering us on.

We spent hours wrapped in this magical bubble, designing and dreaming, the shop transforming into a hive of inspiration. I found myself sharing stories of my childhood, the moments of triumph and frustration as I learned to sew, and the invaluable lessons my grandmother had imparted—like the importance of patience and the beauty of imperfection. They listened intently, their eyes wide as I revealed the warmth that had been my compass, guiding me back to this very place.

Just as we were immersed in our creations, the bell above the door jingled again. A familiar face appeared—Maggie, my best friend since childhood, her blonde hair tied in a messy bun, a paint-splattered apron draped over her shoulders. "I could smell creativity from a mile away!" she declared, her eyes brightening at the sight of us huddled around the table. "What's happening here?"

As I welcomed her with open arms, she scanned the scene, her gaze landing on the scattered fabrics and my sketches. "Oh wow, this is amazing! Are you actually going to make that dress?"

I nodded, my heart swelling with excitement. "I am! And these girls have been so inspiring, helping me refine the ideas."

Maggie leaned over to admire the lace, her expression shifting to one of reverence. "Your grandmother's lace? That's so special! It'll bring such a beautiful energy to your design."

With Maggie's presence, our dynamic shifted. The camaraderie of friends reignited the creative spark, and soon the shop became a whirlwind of fabric, laughter, and shared stories. We took turns trying on various swatches, pretending to strut down invisible runways, tossing out outrageous design ideas with wild abandon.

In those moments, I realized how powerful it was to collaborate, to let go of my solitary approach to creativity and embrace the joy that came from shared vision. Ideas were bouncing around like confetti, and soon we decided to host an impromptu mini fashion show right in the shop. We draped fabric over ourselves, each of us becoming a canvas for our collective imagination.

Maggie twirled in a vibrant red tulle, embodying a fairy-tale princess, while the fiery-haired girl spun around in an electric blue satin, claiming her role as a modern-day diva. Laughter echoed through the aisles, mingling with the vibrant fabric that surrounded us, as the fabric shop transformed into a stage, alive with possibility.

As the sun dipped lower, casting a golden glow through the windows, I felt an overwhelming sense of gratitude wash over me. Here I was, surrounded by laughter and creativity, the weight of my week's worries melting away. I glanced around at the faces of my friends and the new companions I had made that day, their smiles bright against the backdrop of our whimsical creations.

The evening unfolded with stories that spilled out like threads from an unraveling spool. We shared our dreams and fears, the fabric of our lives weaving together in a beautiful tapestry of friendship. The more we spoke, the more I felt the barriers of doubt and insecurity slip away, replaced by a warm embrace of acceptance and encouragement.

As the sun set, casting hues of orange and pink through the shop, I felt a renewed sense of purpose. I was not merely creating a dress; I was crafting a narrative, a reflection of the bonds that tethered us to one another and to the past.

When I finally gathered my sketches and our assorted fabric swatches to take home, I felt a sense of completion. It was more than just a project; it was a promise to honor my grandmother while forging my own path, one where creativity and connection thrived.

With Maggie beside me, we stepped out into the cool evening air, laughter spilling out of the shop as we waved goodbye to our newfound friends. The stars began to twinkle overhead, the world outside bustling with life, yet inside me, there was a serene certainty. I felt empowered, ready to embrace my journey—one woven with threads of resilience, love, and the shared joy of creation.

That night, as I sat at my sewing machine, the delicate lace unfolding before me like a whisper of history, I reflected on how far I had come. My grandmother's spirit infused every stitch, reminding me that I was part of a larger narrative—one that would continue to unfold, fueled by passion, creativity, and the bonds I had nurtured along the way. Each thread I wove was not just a connection to my past but a foundation for the future I was determined to create, where dreams danced freely, unbound by expectations, and stitched together by the pure joy of crafting a life rich with meaning.

Chapter 12: The Threads of Doubt

The air in Manhattan was electric, tinged with the faint scent of pretentious coffee and the lingering aroma of baked goods from a nearby café. I navigated the city streets with a purposeful stride, the heels of my boots clicking against the cracked pavement, a sound that had once filled me with confidence but now felt like a countdown to my impending doom. The skyline loomed overhead, its steel and glass glinting in the sunlight, each towering building a reminder of dreams I had spun into existence. Today, however, those dreams felt more like a web of deceit, each thread fraying under the weight of doubt.

My latest collection had launched with all the fanfare I could muster, a kaleidoscope of color and fabric that had danced down the runway just days ago. Yet now, as I scrolled through my social media feed, my heart dropped into my stomach like a stone. An influencer, a beacon in the world of fashion, had publicly torn apart my hard work. Her words, laced with biting sarcasm, claimed my designs were derivative and uninspired, devoid of the creativity that once defined my brand. I could almost feel her icy gaze through the screen, scrutinizing every stitch and seam of my garments, dissecting my soul with the precision of a surgeon.

A nervous flutter settled in my chest, and I quickly closed my phone, the buzzing of notifications suddenly sounding like a swarm of angry bees. I leaned against the cool brick of a nearby building, its surface rough against my palm. The sounds of the city faded into the background—the laughter, the honks of taxis, the cacophony of life. In that moment, I felt isolated in a crowd, a lone figure adrift in a sea of judgment. I had always prided myself on my originality, but now that conviction wavered, each compliment I had ever received transforming into a potential lie.

Blake, my rock and unwavering support, sensed my turmoil. He approached me, his dark hair tousled and those stormy blue eyes sparkling with concern. I had always admired how he navigated the fashion world with the grace of a gazelle and the tenacity of a bull. But today, his ambition felt suffocating, as if he were pushing me towards a cliff, urging me to leap into the unknown when I was still struggling to find my footing.

"Let's talk about it," he said, his voice low and soothing, like the gentle lapping of waves against a rocky shore.

I shook my head, pushing away the worry that draped itself around me like a heavy cloak. "No, I just... I can't right now. I need some air."

"Running away won't fix this," he pressed, his brow furrowing. "You need to confront it head-on."

His words echoed in my mind, but they felt like shards of glass, cutting through my fragile state. I could feel the walls closing in, and I desperately wanted to flee rather than engage in what felt like an inevitable fight. I turned away, my breath quickening as I made my way down the street, each step a rebellion against the world I had crafted and a retreat into the shadows of my self-doubt.

As I wandered, I found myself gravitating towards Central Park, its lush greenery a stark contrast to the concrete jungle surrounding it. The air was infused with the sweetness of autumn leaves, crisp and vibrant. I inhaled deeply, attempting to fill my lungs with tranquility, but all I could taste was bitterness. The park, usually a sanctuary, now felt like an echo of my insecurities. Joggers zipped by, their faces set in determination, while couples strolled hand in hand, laughter spilling from their lips like music. I envied them, their carefree existence, while I felt like a ghost in my own life.

I took a seat on a weathered bench, watching as the world moved around me in perfect harmony, each person a vibrant thread in the tapestry of the city. I pulled out my sketchbook, its pages blank and waiting for inspiration that felt so elusive now. I flipped through past designs—bold, unique, full of life. The colors practically sang from the pages, yet today they fell silent. My pencil hovered above the paper, my mind swirling with the echoes of that influencer's voice, each critique amplifying the silence.

In the midst of this turmoil, Blake's words lingered in my mind, a reminder of my own resolve. Confrontation. That was the key. But what if confrontation meant facing my own failures? What if it meant exposing the cracks in my carefully curated facade? The mere thought of it sent a shiver down my spine, yet I knew that hiding would only prolong my pain.

As dusk approached, the park transformed, the warm hues of sunset spilling across the sky, casting a golden glow on the trees. I drew in a breath, letting the crisp air fill my lungs. Each inhale felt like an act of defiance against the weight of my self-doubt. I was not just a designer; I was a dreamer, a creator, and I had poured my heart into every stitch of my collection.

Suddenly, a realization hit me like a jolt of electricity. I had a choice. I could allow this moment of public scrutiny to define me, to shrink away into obscurity, or I could rise above it, allowing it to fuel my creativity instead. My designs were extensions of my identity, flawed and raw yet undeniably mine. I had always believed that vulnerability was strength, and perhaps it was time to embrace that belief wholeheartedly.

With newfound determination, I snapped my sketchbook closed, a smile creeping onto my lips. The vibrant city around me seemed to pulse with life, a reminder that I was still part of it. As I stood up, I felt lighter, the burden of self-doubt beginning to lift, revealing the bright future that lay ahead. With every step I took back towards the chaos of fashion week, I felt the threads of doubt unraveling, making way for the rich tapestry of hope and resilience that I was ready to weave anew.

As I strode back through the vibrant streets of New York, each step became a silent mantra, a reminder of my resolve. The chaos of the city enveloped me, its heartbeat thrumming in time with my own, a peculiar harmony emerging from the discord of doubt. I passed storefronts bursting with bold fashion statements—floral prints, oversized jackets, shimmering accessories—each one a testament to the audacity of creativity. The sight stirred something within me, a flicker of the flame that had once burned so brightly in my soul, before the winds of criticism had snuffed it out.

The evening air was brisk, carrying whispers of autumn leaves and the distant aroma of roasted chestnuts. My feet led me to a quaint little café, its windows adorned with twinkling fairy lights that sparkled against the dusky backdrop. As I pushed open the heavy wooden door, a bell jingled softly above me, announcing my arrival to the cozy haven within. The warmth enveloped me like a hug, dispelling the chill that had settled around my heart.

I chose a small table in the corner, the wooden surface scarred but polished from years of stories shared over steaming cups of coffee. The barista—a wiry man with an artistic flair in his tattoos—greeted me with a nod and an easy smile. I ordered a chai latte, hoping its spiced richness would rekindle the warmth I had momentarily lost. As I waited, I took out my sketchbook, the blank pages now a canvas for my renewed determination.

The café buzzed with chatter, the air punctuated by laughter and the clinking of cups. I allowed myself to be swept up in the atmosphere, a kaleidoscope of vibrant conversations swirling around me. Yet, even amidst this energy, my thoughts danced restlessly, flitting between insecurities and aspirations. It was then that I noticed a couple seated at a nearby table, their ease with each other radiating warmth. They shared whispered secrets and soft laughter, their fingers entwined as if they were coconspirators in a beautiful adventure.

In that moment, I realized how essential connection was—not just with others but with myself. I had spent so long chasing validation from external sources, striving to please an audience that often wielded the power to uplift or dismantle. Perhaps, in this tangled web of doubt, the key was to connect with the essence of who I was as a designer, to remember why I had ventured into this whirlwind of fabric and thread in the first place.

The barista returned, placing my latte in front of me, steam curling into the air like a dancer taking the stage. I wrapped my hands around the warm cup, letting its heat seep into my skin, grounding me. With a renewed sense of purpose, I opened my sketchbook, feeling the pencil flow against the paper, bringing to life the images that danced in my mind.

Each stroke was an act of defiance, a refusal to be defined by someone else's critique. I sketched silhouettes that spoke of strength and vulnerability, textures that embodied the tumult of my emotions. As I worked, I could almost hear the fabric whispering stories of resilience, echoing my own journey of triumphs and tribulations.

Time slipped away unnoticed, the world outside fading into a blur as I lost myself in the rhythm of creativity. When I finally paused to catch my breath, the sun had dipped low, painting the sky in hues of lavender and gold. I took a moment to survey my sketches, each one a small rebellion against the doubts that had threatened to consume me.

With a sigh of contentment, I gathered my things, the sketches folded neatly in my bag. As I stepped back into the crisp night air, I felt lighter, the weight of criticism replaced by the buoyancy of self-acceptance. I glanced at my phone, the notifications now a dull hum, and smiled. The chaos of social media could wait; tonight, I had reclaimed my narrative.

Making my way back towards my studio, I noticed the neon glow of signs illuminating the streets, reflecting the vibrant tapestry of life that surrounded me. I passed a group of street performers, their laughter mingling with the sound of a guitar strumming a familiar tune. It struck me how each note resonated with the spirit of creation, the heart of artistry, and I couldn't help but feel a kinship with them. Here, in this vibrant city, the tapestry of creativity was woven together, a collective heartbeat echoing through the night.

Arriving at my studio, I paused at the entrance, my heart racing with anticipation. The door creaked open, revealing a space filled with fabric swatches and half-formed ideas dancing in the dim light. The chaos of the room mirrored the chaos in my mind, yet tonight, it felt inviting rather than intimidating. I flicked on the lights, the bulbs casting a warm glow across the room, and set to work, eager to breathe life into my vision.

In the days that followed, I found solace in the creation process. My fingers flew over fabric, each snip of the scissors and each stitch of the needle reinforcing my commitment to authenticity. I poured my heart into the designs, seeking not perfection but a reflection of the tumult I had experienced. I wanted each piece to resonate with the truth of my journey, an embodiment of resilience and vulnerability, an invitation for others to connect with their own stories.

Blake began to notice the shift in me, the way my laughter echoed in the studio, how my eyes sparkled with the thrill of creation. He would peek in occasionally, a teasing grin on his face as he brought me coffee or fabric swatches, his presence a grounding force that reminded me of the beauty in collaboration. Despite our earlier tensions, I found comfort in his unwavering belief in my talent, even when I faltered.

One evening, as we worked side by side, I paused to catch his gaze. "Thank you for believing in me," I confessed, my voice barely above a whisper. The weight of my earlier fears began to lift, leaving behind the sweet taste of gratitude.

He smirked, tossing a playful glance my way. "I always knew you had it in you. It was just a matter of time before you remembered."

His words wrapped around me like a warm embrace, a gentle reminder that I was not alone in this chaotic world. I had my battles, but I also had allies, people who saw the light in me even when I couldn't see it myself.

And so, I continued to create, each piece a reflection of my evolving narrative. In the heart of the city, amidst the chaos of fashion, I found a sense of belonging not in the validation of others, but in the connection I forged with my true self. I was ready to step back into the limelight, not as a shadow of doubt but as a beacon of hope, a tapestry woven with threads of resilience and grace, eager to share my story with the world.

The days slipped by like sand through my fingers, each one a delicate reminder of both my vulnerability and my resolve. The studio, once a cacophony of chaos and doubt, had transformed into a sanctuary of creation. Each morning, I arrived earlier than necessary, the first rays of sunlight piercing through the windows, illuminating the fabric strewn across the tables like remnants of my scattered thoughts. The air was always tinged with the earthy scent of cotton and silk, a fragrant promise of the magic I was determined to weave.

As I immersed myself in my designs, the outside world began to fade. The barista at the café had become a familiar face, a comforting presence who anticipated my order and smiled knowingly as I sketched ideas at my favorite corner table. I found myself sketching with fervor, my pencil dancing across the pages like a conductor leading an orchestra. Each line was a note, each curve a melody, harmonizing into a collection that began to reflect my true self rather than the diluted version that had once sought approval.

Blake, ever the pragmatist, observed my transformation with a mixture of pride and relief. He often popped by with fabric samples or new ideas, his dark eyes lighting up as he watched me work. Yet, it was in the moments of silence, when we were lost in our respective worlds, that I felt the most profound connection with him. The air would hum with unspoken understanding, a palpable energy that kept the shadows of doubt at bay.

Despite our burgeoning camaraderie, the specter of that influencer's words lingered at the edges of my mind, a ghost that threatened to reemerge when I least expected it. I resolved to address it, determined to rise above the criticism rather than let it haunt me. As I prepared for the upcoming showcase, I wanted to invite the very doubts that had once paralyzed me into the light, to showcase them in all their raw glory.

The evening of the showcase dawned with the promise of excitement and a hint of apprehension. The air buzzed with anticipation as the venue—an old, converted warehouse—buzzed with the sounds of fashion enthusiasts and industry insiders. I stood backstage, my heart thundering against my ribcage, my fingers nervously drumming against my thigh. The bright lights above cast a warm glow, creating a surreal atmosphere that felt almost dreamlike.

Blake was at my side, his presence a grounding force in the midst of chaos. "You're ready for this," he whispered, squeezing my shoulder reassuringly. His confidence in me stirred something deep within, a flicker of determination that began to outshine the lingering shadows. I could feel the weight of his gaze, a silent promise that I was not alone in this endeavor.

As the first model stepped onto the runway, I held my breath, the world around me fading as I focused on the vision I had brought to life. The fabric flowed gracefully, the colors vibrant and alive, each piece echoing the resilience I had discovered within myself. The audience's reactions were immediate—gasping in awe, murmuring appreciation. Each step the model took felt like a victory for me, a triumphant rebuttal to the doubts that had once threatened to consume me.

Then came the moment that shifted everything. The fourth model emerged, draped in a gown that shimmered like the twilight sky. As she walked, I felt a swell of pride and vulnerability collide within me, a wave of emotion that threatened to spill over. The audience responded with an eruption of applause, their approval washing over me like a warm tide. It was intoxicating, the validation I had longed for, yet this time it felt different. It was not merely about external acknowledgment but about the affirmation of my journey, the transformation I had undergone.

As the final model exited the runway, the applause crescendoed, a deafening roar that filled the room with an electric energy. I stood at the edge of the stage, heart racing, eyes brimming with unshed tears. Blake's beaming smile was my anchor, grounding me in the moment. The weight of self-doubt began to lift, replaced by an exhilarating sense of possibility.

In the aftermath, as guests mingled and the energy buzzed, I was surrounded by praise and admiration. It felt surreal to hear my name woven into conversations, a testament to my journey from obscurity to a place of recognition. Yet amidst the euphoria, I felt an overwhelming urge to seek out the very critic who had ignited my spiral of doubt.

With Blake by my side, I ventured through the crowd, the vibrant conversations swirling around us like confetti. When I spotted her—a vision in designer attire, laughter bubbling from her lips—I approached with a mix of trepidation and determination. She was surrounded by admirers, her influence palpable.

"Excuse me," I said, my voice firm yet polite as I stepped into her circle. Her gaze flicked to me, and for a moment, time suspended as the air crackled with tension. "I'm the designer behind the collection you reviewed."

Her expression shifted, surprise mingling with curiosity. "Oh! You're the one," she said, a hint of amusement dancing in her eyes. "I didn't expect to see you here."

"I wanted to thank you," I replied, the words spilling forth before I could second-guess myself. "Your critique pushed me to rediscover my creativity and authenticity. This collection is a reflection of that journey."

The surprise on her face deepened, replaced by an inscrutable expression. "I appreciate that," she replied, her tone shifting to one of genuine interest. "Criticism can be harsh, but it's meant to challenge artists to grow."

Blake stood beside me, his presence reinforcing my resolve. "And grow she did," he said, a hint of pride lacing his voice.

The influencer regarded me with newfound respect, her earlier judgment softened by the sincerity of my words. "I'd love to hear more about your process. It seems you have a unique vision."

As we delved into a conversation about inspiration and creativity, I felt a weight lift from my shoulders. The shadows that had haunted me began to dissipate, replaced by a bright clarity. In that moment, I realized that my journey was not solely defined by the opinions of others. It was the unwavering belief in myself that mattered, the courage to face my doubts head-on and to forge a path illuminated by my own creativity.

The night continued, the mingling of laughter and conversation echoing around me, yet I felt anchored in my truth. I was a designer, a creator, an artist—not merely defined by external validation but by the very essence of my spirit. With each conversation, each connection made, I built bridges rather than walls, weaving a network of understanding and support.

As the evening came to a close, I stood by the window, gazing out at the cityscape, a constellation of lights twinkling in the distance. Blake joined me, leaning against the wall, a sense of contentment radiating from him. "You did it," he said softly, the warmth in his voice wrapping around me like a gentle embrace.

I smiled, a sense of fulfillment coursing through me. "No, we did it," I corrected him, knowing that this journey was not one I had walked alone.

In that moment, I embraced the beauty of my craft—the intricate dance between vulnerability and strength, doubt and creativity. The city outside continued its rhythm, alive with possibility, and I felt ready to step into the next chapter of my journey, not as a solitary figure, but as part of a vibrant tapestry woven together by the threads of our stories, hopes, and dreams. Together, we would create something beautiful, something authentically our own, and I knew that the world was waiting with bated breath to see it unfold.

Chapter 13: Patterns of Forgiveness

Morning light streamed through the window like a gentle caress, illuminating the faded floral wallpaper of my childhood home. I could almost hear the echoes of my mother's laughter intertwined with the chirping of birds outside, a reminder of simpler times when life seemed less complicated. Yet, that same light felt blinding today, forcing me to confront the tangled web of emotions I had been so expertly avoiding. With every minute spent in bed, surrounded by the ghosts of past conversations and unresolved feelings, I felt more like a prisoner than a daughter. The familiar scent of brewed coffee wafted through the house, coaxing me from beneath the weight of my tangled sheets. It was both comforting and provoking, urging me to rise and face the day, as if my love for caffeine could somehow overshadow the turmoil bubbling within me.

    I slid out of bed, the wooden floorboards creaking beneath my weight, each sound a reminder of the years that had drifted away, laden with regrets and unspoken words. As I padded to the kitchen, the sun poured into the room, casting warm golden rays across the tabletop, illuminating the mismatched mugs that lined the shelves. I reached for my favorite—a chipped ceramic cup that had once belonged to my grandmother. Its surface was rough, a mosaic of paint and age, but it felt like home in my hands. I filled it to the brim, savoring the rich aroma that danced in the air, a bittersweet reminder of mornings spent laughing over breakfast with my family.

    With coffee in hand, I sank into the worn leather armchair in the corner, its embrace enveloping me like a hug from a dear friend. It had seen countless moments of joy and sorrow, much like me. I took a sip, the warmth spreading through me like a whisper of courage, nudging me toward the conversation I desperately needed to have. Today, I would reach out to Blake. The mere thought of it sent a jolt of anxiety racing through me. We hadn't seen each other since our last project spiraled into chaos, emotions flaring up like fireworks before crashing down in a shower of sparks. But something within me—a flicker of hope perhaps—insisted that we could salvage what we had.

The coffee shop down the street was a local gem, nestled between a thrift store overflowing with forgotten treasures and a bookstore that smelled of old paper and adventure. It had once been our go-to spot, a sanctuary where ideas flowed as freely as the coffee. The thought of stepping back into that familiar haven made my heart race. I had cherished those moments—his laughter mingling with the sound of steam rising from the espresso machine, the way his eyes lit up when he discussed a new concept, his passion contagious. I yearned for that connection again, to reclaim a piece of us that felt lost.

As I walked through the door, the bell above it jingled cheerfully, announcing my arrival. The aroma of freshly ground beans enveloped me, pulling me in like a warm blanket. I spotted Blake in the far corner, his head bent over a notebook, the sun catching the dark curls that framed his face. My heart raced, a mix of excitement and apprehension. I hadn't anticipated how seeing him would stir up a cocktail of emotions. Would he welcome me? Would he even want to see me after everything?

"Hey," I said, the word slipping out almost shyly as I approached the table. He looked up, surprise flickering across his features, quickly replaced by a tentative smile that sent a flutter through my chest.

"Hey," he replied, the warmth in his voice wrapping around me like the steam rising from his cup. There was an awkward pause as I slid into the chair across from him, the air thick with unspoken words. My fingers danced over the rim of my mug, unsure of how to navigate the depths of our history.

"Wow, this feels weird," I blurted out, my nerves bubbling to the surface. "Like, really weird."

Blake chuckled softly, a sound that tugged at the corners of my heart. "Yeah, it does. But not in a bad way, right?"

"No, not bad," I said, feeling a smile tug at my lips. "Just... strange. I wasn't sure you'd want to see me."

He shrugged, his eyes searching mine. "Honestly, I wasn't sure either. But I'm glad you reached out."

Our conversation wove between moments of silence and bursts of laughter, a delicate dance of vulnerability. We exchanged stories about our lives since that chaotic project, each word breaking down the walls we had built. As I listened to him talk about his recent travels, his eyes bright with enthusiasm, I felt a spark of the camaraderie we once shared—a bond that had felt frayed but was now beginning to mend. It felt good to laugh again, to share in the simple joys of life, even amidst the complexity of our emotions.

I took a deep breath, feeling the weight of my confession build within me. "I've been thinking a lot about everything," I admitted, my voice barely above a whisper. "About us. I need your support—not just as a collaborator, but as a friend. I've realized that I can't keep running from my emotions, and I definitely can't keep blaming you for my struggles."

His gaze softened, the tension in his shoulders easing. "I've missed you, you know. It was tough navigating all that without you."

His words struck a chord deep within me, resonating with my own longing. "I've missed you too," I said, my voice trembling slightly. "I'm sorry for how I acted. I was scared, and I didn't know how to deal with it. But I want to move forward. I want to forgive myself, for my mistakes, for my fears... and I want to forgive you too."

The air between us shifted, charged with a sense of understanding. In that moment, I realized that forgiveness was not merely about absolution but about recognizing our shared humanity. It was about accepting that we were both flawed, navigating a world that often felt overwhelming. And as I looked into his eyes, I felt a sense of hope blossoming—a fragile yet beautiful beginning, like the first blooms of spring peeking through the remnants of winter. The journey ahead would not be easy, but for the first time in a long while, I felt ready to embrace it.

The laughter between us danced in the air like the steam from our mugs, weaving threads of warmth and nostalgia. As Blake spoke about his recent adventures—his hiking escapades in the Rocky Mountains, where he'd nearly lost a shoe to a particularly ambitious squirrel—I found myself captivated, not just by his words, but by the way his face lit up. Those moments of shared joy felt like the first rays of sunshine breaking through a long, dreary winter. I was reminded that beneath the weight of our unspoken grievances lay a friendship worth salvaging.

Each story he told unraveled more of the distance that had formed between us, creating a tapestry of connection that felt both familiar and exhilaratingly new. His animated descriptions of the breathtaking landscapes he had encountered painted vivid images in my mind. I could almost hear the rustling leaves, the crunch of gravel underfoot, and the crisp mountain air filling my lungs. The idea of exploring the world alongside him again sparked a long-forgotten excitement within me, a reminder that adventure still lay ahead, even if our paths had twisted through shadows.

"Did you ever see the sunrise from the top?" I asked, leaning forward, completely entranced by the glint in his eyes.

"Once," he replied, his gaze drifting as he conjured the memory. "It was breathtaking—like nature was putting on a show just for me. I remember feeling so small, but in a good way. Like all my problems were just tiny dots on the horizon."

I nodded, the imagery settling in my chest. "I've always wanted to experience something like that," I confessed, suddenly aware of how much I craved the beauty of life outside my own bubble. "Just a moment to step back and breathe. But lately, I've felt so... stuck."

Blake's expression softened, and he leaned back, arms crossed as he regarded me thoughtfully. "Stuck can feel suffocating, can't it? I get that. Sometimes it's easy to forget that we're allowed to step back and reassess things."

His words resonated with me. I had spent so long entangled in my insecurities, weighed down by expectations—both others' and my own. The realization that I could simply choose to step back and reassess felt revolutionary, a fresh breeze cutting through a stifling room. My fingers tightened around my mug as I thought about all the things I wanted to do—projects I wanted to start, places I wanted to visit, dreams I had shelved away like dusty keepsakes.

"I want to go back to painting," I said suddenly, the thought spilling out before I could second-guess myself. "It's been ages since I've let myself create something just for the sake of it. I used to love losing myself in the colors and textures, and somewhere along the way, I forgot how much it meant to me."

His eyes sparkled with encouragement, and I could see him processing this revelation. "You should. What's stopping you?"

"Fear, mostly," I admitted, a hint of shame creeping in. "Fear that I'm not good enough, or that it won't be worth the time. Or worse, that I'll pour my heart into it and it will just... be mediocre."

"Have you ever seen a piece of art that was truly 'mediocre'?" Blake countered, leaning forward, the corners of his mouth twitching upward. "Art is subjective, right? It's more about the process than the product. You should paint just for you, without any pressure. And who knows? You might end up creating something amazing."

His unwavering belief in me felt like a warm embrace, one that wrapped around my worries and squeezed them tight. It was easy to get lost in self-doubt, especially when it came to something so personal. But hearing him speak reminded me that art was not merely about the end result; it was about the journey—the emotions poured onto the canvas, the colors splashed with reckless abandon, and the moments of clarity it brought.

"I think I need to find a way to let go," I mused, my voice softer now. "To embrace the messiness of it all."

Blake nodded in agreement, his expression earnest. "That sounds like a beautiful way to move forward. Just remember, you're not alone in this. I'm here, cheering you on, no matter what it looks like."

His words enveloped me like a comforting blanket, soothing the nagging doubts that had kept me frozen in place. I could almost envision the vibrant swirls of paint dancing across the canvas, each stroke a step toward reclaiming a part of myself that had been lost.

"Thank you for being so supportive," I said, my voice barely above a whisper. "I can't tell you how much it means to me."

"Of course," he replied, his tone sincere. "But I'm also going to need your support in return. I've been struggling to figure out what's next for me, too. I think I might want to delve into writing, but it feels daunting, you know?"

My heart swelled at the thought of him exploring this new avenue, and a smile broke across my face. "You're an incredible storyteller! I'd love to read anything you write."

He chuckled, shaking his head. "You're just saying that."

"No, really!" I insisted. "You have a gift, and you shouldn't doubt that. Just like I shouldn't doubt my art."

We exchanged a knowing look, the kind that bridges unspoken fears with shared encouragement. There was a powerful understanding in that moment, a realization that we were both navigating our own paths toward self-acceptance and authenticity.

As the sun dipped lower in the sky, casting a warm glow across the café, I felt a sense of peace settling in my chest. It was as if the universe had conspired to bring us together at this moment, wrapping us in a cocoon of possibility. I was reminded that while our past had been riddled with misunderstandings, the future still held the promise of growth, laughter, and connection.

"I guess we can both be each other's cheerleaders," I suggested, feeling lighter as the words tumbled out. "Let's keep each other accountable. I'll start painting again if you start writing."

He grinned, that boyish charm lighting up his features. "Deal. And who knows? Maybe we can even collaborate on something one day. A fusion of art and words."

"Now that sounds like a beautiful disaster waiting to happen," I laughed, picturing chaotic paint splatters mingling with whimsical prose.

"Exactly," he said, his eyes twinkling with mischief. "Just think of it as a way to embrace the messiness together."

With a newfound determination blossoming between us, I realized that forgiveness wasn't just an end goal but a path—a way to navigate the intricate dance of relationships, allowing space for growth, vulnerability, and laughter. In this cozy café, amidst the aroma of coffee and the clinking of cups, I felt the weight of the world begin to lift. Together, we could face our insecurities, paint our dreams, and maybe, just maybe, find our way back to each other in the process.

As we continued to share stories, the world around us faded into a comforting blur, the bustling café a mere backdrop to our rekindling connection. The gentle hum of conversation mixed with the rhythmic clinking of cups, creating an ambiance that felt both familiar and inviting. Sunlight streamed through the large windows, casting playful shadows across the polished wooden floor, illuminating dust particles that danced lazily in the air. I could almost hear the whispers of the past echoing between us, tales of dreams forged in the warmth of coffee cups and laughter.

A sense of urgency coursed through me, an insistent reminder that this moment was too precious to let slip away. "What if we set a date to share our first creations?" I proposed, excitement bubbling in my chest. "Like a mini art and writing showcase just for ourselves? It could be our own little ritual." The idea felt exhilarating, a tangible promise of our commitment to support one another.

Blake raised an eyebrow, a smirk tugging at the corners of his mouth. "A showcase? You mean like a gallery opening, complete with pretentious art critiques and overpriced wine?"

I laughed, shaking my head. "More like two friends sharing their heart and soul over coffee, minus the judgment and lofty expectations. Just us, our art, and maybe some snacks."

"Snacks are crucial," he agreed, nodding seriously. "But you realize we'll need a venue, right? I mean, my apartment doesn't exactly scream 'artistic haven.'"

"Who needs a venue?" I countered, leaning closer, enthusiasm spilling from every word. "We could turn your living room into a makeshift gallery. We can drape a sheet over the couch for a backdrop, scatter your novels around as décor, and voilà! Instant ambiance."

His laughter was infectious, a rich sound that made my heart flutter. "You have a point there. My couch does need a little character."

The thought of transforming his living room into a creative haven ignited a spark of joy within me. It was more than just a showcase; it was a celebration of our journeys—a way to reclaim the pieces of ourselves we had almost lost. "Let's set a date," I urged, a mischievous grin on my face. "How about next Saturday? We can each present our work, and afterward, we'll feast on whatever snacks we can scrounge up. Maybe even a celebratory pizza?"

"Pizza? Now you're talking!" Blake's eyes gleamed with mischief. "Deal. Next Saturday it is."

As we sealed our pact with laughter, the air between us crackled with a fresh electricity, the kind that hinted at new beginnings. I felt lighter, as if a weight had been lifted from my shoulders. The fear that had gripped me for so long was starting to dissolve, replaced by anticipation and the thrill of possibility. It was a feeling I had nearly forgotten—a reminder that there was still beauty to be found in the chaos of life.

Later that evening, as I sat alone in my room, surrounded by the remnants of my day—scattered sketches, paintbrushes still wet from the afternoon—I felt a stirring of creativity bubbling up within me. The blank canvas loomed in the corner, its stark whiteness both daunting and inviting, like a portal into uncharted territory. My heart raced at the thought of painting again, a sensation akin to standing at the edge of a cliff, ready to leap into the unknown.

With a deep breath, I gathered my brushes, the familiar textures grounding me. Each stroke felt like a release, an exploration of emotions I had kept bottled up for too long. The colors swirled together—vivid blues clashing with fiery reds, soft yellows mingling with deep purples—as I lost myself in the process. With every flick of my wrist, I shed layers of insecurity, transforming fear into a vibrant display of emotion. I was no longer painting for an audience; I was creating for myself, embracing the glorious messiness of it all.

Hours slipped away unnoticed, the outside world fading into the background as I became fully immersed in my creation. My mind wandered to Blake, to our plans for the upcoming showcase. The thought of unveiling my art to him filled me with both excitement and trepidation. Would he see the essence of my struggles reflected in the colors? Would he understand the journey that led me to this moment?

As the sun dipped below the horizon, casting a warm glow throughout the room, I finally stepped back to assess my work. The canvas was a riot of color, a tapestry of emotion that mirrored my tumultuous journey. I felt a profound sense of accomplishment wash over me—a realization that this was only the beginning.

In the days that followed, I found myself caught in a delightful whirlwind of creativity. Each morning, I awoke with a renewed sense of purpose, eager to dive into my art and connect with Blake in ways I hadn't imagined possible. Our conversations flowed effortlessly, a delightful mixture of encouragement and playful banter as we exchanged ideas and inspirations. We shared snippets of our creative processes, often leading to late-night phone calls filled with laughter and impromptu brainstorming sessions.

Yet, amid the exhilaration of our newfound connection, an undercurrent of anxiety began to bubble to the surface. As the showcase drew nearer, the looming prospect of vulnerability began to weigh on me. The thought of exposing my heart, of unveiling my struggles and triumphs for Blake to witness, filled me with trepidation. What if my art didn't resonate with him? What if he saw the cracks I had worked so hard to conceal?

As I poured my fears onto the canvas one evening, I decided to paint a piece that encapsulated my journey of forgiveness—the struggle to accept my flaws, to embrace the imperfections that made me human. I envisioned a figure standing at the edge of a cliff, arms outstretched toward the horizon, a blend of light and shadow swirling around them. It would symbolize the delicate balance between vulnerability and strength, an homage to the journey we all undertake in search of acceptance.

With each stroke, I felt the weight of my anxiety begin to lift. I was pouring my heart into this piece, allowing my fears to transform into something beautiful. The act of creation was liberating, reminding me that vulnerability could lead to connection, and connection could ultimately pave the way for healing.

As Saturday approached, I could feel the palpable tension in the air—a mixture of excitement and nervous anticipation. I spent the afternoon preparing Blake's living room, draping a soft sheet over the couch and scattering my sketches and paintbrushes like scattered stars across the floor. Each detail felt significant, a reflection of the bond we were building, one that was rooted in mutual support and understanding.

When the time finally arrived, I stood in front of the mirror, taking a deep breath to calm my racing heart. My reflection stared back at me, a mixture of apprehension and determination etched across my face. I was ready to share not just my art, but a piece of my soul. As Blake entered the room, his eyes widened with surprise and delight, and I felt a warmth bloom in my chest.

We exchanged shy smiles before he motioned for me to begin. With the glow of the fairy lights twinkling above us and the aroma of fresh pizza wafting through the air, I took a step forward. I opened my heart and let the words flow, revealing the story behind each piece, my fears laid bare but met with understanding.

In that moment, surrounded by the comforts of friendship and creativity, I knew I was finally embracing the patterns of forgiveness—not just for Blake but for myself. As I looked into his eyes, I saw not judgment, but acceptance. And in that acceptance, I discovered the true essence of friendship—the ability to weather storms together, to grow, and to celebrate each other's victories. We were two artists standing on the precipice of our dreams, ready to leap into the unknown, together.

Chapter 14: The Fashionable Affair

The sun hung low in the sky, casting a warm, golden hue over the streets of Asheville, North Carolina. The mountains cradled the town like a secret, their rugged silhouettes softened by the late afternoon light. With every breath, I inhaled the scent of fresh pine mingling with the distant aroma of artisanal coffee wafting from the local café, where friends gathered, laughter spilling out like confetti. It was in this vibrant tapestry of life that Blake and I found ourselves, two kindred spirits reigniting a flame that had once flickered into embers.

As we stepped into the cozy confines of the old warehouse that would host our charity fashion show, my heart raced with anticipation. The raw, industrial space was a canvas of potential; exposed brick walls adorned with splashes of local art and the occasional oversized window filtering the sunset's hues into a dance of light and shadow. I could almost hear the heartbeat of the place, the whispers of artists and creators who had once filled it with dreams and colors.

Blake leaned against a weathered beam, his silhouette backlit by the warm glow seeping through the window, creating an ethereal aura around him. His eyes sparkled with the mischief and creativity I remembered so well, the kind that sparked ideas like fireworks on a summer night. "What do you think?" he asked, gesturing with a flourish to the expansive space before us. "Should we turn it into an enchanted forest, or perhaps a vintage Parisian street?"

"Why not both?" I replied, excitement bubbling within me. "Imagine a whimsical forest adorned with fairy lights and fabric draped like the streets of Montmartre. Models gliding down a runway that feels like a dreamscape."

He chuckled, the sound warm and infectious. "A fashion fairy tale, then. I love it. We can mix earthy tones with vibrant colors. Think flowing fabrics that mimic nature—like a walking garden."

As we brainstormed, I could see the wheels turning in his mind, a whirlwind of inspiration that pulled me into its orbit. The thought of fusing our styles sent a thrill racing through me. My designs were often bold and avant-garde, embodying a spirit of rebellion, while Blake leaned towards the romantic and ethereal. Together, we could create something truly magical—something that spoke to the heart of our community and celebrated the artistry that thrived here.

We mapped out our ideas on a massive whiteboard, sketching concepts that flowed like the very fabric we envisioned. Each stroke felt like a declaration of our renewed friendship, a promise that we were no longer just two artists struggling in our own corners of the world. We were collaborators, partners in crime, united by our love for fashion and our desire to make a difference.

The project brought a sense of urgency, but in the best possible way. As we pieced together plans for our show, I felt a blossoming within me, a surge of confidence that had been dormant for far too long. I couldn't remember the last time I had felt this alive, this inspired. There was a synergy between us, a current that pulsed beneath our words and ideas. With each concept we generated, our laughter echoed against the warehouse walls, intertwining with the dreams of those who had come before us.

Days turned into nights, each moment punctuated by the scent of coffee, the hum of music, and the rustle of fabric as we transformed the space into a sanctuary for artists. We reached out to local talent, inviting musicians, painters, and dancers to lend their skills to our show. This was more than just a runway—it was a celebration of community, a manifestation of love for the arts. I felt the joy of connection with each artist who joined our cause, the realization that we were all weaving our unique threads into a vibrant tapestry.

As the event approached, we held meetings that spiraled into creative chaos, fueled by passion and the occasional slice of pizza. I marveled at how effortlessly Blake balanced his creativity with my exuberance, the way he anchored me when my ideas threatened to float too far from reality. I saw in him a gentle confidence, a man who believed in the power of art to heal and unite, to evoke emotion and spark change.

One evening, as we worked late, the moonlight spilled through the windows, bathing the room in a silvery glow. I turned to him, my heart brimming with gratitude. "I never thought I'd find this again," I confessed, my voice barely above a whisper. "This spark. This connection."

Blake met my gaze, his expression serious yet tender. "Neither did I. But it's not just about fashion; it's about friendship, right? We're not just creating clothes; we're creating a space for people to express themselves."

His words resonated deeply, echoing the very essence of what we were trying to achieve. In that moment, surrounded by sketches and swatches, I realized how much I cherished this partnership—not just as collaborators but as friends, as confidants in a world that often felt overwhelming and chaotic.

As the final touches were made in preparation for the show, my excitement swelled, a sweet anticipation laced with nervous energy. I imagined the evening unfolding: the lights dimming, the audience murmuring in hushed awe, and our designs coming to life on the runway, a visual symphony of color and texture. I could almost hear the applause, the cheers of support from a community that had always inspired me.

This fashion show was more than an event; it was a celebration of resilience, a testament to the beauty of collaboration. With Blake by my side, I felt invincible, ready to embrace whatever lay ahead. The vibrant world we were crafting together would not just showcase our creativity; it would echo the heartbeat of our town, a reminder of the artistic spirit that thrived in every corner of Asheville.

The day of the fashion show arrived like a freshly painted canvas, filled with promise and potential. The warehouse buzzed with an energy that crackled in the air, a palpable excitement that made the hairs on my arms stand on end. I could hardly believe how far we had come from our initial brainstorming sessions, those playful exchanges of ideas now transformed into a vibrant reality. Everywhere I looked, local artists busily set up their displays, their passion evident in the meticulous way they arranged their works. Each corner of the venue told a story, each painting, sculpture, and piece of jewelry beckoning for attention, eager to share its tale.

As I navigated through the space, my heart danced in sync with the rhythm of the music echoing from the makeshift stage. Blake stood at the far end, his silhouette framed by the warm glow of string lights that twinkled above like stars newly spilled from the heavens. He was in his element, adjusting the runway with a precision that was equal parts artistry and determination. A surge of pride washed over me. We had poured our hearts into this endeavor, and I knew that this night would be a celebration not just of fashion but of friendship and creativity.

The models arrived one by one, each adorned in our designs that blended earthy tones with bursts of color, flowing fabrics draping gracefully around their forms. I watched as they transformed before my eyes, the ethereal qualities of our creations melding with the unique personalities of each woman and man. It was a symbiotic relationship; the clothes enhanced their beauty, and they brought the garments to life, twirling and posing as they practiced their walks.

"Look at them," Blake said, his voice a mix of awe and satisfaction. "They're not just wearing clothes; they're embodying a vision."

I nodded, my chest swelling with a mix of excitement and nervousness. "And they're doing it with such grace. I can't wait for the audience to see how our designs move."

In those moments leading up to the show, we darted between the chaos and beauty of the preparations. I found solace in the little things—the way the light bounced off the sequined fabric of one dress, or the feel of the soft silk against my fingertips. Each piece was a labor of love, a testament to the late nights spent sketching and sewing, fueled by endless cups of coffee and a shared determination to create something unforgettable.

Backstage, the air was thick with anticipation. I flitted around, checking on hair and makeup, adjusting the fit of a particularly intricate dress that flowed like water. The nervous energy was infectious, propelling everyone into a whirlpool of laughter and last-minute adjustments. I caught sight of Blake, deep in conversation with one of the musicians who would perform during the intermission. The way he animatedly gestured with his hands, his eyes bright with enthusiasm, reminded me of a child telling a story—a fitting role for someone so deeply passionate about art.

"Are you ready?" he called out to me, his voice cutting through the buzz like a bell.

"Ready as I'll ever be!" I replied, a nervous laugh escaping my lips. I felt as if I were standing on the precipice of something monumental, the butterflies in my stomach flapping wildly, threatening to lift me off the ground.

As the lights dimmed, a hush fell over the audience. The murmur of anticipation transformed into an excited silence, an electric atmosphere that ignited my senses. I stood at the edge of the runway, peering through the curtains, my heart pounding with each passing second. I could see familiar faces among the crowd—friends, family, local artists, all here to support us. The warmth of their presence enveloped me, grounding me in the moment.

With a deep breath, the show commenced. The first model stepped onto the runway, and the audience collectively exhaled, a ripple of awe sweeping through the room. The fabric shimmered under the lights, capturing every hue of the rainbow, transforming the model into a living piece of art. I felt my breath catch in my throat, an overwhelming sense of pride surging through me. This was our creation, our vision taking flight before our very eyes.

One by one, the models glided down the runway, each showcasing a unique design that told its own story. I could see the joy on their faces, the confidence that radiated from within as they embraced their roles as living canvases. Each twirl and pose was met with applause, the audience erupting into cheers that made my heart sing. Blake joined me at the side of the stage, our hands brushing together for just a fleeting moment, a silent acknowledgment of what we had achieved.

"This is incredible," he murmured, his eyes shining with pride. "We did this together."

"Together," I echoed, feeling the weight of our shared journey settle comfortably around my shoulders. The event was a celebration of more than just fashion; it was a testament to the power of collaboration and friendship.

As the final model made her entrance, wearing a breathtaking gown that billowed like clouds, the audience erupted in applause. The sound washed over me like a warm wave, enveloping me in a cocoon of joy. I turned to Blake, our eyes meeting in a moment of unspoken understanding. This was what we had envisioned—a night that celebrated not just our designs but the artists who poured their hearts into their work, the community that thrived on creativity, and the rekindling of our friendship.

When the show concluded, we took to the stage for a bow, our hands raised high, basking in the glow of the audience's appreciation. I could hardly contain my emotions; tears welled in my eyes as I scanned the crowd, catching sight of familiar faces beaming with pride. I realized in that moment how far we had come, how much this journey had meant not only for us but for everyone who had joined in this artistic endeavor.

As the applause echoed in my ears, I knew this was just the beginning. Our journey together had awakened a creative spark within me that I had thought long extinguished. With Blake by my side, I felt ready to take on the world, one stitch at a time, crafting not only fashion but a future woven together by friendship, passion, and the unwavering belief in the power of art to bring people together. The night shimmered with promise, and as we stepped off the stage, I felt an exhilarating sense of possibility lingering in the air, whispering that our story was far from over.

The evening air was thick with a mixture of exhilaration and satisfaction as Blake and I descended from the stage, our hearts still racing from the applause that echoed in our ears. The warehouse, now transformed into a sanctuary of artistry, pulsed with life as guests mingled, their laughter blending harmoniously with the soft notes of live music. The atmosphere was electric, each conversation a tapestry of shared joy and creativity, woven together by the vibrant threads of our collective efforts.

As I surveyed the scene, I noticed local artists eagerly engaging with attendees, their passion for their work palpable in the way they animatedly discussed their creations. One corner of the venue was dedicated to paintings that captured the essence of Asheville's breathtaking landscapes—rolling hills kissed by the orange glow of sunset, vibrant streets bustling with life. Nearby, a sculptor deftly demonstrated her craft, molding clay into whimsical forms that danced in the light. I marveled at the impact of our show, how it had transformed not just the warehouse, but the very spirit of our community.

"Look at them," Blake said, his voice filled with awe. "This is what we set out to do—connect people through art."

I nodded, feeling a swell of gratitude. "I never imagined we could create something that resonates so deeply. It's like a living gallery."

As the night unfolded, I found myself drifting from one group to another, soaking in the creativity that flowed around me. I stopped to chat with a painter named Mia, whose brushstrokes seemed to capture the heartbeat of the mountains themselves. She spoke of her love for the landscape, the way each sunrise inspired her to create. "It's like each painting is a conversation between me and the world," she said, her eyes alight with passion.

I shared my journey into fashion, how every fabric choice felt like a chapter in a story waiting to be told. Mia listened intently, nodding as if she understood the language of creation that connected us. We spoke for what felt like hours, a seamless exchange of ideas and dreams that left me invigorated. I couldn't help but think how this evening had become a kaleidoscope of artistry, each interaction a unique design contributing to the overall tapestry.

Blake rejoined me, holding two glasses of sparkling cider, his expression a mix of pride and disbelief. "I never thought we could pull this off," he admitted, handing me a glass. "This was beyond anything I imagined."

We clinked our glasses together, the delicate sound resonating like a promise of more adventures to come. "To more nights like this," I toasted, feeling a rush of gratitude for the bond we had rekindled.

As the night wore on, the atmosphere shifted into something more intimate. The lights dimmed slightly, and the musicians took center stage, strumming soothing melodies that wrapped around us like a warm embrace. I watched as couples began to dance, the flickering candlelight casting soft shadows on their smiling faces. It felt as if the entire room had stepped into a dream, where worries faded and joy reigned supreme.

Blake and I exchanged a glance, a silent agreement passing between us. "Shall we?" he asked, extending his hand toward the dance floor.

With a mixture of excitement and nervousness, I took his hand, feeling the warmth radiate from him. We stepped onto the floor, the music washing over us, and I was suddenly acutely aware of the world around us melting away. In that moment, it was just the two of us—lost in our own bubble of creativity, friendship, and shared dreams.

As we danced, I couldn't help but notice how fluidly we moved together, as if the rhythm of our hearts synchronized with the music. Blake spun me around, a mischievous glint in his eye, and I laughed, the sound blending into the melodies that floated through the air. It was a beautiful reminder of how far we had come, how much we had grown—not just as artists, but as friends who understood the nuances of each other's souls.

In the midst of the dance, Blake leaned closer, his voice a soft whisper against my ear. "You know, I've been thinking... this isn't just about fashion or art. It's about creating a platform for voices that need to be heard."

I pulled back slightly, searching his gaze. "What do you mean?"

He took a breath, his expression serious. "I want to continue this, to make it bigger. We could do workshops, invite more artists, expand our reach. We could create a movement."

My heart raced at the thought. A movement. The idea was intoxicating, a rush of adrenaline and inspiration flooding through me. "You're right," I said, my voice rising with excitement. "We could turn this into an annual event, make it a staple in the community."

The spark of ambition ignited between us, igniting a conversation that felt like brainstorming a new dream. We discussed everything from potential themes for future shows to collaborations with local schools, inviting young artists to participate and showcase their talent. Each idea flowed easily, the creative synergy between us undeniable.

As the music swelled around us, I felt a deep sense of purpose blooming within me. It was thrilling to think that our friendship and artistic collaboration could give birth to something larger than ourselves. It was as if the universe had conspired to bring us together, to fuel a passion that burned brightly in both our hearts.

When the final song echoed through the warehouse, the audience erupted into applause once more. I glanced at Blake, our smiles mirroring the elation coursing through us. This night had been more than just a showcase; it was the beginning of a new chapter, a promise of what we could accomplish together.

As the crowd began to disperse, I noticed a group of young artists huddled together, their faces lit with excitement. They approached us, their eyes gleaming with admiration. "Your show was amazing!" one girl exclaimed, her voice bursting with enthusiasm. "We've always wanted to get involved in something like this!"

Blake and I exchanged glances, an unspoken agreement forming between us. "We'd love to have you involved in future events," I said, my heart swelling with the prospect. "Let's make this a space where everyone can share their voice."

The thrill of connection wrapped around me like a warm blanket. Each person in the room felt like a vital thread in the tapestry we were creating—a community woven together by the threads of art and friendship.

As the last guests trickled out, Blake and I began to gather our things, our hearts still buoyant from the night's events. The warehouse, now dimmed and quiet, held echoes of laughter and dreams yet to be fulfilled. "What do you think will happen next?" Blake asked, a twinkle in his eye.

I paused, contemplating the journey ahead. "I think we're just getting started," I replied, my voice steady. "Together, we can create something that not only showcases fashion but uplifts the entire community."

With a shared vision that radiated hope, we stepped into the cool night air, the stars twinkling above us like the endless possibilities that lay ahead. In that moment, I felt a profound sense of belonging—not just to Blake, but to the vibrant world of art and creativity that awaited us. The journey ahead shimmered with promise, and I was ready to embrace it all.

Chapter 15: The Runway of Resilience

The air was thick with the scent of fresh paint and linseed oil, mingling with the sweet aroma of caramel popcorn wafting from a nearby vendor's cart. As I stepped into the historic theater, its gilded edges and marbled columns seemed to whisper tales of grandeur and forgotten dreams. It was here, beneath the heavy velvet drapes and shimmering chandeliers, that we would unveil our charity fashion show—a project born from a blend of hope and relentless ambition. Each day leading up to this moment, the anticipation coursed through my veins, an intoxicating mixture of exhilaration and dread that felt oddly familiar.

Backstage was a frenzy of movement. Models darted between racks of meticulously designed garments, their laughter punctuated by the sharp clicks of high heels on the polished wooden floor. I stood among them, clutching my sketches, feeling both like a proud architect unveiling a masterpiece and an anxious artist peeking through the curtain. The soft glow of dressing room lights cast a warm hue on my creations, each piece a vibrant splash against the backdrop of anxieties waiting to unfurl.

Blake's laughter broke through my spiraling thoughts, a low rumble that steadied my heart. He emerged from the crowd, his presence a calming force amid the chaos. With tousled hair and an easy smile, he seemed at home in this whirlwind. "You're not going to let the spotlight scare you, are you?" he teased, arching an eyebrow in that infuriatingly charming way he had. The confidence radiating from him felt like a lifebuoy thrown into my stormy sea of self-doubt.

"No," I said, trying to mirror his nonchalance, though the tremor in my voice betrayed me. "Just... waiting for it to swallow me whole."

He stepped closer, his warmth enveloping me like a comforting blanket. "You've put your heart into this. When those lights shine, remember that you're sharing a piece of yourself. That's powerful."

His gaze held mine, grounding me in the moment, and for a heartbeat, the chaos faded.

The theater pulsed with a rhythm of its own; the orchestra was tuning, and the audience's murmur swelled like a distant wave, lapping at the shore of my resolve. I took a deep breath, inhaling the mingled scents of anticipation and polish. Each inhale pushed me deeper into my resolve, sparking memories of late nights spent stitching seams and perfecting silhouettes. Each garment was more than fabric; it was a chapter of my journey, woven with threads of my triumphs and tears.

As the backstage chatter crescendoed, I turned my attention to the models preparing to don my designs. Each one had a distinct aura—some radiated confidence, while others exuded a shy grace that reminded me of my own insecurities. I could feel their energy reflecting my own; we were a tapestry of vulnerability and strength, interwoven with the hopes that tonight would be a turning point.

The stage was set, the lights dimmed to a sultry glow that whispered of secrets and dreams. A palpable hush fell over the crowd, their expectant eyes eagerly scanning the entrance where the models would soon emerge. My heart raced in tandem with the quickening pace of the music as I caught sight of the first model, her stride unwavering, embodying the very essence of the creations that adorned her.

And then came the applause, a warm wave that rolled through the audience, crashing against the shores of my doubt. With each stride, my designs came alive, swirling around her like leaves dancing in an autumn breeze. The lights caught the shimmer of sequins and the vibrant hues of fabrics, igniting a spark in my chest. My heart swelled as I realized that this moment was not solely about the clothes. It was a celebration of resilience, a testament to the battles fought both on and off the runway.

As the show unfolded, I found solace in the applause that echoed like a heartbeat, a rhythm that carried my dreams. With every step, the world outside melted away, leaving only the music and the moment. I could see Blake leaning against a pillar, his smile bright as he cheered for me in silence, his eyes twinkling with pride. I thought about how far we'd come, how our laughter had filled countless late-night conversations over steaming cups of coffee and midnight snacks. This was more than just a fashion show; it was a reflection of our shared journey, an embodiment of all our hopes and fears intertwined.

Then, as if the universe conspired to amplify my joy, the final model strode down the runway, adorned in a gown that flowed like liquid gold, its fabric catching the light in mesmerizing waves. The audience's applause swelled, a crescendo of sound that enveloped me like a warm embrace. I could feel the weight of my insecurities lifting, replaced by a vibrant energy that surged through my veins. This was validation, a chorus of encouragement ringing in my ears, assuring me that I had done more than just create; I had connected.

In that fleeting moment, I realized that the vulnerability I had feared was, in fact, my greatest strength. The thrill of sharing my work, of letting others glimpse the raw essence of who I was, transformed the stage into a sanctuary. As the show came to a close, I took a breath, savoring the sweet taste of triumph that lingered on my tongue. The applause, the laughter, the joy—it was a symphony of resilience, a reminder that we all wear our battles like badges, and every piece of fabric tells a story worth sharing.

With each beat of my heart echoing the rhythm of the audience's cheers, I knew that this runway was not just a stage; it was a testament to the power of dreams. And in the company of Blake, who stood resolute in his belief in me, I felt ready to embrace whatever came next, armed with the knowledge that vulnerability could indeed lead to beauty and connection.

The final echoes of applause still reverberated in the air, a lingering testament to the night's triumph, as I stepped away from the chaos of backstage. The mingling scents of hairspray and warm body heat faded, replaced by the cool breeze of the Chicago evening, fresh and invigorating. A soft glow from the streetlights illuminated the cobblestones beneath my feet, transforming the world outside the theater into a stage of its own. It was as if the universe had conspired to welcome me into this new chapter, the night air whispering promises of what lay ahead.

I walked slowly, my heart still dancing to the rhythm of the show. Each step felt lighter, unburdened by the weight of self-doubt that had previously clung to me like a second skin. The vibrant fabric of my designs lingered in my mind, each piece a part of my story, like the glimmer of stars scattered across an indigo sky. I could see them now—bold and unapologetic, echoing the very essence of resilience that had pulsed through the theater just moments ago.

As I strolled down Michigan Avenue, the world buzzed with life. The laughter of late-night revelers floated from nearby cafés, their chatter weaving a tapestry of joy and connection that resonated within me. I felt an odd kinship with these strangers, united by the common thread of celebration. In the distance, a street musician played a lively tune, his fingers dancing over the strings of an old guitar. I paused, letting the music wash over me like a balm, a fitting soundtrack to the whirlwind of emotions still swirling in my chest.

I pulled out my phone, glancing at the time. Blake had promised to meet me outside for a celebratory drink, and the thought made my heart flutter. Our moments together had become a cherished ritual, each encounter a patchwork of laughter, deep conversations, and the unmistakable connection that had blossomed between us. With each passing day, I found myself unraveling more around him, revealing layers I had kept tightly bound for so long.

As I turned the corner, the neon glow of a cozy bar caught my eye. Its inviting warmth contrasted sharply with the crisp night air, beckoning me to step inside. The rich wooden doors creaked as I entered, the ambiance filled with the low murmur of voices and the clinking of glasses. I spotted Blake at a table in the corner, his back to me, a picture of casual elegance in his navy blazer that complemented the worn jeans and crisp white shirt he wore. He turned at the sound of my approach, his smile lighting up the dimly lit room.

"There you are," he said, his voice smooth like the bourbon he had ordered, as he stood to pull out my chair. "I was starting to think you'd floated away with the applause."

I laughed, a sound that felt foreign yet familiar, like discovering a long-lost part of myself. "I almost did, but I managed to keep my feet on the ground—barely." I took a seat, the warmth of the atmosphere wrapping around me like a hug.

After ordering a couple of drinks, we fell into a rhythm of easy conversation, our laughter mingling with the bar's ambiance, each anecdote shared a step closer to unraveling the threads of our lives. "You should have seen the look on your face when the first model stepped onto the runway," Blake teased, leaning closer, his eyes glinting with mischief. "It was like you'd just seen a ghost."

I rolled my eyes, playfully swatting his arm. "Hey, it's not every day your work is paraded in front of a crowd. It was an emotional rollercoaster."

"More like a runaway train," he chuckled, his voice warm, wrapping around my nerves like a soft blanket. "But you handled it like a pro. I could see the pride in your eyes when you watched the models."

In that moment, as our eyes locked, I felt an undeniable connection, a tether that pulled me toward him. There was something intoxicating about sharing this journey with him, as if he were a vital piece of my evolving narrative. "Thank you for being there," I said softly, vulnerability lacing my words. "I don't think I could have done it without you."

He paused, the warmth in his expression shifting to something deeper. "You would have, you know. You're stronger than you give yourself credit for." His gaze held mine, a quiet intensity that sent a thrill through my core. In his presence, my insecurities felt small, diminished by the unwavering belief he seemed to have in me.

As we toasted to the night's success, our glasses clinked softly, a melodic promise that echoed with every heartbeat. The bourbon warmed my insides, a slow burn that mirrored the flickering flames of hope ignited within me. Our conversation ebbed and flowed, seamlessly weaving between lighthearted banter and deeper revelations about dreams and fears, about love and the complexities of life.

"Do you ever think about what's next?" he asked, a spark of curiosity dancing in his eyes. "For your designs, I mean."

I leaned back, contemplating the question as the room pulsed around us. "Sometimes. I want to create pieces that tell stories—clothes that resonate with people on a personal level. Fashion isn't just about what you wear; it's about how it makes you feel, how it empowers you." The words flowed easily, each syllable wrapped in a passion that had lain dormant for far too long.

"And what about you?" I countered, sensing the dreams behind his playful exterior. "What's next for Blake?"

He hesitated for a moment, the weight of his thoughts etched across his features. "I've been thinking about starting my own photography project. Something that captures the essence of people in their most authentic moments. I want to show the world what they don't often see."

The sincerity in his voice sent a shiver down my spine. "You'd be amazing at that," I said, my admiration unmasked. "Your eye for detail is incredible. I can already picture your work hanging in galleries."

The corners of his mouth turned up, a mixture of gratitude and something deeper flickering in his gaze. "Maybe we'll both be hanging our dreams side by side someday," he said, his voice low and earnest.

In that instant, a vision unfolded in my mind—our dreams entwined like threads in a tapestry, vibrant and strong. As I looked into his eyes, I felt a burgeoning sense of possibility, a reminder that resilience isn't just about bouncing back; it's about forging ahead, hand in hand with those who lift us up.

The night continued to unfurl, our laughter mingling with the music that swirled around us, each moment a step deeper into a shared journey that felt both exhilarating and comforting. Outside, the world danced on, but within this little haven, I felt a blossoming sense of belonging, an unshakeable bond that whispered of promises yet to be fulfilled. With each passing minute, I knew that whatever challenges awaited us, I was ready to face them head-on, emboldened by the strength we found in one another.

The bar buzzed with a frenetic energy, yet within our little corner, a bubble of intimacy enveloped Blake and me. The muted sounds of laughter and clinking glasses created a symphony that underscored our shared ambitions. With each sip of bourbon, warmth unfurled in my chest, a liquid courage bolstering my resolve to explore the depths of my dreams and those of the man across from me.

The night deepened as we traded aspirations like precious tokens, each revelation illuminating the path ahead. "You know," I mused, tapping my glass thoughtfully, "it's incredible how tonight felt like a turning point. It was more than just a show; it was a gathering of souls, all willing to embrace vulnerability for the sake of art."

Blake nodded, his eyes shimmering with understanding. "Exactly. It's like we were all part of something bigger—a collective heartbeat. And that's where the magic lies. In the connection."

His words resonated, sending ripples of inspiration through my mind. I envisioned a collection that encapsulated that very spirit of connection, pieces that spoke not just of fabric and thread but of the stories that wove us together. "What if I created a line inspired by moments of vulnerability? Each piece could tell a story of resilience, capturing the essence of what it means to share our true selves."

A thoughtful silence enveloped us as Blake considered my idea. "That sounds powerful. You could partner with artists from different backgrounds, incorporate their stories into your designs. It would turn every garment into a conversation starter, a canvas for the soul."

The enthusiasm bubbled within me, igniting a flurry of ideas. The possibilities seemed endless, each more enticing than the last. "We could host a pop-up event—bring together models, artists, and people who have inspiring stories. Let the runway be a platform for their voices," I suggested, my excitement bubbling over.

He leaned forward, his eyes brightening. "And we can document it all! Your designs, their stories, captured through photography. It would make for a breathtaking collection."

As the conversation unfolded, the fabric of our shared vision began to take shape, intricate and rich. The night, once filled with the sweet thrill of success, transformed into a blueprint for the future, a canvas painted with our aspirations. With Blake by my side, the fears that once held me captive faded into the background, replaced by an unshakeable conviction that together, we could create something remarkable.

When we finally left the bar, the Chicago streets were alive with the pulse of nightlife, shimmering under the soft glow of street lamps. The brisk air invigorated me, a refreshing reminder of the vibrant world outside our intimate bubble. As we walked side by side, laughter bubbled up between us, each shared glance sparking a connection that felt almost palpable.

"Do you ever think about how quickly life can change?" I mused, my breath visible in the chilly night air. "One moment, you're anxious about a show, and the next, you're brainstorming a new collection."

"Absolutely. Life has a way of surprising us, doesn't it?" Blake replied, his voice thoughtful. "It's all about seizing those moments when they come. That's what makes it all worthwhile."

As we strolled down Michigan Avenue, the iconic skyline loomed above us, a backdrop of dreams realized and futures yet to be written. The thrill of the unknown wrapped around me like a warm shawl, encouraging me to embrace every possibility with open arms. It was in this moment that I felt a shift within me, a deeper understanding of what resilience truly meant. It was about not just bouncing back from setbacks, but embracing change, welcoming the unpredictable nature of life as an adventure waiting to unfold.

Arriving at the nearby park, we took a moment to pause, the tranquility of the lush greenery a soothing contrast to the city's frenetic pace. The park was alive with the gentle rustling of leaves and the distant sounds of laughter. Blake leaned against a tree, his expression contemplative as he gazed up at the stars twinkling overhead. "You know, it's easy to forget that there's a whole universe out there, just like it's easy to forget how significant our little moments can be."

"Like this one?" I asked, feeling bold enough to step closer. The air between us shimmered with unspoken words, a palpable tension that danced in the cool night.

"Exactly." His gaze met mine, and in that moment, the world around us faded. The laughter of distant revelers, the rustling leaves, the city's heartbeat—it all became a mere backdrop to the connection that crackled in the air between us.

With a nervous thrill, I ventured a step closer, the space between us shrinking. "I've found that sharing my work has opened up so many doors, but it's also made me realize how much I want to share my life with the people who matter."

Blake's expression softened, his eyes searching mine as if trying to unearth the depths of my heart. "You matter to me, you know. More than just as a designer or a colleague. There's something incredibly special about you."

The sincerity in his voice sent a rush of warmth through me, igniting a spark of hope I had dared not acknowledge. "I feel the same way," I admitted, my heart racing as the truth slipped past my lips.

As if on cue, a shooting star streaked across the sky, a dazzling trail of light that ignited the darkness. We both looked up, momentarily entranced, the magic of the moment swelling around us. "Make a wish," Blake urged, his voice a soft whisper filled with promise.

With my heart pounding, I closed my eyes and wished for clarity, for strength to follow this newfound path alongside him. When I opened my eyes, I found him still watching me, his expression a blend of awe and something deeper, a quiet understanding passing between us.

"Whatever comes next, we'll figure it out together," he said, and the conviction in his voice sent a shiver of excitement down my spine.

That night felt like a turning point, a culmination of dreams intertwining and blooming under the vast expanse of the starry sky. With Blake at my side, I was no longer just a designer or a dreamer; I was a woman ready to embrace the unknown, to create a narrative woven from resilience and connection.

As we walked back to the theater to retrieve my things, the city pulsed around us, a living tapestry of stories waiting to be told. I felt a sense of purpose, a drive to not only share my designs but to inspire others to embrace their own vulnerabilities, to wear their stories proudly like the garments I created. Together, Blake and I would carve a path through this world, armed with dreams, laughter, and the unshakeable belief that resilience can indeed be a beautiful thing.

Under the glow of the city lights, our shared laughter echoed through the night, a symphony of possibility that promised to unravel new adventures waiting just beyond the horizon.

Chapter 16: Threads of Fate

A rush of adrenaline coursed through my veins as I stood backstage, my heart pounding against my ribcage like a drumbeat at a rock concert. The dim lighting and the scent of fresh paint mingled with the lingering aroma of popcorn from the concession stand, creating an intoxicating blend of anticipation and nostalgia. I could hear the murmur of the audience, a gentle wave of conversation that flowed in and out of focus, punctuated by bursts of laughter and the rustle of programs being flipped. Tonight was not just any night; it was a celebration of creativity, a tapestry woven from the dreams of artists and the hope of a community.

Blake stood beside me, his hands shoved deep into the pockets of his tailored suit, the faintest line of worry creasing his brow. He was usually a beacon of calm, but I could see that even his confidence was wavering. The stage lights flickered like stars, casting fleeting shadows across his face, amplifying the storm brewing behind his hazel eyes. "Did you hear back from the sponsor?" he asked, his voice low and strained, as if he were afraid to voice the possibility that hung in the air.

I shook my head, the knot in my stomach tightening with each passing moment. The promise of financial support that had initially given us the courage to dream big had slipped through our fingers like sand. The news had come like a winter chill, unexpected and biting, sending a shiver down my spine. Our charity show was built on the belief that we could make a difference, that our combined efforts would spark a change in the community. But now, with a major sponsor withdrawing at the last minute, that belief felt like a fragile paper boat bobbing in a raging sea.

As the reality of our situation set in, I watched the panic bloom in Blake's eyes, mingling with the determination that always burned so brightly in him. It was a fire I admired, one that had inspired so many in our circle. And yet, standing there in the backstage shadows, I could see how heavy the weight of this setback had settled on his shoulders. I stepped closer, placing a reassuring hand on his arm, feeling the tension coiled within him. "We can figure this out," I whispered, hoping to ignite a spark of optimism amidst the gathering storm.

Blake nodded, though the uncertainty lingered in his gaze. "We need a plan," he said, urgency threading through his words. "There's no time to waste. The show must go on."

With a shared glance that spoke volumes, we both turned our attention to the small army of friends and volunteers bustling around us. They were the heart of this endeavor, their passion palpable in the electric air. The sound of laughter, the clinking of glasses, and the rustling of fabric as costumes were hurriedly adjusted filled the space, creating an atmosphere thick with enthusiasm. We needed that spirit now more than ever.

"Let's gather everyone," I said, my voice rising above the din. It was time to rally the troops. I could feel the weight of responsibility resting heavily on my chest, but I also felt a glimmer of resolve. If there was one thing I had learned through all of this, it was that people were often willing to rise to the occasion, to join hands in the face of adversity.

The small gathering quickly turned into a whirlwind of ideas and energy, each face lit with the determination to keep our dream alive. We huddled together, a motley crew of artists, friends, and local patrons, each one invested in the outcome of the night. Ideas flew like confetti in the air, each suggestion building on the last. Social media buzzed around us, a platform that could amplify our voices and bring our community together.

As we brainstormed, I felt a surge of gratitude for the diversity of our little collective. There was Clara, her curly hair bouncing as she spoke, her voice rising with enthusiasm, drawing everyone in. She had a knack for words, a way of stringing them together that made even the most mundane ideas seem like brilliant epiphanies. Then there was Marcus, an artist known for his vivid murals that seemed to breathe life into the walls of our town. His laughter was infectious, and he threw out ideas with a creativity that electrified the group.

Together, we crafted a plan that felt like a lifeline. We would utilize social media to raise awareness, to tap into the pulse of our community and let them know we needed them now more than ever. The idea spread like wildfire, igniting passion in our hearts. We would share our journey, the struggles, and the dreams, inviting our neighbors to join us in making this event a success.

As I looked around at the faces of my friends, I felt an overwhelming sense of belonging. We were not just fighting for a charity show; we were fighting for each other, for the very essence of our community. In that moment, I understood the true meaning of collaboration and resilience. It wasn't just about keeping the lights on for one night; it was about igniting hope, about stitching together the frayed edges of our shared aspirations into something beautiful.

The minutes flew by like the soft flutter of butterflies, each second steeped in urgency and determination. As our plan began to take shape, the energy around us transformed into a palpable force, each person leaning into the challenge with a fervor that was nothing short of inspiring. I could see Blake, his features softening, a small smile breaking through the tension as he observed the contagious enthusiasm of our friends. It was as if a veil had been lifted, revealing a pathway forward, illuminated by the collective glow of our resolve.

The stage lights dimmed further, casting a gentle glow on our gathered group. In that moment, I felt something shift within me—a profound understanding that our journey was more than just about a charity show. It was about weaving together our stories, our hopes, and our dreams into a tapestry that was vibrant and full of life, one that would resonate far beyond the boundaries of our small town.

The air hummed with anticipation as we launched into our frantic campaign, fingers flying across keyboards, eyes glued to screens, fueled by an electric mix of determination and sheer necessity. Social media transformed from a simple platform for sharing memes and mundane updates into a vibrant megaphone through which we could broadcast our plight. We created a flurry of posts that painted a picture of the charity show—not just as a mere event, but as a heartfelt endeavor brimming with purpose and community spirit. Each carefully crafted word was designed to stir the hearts of those who read it, encouraging them to join us in our quest.

I watched as Clara expertly maneuvered the digital landscape, her charisma spilling over into every post. Her infectious enthusiasm was magnetic; it could draw in even the most disinterested observer. "Join us for a night of laughter, love, and local talent!" she exclaimed in one of her posts, punctuating her words with vibrant emojis that danced across the screen. Her passion was a flame, and as we worked side by side, I felt myself being drawn into that warmth, the cold tendrils of doubt loosening their grip on my heart.

Blake stood nearby, his face illuminated by the glow of his phone, as he connected with local businesses, imploring them to contribute in any way they could. "Every bit helps," he reminded me, his voice steady despite the whirlwind surrounding us. The sight of him, so resolute and unyielding, filled me with a renewed sense of purpose. We were all in this together, a makeshift family united by a common goal that was rapidly evolving from a simple charity show into a community rallying point.

In the midst of our online frenzy, a notification flashed across my screen—one of our friends had shared a heartfelt message, recounting how our last show had impacted her family, drawing them out of a dark place and back into the light. Her words resonated deeply, and as I read them aloud to the group, I could see the collective spirit strengthen. It was proof that our efforts mattered, that even the smallest flicker of kindness could ignite a flame of hope in someone's heart.

By the time the sun dipped below the horizon, painting the sky in shades of pink and gold, we had transformed our anxiety into action. The once-distant dream of saving the charity show felt tangible now, a shared vision that linked us all. As dusk settled over the town, casting an amber glow on the buildings, I felt an exhilarating sense of community spirit envelop us, wrapping around our shoulders like a cozy blanket on a chilly evening.

As the night wore on, we planned a gathering at the local park to further engage the community. It would be a mini event—an open mic night where locals could come, share their talents, and support our cause. The idea sparked enthusiasm; laughter bubbled up from our group like soda fizzing in a glass, buoyed by the promise of connection and creativity. Clara suggested bringing in food trucks, a concept that made everyone nod in agreement, imagining the mouthwatering scents wafting through the air. The thought of sharing a meal, surrounded by laughter and music, painted a vivid image in my mind, one that was hard to resist.

We spent hours meticulously outlining the details, our spirits buoyed by a sense of camaraderie. We drew up a list of potential local artists and musicians, people we knew could pour their hearts out on stage and draw in an audience. As the final details of our makeshift festival began to solidify, I could feel a current of hope coursing through me, fueled by our shared purpose.

"Let's make this special," Blake said, his voice steady but laced with excitement. "We want to not only raise money but also celebrate what we can achieve together." The light in his eyes was infectious, and I could see everyone around me nodding in agreement, caught up in the fervor of possibility.

As the clock ticked closer to midnight, we wrapped up our planning, and exhaustion began to settle in like a soft blanket. Clara and Marcus exchanged ideas for their performances, the anticipation bubbling over as they contemplated their creative potential. I took a moment to step outside, the cool night air brushing against my skin like a gentle caress. I closed my eyes, allowing the sounds of the bustling preparation to fade into the background, replaced by the soft rustle of leaves and the distant hum of conversation.

In that stillness, I reflected on how this journey had transformed me. I was no longer just a bystander in my own life; I was an active participant, learning the delicate art of collaboration and the power of vulnerability. The moments of doubt that had once plagued me began to dissolve, replaced by a growing sense of confidence. I was part of something much larger than myself—a movement fueled by compassion and creativity.

The following days blurred together in a whirlwind of activity. Flyers were printed and distributed, and our social media campaign gained traction as more people began to rally behind us. The local businesses responded with an outpouring of support, donating goods, services, and money to help ensure our success. The community began to coalesce around us, igniting a fervor that felt like the first spark of spring thawing the icy grip of winter.

As we drew closer to the day of the open mic event, I found myself reflecting on the profound connection we had nurtured within our community. People who had once walked past each other without a second glance were now engaging in conversations, offering their talents, and coming together for a common purpose. It was a reminder that hope could be a powerful force, one capable of bridging gaps and forging connections between strangers.

On the eve of the event, as I stood in front of the mirror adjusting my outfit, I caught a glimpse of my own reflection and realized I had changed too. The girl who once feared rejection had learned to embrace vulnerability, to stand tall amidst uncertainty. With every challenge we faced, I felt the threads of fate weaving together our stories, intertwining our lives in a tapestry that was vibrant and full of life. We were not just striving to save a charity show; we were crafting a narrative that would echo through our town, reminding everyone that together, we could face any storm.

The day of our open mic event dawned bright and clear, the sun spilling its golden rays across the town like a painter with an infinite palette. I woke to the sound of birds chirping outside my window, their melodies mingling with the faint hum of traffic in the distance. The air was crisp with the promise of autumn, a gentle reminder that change was always just around the corner. I took a moment to breathe in the sweet scent of crisp leaves and fresh coffee wafting from the kitchen, savoring the warmth of anticipation that danced in my chest. Today wasn't just another Saturday; it was the culmination of our efforts, a celebration of resilience, creativity, and community.

As I dressed, slipping into a vintage floral dress that swayed gently around my knees, I felt a surge of excitement bubbling within me. Every detail of the event replayed in my mind—the vibrant flyers plastered on local storefronts, the enthusiastic responses flooding our social media pages, and the countless volunteers who had come together to transform the park into a magical venue. We had created an inviting space filled with laughter and joy, adorned with twinkling string lights and colorful bunting that fluttered like cheerful flags in the soft breeze.

Once dressed, I made my way to the park, where the smell of fresh popcorn and grilled hot dogs wafted through the air, mingling with the sweet aroma of cinnamon from the nearby vendor selling warm apple cider. The sound of chatter and laughter enveloped me as I approached the grassy area we had chosen for our stage. My heart swelled as I took in the scene: friends were setting up chairs, musicians were tuning their instruments, and the park seemed to pulse with a palpable energy, vibrating with the anticipation of what was to come.

Blake was already there, a flurry of motion as he directed the final touches, his usual charm on display as he coaxed volunteers into action. His white button-up shirt was rolled up at the sleeves, revealing the sinewy muscles of his forearms, which flexed as he gestured animatedly. "You're just in time!" he called out, his voice buoyant amidst the chatter. "We need more chairs over here!"

I joined him, and together we arranged the seating in a semicircle, creating an inviting atmosphere that encouraged connection. With every chair we placed, I could feel the excitement swelling like a tide, ready to wash over us as the event unfolded. "I can't believe we pulled this off," I said, glancing around at the crowd that had begun to gather. "Look at all these people!"

Blake's eyes sparkled with enthusiasm. "And it's just the beginning," he said, stepping back to admire our handiwork. "I have a feeling this is going to be one for the books." His belief in our efforts, his unshakeable faith in the community, made me feel lighter, as if the weight of our earlier challenges had been transformed into something altogether magical.

As the sun climbed higher, casting a warm glow over the park, the first performer stepped onto the stage—a local poet named Lena, whose words always resonated with raw honesty. The crowd hushed, leaning forward in their seats as she began to speak, her voice weaving through the air like silk. Each verse was a thread connecting us all, capturing the struggles and joys of our shared experiences. I watched as her words wrapped around the audience, binding us together in a tapestry of understanding.

In between performances, laughter erupted as Marcus took the stage with his guitar, strumming a lively tune that beckoned a few brave souls to the front to dance. It was contagious; the way he engaged with the crowd, pulling them in with every note, reminded me of how powerful art could be in bridging the gaps between strangers. A small circle formed, filled with friends and neighbors moving in sync, their faces alight with joy. I found myself clapping along, caught up in the infectious energy.

As the day stretched on, each performance became a thread in the fabric of our community, binding us tighter together. The musicians, poets, and storytellers poured their hearts into their art, sharing snippets of their lives, their dreams, and their fears. I could see people in the audience nodding along, recognizing pieces of themselves in the stories shared. The laughter, the sighs, the shared glances—it was a symphony of connection that resonated deeply within me.

As the sun began to dip low in the sky, casting a warm orange hue across the park, I took a moment to step back and breathe it all in. I was surrounded by laughter, the sounds of clinking glasses and the soft rustle of food wrappers, all intertwined with the melodies that floated through the air. It was a celebration, yes, but it was also a reminder of the power of community, of people coming together to support one another, to lift each other up when the world seemed intent on pushing us down.

"Hey, can I steal you for a minute?" Blake appeared beside me, a playful grin on his face, his eyes sparkling with mischief. "I think it's time for us to make our big announcement."

I nodded, my heart racing in anticipation. We had decided to share our story, to bring everyone into the fold of our journey—the highs and lows, the uncertainty and the triumphs. As we made our way to the makeshift stage, I could feel the warmth of the crowd enveloping me, a reminder that we were all in this together.

Blake took a deep breath, stepping forward to address the gathering. "Thank you all for being here today. What we're celebrating is not just an event, but the spirit of our community!" He gestured toward the performers, the volunteers, the smiling faces of friends and neighbors. "Each of you has played a vital role in keeping this dream alive. The support we've received has been overwhelming, and it's proof that when we stand together, we can overcome anything."

His words reverberated through the crowd, and I felt a swell of pride. This was what we had hoped for—an opportunity to showcase the strength of our bonds, the beauty of our shared experiences. I took a step forward, joining him at the forefront. "We've faced challenges along the way, but we learned something invaluable: that passion ignites hope, and when we come together, we can create something truly beautiful."

A ripple of applause echoed in response, the sound of clapping mingling with cheers and laughter, creating a symphony of encouragement that filled my heart to bursting. In that moment, I realized how far we had come, how much we had grown—not just as individuals, but as a collective force of nature.

As we wrapped up our announcement, I looked out over the sea of faces illuminated by the golden hues of the setting sun, each person a unique thread in the tapestry we had woven. Their smiles, their laughter, and their willingness to support one another created a vibrant mosaic of hope and resilience, a testament to the strength found in community.

The evening rolled on, each performance becoming a thread binding us closer together. By the time the final act took the stage—a young singer with a voice that soared like a bird in flight—the park was filled with a warm glow, not just from the string lights overhead, but from the palpable sense of connection that filled the air.

I glanced at Blake, who stood beside me, his eyes reflecting the twinkling lights above. He smiled, and I could see the pride shining in his expression. In that moment, we were no longer just individuals fighting for a cause; we were part of something larger, a tapestry woven from the hopes and dreams of everyone who had joined us.

As the final notes drifted into the night, I felt a profound sense of gratitude wash over me. The threads of fate had brought us together, and I knew that this was just the beginning of a much greater journey.

Chapter 17: A Patterned Heart

The backstage atmosphere is electric, charged with a palpable anticipation that dances in the air like the first hints of summer. I can almost taste the thrill of the moment as I peer through the curtains, my heart thumping in sync with the rhythmic pulse of the music that begins to swell in the auditorium. It's as if the very walls are infused with the dreams and ambitions of everyone involved, each breath drawn filled with the scents of hairspray, fresh fabric, and the bittersweet tang of hope. This charity show, this celebration of creativity and resilience, is not merely an event; it's a testament to everything we've fought for.

Each model gliding down the runway embodies a story, a piece of our shared journey stitched into the seams of their garments. The spotlight glistens against the iridescent fabrics, casting kaleidoscopic reflections that shimmer like fragments of our past—some bright, some shadowed. As the first model steps onto the runway, her confidence radiates, and I can't help but feel a swell of pride surge through me. This is our creation, a culmination of late nights, laughter, and tears, poured into every thread and bead.

But as I'm caught in the mesmerizing rhythm of the show, my heart jolts like a startled rabbit when my eyes dart to the audience. There she is—my mother, perched in the third row, her presence slicing through my elation like a knife through silk. Her hair, as familiar as the smell of vanilla from my childhood, is pinned back, a few rebellious strands framing her face. The years have etched their marks upon her, yet her eyes shine with an intensity that makes it difficult to breathe. I feel a rush of conflicting emotions: a fierce pride in what I've accomplished, a bitter resentment bubbling up from years of unanswered questions, and an undercurrent of longing that I thought I had buried.

I catch myself wondering what she sees when she looks at me now. Does she see the girl who once sought her approval in every school project, in every artwork? Or has she conjured up the ghosts of my failures, the teenage rebellion, and the misunderstandings that drove us apart? The models continue to glide down the runway, but my attention is glued to her, my heart twisting with each step they take.

Then, amidst the sea of faces, I spot Blake. Our eyes lock, and for a moment, the chaotic world around us fades into a blur. The warmth in his gaze wraps around me, a stark contrast to the icy grip my mother's presence has on my heart. It's an unspoken understanding, a connection that weaves through the air between us, binding our past struggles and present hopes. He nods slightly, a reassuring gesture that feels like an anchor in this storm of emotions.

His own journey has not been without its trials; we've shared laughter and heartache, moments when we thought we'd lose everything. And yet, here we stand, our paths converging again in this moment of triumph. I can see in his eyes that he too feels the weight of the moment—his dreams reflected in the shimmering fabric, each piece a fragment of our shared narrative. The connection between us is deeper than any of the intricate designs that swirl around the runway, something raw and beautiful, untarnished by the fears that once kept us apart.

As the show progresses, my heart beats in tandem with the music, the bass reverberating through my chest, drowning out the tumultuous thoughts that threaten to overwhelm me. The audience is enraptured, their gasps of admiration echoing off the walls. I find solace in the energy surrounding me, the joy of creation swirling around like confetti. I can feel my team's eyes on me, watching my reactions, gauging my emotions, and in this moment, I know I have to focus.

I take a deep breath, letting the air fill my lungs, willing the swirling feelings to settle. I turn my attention back to the runway. Each model embodies a fragment of my soul—the bold patterns and bright colors a reflection of my dreams, each design crafted with love and intent. This show isn't just about showcasing talent; it's about healing, understanding, and embracing our imperfections.

But the reality of my mother's presence lingers in the back of my mind like an unwelcome guest. I can't help but wonder what she thinks of me now, the girl who once craved her approval, now a woman crafting her own destiny. I can see the flicker of recognition in her eyes as she watches the pieces walk by, and for a moment, I imagine her thoughts. Does she feel pride? Regret? Or perhaps the wistful ache of a bond strained by years of distance?

As the last model walks the runway, a wave of relief washes over me. The applause is deafening, the cheers a symphony of celebration that fills the space, momentarily pushing aside the turmoil in my heart. I step forward, ready to join my team for the final bow, but I can't shake the feeling that I must confront my mother. The urge to bridge the chasm between us burns brightly, a desire to understand and be understood.

As we take our bows, the light dances around me, illuminating the faces in the crowd. I look toward my mother again, and the moment feels suspended in time. She smiles, and for the first time in years, I see not just a mother, but a woman, someone who has faced her own battles, her own doubts.

The music fades, and the applause swells to a crescendo. I take a step back, drawing in a deep breath, preparing to make my way toward her, ready to confront the tangled emotions that have held me captive for so long. Each step feels heavy yet exhilarating, and as I approach, the vibrant world of fabric and design fades into the background. In this moment, all that matters is the connection I've longed for—a conversation long overdue.

The distance between my mother and me seems to stretch impossibly wide as I weave through the backstage chaos, the rhythmic thrum of the audience's applause echoing in my ears like a heartbeat. The vibrant fabrics and designs, once the sole focus of my world, fade momentarily as my heart races with a cocktail of anxiety and determination. I can feel my pulse quickening, a frantic rhythm, each beat echoing the uncharted territory of emotions I am about to traverse. My team's jubilant laughter and shouts of excitement blur into the background, the victorious atmosphere overshadowed by the weight of my mother's gaze.

As I approach, her expression shifts subtly, transforming from awe to something more complex, a blend of emotions that seems to mirror my own tumultuous feelings. Her smile falters as I draw closer, and I wonder what she sees in me now—an ambitious designer blossoming into her own, or the little girl still seeking approval? I can't quite decipher the depths of her expression, but I can feel the air thickening between us, charged with unspoken words and years of silence.

The last remnants of the show hang in the air like a gentle breeze, each memory of laughter, disappointment, and triumph woven into the fabric of the evening. I take another step forward, and suddenly the applause feels like a distant thunder, the world around us softening as I reach my mother's side. She rises slightly, her posture straightening as if bracing for an impact, and in that moment, I realize how much has changed and how much remains the same.

"Mom," I say, my voice steady but quivering with anticipation. The word feels both familiar and foreign, like a long-lost melody.

She gazes at me, her eyes shimmering with something indefinable—perhaps regret, or the bittersweet tinge of nostalgia. "You've done so well," she finally breathes out, her voice breaking slightly, as though the words have been caught in her throat for far too long.

I can sense the weight of her pride and the uncertainty mingling in her tone. "Thanks. It means a lot, coming from you," I reply, the warmth of her compliment flickering like a candle flame, both illuminating and fragile. My heart races, an erratic beat that mirrors the fluttering emotions trapped between us.

"I wanted to come tonight," she continues, her gaze flickering over the remnants of the show—still-vibrant fabrics and the remnants of excitement left in the air. "I didn't know if you'd want to see me."

The admission catches me off guard, tugging at the threads of vulnerability I've tried so hard to keep at bay. "I didn't think you would," I admit, the honesty spilling out like a river breaking through a dam. "I figured you'd have better things to do."

A shadow of hurt crosses her face, and I can see the layers of history etched into her features. "I've missed so much, haven't I?" she whispers, and her voice trembles, echoing the truth that has haunted us both. The air thickens with the gravity of our shared past, and I feel the impulse to reach out, to bridge the chasm between us with a gesture, but fear keeps my hands at my sides.

"We've both been busy," I say lightly, trying to infuse levity into the moment, but the attempt feels clumsy. The weight of the words lingers in the air like an unwelcome guest, a reminder of the years lost in silence.

"I've been trying to make sense of everything," she says, her gaze dropping to the floor for a brief moment before returning to me, filled with a quiet resolve. "I've been watching you from a distance, and I realize now how wrong I was."

Each word is like a gentle prod, peeling back the layers of my heart, unraveling the defenses I've wrapped around myself. I think of the late-night phone calls that went unanswered, the milestones she missed, and the hollow feeling of longing that accompanied every small success. "I didn't understand why you... why we..." My voice falters, a fragile thread pulling at the corners of my resolve.

A small breath escapes her lips, and she takes a step closer, her sincerity palpable. "I was afraid, you know? Afraid of how much you were growing away from me. It felt easier to step back than to confront that."

It's like a mirror, reflecting not only her fears but my own—the hesitance to embrace change, to confront the reality of our strained relationship. "I wished you'd fought harder," I admit, my voice barely above a whisper. "But I get it now. I've fought my own battles, and sometimes it's easier to run than to face the music."

The sincerity between us swells, igniting a flicker of hope. The crowd is still cheering, but we exist in a bubble, a world constructed from shared memories and unspoken words. For the first time in ages, I feel the promise of understanding shimmering in the air, a chance to weave new threads into our relationship, ones infused with honesty and vulnerability.

"I want to know you again," I finally say, each word heavy with intention. "I want us to talk, really talk, about everything."

A tentative smile breaks across her face, and in that moment, it feels like a door has creaked open, revealing the light beyond. "I'd like that," she replies, the hope in her eyes blossoming like spring flowers after a long winter.

As we stand there, the applause fading into the distance, I feel a rush of warmth enveloping us—a fragile yet resolute bond beginning to form amidst the vibrant chaos of the evening. My past and present coalesce, and I realize that this moment, amidst the remains of our shared ambitions, is merely the beginning. The journey ahead may be fraught with challenges, but for the first time, I'm willing to face them. Together.

Blake's presence lingers at the edge of my mind, a comforting reminder of the connections we build through shared experiences.

I steal a glance toward him, and our eyes meet once more, a silent agreement passing between us. The support I see there fills me with courage, solidifying my resolve to face this new chapter with an open heart.

As the applause swells again, I squeeze my mother's hand gently, the warmth of her touch sending ripples of reassurance through me. In this vibrant world, as our paths intertwine once more, I finally understand: we are all works in progress, beautifully imperfect, yet capable of growth and connection. And tonight, beneath the bright lights of hope, I'm ready to embrace the journey ahead.

The warmth of my mother's hand in mine lingers, a tether binding us in this moment amidst the vibrant chaos of the charity show. I can still hear the fading echoes of applause, the sound waves bouncing around the room, yet all that truly exists is the soft crackle of electricity between us, a promise unspoken but profoundly felt. It is as if time has slowed, allowing us to wade through the tangled waters of our past and tentatively approach the shores of understanding.

As I stand there, gazing into her eyes, I find myself flooded with memories—the scent of her vanilla-scented candles flickering in the evening light, the stories she wove into bedtime tales, and the warmth of her laughter mingling with the melodies of our shared lives. Yet those memories are intertwined with the shadows of disappointment, the times she felt distant, and the conversations left unspoken. I feel the weight of everything that has brought us to this moment, a mixture of hope and trepidation blossoming like flowers in the first thaw of spring.

"Let's get out of here," I suggest, my voice breaking the fragile silence. The buzz of the show feels overwhelmingly vibrant, and I crave an escape, a space where the world can recede, leaving just the two of us to navigate this delicate landscape of reconciliation.

She nods, her eyes shining with a glimmer of anticipation. "Yes, I'd like that." Together, we make our way to a quieter corner of the venue, away from the revelers still basking in the afterglow of the show.

The soft glow of string lights overhead casts a warm halo around us, creating an intimate atmosphere that feels worlds apart from the frenetic energy of the runway. I settle onto a plush, vintage sofa that has seen better days, the upholstery a deep emerald green that recalls the forests of my childhood. My mother joins me, her movements hesitant yet purposeful, and as we sink into the cushions, a comfortable silence envelops us.

"What did you think of the show?" I ask, turning to face her, my curiosity bubbling to the surface like the effervescence in a freshly poured glass of champagne.

She chuckles lightly, a sound reminiscent of the gentle wind rustling through leaves. "It was breathtaking. I had no idea how talented you've become." Her words are warm, yet I can detect the undertone of something deeper—perhaps admiration mixed with the ache of missed moments. "The designs were so... you. I could see your heart in every piece."

A blush creeps into my cheeks, the compliment wrapping around me like a cozy blanket on a cold winter's night. "Thank you. It's been a journey. Each collection tells a story, our story."

As I speak, I can't help but reflect on the countless hours spent hunched over sketches, the trials and errors, and the moments of doubt that had threatened to drown me in despair. Yet here we are, on the precipice of something new, a chance to rewrite the narrative that has kept us apart for so long.

"I want to understand," my mother says, her voice imbued with sincerity, pulling me from my reverie. "I want to know how you've felt all these years."

My heart stutters, the words choking in my throat. I've carried the weight of my emotions like a heavy coat, too burdened to take it off. "It was hard, Mom. I missed you. I missed the connection we used to have."

A flicker of pain crosses her face, and I realize this is not just about me; it's about her too. "I thought I was doing what was best. I thought giving you space would help you grow."

"Maybe," I reply cautiously, "but I needed you there. I needed to know that you believed in me, even when I faltered."

Her expression softens, and I can almost see the gears turning in her mind. "I do believe in you," she reassures me, her voice steady and true. "I've watched you grow from afar, always proud but afraid to step in."

"I get that now," I reply, sensing a thawing in my own heart. "We both made choices that led us here, and it's okay to acknowledge that."

We linger in this moment, a tapestry of emotions unfurling before us, threads weaving together the past with hope for the future. The subtle rustle of the crowd ebbs in the background, but here, cocooned in our own world, it feels like we've entered a sanctuary.

I glance around, noticing the twinkling lights casting a gentle glow over the venue, illuminating the faces of friends and colleagues celebrating a successful night. Yet, despite the joy surrounding us, my focus remains solely on my mother. The barriers that once felt insurmountable seem to soften, as if the air has turned warm and forgiving.

"What's next for you?" she asks, a genuine curiosity igniting her tone.

My heart leaps at the question. "I want to expand my brand, maybe even explore sustainable fashion. There's so much potential, and I want to create pieces that resonate with people, that tell their stories too."

Her eyes widen, a spark igniting behind them. "That sounds incredible. You've always had a gift for connecting with people through your art."

I smile at her words, the validation a soothing balm to my soul. "I hope so. I want to create something meaningful, not just pretty clothes. I want people to feel empowered when they wear what I design."

As we talk, the initial tension dissolves, replaced by a comfortable rhythm that feels like music—harmony rising from the remnants of dissonance. With each word exchanged, it's as if we're stitching together a new narrative, one filled with promise and understanding.

In the distance, I can see Blake talking animatedly with some of our friends, his laughter ringing out like a melodic note in the symphony of the evening. He catches my gaze and offers a soft smile that sends warmth flooding through me. I know he senses the shift between my mother and me, the subtle transformation that signifies a step forward.

"I want to meet him," my mother suddenly says, breaking into my thoughts.

I blink in surprise. "You want to meet Blake?"

"Yes. If he's someone you care about, I'd like to understand that part of your life too."

A flutter of nerves dances in my stomach, but I nod, the idea of introducing them stirring a mix of excitement and apprehension. "Okay, let's go say hi."

As we rise from the sofa, I feel a renewed sense of purpose, a determination to bridge the gaps that have long divided us. With each step toward Blake, the remnants of fear dissipate like fog under the morning sun, replaced by a budding sense of hope that perhaps, just perhaps, we can cultivate something beautiful from the soil of our shared experiences.

Blake turns as we approach, his expression shifting from casual laughter to a soft smile that lights up his face when he sees me. "You two look like you're having a moment," he teases lightly, yet there's an undertone of respect that makes my heart swell.

"This is my mom," I say, introducing her with a mix of pride and nerves.

"Hi, it's lovely to meet you," he extends a hand, and I watch as they exchange greetings, a curious connection sparking between them.

"I've heard so much about you," my mother responds, her voice warm, and I feel the shift in the atmosphere, the subtle intertwining of our lives as they begin to converge.

Blake smiles, an easy confidence radiating from him. "All good things, I hope?"

My mother chuckles, a sound like tinkling wind chimes, and I know in that moment that we are on the precipice of something transformative. Perhaps our paths had been jagged and broken, but now they seem to be weaving together anew, a tapestry richer and more intricate than I ever could have imagined.

In this vibrant, chaotic world, I can finally see a future unfurling before us—one of connection, understanding, and love. It feels like the dawn of a new beginning, the promise of brighter days ahead, stitched together with the threads of our shared stories and experiences.

Chapter 18: The Loom of Destiny

The evening air held a softness that wrapped around me like a favorite sweater, its warmth contrasting with the coolness of the autumn twilight settling over the city. The lights of the charity gala flickered like fireflies, a kaleidoscope of colors dancing off the polished marble floors and sparkling crystal chandeliers. I had poured my heart and soul into this event, and the buzz of triumph still reverberated in my chest. People laughed and mingled, glasses clinking, the melody of soft jazz weaving through the lively chatter. Yet, amid the elation, a heaviness loomed, thickening the air around me—a weight I knew all too well.

As I stepped outside onto the terrace, the gentle rustling of the nearby oak trees whispered secrets of their own. The city skyline, with its towering skyscrapers, stretched into the horizon, silhouetted against a canvas of deep indigo and soft gold. I took a deep breath, feeling the night settle in, both beautiful and bittersweet. My heart raced not from the adrenaline of the event but from the impending confrontation that awaited me inside.

My mother had arrived unannounced, her presence a storm brewing beneath the facade of polite pleasantries we had maintained for far too long. The years of silence between us had woven an intricate tapestry of hurt and misunderstanding, and tonight felt like the final thread would be pulled, unraveling everything we had built—or failed to build. As I stood there, gazing at the city I had tried to embrace, my thoughts drifted back to a time when I had idolized her.

In my mind's eye, I was a child again, perched on the edge of my bed, listening to her recount stories of her youth with a spark in her eyes that felt almost mythical. I could still smell the faint scent of lavender from her perfume as she would lean down to tuck me in, the warmth of her presence enveloping me like a cocoon.

But those memories now felt like fragments of glass, beautiful yet sharp, reminding me of the many ways she had disappointed me over the years. The familiar ache throbbed in my chest as I recalled the countless times I had longed for her approval, her affection, only to be met with indifference.

Blake stood beside me, his quiet strength a constant reassurance, though he remained a few paces back, sensing the gravity of the moment. The subtle shift in his demeanor, the way his eyes crinkled at the corners when he smiled, told me that he understood this was not just another familial squabble. It was the intersection of our past and present, a collision of hearts that had been strained too long.

"Are you ready?" he asked softly, his voice barely above the murmur of the wind.

I nodded, swallowing hard, forcing a smile that didn't quite reach my eyes. "Ready as I'll ever be."

With each step back inside, I felt the weight of the room shift, the air thick with anticipation and unspoken words. The grand hall, illuminated by the soft glow of candlelight, suddenly felt stifling, as if it were a living entity holding its breath in the face of our impending confrontation. I spotted my mother across the room, her posture erect, hands clasped tightly in front of her. She looked like a queen surveying her kingdom, regal yet distant, and my heart twisted in an all-too-familiar dance of dread and longing.

"Go," Blake urged, his voice a gentle nudge toward the inevitable.

I took a deep breath, the kind that fills your lungs and makes you feel alive, and walked toward her, each footfall echoing with uncertainty. The world around me faded into a blur as I honed in on the woman who had shaped so much of my life, both in the way I adored her and in the way I had learned to shield myself from her.

"Mom," I said, my voice surprisingly steady despite the tumult swirling inside me.

She turned slowly, her eyes narrowing as if trying to dissect the emotional puzzle standing before her. "Congratulations on the event, dear. You did wonderfully."

"Thanks," I replied, my words clipped as I fought against the swell of feelings threatening to surface. "But we need to talk."

There was a moment of hesitation, a flicker of apprehension in her eyes, before she nodded curtly. "Fine. Let's find somewhere quieter."

We settled in a cozy nook, the soft glow of a nearby lamp casting a warm hue around us, and for the first time in years, I allowed myself to fully confront the churning emotions I had buried deep within me. I looked into her eyes, searching for the connection that had long been lost, and began to speak.

"I've spent so long feeling invisible to you, like my achievements were just footnotes in your life," I admitted, my voice a fragile whisper laced with years of pent-up frustration. "I've felt like I've had to earn your love every single day."

Her expression shifted, the corners of her mouth tightening as if my words had physically struck her. "You think I didn't care? I've always cared! I just... had my own battles."

The statement hung in the air between us, heavy with unfulfilled promises and unspoken pain. My heart thudded painfully in my chest as I pushed through the fear that had gripped me for so long. "But you never let me in. You never let me see those battles."

As the conversation flowed, the years of resentment, hurt, and misunderstanding unfurled between us like a threadbare tapestry, revealing the raw, unfiltered truth of our relationship. I watched as the walls around her began to crack, each admission and confession drawing us closer, dismantling the fortress she had built to shield herself from vulnerability.

"I was afraid," she finally admitted, her voice trembling as tears glimmered in her eyes. "Afraid of failing you, afraid of being what you needed."

In that moment, a wave of empathy washed over me, and I realized that her struggles were just as real as my own. Forgiveness was no longer a distant concept; it was an act of reclaiming my narrative, an opportunity to weave a new story where we both could exist without the shadows of our past.

The room shifted, the tension now palpable, a delicate web woven from the threads of our unspoken history. My mother sat across from me, her face a canvas of emotions—regret, longing, perhaps even a flicker of hope. I could see the effort it took for her to lower her defenses, to let her heart peek through the cracks of years spent in silence. The light flickered overhead, casting shadows that danced like memories, and for the first time, I could feel the weight of our shared experiences pulling us closer instead of pushing us apart.

"I spent so long thinking you had it all together," I continued, my voice softer now, gentler. "Every time you achieved something, it felt like a reminder of my own shortcomings. I just wanted you to notice me." My words spilled out in a rush, the floodgates finally breached. "I wanted you to see me, not just as your daughter but as someone with her own dreams and struggles."

Her eyes widened, and for a moment, I thought I saw a spark of understanding. "I never meant to overshadow you," she replied, her voice quaking as if it might break under the weight of her honesty. "I thought I was protecting you from my failures, from the chaos of my life."

The air between us shimmered with the truth, illuminating the dim corners of our hearts. I could feel the corners of my own walls softening, the hard edges rounding off as the conversation unfolded. "But in trying to protect me, you pushed me away," I murmured, feeling the warmth of tears prickle at my eyelids. "I've carried that loneliness for so long. It shaped me into someone who felt like she had to fight for every ounce of love."

"I thought I was doing what was best," she said, her voice choked with emotion. "In my own way, I thought I was teaching you strength."

"That's the thing," I interjected, frustration slipping back into my tone. "Strength is not just about enduring; it's about allowing others in. It's about vulnerability." I could see her grappling with my words, her expression shifting like the shadows cast on the wall behind her, revealing the cracks and crevices of her own past.

For a fleeting moment, I pictured us as a patchwork quilt, each piece a different story, stitched together yet fraying at the edges. In that metaphorical image, I recognized that we were both trying to navigate a complicated pattern of love and pain, and perhaps together we could sew a new design, one that acknowledged our struggles while celebrating our strengths.

"I know I failed you as a mother," she confessed, her voice barely above a whisper. "And for that, I am so sorry. I never wanted you to feel like you were unworthy of love. You are the most amazing person, and I took that for granted."

My heart ached with the weight of her confession, a cocktail of sorrow and understanding swirling within me. "I'm learning to accept that you were doing the best you could, just like I'm doing the best I can," I said, my tone shifting towards something more hopeful. "It doesn't excuse the hurt, but it helps me to see the woman behind the mother I've criticized."

The silence that followed was not one of discomfort but a sanctuary, a space for healing. I watched as she wiped away a tear that slipped down her cheek, her vulnerability laid bare, and in that moment, I felt a flicker of warmth that had been absent for so long.

It was as if we had begun to rewrite the script of our lives, each word a step toward reconciliation.

"I want to know you," I said, leaning forward, the earnestness in my tone palpable. "Not the persona you've created, but the real you—the woman who has dreams, fears, and failures, just like me."

She nodded slowly, a tentative smile forming as the tension in her shoulders eased slightly. "And I want to know you as well. The woman you've become. Tell me about your dreams."

And so I did, weaving tales of my aspirations, the colors of my hopes spilling out like paint on a canvas. I spoke of my passion for art, the thrill of creating something from nothing, and how I yearned to showcase my work, to have it resonate with others. As I spoke, I could see her leaning in, her expression transforming from one of distant concern to genuine interest, her focus sharp as if I were unveiling a masterpiece right before her eyes.

"Art is a window into the soul," she mused, her eyes sparkling with newfound appreciation. "I never understood how much it meant to you. I should have asked sooner."

The conversation flowed effortlessly, the earlier discomfort dissipating like fog under the morning sun. I felt lighter with each word, the years of resentment falling away like autumn leaves surrendering to the wind.

In the depths of that exchange, I realized that this moment was not just about forgiveness; it was about building a bridge between two islands that had drifted apart. With Blake silently offering his unwavering support nearby, I felt an unexpected swell of gratitude. His presence grounded me, allowing me to navigate this emotional terrain with the kind of strength I hadn't known I possessed.

"Maybe we can create something together," I suggested, the idea blooming like a flower pushing through the cracks in concrete. "A piece of art that tells our story. Something that reflects both our journeys."

Her eyes lit up, a mixture of surprise and joy radiating from her. "I'd love that," she replied, her voice brimming with excitement. "A collaboration, a merging of our worlds."

As we spoke of colors and textures, dreams and aspirations, I noticed the shadows that had long haunted us beginning to recede. It was a small step, but one filled with promise—a promise that the threads of our lives could intertwine anew, forming a tapestry vibrant with understanding, connection, and love.

The evening drew to a close, the gala fading into a memory of laughter and success, but in our hearts, something new was being born. With each shared smile and unguarded moment, we were stitching a fresh narrative, one where forgiveness and love could flourish. In that cozy nook, amid the laughter of friends and the music that swirled around us, I found myself not just as her daughter but as an artist ready to embrace the beauty of a new beginning.

As the evening wore on, a gentle breeze swept through the open terrace, its cool touch a reminder of the world outside. Laughter and music drifted from the ballroom, yet within our little sanctuary, the air buzzed with an electric energy. My mother's eyes sparkled with newfound hope, a flicker of the vibrant woman I had once known, buried beneath layers of expectation and disappointment. She leaned closer, the distance between us shrinking not just physically but emotionally, as if she were unearthing a treasure long forgotten.

"Tell me more about your art," she urged, her curiosity infectious. I could feel her enthusiasm like a wave crashing over me, washing away the last vestiges of apprehension.

"It's hard to explain," I began, the excitement bubbling within me like effervescent champagne. "Each piece is a story, a fragment of my soul. Sometimes, it's the chaos of colors that speaks to me, while other times it's the stillness of a single line, a simple stroke that captures a fleeting moment." I gestured as I spoke, my hands painting vivid images in the air. "I draw inspiration from everything around me—the city's heartbeat, the people who weave through my life, the bittersweet memories that linger like the scent of rain on pavement."

Her expression softened, and I could see the flicker of recognition in her eyes as if she were suddenly tuning into a frequency she had long forgotten. "I've never thought about art that way," she said slowly, as though the concept was settling in her mind, rearranging her understanding of what creativity meant. "It's a language of its own."

"Exactly!" I exclaimed, my heart racing with excitement. "And it doesn't just exist on canvas. It's everywhere—in the way sunlight filters through the trees, the laughter of children playing in the park, even in the melancholy of a rainy day. It's all interconnected, like threads in a tapestry."

I watched her absorb my words, the corners of her mouth turning upward as she leaned back, considering the newfound perspective. "You make it sound so beautiful, so alive," she murmured. "I wish I could see the world through your eyes."

"Maybe you can," I suggested, feeling a surge of optimism. "Art can be a journey. We can explore it together. I could show you the hidden corners of the city that inspire me. We could visit galleries, attend workshops—whatever you want."

A deep breath escaped her lips, and for the first time, I sensed the possibility of something blooming between us. "I'd like that," she replied, her voice steady, the hint of a smile teasing her lips. "I've spent so many years wrapped in my own world. It's time I stepped outside."

The sincerity in her eyes ignited a flame of hope within me. I hadn't just peeled back the layers of our past; I was also igniting a potential for a shared future, a blossoming of understanding that had seemed impossible not long ago. "We can start small," I proposed, an idea sparking in my mind. "There's an artist collective downtown that showcases emerging talent. We could go this weekend. I'd love to hear your thoughts."

"Is it the one by the old factory?" she asked, her interest piqued. "I've seen the murals from the street. They looked stunning."

"Yes! Those murals tell stories of the city's history, its struggles and triumphs," I replied, enthusiasm threading through my words. "Each one is a conversation between the past and the present, a beautiful reminder that art can transform spaces and lives."

Her nod of approval was like the first rays of sunlight breaking through a cloudy sky. It felt like a pact, one forged not in words but in shared excitement and hope. As we spoke, I felt the tension of our years of silence dissolve, leaving behind a warm current of connection that wrapped around us like a soft blanket.

Suddenly, Blake appeared at the edge of our intimate enclave, his presence grounding and supportive. He had a soft smile on his face, a knowing look that spoke volumes. "I hope I'm not interrupting," he said, but his tone indicated he had been listening, quietly taking in the unfolding transformation.

"Not at all," I replied, grateful for his unwavering support. "We were just discussing the world of art and how it's more than just colors on a canvas."

His gaze flicked to my mother, and I could see the moment he recognized the shift in our dynamic. "Sounds like a fascinating conversation. I'd love to hear more about the artist collective," he added, effortlessly drawing into our circle. "What do you think, Mrs. Kinsley? Are you ready to dive into the world of art?"

My mother laughed softly, the sound light and carefree, banishing the shadows that had loomed over us for far too long. "I think I might be," she replied, her voice vibrant with newfound enthusiasm. "I've been missing out on so much. Perhaps it's time I learned to appreciate the world through a different lens."

As Blake joined our conversation, his warmth infused the air, creating a sense of camaraderie that felt surreal. We spoke about art, music, and the quirks of life in the city, the three of us weaving a tapestry of stories that illuminated the evening. I could see the way Blake's easy laughter coaxed my mother from her shell, his kindness gently prying open the door to her heart.

The light began to shift as the sun dipped below the horizon, casting golden rays across the room, and I felt a warmth blossom in my chest. There was magic in the air, a sense of rebirth echoing through the walls of the venue. In this moment, I recognized how the fabric of our lives had intertwined, each thread vibrant and rich with potential.

When the evening finally drew to a close, my heart felt as if it had expanded, filling the space between us with something profound. My mother and I stood side by side, gazing out at the twinkling lights of the city, which seemed to pulse in time with the beat of our newly rekindled relationship.

"Thank you for tonight," she said, her voice soft but resolute. "I didn't know I needed this. I'm grateful for your courage to speak up."

And just like that, a lightness settled over me, an assurance that we were beginning a new chapter together—one where forgiveness thrived and connection blossomed like spring after a harsh winter. The past no longer held power over us; we had begun to forge a new narrative, one where understanding and love could flourish.

As we stepped back into the thrumming heart of the gala, I glanced at Blake, his eyes glinting with pride and affection. In that moment, surrounded by the laughter and vibrancy of life, I felt a sense of belonging that had eluded me for far too long. The journey ahead was uncertain, but with each passing moment, I realized that it was ours to shape. Together, we could paint a future that was as rich and intricate as the art I adored—one filled with vibrant colors, stories, and, most importantly, love.

Chapter 19: Tangled Up in You

The Riverwalk sprawled beneath a tapestry of stars, each light flickering like a tiny wish whispered into the night. I could hear the soft lapping of the water against the wooden pylons, a rhythmic serenade that mingled with the laughter of couples meandering nearby. Each step I took beside Blake felt imbued with a peculiar energy, as though the very air around us was charged with unspoken words and shared dreams. The city thrummed with life, but within this bubble of our own, everything else faded into the background, a distant hum of existence that I could tune out at will.

The streets, adorned with string lights that twinkled like fireflies caught in a summer's dusk, beckoned us to explore. I had often walked this path, but tonight, the familiar scenery felt new—painted in hues of possibility. The scent of street food wafted through the air, spicy and sweet, but it was the warmth radiating from Blake's presence that captivated me most. He walked with an easy grace, the kind that made me forget to breathe as my heart quickened its pace, matching the footsteps echoing in my chest.

As we passed a local artist showcasing his vibrant paintings, I paused, momentarily entranced by a canvas splashed with the bold colors of sunset over the water. It mirrored the shifting feelings I had for Blake—intense, unpredictable, yet breathtaking in its beauty. "Look at that one," I murmured, gesturing toward the canvas. "It's like the world is melting into each other."

He leaned closer, his shoulder brushing against mine, igniting a rush of warmth that spread from my skin to the depths of my being. "It does have that... ethereal quality," he replied, his voice a deep, rich melody that wrapped around me like a favorite song. I could feel the heat radiating from his body, as if he, too, felt the pull of this moment.

Blake turned to me, his eyes capturing the glint of the lights as they danced in the depths of his gaze. "You have a knack for finding beauty in everything, don't you?" The compliment rolled off his tongue, smooth and sincere, and my cheeks flushed with a mix of pride and embarrassment.

"It's easier to see it when you're not caught in the storm," I confessed, glancing down at the cobblestone path beneath our feet. The truth of my words hung between us, a delicate thread binding my past to the present.

In that moment, he reached out, his fingers brushing against mine, and an electric current surged through me, igniting every nerve ending in my body. My breath hitched, and the world around us slipped away. All the heartache, the doubts, the fears of being more than friends faded like shadows at dawn. The tension that had woven itself into the fabric of our relationship began to unravel, each thread revealing the vibrant colors of our shared connection.

I turned to meet his gaze, feeling the weight of his eyes on me, deep and searching. The softness in his expression spoke volumes, urging me to let go of the past and step into the unknown. "What if we don't go back?" he asked, the question lingering in the air like a challenge. The sincerity in his voice sent a shiver of excitement through me.

"What do you mean?" I asked, half-daring to hope.

His smile widened, revealing a hint of mischief. "What if we let tonight carry us where it wants to go? Just you and me, no walls."

I swallowed hard, my heart racing as the possibility of it all wrapped around me. "You mean... like a date?"

"Something like that," he replied, his voice low, thick with emotion.

For a heartbeat, I hesitated, the weight of my past flickering in my mind like a faulty neon sign. But as I looked into Blake's eyes, all I could see was the promise of adventure, the thrill of diving into something real and vibrant.

"Okay," I whispered, and in that single word, I felt the chains of doubt fall away.

As we walked, hand in hand now, the world began to shift again. Laughter floated through the air, weaving around us like a melody that pulled us deeper into this new chapter. I could hear the gentle strumming of a guitar somewhere ahead, a street performer pouring his heart into every chord, and the sound beckoned us closer.

The music wrapped around us, weaving a tapestry of sound that matched the pulse of my heart. We stood together, swaying to the rhythm as if the universe itself was guiding us through this delicate dance. The crowd around us faded, and it was just Blake and me, lost in our own world, our laughter rising above the strum of the guitar.

He pulled me closer, his arm sliding around my waist, and the heat radiating from him felt like home. I rested my head against his shoulder, the scent of him—a mix of cedar and something distinctly him—calming my racing thoughts. This moment, this feeling, was intoxicating, and I knew I would chase it as long as it led me to him.

As the last notes of the song faded into the night, the air buzzed with an exhilarating kind of magic. I looked up at Blake, my heart full and my mind swirling with dreams of what might unfold. We were standing at the precipice of something new, something beautiful, and all it took was the courage to reach out and hold on tight.

In that instant, I realized that love wasn't just a fairytale; it was this—messy, electric, and undeniably real.

The warmth of Blake's arm around my waist felt like a protective shield against the world, yet simultaneously invited me to explore the unknown depths of my emotions. We meandered further along the Riverwalk, the murmur of the water beneath us offering a soothing backdrop to our laughter. Each step felt deliberate, as if we were carving out a new path not just in the city but within our lives. I could feel the anticipation simmering between us, palpable and intoxicating.

The energy of the night thrummed in my veins, and I found myself captivated by the way the streetlights cast playful shadows over Blake's features, emphasizing the sharp angles of his jaw and the softness of his eyes. His laughter was a melodic invitation, coaxing me into a world where our friendship might blossom into something deeper, something I had longed for yet feared to touch.

"Let's grab a bite," he suggested, his voice warm and inviting, like a crackling fire on a chilly evening. I nodded, not even pausing to consider what I might want to eat. The thought of sharing a meal with him felt like a celebration—a small, intimate acknowledgment of the journey we were about to embark upon.

We wandered toward a quaint bistro tucked away from the main thoroughfare, its outdoor seating draped in twinkling fairy lights that mirrored the stars overhead. The scent of rosemary and garlic wafted through the air, wrapping around me like a comforting embrace. As we settled into a cozy corner table, the world outside faded further, creating a cocoon of warmth and intimacy that felt all too perfect.

"What do you recommend?" I asked, scanning the menu, but my focus was split between the food and the man seated across from me. His eyes sparkled with mischief as he leaned forward, his elbows resting on the table, the faintest hint of a smile playing on his lips.

"Anything is good, but you should definitely try the risotto. It's like a hug in a bowl."

I chuckled, picturing the dish wrapped in layers of creamy goodness. "A hug in a bowl, huh? Sounds like exactly what I need." Our shared laughter filled the air, drawing curious glances from nearby diners, but I didn't care. In this moment, with Blake, I felt alive.

As we placed our orders, the conversation flowed effortlessly, transitioning from light-hearted banter to deeper revelations. I found myself sharing stories I had kept close to my heart—fragments of my childhood, dreams I had let slip away, the moments that had shaped me into the woman I was today. Blake listened intently, his gaze never wavering, as if he was committing every word to memory. His presence was a warm anchor, grounding me even as I drifted through the currents of vulnerability.

"I think we all carry our past like a badge," he said, his tone reflective. "It's what shapes us, even if we don't always see it that way."

His insight resonated within me, sending ripples of understanding through my core. "You're right. Sometimes it feels heavy, though, like I'm dragging it behind me."

Blake nodded, a flicker of empathy in his eyes. "But you don't have to. It's part of you, not the whole of you."

As he spoke, something shifted in the air, a promise forming between us, illuminated by the soft glow of the bistro lights. We were no longer just friends sharing a meal; we were explorers of uncharted territories within our hearts.

Our meals arrived, steaming bowls of risotto accompanied by a generous sprinkle of herbs and a hint of lemon zest. The first bite sent waves of flavor cascading through my senses, and I closed my eyes in delight. "This really is a hug in a bowl," I declared, eliciting a soft laugh from Blake.

As we ate, the laughter ebbed and flowed, punctuated by moments of comfortable silence where words were unnecessary. With each shared smile and lingering glance, I felt the unbreakable bond we had crafted over the years deepen into something more potent. The world outside faded further into the background, and for the first time, I dared to imagine a future colored by the richness of what was blossoming between us.

After we finished our meal, Blake leaned back, surveying the bustling street beyond. "How about dessert?" he proposed, his eyes twinkling with mischief. "I know a place that serves the best chocolate cake."

"Chocolate? You had me at 'cake,'" I replied, the thrill of spontaneity coursing through me. We paid our bill and stepped into the cool evening air, where the sounds of the city became a symphony around us. The laughter of passersby, the distant strum of a guitar, the gentle rustle of leaves—it was a perfect night, vibrant and alive.

As we walked, I caught myself stealing glances at him, noticing the way his smile lit up his face, how the moonlight danced in his hair. The weight of the world outside seemed to lift with each shared moment. With Blake, I felt seen, understood, and cherished, as though I had finally found the missing piece to a puzzle I hadn't realized I was trying to solve.

We reached the bakery, its windows filled with decadent displays of pastries, each more alluring than the last. I could already feel the anticipation buzzing in the air, a sweet promise of indulgence. "You have to try the chocolate cake; it's practically a legend around here," Blake insisted, his enthusiasm contagious.

"Then lead the way, oh wise chocolate connoisseur," I teased, stepping inside. The warmth enveloped us like a soft blanket, and the rich scent of cocoa wrapped around my senses, making my heart flutter in anticipation.

After ordering a generous slice of cake, we settled at a small table near the window, where the world outside buzzed with life. As Blake slid the plate toward me, our fingers brushed again, and I felt that familiar jolt, a reminder of the electricity that danced between us.

"Okay, here's the moment of truth," he said, his eyes sparkling with anticipation as I took my first bite. The cake melted on my tongue, rich and decadent, and I couldn't help but let out a satisfied moan.

"Okay, you were right. This is definitely worth it," I said, grinning at him.

Blake chuckled, clearly pleased with my reaction. We shared bites, laughter bubbling between us, the sweetness of the cake a perfect metaphor for the sweetness of the moment. With every glance and shared smile, the walls that had once separated us began to dissolve, replaced by an unspoken understanding that felt as natural as breathing.

The night stretched on, each moment layered with laughter and shared secrets. With every passing second, I could feel my heart weaving itself more tightly with Blake's, our fates becoming intricately entwined in the fabric of our burgeoning romance. In that quaint little bistro, amidst the sweet chaos of the world outside, I realized I had finally stepped into a story that was ours—rich with possibility and glowing with the warmth of love yet to fully bloom.

The echoes of laughter and the soft clinking of glasses created a melodic backdrop as we emerged from the bakery, our spirits buoyed by the richness of the chocolate cake and the sweetness of shared moments. The cool night air embraced us, carrying the distant sounds of the Riverwalk—musicians strumming lively tunes, the gentle rustle of leaves stirred by a playful breeze, and the laughter of revelers who found their own stories within this vibrant city.

As we strolled, our fingers intertwined naturally, as if they had always belonged that way. I could feel Blake's warmth radiating through the small gap between us, an invisible tether that pulled me closer, urging me to lean into the comfort of our connection. The world around us began to blur, becoming little more than a canvas splashed with colors of possibility, each hue echoing the emotions we were finally daring to explore.

"Where to next?" I asked, my voice a playful lilt, barely concealing the giddiness bubbling inside me. The night stretched before us like an open invitation, full of undiscovered adventures and late-night secrets.

"How about we find a spot with a view?" he suggested, a hint of mischief glinting in his eyes. "I know a place."

His enthusiasm was infectious, igniting a spark of curiosity in me. As we walked further along the river, the lights danced on the water's surface, illuminating the path with a shimmering glow. The city felt alive around us, each corner holding stories waiting to be unraveled. I could almost hear the whispers of the past echoing in the alleyways and street corners—the love stories, heartbreaks, and triumphs that shaped the very essence of this place.

We rounded a bend and discovered a hidden staircase that led up to a small park overlooking the river. It was a gem nestled among the chaos, filled with the soft sounds of nature mingling with the urban landscape. As we climbed, anticipation bubbled within me, and I felt like we were leaving the world behind, stepping into our own secluded paradise.

At the top, the view opened up, revealing the sparkling expanse of the river, framed by the vibrant lights of the city. "Wow," I breathed, taking in the sight before me. The landscape stretched infinitely, the stars twinkling above like scattered diamonds, mirroring the lights below. It was breathtaking, but even more so was the way Blake's presence seemed to heighten everything around us.

"Isn't it beautiful?" he said softly, standing beside me, his shoulder brushing against mine.

I turned to him, finding his eyes lit with wonder, and suddenly the view didn't matter as much as the man beside me. "It is. But I think it might be more about who I'm sharing it with."

His gaze shifted, a spark igniting between us as the moment hung in the air like the lingering taste of chocolate on my lips. The tension from earlier returned, electrifying the space around us, pulling us closer together. Without thinking, I reached for his hand, feeling the warmth envelop me in a way that felt both grounding and exhilarating.

We leaned against the railing, watching as the river mirrored the night sky, our reflections intertwined with the shimmering lights. I could feel the weight of unspoken words hanging between us, urging me to voice the thoughts swirling in my mind.

"Do you ever think about how everything we've gone through has led us to this moment?" I asked, my voice barely above a whisper.

Blake turned to me, his expression serious yet gentle. "All the time. It's like the universe conspired to bring us here."

The sincerity in his voice made my heart swell. "I spent so long wondering if I would ever find someone who truly understood me. I feel like I've been living in black and white, and now... it's all in color."

A smile spread across his face, his eyes shining with something I couldn't quite place—was it hope? Or perhaps a shared longing? "You deserve to live in color. We both do."

With the weight of our pasts dissipating into the night, I felt the thrill of what lay ahead—the promise of laughter, adventure, and the undeniable pull of something more.

As if compelled by an unseen force, I leaned in closer, my heart pounding in my chest. The moment hung suspended, and the world around us faded into nothingness. And then, in a surge of courage, I closed the gap between us, my lips brushing against his in a tentative kiss. It was soft and sweet, filled with the uncharted territories we were beginning to explore together.

Time stood still as the kiss deepened, igniting a fire that spread through me, bright and consuming. My mind raced, caught in a whirlwind of emotions that swirled around us like the autumn leaves dancing in the breeze. Every brush of his lips sent ripples of warmth cascading through me, erasing any lingering doubts.

When we finally pulled apart, breathless and wide-eyed, the world seemed to shift again, falling into place in a way I hadn't anticipated. "Wow," I managed, my voice barely a whisper, the weight of the moment settling comfortably in the pit of my stomach.

Blake chuckled softly, a playful light dancing in his eyes. "Yeah, wow."

We stayed there for a while, our fingers still entwined as we basked in the glow of our shared moment, the city humming around us like a well-loved song. A sense of clarity washed over me—this was what I had been waiting for. The simplicity of being with someone who understood my heart and all its quirks felt like coming home.

As the night wore on, we began to share our dreams—small aspirations and grand desires, woven together in a tapestry of hope. I spoke of wanting to travel the world, to write stories that would leave an impact. Blake, in turn, shared his love for music and his dream of one day performing on a stage that spanned the globe.

"I can picture it," I said, picturing him on a vibrant stage, the crowd roaring as he played. "You're going to make that happen."

He shrugged, a hint of self-deprecation lacing his words. "It feels impossible sometimes."

"Nothing is impossible when you have the right person cheering you on," I replied, my voice steady, my gaze locking onto his. "And I want to be that person for you."

The sincerity in my words hung between us, solid and unyielding. The laughter faded, replaced by a shared understanding that we were on the brink of something extraordinary.

With the city lights twinkling beneath us and the stars shimmering overhead, I realized that we were no longer just two friends navigating the tumultuous waters of our emotions. We were co-authors of a narrative that was just beginning to unfold—one filled with color, warmth, and the promise of a future steeped in love and adventure.

As we descended the staircase and walked back toward the Riverwalk, I felt lighter, the burdens of the past all but forgotten. The world around us shimmered with possibilities, a reminder that every moment mattered, every heartbeat a step closer to a life we would build together. And in that simple truth, I found my anchor, knowing that no matter what challenges lay ahead, we would face them side by side.

Chapter 20: The Color of Competition

The bright city lights of New York glimmered against the night sky like a cascade of diamonds, a dazzling spectacle that wrapped around me like a warm embrace. My feet pattered against the polished marble floor of the gallery, echoing softly as I meandered through the curated space, each corner revealing a world of fabric and artistry that thrummed with life. The air was rich with the scent of fresh paint and polished wood, intermingled with a hint of champagne that danced on the tongues of the stylish crowd. I inhaled deeply, letting the atmosphere infuse my senses, while my heart swelled with pride at the success of our charity show that had just unfolded—a whirlwind of colors, creativity, and camaraderie.

Yet, beneath the surface of that elation, a more insidious tension simmered. Whispers skittered across the room like quicksilver, sliding into my ears unbidden. They spoke of a newcomer, Nora Sinclair, a designer whose pieces fluttered through the industry like wildflowers blooming in a concrete jungle. I could almost see the murmurs taking flight, darting between the guests like butterflies, their colors vibrant and irresistible, igniting a disquieting spark of competition. The very thought of it made my pulse quicken, a frantic beat that drummed against my ribcage as if trying to escape the cage of my insecurities.

I turned my gaze to the gathering crowd, each person a tapestry of style and ambition, and felt my heart sink a little deeper. Nora, it seemed, was a breath of fresh air, her designs marked by an ethereal quality that seemed to captivate everyone around me. Her flowing fabrics and daring silhouettes contrasted sharply with my own work—while I often embraced the structured lines and classic styles, she danced on the edge of avant-garde, with drapes that seemed to have minds of their own and colors that echoed the chaos of a sunset.

Each piece she presented had a life, an undeniable magnetism that drew eyes and whispered promises of innovation and adventure.

Blake, ever the pillar of strength in my life, stood beside me, his presence a reassuring balm against the rising tide of anxiety. He was my anchor in this sea of uncertainty, his gaze steady as he surveyed the room. His dark hair tousled just enough to lend him that effortlessly handsome look, and his smile, when he turned to me, was like sunlight breaking through clouds. "Don't let it get to you," he said softly, his voice a low rumble that vibrated through me. "Remember, your vision is unique. Embrace it."

I nodded, forcing a smile that felt more like a grimace as I fought to swallow my self-doubt. "It's hard, you know? Every time I see one of her designs, I can't help but think that I'm... old news." The words spilled from my lips like a confession, each one heavy with the weight of my insecurity. I felt exposed under Blake's unwavering gaze, as if he could see straight into the depths of my turmoil.

"Competition is just that—a challenge," he replied, his eyes narrowing slightly, urging me to see reason. "It's not about erasing your identity; it's about refining it. You can't let her brilliance dim your own light." His words wrapped around me, a soothing thread of reassurance, yet still, the creeping tendrils of doubt wound tighter around my heart.

The clinking of glasses and the hum of conversation swirled around us, a lively background to the internal chaos I faced. I wanted to believe Blake, to absorb the truth behind his words, but the echo of Nora's talent resonated too loudly in my mind. I could almost picture her at her drafting table, sketches scattered like fallen leaves around her, each line a testament to her boldness. I could imagine her laughter—a bright, contagious sound that could light up the most stifling of rooms.

Just as I began to sink deeper into my insecurities, a familiar face broke through the crowd—a fellow designer, Jessica, whose face glowed with enthusiasm. She glided toward us, her dress shimmering like liquid silver, and I felt an involuntary lift in my spirits. "Have you seen her collection?" Jessica asked, her eyes wide with excitement. "It's breathtaking! I mean, she's not afraid to push boundaries. It's really something to behold."

I swallowed hard, a lump forming in my throat as I forced a smile. "I've heard," I replied, my voice teetering between enthusiasm and defeat. The weight of Jessica's praise felt like a mountain, and I stood at the foot of it, peering upward, wondering if I would ever reach that summit.

"You should go see it!" Jessica urged, her energy infectious. "It's at the boutique on Fifth Avenue. You have to experience it for yourself."

Blake looked at me, his expression a mixture of encouragement and curiosity. "What do you think?" he asked, his voice laced with genuine interest.

"Maybe," I said, but even to my ears, it sounded half-hearted. My heart raced at the idea of stepping into the world of Nora Sinclair, a space that suddenly felt foreign and intimidating. What if I stepped into that boutique, only to find myself drowning in the brilliance of her designs? What if they held a mirror to my inadequacies, reflecting everything I feared I wasn't?

As the night wore on, I forced myself to engage with the vibrant crowd, laughing and sharing stories, yet I couldn't shake the specter of competition lurking in the back of my mind. The celebration of our charity show, a triumph we'd all worked so hard for, felt tainted by the looming shadow of insecurity. It was a dance of dichotomies—joy and fear waltzed together, an unsettling choreography I couldn't seem to escape.

But as I watched Blake converse animatedly with Jessica, a flicker of resolve ignited within me. Perhaps Nora's brilliance didn't have to eclipse my own. Perhaps this was a moment to embrace the challenges, to evolve rather than retreat. After all, even the brightest stars need the dark of night to shine the brightest. The realization swelled within me, a budding hope that whispered I could carve out my place in this ever-shifting landscape of fashion, as long as I dared to embrace my own unique voice.

A week after the show, I found myself wandering the streets of SoHo, the sun casting a warm glow on the cobblestone pathways, each step echoing the rhythm of my restless thoughts. The neighborhood buzzed with energy—artists displayed their works in the open air, eclectic shops beckoned with promises of treasures hidden within, and the scent of artisanal coffee wafted through the crisp autumn air. Yet, amidst the vibrancy, a disquiet pulsed within me, much like the unpredictable rhythm of the city itself.

The boutique on Fifth Avenue loomed ahead, its windows draped with Nora Sinclair's latest collection—a kaleidoscope of colors and textures that seemed to vibrate with life. The fabric flowed like water, and the daring cuts were a seductive challenge to convention. A bold sign, "Nora Sinclair," glinted in the sunlight, each letter a testament to a name that had quickly become a beacon of fresh inspiration and fierce competition. I hesitated outside, my heart fluttering like a caged bird, a tempest of emotions swirling in my chest.

Blake had encouraged me to come here, to witness firsthand what had everyone so captivated, but as I stood on the threshold, a rush of self-doubt washed over me. What if stepping inside only confirmed my fears? What if Nora's designs would illuminate all the shadows lurking in my creative spirit? A deep breath steadied me, and I pushed through the glass doors, the chime of the bell announcing my arrival as if heralding a new chapter.

The interior was a seamless blend of elegance and avant-garde—exposed brick walls adorned with vibrant artworks, the air humming with a curated playlist of modern melodies. The staff, clad in Nora's designs, moved gracefully, their movements as fluid as the garments they wore. As I navigated through the space, I felt like an interloper in a world bursting with color, where every stitch and thread told a story I had yet to unravel.

I caught glimpses of other patrons, their eyes widening in delight as they examined the pieces. Gowns swirled around mannequin forms, each a bold proclamation of creativity and craftsmanship. One dress, in particular, caught my eye—a floor-length creation in hues of indigo and teal, the fabric cascading like waves, capturing the essence of the ocean. It seemed to dance in the soft light, as if it possessed a heartbeat of its own, and I felt an almost magnetic pull toward it.

"Isn't it divine?" a voice chimed beside me, pulling me from my reverie. A woman with bright red hair and a pixie cut smiled, her eyes sparkling with enthusiasm. "Nora really knows how to breathe life into fabric, doesn't she?"

I managed a nod, my heart still racing as I forced a smile. "It's stunning," I replied, my voice steady, though uncertainty still danced beneath the surface.

"Are you a designer too?" she asked, her tone inviting, as if she were extending a hand across an invisible divide.

I hesitated for a moment before replying, "Yes, I am. Just trying to find my place in this world." The honesty slipped out before I could reel it back in, and I felt a twinge of vulnerability exposing my insecurities to a stranger.

"Trust me, it can be daunting," she said, her expression softening. "But each of us has our own unique voice. I came here hoping to find inspiration and figure out what I want to create next. Nora's pieces are incredible, but that doesn't mean there isn't room for everyone."

Her words felt like a lifeline, and for a moment, the heaviness in my chest lightened. Perhaps it was true—perhaps this was a journey shared by many, a vibrant tapestry of talents interwoven with threads of ambition, fear, and creativity.

As I continued to browse, the beauty of Nora's designs began to wash over me, each piece whispering stories of elegance and innovation. The colors blended like a painter's palette, each choice bold yet perfectly balanced. I found myself stepping closer to the indigo dress, my fingers grazing the fabric, and in that moment, I imagined the possibilities of my own creations.

What if I embraced a more adventurous palette? What if I fused elements of my style with the boldness I admired in Nora's work? A rush of adrenaline surged through me at the thought, igniting a spark of creativity that had been dulled by doubt. My vision flickered before my eyes, a collage of colors and textures waiting to be brought to life.

Just then, a figure entered my periphery—tall and commanding, with an air of confidence that filled the space around him. Nora Sinclair herself strode into the boutique, her presence electric, exuding a mix of poise and passion. She wore a tailored outfit that was both sharp and flowing, the fabric catching the light as she moved. Her dark hair framed her face, accentuating her sharp cheekbones, and her gaze swept across the room, keen and observant.

I held my breath as I watched her interact with customers, each word dripping with enthusiasm as she shared the inspiration behind her designs. There was a warmth to her, an openness that belied the fierce competition she embodied. It was impossible not to admire her talent, her dedication, and the ease with which she navigated this whirlwind of creativity. But even amidst my admiration, the familiar pang of insecurity twisted in my gut.

"Are you okay?" The woman beside me noticed my sudden tension, concern etched on her face.

I forced a laugh, the sound brittle yet genuine. "Just feeling a bit overwhelmed. It's impressive to see someone so talented in person."

"Don't compare yourself to her," the woman said gently. "Instead, think about what you can learn. Every designer brings something different to the table. Find your unique voice, and let it resonate."

Her encouragement wrapped around me like a warm embrace, and I nodded, absorbing her words. The realization settled in my mind like a seed, taking root within me. This was not a contest of overshadowing but rather a celebration of expression.

As Nora continued to engage with the crowd, I felt an unexpected swell of determination. Perhaps my insecurities would always linger, but I was more than just my fears. I had a vision—a distinct style that told my own story, waiting to be shared. In that moment, a flicker of hope ignited within me, a resolve to embrace the colors of my journey rather than shy away from them.

The boutique pulsed with creativity, a heartbeat of passion that resonated with every designer present. With each glance, each whisper of fabric, I felt my spirit begin to unfurl. It was time to step into the light, to embrace the vibrant spectrum of my own identity. The whispers of competition might linger, but they would no longer define me. I was ready to paint my canvas, unapologetically bold, and full of life.

The rhythmic thump of my heart resonated within me as I stood at the threshold of my own aspirations, the boutique's atmosphere pulsating with an electric energy that seemed to lift the very air around me. Surrounded by Nora Sinclair's dazzling creations, I felt a shift within—a burgeoning awareness that the pulse of creativity didn't just belong to her; it could belong to me too. I turned back to the red-haired woman who had offered me such kind encouragement, her presence a beacon of solidarity amidst my swirling thoughts.

"What's your name?" I asked, genuinely curious, eager to forge a connection in this land of artistic warriors.

"Jenna," she replied, her smile wide and welcoming. "I'm a textile artist, still figuring out where my work fits in this ever-changing industry. I've seen a few pieces of yours at local shows—they're exquisite! I'd love to see what you come up with next."

The compliment sent a ripple of warmth through me, a reminder that even within the vastness of competition, connections could still be forged. "Thank you," I said, my cheeks flushing with the unexpected praise. "I'm trying to find my voice, you know? It feels like everyone is shouting, and I'm still whispering."

Jenna nodded, her eyes sparkling with understanding. "We all start as whispers. It's the journey that amplifies our voices." Her words resonated like the finest silk gliding across bare skin, delicate yet powerful.

As I wandered deeper into the boutique, I allowed myself to absorb the creativity enveloping me. Each dress was a symphony of color and texture, a marriage of modernity and tradition that ignited my imagination. I envisioned my own pieces among them, a reflection of my journey—a vibrant dance of fabrics and emotions interwoven with my personal experiences. With each step, I could see the fragments of my own designs beginning to crystallize in my mind, merging with the inspiration I drew from Nora's work.

But just as I felt a flicker of excitement spark within, I heard a familiar voice from across the room. "You know, they say imitation is the sincerest form of flattery." The voice dripped with sarcasm, cutting through the air like a knife. I turned to see Nora standing there, arms crossed, her expression a mask of confidence that concealed an undertone of rivalry. The way she looked at me, a mix of curiosity and challenge, sent a shiver of apprehension racing down my spine.

"Isn't that right?" she continued, stepping closer, her presence both captivating and intimidating. "So many designers feel the need to jump on the latest trend, forgetting what makes them unique."

I clenched my jaw, feeling as though I had been caught in an unspoken battle of wills. "I believe inspiration is everywhere," I replied, my voice steady despite the unease gnawing at me. "It's how we interpret that inspiration that defines our work."

Nora's lips curled into a sly smile, one that felt like a challenge. "True, but if you're going to swim in these waters, you'd better be prepared to make a splash."

The air crackled between us, charged with a mixture of admiration and animosity. I could feel Jenna's presence beside me, her supportive gaze bolstering my resolve. I couldn't let Nora's words wound me; instead, I had to embrace the moment, recognizing that competition, though daunting, was also a catalyst for growth.

As Nora strolled away, her presence leaving a tangible tension in the air, I turned back to Jenna. "She's something, isn't she?"

"She's fierce," Jenna acknowledged, a hint of awe in her voice. "But that's the nature of this industry. It pushes you to find your limits."

Feeling a surge of determination, I nodded, appreciating the shared camaraderie in the face of competition. "You're right. I'm ready to push back."

With newfound purpose, I made my way to the boutique's counter, where an elegant assistant stood, tapping away on a tablet. "Could you let me know when you have any events showcasing emerging designers? I'd love to participate," I said, my heart racing with the thrill of taking initiative.

"Absolutely," she replied, her demeanor professional yet warm. "We often host pop-up events for local talent. I'll make sure to keep you in the loop."

The prospect sent a thrill of excitement coursing through me. Here was a chance to not just exist but to thrive, to step into the light with my creations. With each passing moment, the seed of my confidence began to sprout, fueled by the belief that I could stand my ground, even in the face of formidable talent like Nora's.

Leaving the boutique, the cool autumn air enveloped me, invigorating my spirit. The sky was a deep blue, brushed with strokes of gold and pink as the sun began its descent. I pulled my coat tighter around me, the chill mirroring the competition that loomed ahead. But instead of retreating into my insecurities, I embraced the briskness as a reminder of the journey that lay before me.

Over the next few weeks, I channeled my energies into my work, my sewing machine becoming my sanctuary. The clatter of the needle against the fabric was a soothing rhythm, a mantra that fueled my creativity. I began sketching designs that fused my traditional style with the bold colors I had admired in Nora's collection. Each piece told a story—one of resilience, passion, and growth.

Every morning, I would stop by my favorite café, a quaint spot where the aroma of fresh coffee danced with the laughter of locals. It became a ritual—sipping a velvety cappuccino while pouring over my sketches, the world around me fading into a backdrop of inspiration. My conversations with Blake, filled with laughter and support, fortified my resolve, reminding me that I was not alone in this journey.

One evening, as I wrapped up a particularly challenging piece, Blake joined me at my workspace. He plopped down beside me, his gaze shifting from my designs to me, a playful grin spreading across his face. "You've been busy," he teased, reaching out to touch a vibrant silk swatch draped over my table. "Is this what I think it is?"

"It's my interpretation of the autumn harvest," I said, a glimmer of excitement lighting my eyes. "Each piece reflects the colors and textures of the season—rich golds, deep reds, and earthy browns."

Blake studied the fabric, the shadows of creativity mingling with admiration in his eyes. "It's beautiful. You're not just finding your voice; you're amplifying it."

The compliment filled me with warmth, a gentle reminder of how far I had come. I glanced around my workspace, a kaleidoscope of swatches and sketches, remnants of late nights and boundless creativity, and I knew I was ready for the next step.

The day of the pop-up event arrived, a whirlwind of excitement that sent butterflies flitting through my stomach. I arrived early, my heart racing as I set up my station, the booth a reflection of my artistic vision. Draped fabrics hung elegantly, each piece poised to tell a story. As the crowd began to trickle in, I felt a mix of apprehension and exhilaration.

Jenna appeared at my side, her eyes alight with excitement. "You did it! Look at all these people!"

The gallery buzzed with energy, a vibrant tapestry of creativity and passion. I caught sight of Nora across the room, her presence magnetic as she mingled with guests, exuding confidence and charm. The contrast between us was palpable, yet instead of feeling overshadowed, I felt emboldened.

As the event unfolded, I engaged with visitors, sharing the inspirations behind my designs. The conversations flowed like wine, laughter mingling with compliments as I witnessed my creations coming to life in the hands of others.

In that moment, surrounded by art and ambition, I understood that competition didn't mean erasing myself; it meant embracing the diverse spectrum of creativity that surrounded me. My journey was intertwined with those of others, a mosaic of stories and expressions waiting to be shared.

As the evening drew to a close, I stood in the midst of the vibrant chaos, a sense of fulfillment washing over me. The air hummed with energy, and in that atmosphere of shared passion, I felt a connection to every artist, every dreamer, and every whisper of creativity that had paved my path. I was not merely a contender in a race; I was a storyteller, a creator, and above all, I was ready to paint my own canvas in vivid colors, unafraid of the shadows that would inevitably dance alongside me.

Chapter 21: Stitches of Deception

The crisp autumn air had settled over Manhattan like a gossamer shawl, delicate yet intoxicating, with each inhalation carrying the sweet scent of falling leaves mixed with the faint whiff of roasted chestnuts from a nearby vendor. I stood by the tall, glass-paneled windows of my tiny studio apartment, the skyline stretching out like a jagged heartbeat of the city. The sun dipped low, splashing golden hues across the concrete jungle, and I could feel the pulse of New York weaving its way into my veins. My gaze drifted down to the street where tourists bustled, their laughter rising in a buoyant symphony that contrasted sharply with the tense silence in my mind. Nora, the rising star of the fashion world, had become the center of a storm, and I was, in some twisted way, drawn to the chaos.

Her designs had once filled me with a fiery admiration, a reverence for the way she could transform the mundane into the magnificent, each stitch telling a story of aspiration and artistry. But now, whispers coiled around her name like smoke, and the allure of her fame felt tainted, laced with betrayal. Rumors, vicious and relentless, crawled through the industry like a predatory beast, gnashing its teeth. It was said that Nora's latest collection bore striking similarities to the work of lesser-known designers, their voices drowned out by the roaring clamor of her rising fame. A part of me relished the unfolding drama; it was a spectacle, a front-row seat to the unraveling of a carefully curated image, yet beneath that surface delight lay a seed of discomfort.

Nora had always presented herself as the epitome of confidence, a shimmering figure in the chaotic world of high fashion. But the glitz and glamor hid something deeper—a relentless pressure that I could almost taste. The shiny façade she wore like armor began to crack under the weight of expectation, and I couldn't help but feel a surge of empathy. I recalled the sleepless nights I'd endured, my own struggles looming like shadows in the corners of my mind. The whispers of failure echoed relentlessly, growing louder as the industry chewed up and spat out hopefuls like so much detritus. I had been one of those hopefuls, clinging to dreams that felt as elusive as the morning mist, and here was Nora, entwined in her own web of ambition and despair.

With a heavy heart, I pulled on my oversized cardigan, the fabric soft and comforting against my skin. I had become accustomed to seeking refuge in the small pleasures of life—sipping on steaming cups of chamomile tea while wrapped in my sanctuary of fabric swatches and design sketches. Today, however, the weight of Nora's predicament tugged at my spirit. As the sun dipped lower, shadows danced across my floor, a reminder that time was relentless and unforgiving.

The streets of Manhattan beckoned. I slipped on my boots, their scuffed leather a testament to countless adventures, and headed out, drawn toward the heart of the city. As I walked, I observed the ebb and flow of life around me—the street performers' vibrant energy, the laughter of children darting between adults like fireflies in the twilight. Each face told a story, a snapshot of hopes and dreams woven together in this grand tapestry of existence. But somewhere, within the fabric of it all, I felt the frayed edges of ambition that were all too familiar.

As I turned the corner onto Broadway, a poster caught my eye. Nora's face, radiant and poised, smiled back at me, but there was a flicker of something beneath the surface—an uncertainty that made her beauty seem almost fragile. It struck me then that fame was a fickle friend, capable of bestowing unimaginable joy one moment, only to rip it away the next. The very essence of the fashion industry, with its allure of glamour and prestige, often felt like a masquerade, where masks were worn to hide insecurities and the fear of inadequacy.

The quaint café on the corner, with its tiny round tables and mismatched chairs, offered a perfect escape. I slid into a corner seat, the faint hum of conversation wrapping around me like a warm embrace. The barista, a spirited woman with brightly colored hair, greeted me with a smile that made the world feel a little lighter. "The usual?" she asked, already preparing my favorite chai latte, rich with spices and sweetness. I nodded, grateful for the small comfort amidst the swirling uncertainties that surrounded me.

As I waited, I pulled out my sketchbook, the pages filled with half-formed ideas and fragments of inspiration. I sketched absentmindedly, my pencil gliding over the paper as I lost myself in the rhythmic motion. Designs began to take shape—flowing lines and intricate details that whispered of hope and resilience. Each stroke was a reminder of the passion that had initially drawn me to fashion, a rebellion against the mundane, a chance to create something beautiful amid chaos.

My thoughts wandered back to Nora, to the pressure she must have felt. Her family's expectations, no doubt an iron grip, squeezing the very breath from her aspirations. It was a narrative I recognized all too well, the suffocating love that sought to uplift yet often pinned dreams beneath its weight. The pressure to succeed, to create, to remain relevant in an industry that thrived on novelty, was a beast that could tear even the strongest apart.

I sipped my chai, its warmth spreading through me, an antidote to the chill creeping in from the autumn air. I envisioned Nora, hunched over her sketches, the ghost of doubt hovering like a specter. Had she too, in her solitude, questioned the cost of her dreams? Had she sacrificed pieces of herself in the pursuit of a glittering illusion? The answer, I suspected, lay hidden beneath the layers of fabric and ambition, stitched together in a fabric of deception that perhaps mirrored my own experiences.

As dusk settled in, painting the sky in hues of indigo and violet, I felt a stirring within—a call to reach out, to offer a lifeline. It was time to peel back the layers of gossip and conjecture that surrounded Nora and delve into the woman beneath the shimmering façade. Perhaps we were not so different after all, bound by the threads of ambition and the weight of expectation, navigating our own intricate designs in the unforgiving world of fashion.

The café buzzed with a kind of electric energy, a comforting chaos of clinking cups and animated conversations. I watched as the world outside melted into a wash of color, the city alive with the frenetic pace that was both exhilarating and exhausting. I couldn't help but feel a sense of kinship with the bustling crowd. They were all chasing something—dreams, success, or perhaps just a fleeting moment of connection in this sprawling metropolis. My mind drifted back to Nora, and I found myself captivated by the complexity of her situation. I wondered if she, too, sought refuge in the small joys of life, even as the looming shadows of criticism threatened to engulf her.

My chai latte had cooled slightly, and I took another sip, savoring the balance of spice and sweetness. I glanced around the café, observing the mosaic of patrons—a couple huddled close, whispering secrets as if the world around them was nothing but a backdrop to their own intimate play, while at a nearby table, a young woman in oversized glasses typed furiously on her laptop, her brow furrowed in determination. Each scene was a vignette, and I felt a strange comfort in the anonymity of their lives, even as I grappled with the weight of my own thoughts.

The more I reflected on Nora, the more I began to see her not as a rival but as a mirror, reflecting my struggles and aspirations. I wondered what lay beneath the polished exterior she presented to the world. The rumors swirling around her were vicious and unrelenting, like sharks circling a wounded seal. She had crafted her image so meticulously, projecting an aura of perfection that now felt increasingly fragile. What did it feel like to be the subject of whispers, to have her very identity questioned?

A part of me, that insidious part that thrived on gossip, initially relished the drama unfolding. But with each passing moment, that delight morphed into something more profound—an aching empathy that resonated deeply within me. It was the same empathy that had crept in when I had faced my own struggles, when the stinging arrows of criticism had pierced through my self-worth. I remembered the long nights spent sewing fabric scraps into semblances of designs, fueled by dreams that often felt just out of reach.

Nora's parents, with their relentless pursuit of excellence, must have loomed over her like a dark cloud. Their expectations could easily stifle the very creativity they sought to nurture. In the fashion world, where individuality was both a weapon and a liability, I could only imagine the internal battles she must wage daily. Perhaps, in their fervor for her success, they had inadvertently shackled her to their dreams rather than allowing her to forge her own path. The thought stirred a cocktail of sorrow and frustration within me; it seemed all too common, a narrative that played out in countless lives, including mine.

As I finished my drink, the warmth of the chai lingered, yet the chill of the impending winter whispered reminders of the harshness that lay ahead. I stood, reluctantly leaving my corner of sanctuary, and made my way through the bustling streets of Manhattan, where the kaleidoscope of life continued unabated. The golden hour cast a soft glow over the buildings, and I found solace in the quiet corners of my mind as I pondered my next move.

Deciding to seek out Nora felt instinctual, as if the universe had conspired to nudge me toward a deeper understanding of her journey. I wandered through SoHo, the chic boutiques and art galleries serving as a backdrop to my thoughts. Each step was imbued with purpose, the cobblestone streets echoing the rhythm of my heart. The city pulsed around me, alive with stories waiting to be uncovered.

When I finally reached Nora's studio, the atmosphere was a mix of chaos and creativity. The large windows looked out onto the bustling street below, the sun filtering in, illuminating swathes of fabric draped haphazardly across tables. A symphony of sewing machines hummed in the background, punctuated by the occasional exclamation of frustration from a designer chasing a deadline. I hesitated at the entrance, uncertainty prickling my skin. What would I say? How could I convey the empathy I felt without overstepping?

Before I could second-guess myself, I pushed the door open, the bell above it jingling as if heralding my arrival. The air inside was thick with the smell of fabric and ambition. I caught sight of Nora, her brow furrowed in concentration as she bent over a dress form, her fingers deftly adjusting the fabric like an artist perfecting a canvas. For a fleeting moment, she looked almost serene, lost in her craft, and I felt a pang of admiration.

"Nora," I called out, my voice steady despite the fluttering of nerves in my stomach. She turned, her expression a mix of surprise and guardedness.

"Can I help you?" she asked, the professional façade slipping into place, but I could see the flicker of vulnerability behind her eyes.

"I wanted to talk," I replied, stepping further inside. "About everything."

Her gaze held mine for a moment longer than necessary, the weight of unspoken words hanging in the air between us. There was a flicker of recognition, perhaps a shared understanding of the burdens we both carried in this relentless industry. The silence stretched, but I pressed on.

"I know things are chaotic right now. The rumors..." I trailed off, unsure of how to navigate this delicate terrain.

"Yeah," she sighed, her shoulders drooping slightly. "It's been a lot. I didn't expect it to hit like this."

"None of us do, do we?" I replied, the honesty spilling from my lips like an unguarded confession. "I've been there, and it's tough. The pressure can feel unbearable. You're not alone in this."

Nora straightened, a flicker of surprise flashing across her face before her expression softened. "It's nice to hear that," she said, her voice barely above a whisper. "I've felt so isolated lately, like everyone is just waiting for me to fail."

"You're more than just your designs, Nora. We all are," I insisted, stepping closer. "You have your own voice, and that matters more than the opinions of others."

For a brief moment, we stood in a fragile truce, two women navigating the turbulent waters of ambition and expectation, each searching for the strength to rise above the noise. And in that moment, the bond of empathy began to weave its intricate patterns between us, stitching together the torn edges of our stories.

The air was thick with tension, a palpable weight that seemed to settle in the crevices of the studio as Nora and I stood amidst the fabric swatches and half-finished garments. I could see her defenses waver for just a moment, and it struck me how often we all built walls around our vulnerabilities. The chaos of the outside world faded into the background, and in that small space, we shared an unspoken understanding, one forged in the fires of ambition and the agony of doubt.

"I always thought that success meant you had it all figured out," she admitted, her voice a fragile thread woven into the fabric of our conversation. "But now, with everything happening, I feel like I'm losing control. It's as if I'm stuck in a whirlwind of opinions and expectations."

I leaned against the edge of a nearby table, the sturdy wood grounding me in this moment. "Control is an illusion, isn't it?" I replied softly, remembering the countless times I had felt the same—like a marionette dancing on strings pulled by unseen hands. "In this industry, we're taught to present a flawless image, but beneath the surface, it's a different story altogether. We're all just trying to find our footing."

Nora's gaze flickered toward the sketches pinned to the wall, a tapestry of her dreams and aspirations. "The collection was meant to be my statement piece. My way of saying, 'I'm here, and I'm talented.' But now..." She trailed off, her voice thick with unshed tears. "Now it feels tainted."

"Art is always personal," I said, feeling the weight of her turmoil seep into my own heart. "Every thread you weave carries a piece of your soul. Don't let the noise drown out your voice."

She studied me then, her expression shifting from guarded skepticism to something softer, more open. "Why do you care so much?"

I chuckled lightly, a sound that felt almost foreign in the gravity of our conversation. "Because I've been in the trenches, too. I've fought my battles, worn my scars, and learned the hard way that vulnerability can be a strength, not a weakness."

There was a moment of silence as Nora considered my words, the hum of sewing machines providing a steady background rhythm, a reminder that life and creativity marched forward even amidst chaos. "I didn't think anyone else understood," she finally confessed, her voice barely above a whisper. "Everyone else seems so caught up in the glamour, the allure. It's suffocating."

The truth of her words resonated with me, a reflection of the double-edged sword that was the fashion industry. "Glamour can be a mask," I said, feeling the honesty spill from me like ink from a pen. "What glitters is not always gold. We're all so busy presenting our best selves to the world that we forget to show our scars. But those scars tell the real story."

Nora nodded, her expression softening as she took in my perspective. "Maybe I've been too focused on what everyone else thinks, trying to prove something instead of just being myself. It's exhausting."

"Authenticity is powerful," I encouraged, sensing the shift in her energy, a faint flicker of hope igniting within her. "Your designs are an extension of you. Let them breathe. Don't be afraid to share your journey, the struggles, the triumphs. People connect with that honesty."

As we stood amidst the remnants of her artistic expression, I felt the invisible threads of our shared struggles begin to intertwine, stitching together a bond forged in mutual understanding. Nora had become more than just a rising star or a figure in the industry; she was a kindred spirit, navigating the labyrinth of ambition and self-doubt with a heart that still yearned to create.

"Can we start over?" she asked suddenly, her voice steady now, a newfound resolve coloring her words. "I want to rework the collection. I need it to reflect who I am, not who others think I should be."

A smile crept onto my face, and I could feel the excitement in the air, electric and alive. "Yes! Let's do that. Let's strip away the noise and focus on what truly matters."

The energy in the studio shifted, a vibrant pulse of creativity igniting between us. We began pulling fabrics, colors bursting forth like an artist's palette, a kaleidoscope of possibilities unfolding. We laughed and talked about our inspirations, drawing from personal experiences and emotions that often lay dormant, suffocated under layers of expectation. With each piece we pulled together, I saw Nora's spirit shine a little brighter, the glow of her creativity slowly emerging from the shadows.

As the hours slipped away, the golden light of the setting sun filtered through the windows, casting long shadows across the floor. It felt as if time had paused for us, the city outside fading into a distant hum as we lost ourselves in the magic of creation. Ideas flowed between us like an intricate dance, a beautiful melding of vision and vulnerability, and for the first time in a long time, I felt my own heart swell with inspiration.

"Do you remember the first time you ever designed something?" Nora asked suddenly, her eyes sparkling with curiosity.

I paused, allowing the memory to wash over me. "It was a simple dress for my little sister's birthday. I scrounged up some fabric from the remnants bin at a thrift store. I felt like a magician, transforming a pile of scraps into something beautiful. She twirled around in it, her face lit up with joy. It was in that moment I realized the power of creation—the ability to evoke emotion through fabric."

Nora smiled, her own memories lighting up her features. "I think we forget that sometimes," she mused, her voice tinged with nostalgia. "We get so caught up in the industry's expectations that we lose sight of the joy of creation."

"That's what makes your designs so special, Nora," I said, catching her gaze. "You infuse them with your heart, and that's something no one can replicate."

The energy in the room shifted again, a surge of determination coursing through us as we embraced this new direction. We began sketching feverishly, laughter punctuating our creative frenzy, each stroke of the pencil filled with renewed purpose. The sun dipped below the horizon, leaving behind a canvas of deep indigo, and the world outside felt like a distant dream, replaced by the intoxicating promise of possibility that enveloped us.

With every new design we crafted, I felt the weight of doubt begin to lift from Nora's shoulders, replaced by an unshakeable sense of self. It was as if we were stitching together not just a collection, but a new narrative, one where authenticity reigned supreme.

And in that moment, I realized that the cutthroat nature of the fashion world didn't have to dictate our paths. We could carve out our own spaces, where vulnerability was a badge of honor and creativity flowed freely, unburdened by the judgment of others.

As we stood there, surrounded by the chaos of fabric and sketches, I felt a profound sense of hope. In the midst of the madness, amidst whispers and shadows, we had discovered something precious—a connection, a friendship, and a shared commitment to embrace our true selves.

The path ahead would undoubtedly be fraught with challenges, but together, we would navigate the winding roads of ambition and artistry, fueled by the resilience we had found in each other. And with that, a new chapter began, woven together by the intricate stitches of our dreams, daring to defy the weight of expectation.

Chapter 22: Finding My Voice

The café nestled in the heart of Charleston's historic district exuded a warmth that wrapped around me like a favorite quilt, its walls adorned with sepia-toned photographs of the city's bygone eras. As the sun dipped low, casting a golden hue through the large windows, the aroma of freshly brewed coffee mingled with the sweet scent of cinnamon pastries, creating an ambiance that felt both intimate and invigorating. I glanced at the rustic wooden tables, each one telling its own story of laughter and conversations that echoed within these walls. It was a gathering place for dreamers and artisans, a space where creativity thrived amid the gentle clatter of cups and the soft hum of chatter.

As I arranged my collection on the makeshift display—a blend of vintage suitcases and handcrafted stands—I felt a flutter of nerves weave through me like the delicate thread of a seamstress's needle. Each piece I had created bore fragments of my heart, stitched together with threads of memory and emotion. I thought of the late nights spent hunched over my sewing machine, the soft whirring sound echoing my thoughts as I poured my dreams into each fabric. With every dress, I sought to encapsulate a moment, an experience, a feeling—like capturing fireflies in a jar, their light flickering with the essence of who I was.

The collection itself was a tapestry of my journey, showcasing vibrant hues that mirrored the sunsets I'd watched from the roof of my apartment. There were flowing skirts that danced with the breeze, reminiscent of my childhood spent twirling in the fields of wildflowers behind my grandmother's house, and structured blazers that echoed my desire for independence and strength. I had named the collection "Rebirth," for it symbolized not only my growth as a designer but also my struggle to emerge from the cocoon of self-doubt that had enveloped me for far too long.

With the clock inching closer to the start of the showcase, I caught sight of familiar faces filtering into the café—friends, family, and fellow designers, all drawn together by an unspoken bond of support and love. I welcomed them with open arms, each hug infusing me with a sense of belonging that I had missed. Their encouragement bolstered my spirit, and I could feel the energy in the room shift, a collective anticipation buzzing in the air like static before a storm. I spotted Blake at the back, his warm smile cutting through the noise and grounding me. He had been my unwavering pillar of support, always believing in my talent even when I struggled to believe in myself.

As I began to present my collection, my voice quivered, but I drew strength from the faces looking back at me. I spoke of inspiration drawn from the streets of Charleston—its cobblestone pathways and wrought-iron balconies, the vibrant blooms that spilled from window boxes and danced along the sidewalks. I wanted my designs to echo that beauty, to capture the essence of the city I loved. With each description of the fabrics—the soft cottons, the shimmering silks—I could see their imaginations taking flight, envisioning the pieces not just as garments but as stories waiting to be lived.

The laughter and murmurs of approval from my audience spurred me on, and as I unveiled the first piece, a flowing sundress adorned with delicate lace, I could feel the energy in the room shift once more. The fabric caught the light, shimmering like the surface of the harbor at sunset, and as I described how the dress was inspired by the very first summer I spent exploring the city, a sense of pride swelled within me. I had woven my soul into every stitch, and now, it was laid bare for all to see.

With each piece I revealed, I felt more alive, my passion spilling forth like paint on a blank canvas. I shared the struggles of overcoming self-doubt, of finding my voice amid the cacophony of critics and competition, and how each dress was a triumph over that doubt. The audience listened, rapt and engaged, as if my journey was a shared experience, a tale of resilience that resonated deep within their own hearts.

Then came the pièce de résistance, a tailored gown that cascaded to the floor in a wave of fabric, adorned with intricate beadwork that sparkled like stars scattered across the night sky. I spoke of the late nights spent perfecting the design, of the countless sketches that had littered my workspace like fallen leaves in autumn. As I recounted the inspiration behind the gown—a chance encounter at a local art exhibit where colors danced across the canvas—I could see tears glistening in some eyes, and a warmth enveloped me, a validation of all the hard work I had poured into my craft.

When I finished my presentation, a hush fell over the café, as if time had momentarily stopped. Then, as if on cue, applause erupted, echoing off the walls like the sound of waves crashing against the shore. I stood there, heart racing, overwhelmed by the outpouring of support and love. It felt like coming home after a long journey, like finding the missing pieces of myself in the embrace of this community. I had stepped out of the shadows and into the light, ready to embrace whatever came next, fueled by the belief that I was, at last, worthy of my dreams.

The café's energy buzzed like the city itself—a vibrant mosaic of personalities and stories colliding in a space filled with creativity. As the applause began to fade, I found myself enveloped in the warmth of familiar faces. My friends approached, their smiles wide and genuine, echoing the delight I felt coursing through my veins. Lila, my college roommate, was the first to reach me, her eyes sparkling with unshed tears, a testament to the beauty she saw in my work.

"Oh my God, you were incredible!" she exclaimed, wrapping me in a bear hug that squeezed the breath from my lungs. "That last dress—seriously, it looked like it stepped right out of a fairy tale!"

I chuckled, brushing a stray hair behind my ear, feeling the heat rise in my cheeks. "Thanks! It's so good to see you! I was worried I might trip over my own feet."

"Please, you glided up there!" She pulled back, her expression shifting to one of mischief. "Blake's going to be unbearable now, you know. You've given him a whole new level of bragging rights."

I glanced over at Blake, who stood at the edge of the crowd, his hands casually tucked into his pockets, a proud smile gracing his lips. The way he looked at me, as if I were the only one in the room, sent a rush of warmth through my chest. There was something about his presence that grounded me, a steadying force amid the whirlwind of emotions swirling around.

As guests began to mingle, the clinking of glasses and laughter created a symphony of celebration. I watched as my friends fawned over the garments, their fingers dancing over the fabrics like they were savoring the texture of fine wine. They asked questions, sharing their thoughts and opinions, and I felt a swell of joy at the connection my work fostered. This wasn't just about fabric and thread; it was about creating an experience, a narrative woven into each piece.

"Can I take a closer look?" One of my fellow designers, Nora, stepped forward, her voice tinged with curiosity. She had always inspired me with her edgy designs and fearless approach to fashion. "Your use of color is bold but still so... refined."

I grinned, feeling a sense of kinship with her. "Thank you! I wanted to channel the energy of the city—the sunsets, the blossoms, all those little moments that make Charleston feel alive."

"Mission accomplished." She inspected the sundress closely, her brow furrowing in concentration. "This lace is exquisite. Did you source it locally?"

"Yeah, from a little shop on King Street. They had the most stunning selection. I just couldn't resist."

Nora nodded, appreciating my choice. "You've captured the spirit of your inspiration beautifully. I'd love to collaborate sometime."

The idea thrilled me, igniting a spark of possibility. Collaborations often felt like a dance, a harmonious blending of styles and ideas, and the thought of working alongside someone as talented as Nora set my heart racing. "I would love that," I replied, excitement lacing my voice. "Let's definitely chat more about it."

As the evening unfolded, the café brimmed with conversations about fashion, dreams, and aspirations. I slipped into a rhythm, moving from group to group, my laughter intertwining with the joyful banter. I felt lighter than air, buoyed by the collective energy surrounding me, the palpable excitement that surged as we exchanged stories and ideas. Each moment felt like a thread weaving into a larger tapestry—a fabric of connection that echoed the essence of my collection.

As I poured drinks for my friends, I caught a glimpse of Blake deep in conversation with a local photographer, his gestures animated as he shared his thoughts about my designs. I admired the way he lit up when he spoke, his passion evident in every word. It was moments like this that reminded me of the depth of our bond. He had always seen me for who I was—an artist striving to find her voice, navigating a world filled with noise and distraction.

When the crowd began to thin out, I felt a tug at my heartstrings, a bittersweet pang as I realized the night was winding down. Lila sidled up next to me, a knowing smile dancing on her lips. "So, what's next for you? This was just the beginning, right?"

I took a deep breath, letting the scent of coffee and vanilla fill my lungs, grounding me in the moment. "I think I want to explore more collaborations, maybe even put together a larger showcase. I feel like there's so much more to say, to create."

Lila's eyes sparkled with excitement. "I can see it! You're on fire, and I don't want you to lose that momentum. You've got to keep pushing, keep creating."

"I will," I promised, the determination in my voice a testament to the resolve blossoming within me. "I finally feel like I'm finding my place in this world, and I don't want to let go of that."

As the last few guests filtered out, Blake made his way back to me, his expression a mixture of pride and affection. "You were amazing tonight," he said, brushing a finger along the delicate beadwork of the gown I was wearing, his touch sending a pleasant shiver down my spine. "You've found your voice, and it's beautiful."

"Thanks," I replied, a soft smile curving my lips. "I couldn't have done it without you. Your support means everything to me."

His gaze held mine, a silent understanding passing between us—a recognition of the journey we had both undertaken, each in our own way. "You're just getting started. I can't wait to see where this takes you."

With the café lights dimming and the last traces of the evening's laughter lingering in the air, I felt a profound sense of gratitude wash over me. I had stepped onto a path filled with uncertainty, yet the night had illuminated the way ahead, each connection and each moment a reminder that I was not alone. I had found my voice amidst the cacophony, a melody uniquely mine, ready to resonate and reverberate through the fabric of this beautiful, chaotic world.

The lingering echoes of applause began to fade into the night, and the café slowly emptied, leaving behind an ambiance rich with the scents of coffee and sweet pastries. I stood near the display, now filled with my collection, a mix of exhilaration and disbelief surging through me. The warm glow of the overhead lights cast a gentle halo around the fabrics, making them look even more ethereal, like remnants of dreams waiting to be worn. I was still floating on the high of sharing my heart with so many people, yet an undercurrent of introspection tugged at me, urging me to reflect on what this moment truly meant.

Blake, still by my side, leaned closer, his voice a soothing murmur amidst the fading chatter. "You know, I've never seen you like this. You're not just a designer; you're a storyteller."

His words wrapped around me, comforting yet challenging, inviting me to look deeper into the significance of what I had just shared. "A storyteller?" I repeated, arching an eyebrow playfully. "I'm not sure about that. I just make pretty things."

"Pretty? No, what you create is powerful. Each piece speaks a language of its own. You've captured your essence, your journey, and the essence of this city. People can feel that."

His gaze was unwavering, urging me to see beyond my self-deprecating tendencies. In that moment, I realized that I had been so focused on the tangible—the fabric, the patterns, the cuts—that I had forgotten the emotional weight of my creations. Every stitch held a memory, and every thread was a part of my narrative. I had begun to weave not just garments, but connections to my past, my community, and ultimately to myself.

"Do you really think so?" I asked, a mix of vulnerability and hope threading through my words. "I mean, does it resonate with everyone?"

Blake nodded, his eyes shining with sincerity. "Absolutely. Look around. People are talking, sharing their thoughts. Your work has sparked something in them. It's not just about fashion; it's about emotion."

As we walked toward the door, I took one last glance at the remnants of the evening—the empty tables, the scattered crumbs of pastries, and the warm glow that seemed to linger in the air, a testament to the magic we had created. Outside, the evening sky was a deep indigo, the first stars twinkling like tiny diamonds scattered across velvet. The streets were hushed, a stark contrast to the lively energy inside the café, yet they felt alive with possibilities, as if the city itself was holding its breath in anticipation.

"Do you want to walk?" Blake suggested, breaking the silence. "I think we need to celebrate."

"Celebrate what?" I laughed, the sound bright and genuine. "I didn't even know if this would work!"

"Exactly! That's what makes it special. You took a leap, and look where it got you. Let's explore, shall we?"

His enthusiasm was infectious. With a nod, I fell into step beside him, the cobblestones beneath our feet cool and familiar. As we strolled through the streets of Charleston, I felt the vibrancy of the city wrap around us like a soft embrace. The sweet scent of magnolia trees mingled with the salty breeze from the nearby harbor, creating a heady mixture that ignited my senses.

We meandered toward Waterfront Park, the sound of gentle waves lapping against the docks providing a soothing backdrop to our conversation. The park glimmered under the faint moonlight, its manicured gardens alive with nocturnal whispers. I spotted a group of friends gathered near the pineapple fountain, their laughter bubbling up like champagne. It was a scene that felt effortlessly picturesque, a moment captured in time where joy reigned supreme.

"Have you ever thought about taking your collection beyond the café?" Blake's voice broke through my reverie, pulling me back to our conversation. "There are so many avenues you could explore—pop-up shops, fashion shows, even online."

I contemplated his words, the thought both thrilling and daunting. "I've dreamed of it, but... what if people don't respond? What if it all falls flat?"

"Then you learn and grow from it," he replied, his tone reassuring. "You've already come so far. Remember tonight? It was just the beginning."

We found a bench and sat, the cool wood beneath us grounding me as I gazed out at the shimmering water. The city felt alive, each light flickering like a heartbeat in the night. It dawned on me that every step I had taken had led me here, to this moment of awakening, where I finally began to understand my voice—not just as a designer, but as a creator of experiences.

"I think you're right," I finally said, my heart fluttering with newfound resolve. "Maybe it is time to take that leap again. I've been so caught up in the fear of judgment that I forgot why I started this in the first place. It's about connection, creativity, and sharing my story."

Blake leaned closer, a satisfied smile breaking across his face. "That's the spirit! And I'll be right here cheering you on."

As the laughter of people around us mingled with the distant sound of music from a nearby street performer, I felt a renewed sense of purpose blossoming within me. Each note from the guitar floated through the air, a reminder that life was a symphony of highs and lows, notes of joy and sorrow intertwined. I envisioned my collection blossoming into something larger, reaching out to embrace a broader audience, echoing the stories of many.

In that moment of clarity, I realized that my journey in fashion was not merely about creating beautiful garments, but about weaving a community together—a tapestry of experiences, struggles, and triumphs. Each collection could tell a different story, invite others to share their narratives, and create a dialogue that transcended the boundaries of fabric and thread.

As we stood to leave, I felt a sense of exhilaration that surged through my veins, propelling me forward. The world was vast, and my dreams felt tangible, just within reach. I had found my voice amidst the chaos, and now it was time to let it sing, to let it soar into the vibrant tapestry of life awaiting me. With Blake by my side, the possibilities felt endless, and I knew that I was ready to embrace whatever came next, armed with the belief that my story was worth telling.

Chapter 23: The Weaver's Dance

The sewing studio hummed with the sound of machines whirring, punctuated by the soft rustle of fabric as I rifled through the vibrant swatches spread across the table. Each piece of cloth held its own story, and I could almost hear whispers of their potential designs as I thumbed through them—bold reds like a fiery sunset, cool blues reminiscent of the Atlantic's depths, and intricate patterns that danced like sunlight on water. The air was thick with creativity, a palpable force that wrapped around us like a cocoon, keeping the world outside at bay.

Blake, ever the patient mentor, sat across from me, his brow furrowed in concentration as he meticulously stitched together the latest ensemble. His hands moved with a grace that belied their strength, fingers deftly guiding the fabric as if coaxing it into life. The soft glow of the overhead lights cast a warm hue over his tanned skin, highlighting the slight smirk that danced on his lips every time he caught me stealing glances in his direction. There was something magnetic about him—an unspoken understanding that made our late-night work sessions feel like an intimate affair. Each shared laugh lingered in the air, heavy with uncharted territory.

As we toiled through the night, the outside world fell away, leaving only the flicker of the sewing machine's light and the comforting rhythm of our collaboration. The studio was a sanctuary, its walls lined with sketches of past creations, remnants of dreams brought to life. Yet, amidst the organized chaos of threads and patterns, my heart was tangled in an emotional fabric that felt both exhilarating and terrifying.

"Pass me that navy silk," he said, his voice low and steady, pulling me from my reverie. I reached for the fabric, our hands brushing momentarily—a fleeting connection that sent shivers down my spine. The heat from that simple touch ignited a flicker of something deeper, a current running between us that neither of us dared to acknowledge. The more we worked, the more I noticed the intensity of his gaze, as if he were trying to decipher the intricate layers of my soul through the art of creation.

With each passing hour, the studio transformed from a mere workspace into a vibrant tapestry of our shared dreams. We danced around the idea of what our showcase would mean for us. For Blake, it was another milestone in his illustrious career; for me, it was a proving ground, a chance to step out of the shadows of my past and into the spotlight of my future. Yet, intertwined in our ambitions was a tension that crackled like electricity, threatening to pull us closer together or push us apart.

"Are you nervous?" he asked one evening, leaning back in his chair, a playful glint in his eyes that made my heart flutter. I could see the hint of vulnerability behind his bravado, the boyish charm that somehow made him even more endearing.

"Terrified," I admitted, my voice barely above a whisper. I let out a nervous laugh, my hands fidgeting with a stray thread. "What if I fall flat on my face?"

He chuckled softly, his gaze unwavering. "You won't. You have a talent that demands to be seen. Just trust yourself."

The sincerity in his voice sent warmth flooding through me, a balm for my insecurities. His faith in me felt like a lifeline, and I clung to it, even as a different kind of tension simmered beneath the surface. It was exhilarating, the way our bodies seemed to gravitate toward one another without conscious thought. The way he leaned in closer as we discussed colors and fabrics, or how our laughter echoed off the walls like a melody that had yet to find its harmony.

That night, as we meticulously draped the final garment—a sweeping gown that captured the essence of a summer's twilight—I sensed a shift in the air. The laughter that had filled the room moments before fell into a charged silence, each heartbeat reverberating against the backdrop of the sewing machines. Our eyes locked, and for a moment, it felt as though the world around us had faded into insignificance.

"Blake..." I began, but the words caught in my throat as his hand brushed against my cheek, a soft caress that sent a jolt of electricity coursing through my veins. I could feel the heat radiating from him, the very air thick with anticipation. In that instant, I could sense the barrier between us—the professional façade we had maintained—cracking, shifting, ready to fall away.

I leaned into his touch, my heart racing as I dared to linger in the moment. This was more than just a shared creative space; it was a crossroads where friendship could give way to something infinitely more complicated. The thrill of it all was intoxicating, leaving me breathless and yearning for more.

The workshop, with its chaotic beauty and comforting chaos, faded away as the weight of unspoken feelings hung between us. It was a fragile moment, suspended in time, and as I searched his eyes for clarity, I wondered if we were about to take a step into a new realm where the rules we had followed no longer applied. Would this change everything? Would the fabric of our relationship, carefully woven together over countless hours, unravel in the face of this burgeoning intimacy?

The air was thick with promise, and I felt like a butterfly poised to burst forth from its cocoon, ready to embrace the world—or perhaps just Blake. In that suspended moment, I understood that whatever happened next could redefine not only our work but also the very essence of who we were becoming together.

The breath of silence wrapped around us like a gauzy veil, each heartbeat reverberating off the walls adorned with our creations. I stood frozen, caught between the warmth of Blake's touch and the trepidation spiraling in my chest. It was a delicious tension, intoxicating and overwhelming, a thread woven tightly into the fabric of our shared dreams. I could feel the magnetic pull between us, a gravitational force that seemed to draw our very beings closer, as if we were two stars destined to collide.

"Why do you always manage to make everything so complicated?" he murmured, his voice low and rich, breaking the spell we had cast. His eyes sparkled with that familiar blend of mischief and sincerity, but beneath the lightness was a current of seriousness that sent shivers down my spine.

I blinked, momentarily at a loss for words. "Complicated? I was just—"

"Just what?" He tilted his head slightly, the barest hint of a smile dancing on his lips. "Just staring at me like I'm a sculpture in a museum? Because I could get used to that."

The playful banter hung in the air, lightening the heavy atmosphere, but I could feel the weight of his gaze pressing against my skin. I laughed nervously, a sound that felt almost foreign amidst the charged air. "More like contemplating the meaning of life while you work your magic over there." I gestured vaguely at the dress in progress, a swirl of navy silk and intricate lace that felt like an embodiment of my aspirations.

He chuckled, but the laugh faded as his expression grew earnest, the corners of his mouth settling into a serious line. "You're not giving yourself enough credit. You've brought this vision to life. It's not just me."

"Maybe," I said, my voice faltering slightly. "But it's hard not to feel like a shadow sometimes, especially next to you."

He shook his head, his brow furrowing in that endearing way that made my heart flutter. "You're no shadow. You're the light that guides this whole operation."

His words hung between us like a lifeline, and for a fleeting moment, I let myself believe them. I had spent countless nights doubting my abilities, drowning in a sea of self-criticism, but here was Blake, infusing me with a sense of validation that felt like a warm embrace. Just then, the weight of my aspirations mingled with an unexpected longing.

"Blake, I—" The words were stuck in my throat, twisting and turning like the fabrics we had draped across the mannequins. I wanted to say so much more, to bridge the gap between admiration and something deeper, but the fear of what lay on the other side held me back.

"I know," he said softly, and the way he said it, like he understood my unspoken fears, sent warmth pooling in my chest. "It's terrifying, isn't it? To be vulnerable with someone?"

"It is," I admitted, my voice barely a whisper. "But it's also exhilarating."

We stood there, suspended in a moment that felt like a dance, two hesitant partners on the edge of a precipice. I was acutely aware of the way his fingers lingered on my cheek, as if he were afraid to pull away, as if breaking contact would shatter the fragile spell we had woven. My mind raced with possibilities, each one more alluring and terrifying than the last.

Finally, the silence broke with the sharp sound of a bell ringing from the nearby clock tower, the chime echoing through the night, a stark reminder that time was slipping away. I stepped back, the sudden absence of his warmth leaving a chill in its wake. "We should... we should get back to work," I stammered, scrambling to gather my thoughts, my heart still pounding in my ears.

"Right," he said, a hint of disappointment threading through his voice. We returned to our tasks, the air thick with unspoken words and unresolved feelings. I busied myself with the gown, my fingers fumbling as I secured the final seams, yet my thoughts drifted like feathers in the wind, tangled in the delicate threads of possibility.

As the night deepened, I could feel the swell of emotions within me, a surge of determination rising like the tide. I didn't want to return to the safe confines of platonic friendship. I wanted to dive into the ocean of whatever this was between us, to explore the depths and currents, even if it meant risking everything.

Blake's laughter echoed through the studio as he shared a joke, his voice cutting through the tension like a warm knife through butter. It was this joy, this infectious energy, that made me realize just how much I admired him—not only for his talent but for the person he was beneath the surface.

"Hey," I called out, finding the courage I didn't know I had. "What if we... what if we took a break? Just for a moment?"

He turned, his eyebrows raised in surprise. "A break? From work? What are we, rebels?"

"Exactly!" I laughed, and the sound surprised me. "Let's be rebels for a night. Just... let's step outside."

Without waiting for his response, I grabbed my jacket and headed toward the door, my heart racing at the prospect of stepping outside our carefully curated world, even if only for a moment. The cool night air welcomed us like an old friend as we stepped into the street, the stars twinkling above like tiny diamonds scattered across a velvet canvas.

"What's the plan, oh fearless leader?" he asked, falling into step beside me, his voice playful but laced with curiosity.

"Let's just wander," I suggested, looking up at the sky, the expanse of stars feeling like a million wishes waiting to be made. "No destination, just... freedom."

The streets of our little town came alive under the moonlight, familiar yet transformed. The hum of late-night life buzzed around us, and I reveled in the way the cool air danced across my skin, invigorating and refreshing. I felt lighter, freer, as if the weight of expectations had slipped away with each step.

Blake kept pace with me, his laughter mingling with the distant sounds of a live band playing in a nearby café, the music weaving its way through the air like a gentle caress. As we strolled, I couldn't help but glance sideways, taking in the way his expression shifted from playful to contemplative, the light of the streetlamps casting soft shadows on his features.

"Is this your way of escaping the pressure?" he asked, his voice softer now, as if afraid to disturb the tranquility enveloping us.

"Maybe," I admitted, my gaze focused ahead. "Or maybe it's a way of finding clarity. A moment to breathe before everything changes."

Blake nodded, his silence encouraging me to continue. "I feel like I've been holding my breath for weeks. This showcase—it's everything I've dreamed of, but I can't shake the feeling that I'm teetering on the edge of something monumental."

"Monumental," he echoed thoughtfully. "That's a powerful word."

"It is," I said, glancing at him. "But sometimes monumental moments come with risks. Like the risk of crossing boundaries we've set."

"Boundaries can be slippery," he replied, his eyes locking onto mine with an intensity that made my heart race anew. "But sometimes, crossing them is the only way to discover what truly matters."

His words hung in the air between us, thick with meaning, and in that moment, I knew. This was the cusp of something remarkable—an awakening of dreams and desires that had long lain dormant. The potential of what we could become together shimmered in the night, just beyond our reach, and for the first time, I felt ready to chase it.

The soft glow of streetlights illuminated the cobblestone streets as we wandered deeper into the heart of our town, a quaint place known for its charm and artistic spirit. Each building whispered tales of history, their façades painted in colors that seemed to capture the essence of a vibrant past. I inhaled the cool night air, the scent of blooming jasmine wrapping around us, mingling with the faint echo of laughter from a nearby pub. It was a melody of life that resonated with the joy of being young and free—if only for a fleeting moment.

Blake walked beside me, his silhouette cutting a striking figure against the illuminated backdrop of the night. I could see the way his eyes sparkled, reflecting the ambient glow, and I realized I wanted to know everything about him—the stories behind those expressive eyes, the laughter lines that hinted at a lifetime of joy, the dreams he nurtured beneath that confident exterior. It was a dizzying thought, how intertwined our lives had become in such a short time, and the idea of a deeper connection both excited and terrified me.

"Let's stop here," I said suddenly, pointing at a small outdoor café nestled under a canopy of twinkling fairy lights. The warmth emanating from the place felt inviting, and the gentle murmur of conversation blended with the soft strains of music playing nearby. We approached the café, the aroma of fresh pastries and rich coffee wafting through the air like a comforting embrace.

As we settled into a cozy nook, I glanced around, taking in the eclectic decor—a whimsical blend of vintage posters and mismatched furniture that echoed the creative spirit of the town. It felt like a sanctuary, a place where time slowed down and the chaos of the world outside faded away.

"Coffee?" Blake asked, his voice breaking through my reverie.

"Absolutely. The stronger, the better," I replied, grinning. "I think I'm going to need it to survive the week ahead."

He chuckled as he flagged down a waiter, his charm effortlessly brightening the atmosphere. As he ordered, I couldn't help but admire the way he navigated the interactions around him—his presence felt larger than life, and I was drawn to him like a moth to a flame.

"Have you always been this magnetic?" I teased when he returned, handing me a steaming cup of coffee.

He smirked, leaning back in his chair. "I'm just a guy who knows how to order coffee. The real magic is in the beans."

"Is that so?" I sipped, the rich flavor enveloping my senses. "And here I thought it was all in the company."

"Touché," he replied, a playful glint in his eyes. "But really, I think you're the one bringing the magic tonight. This whole spontaneous adventure? I'm just along for the ride."

As we settled into easy conversation, the night unfolded like a well-worn tapestry, each word stitching us closer together. We talked about everything—from our dreams for the showcase to childhood memories that evoked laughter and nostalgia. I shared the story of my first disastrous sewing project, a dress that was more akin to a potato sack than a fashion statement, and Blake responded with tales of his own early missteps in the world of design, weaving his experiences into a tapestry of shared understanding.

Yet, beneath the lighthearted banter lay a current of sincerity that made my heart race. I could sense it building, that electric tension we had felt in the studio, and I wondered if it would dare to surface in this moment. The café's warm ambiance enveloped us, but there was still an edge of vulnerability lingering in the air, a promise of more if we only dared to reach for it.

"Have you ever thought about what comes after the showcase?" Blake asked, his tone shifting as he leaned in, his elbows resting on the table.

I paused, the question hanging in the air like an unsung note. "What do you mean?"

"I mean, once you put your work out there, what's next? Are you ready for what that could mean?" His eyes searched mine, and I felt as if he were peeling back layers of my heart, exposing fears I hadn't dared to confront.

A shiver of uncertainty danced along my spine. "Honestly? I've been so focused on the showcase that I haven't allowed myself to think beyond it. But the thought of it—" I took a breath, steeling myself. "It terrifies me."

He nodded, a knowing expression on his face. "It's natural to feel that way. But you have to remember that art, your art, is an extension of you. Sharing it with the world means putting a piece of yourself out there, and that can be both exhilarating and frightening."

"Are you ready for that?" I asked softly. "For your work to be scrutinized, judged?"

"I am," he replied without hesitation, his confidence unwavering. "But it's not just about the judgment. It's about connection. It's about touching people's lives with what we create, and that's worth any risk."

His words resonated within me, a stirring echo of the passion that drove me to pursue this path. But alongside that passion lingered a quiet fear—what if my creations didn't resonate? What if they fell flat?

"Do you really think we can change the world through our art?" I asked, my voice barely above a whisper.

"I believe we can," he said, and there was a sincerity in his gaze that made me believe him. "Art is a language all its own. It can challenge perspectives, heal wounds, and create connections that span beyond time and space."

I found myself captivated, not only by his words but by the depth of his belief. In that moment, I realized he wasn't just speaking of art in general; he was talking about us. About the connection we were forging in this very instant, a bridge crafted from shared dreams and unvoiced desires.

The conversation flowed like the coffee we sipped, rich and warm, until the café began to empty around us, leaving only the remnants of our laughter lingering in the air. As the last few patrons filtered out, I felt the intimacy of our surroundings grow thicker, the space between us diminishing until it was barely there at all.

"Blake," I said, my heart racing as I summoned the courage to voice what had been brewing within me since that night in the studio. "I think we need to talk about—"

Before I could finish, the moment shifted. The door swung open, and a group of friends poured in, their boisterous laughter breaking the spell that had settled around us. The interruption was jarring, like a sudden gust of wind scattering the delicate petals of a flower.

Blake's expression shifted as he glanced at the newcomers, a flicker of disappointment crossing his face before he masked it with a smile. "Looks like our moment was stolen," he said, but the twinkle in his eye didn't dim.

"Not entirely," I replied, though I felt the weight of what had almost transpired linger like an unfinished note in the air.

We spent the next hour mingling with the friends who had joined us, laughing and joking, but in the back of my mind, I felt a sense of longing—a quiet promise left unfulfilled. The connection we had was too palpable to ignore, yet here we were, navigating around it like two dancers avoiding each other on a crowded floor.

As we finally stepped back into the cool night air, I couldn't shake the feeling that we were at a crossroads. The world around us felt charged, full of possibilities and untapped desires. The glow of the streetlamps cast a warm light on the path ahead, and I sensed that whatever lay in store for us, we had crossed an invisible line.

"Where to now?" Blake asked, his playful tone returning as he glanced down the street, eyes sparkling with mischief.

"Anywhere," I replied, the thrill of the unknown coursing through me. "Let's just keep walking. Let's see where the night takes us."

And as we stepped forward, side by side, I felt the weight of the unspoken words still lingering between us—an invitation to embrace the uncertainty, to leap into the unknown, where every thread of our lives could intertwine in ways neither of us could yet fathom.

Chapter 24: The Heart's Fabric

The evening air thrums with an electric energy, laced with the rich aroma of freshly brewed coffee and the soft undertones of jazz swirling through the walls of Café Lark. As I step inside, the dim lighting dances against the exposed brick, casting playful shadows that seem to sway in time with the rhythmic tapping of high heels and the cheerful clinking of ceramic mugs. The café is a melting pot of emotions, a tapestry woven from laughter, hushed conversations, and the occasional burst of applause as friends greet one another with hugs and laughter. My heart races in tandem with the pulse of this vibrant space, each beat a reminder that tonight is mine.

I weave my way through the throng of familiar faces, their expressions an amalgam of encouragement and anticipation. Among the patrons, I catch glimpses of my friends—Becca, with her fiery curls and infectious laughter, her hands animated as she recounts tales from her day. Across the room, there's Eli, a gentle giant whose quiet demeanor hides a sharp wit that can pierce through any veil of pretense. They are my tribe, and their presence is a comforting balm to the frayed edges of my nerves.

My designs are displayed like jewels in a crown, hung carefully on rustic wooden racks that have seen countless artistic endeavors pass through their embrace. Each piece is a story, a fragment of my heart sewn into fabric and thread. There's the ocean-blue gown, its flowing fabric reminiscent of waves crashing against sun-kissed shores, and the fiery red cocktail dress that twinkles under the café's soft lights like the sunset bleeding into the horizon. I glance over at Blake, his silhouette sharp against the backdrop of laughter and chatter. His deep-set eyes hold a warmth that ignites a spark within me, filling the chasm of anxiety that threatens to swallow me whole.

As the clock inches closer to the hour, I can feel the weight of expectation bearing down on me, a tangible force that heightens the sensations around me. The clamor of voices fades, and my world narrows to the stage where I will bare my soul. The spotlight stands ready, a beacon that will illuminate my deepest aspirations and fears. My throat tightens with anticipation, the cool air catching on the rough edges of my nerves, as I take a deep breath and remind myself of why I'm here. This isn't just about the clothes; it's about connection, about sharing my essence with those who've supported me, who've seen the nights when I stitched until my fingers bled and the mornings when doubt clouded my mind.

Finally, the moment arrives. I step onto the stage, each footfall resonating against the wooden floor, a drumbeat heralding the unveiling of my heart. The spotlight casts a warm glow around me, transforming the café into an intimate theater, the audience's faces illuminated by an eager curiosity. I can feel the thrum of their attention, a living thing that wraps around me like a silken shroud, buoying me above the self-doubt that so often threatens to pull me down.

With a deep breath, I begin to speak, my voice a gentle melody rising above the murmur. "Thank you all for being here tonight. Each of you has played a part in my journey, a journey woven with threads of hope, love, and resilience." I catch Blake's eye, his smile unwavering, a beacon guiding me through the fog of my anxiety.

I turn to the first piece, a delicate top adorned with intricate embroidery, each stitch a whisper of my dreams. "This top," I say, my fingers brushing against the soft fabric, "represents the moments of joy I've found in the simplest of things. It's inspired by summer evenings spent beneath the stars, wrapped in laughter and the smell of blooming jasmine." The audience leans forward, captivated, and I can feel their energy flowing toward me, encouraging and invigorating.

As I move through my collection, each piece unfolds like a chapter of my life—there's the knee-length skirt, vibrant and playful, evoking memories of twirling on the old wooden dance floor of my childhood home, the echoes of music reverberating in my bones. I weave anecdotes into the fabric of my presentation, sharing snippets of my life that pulse beneath the surface of my designs. The audience responds, their laughter and gasps painting the air with vivid colors, a tapestry of connection that binds us in this shared moment.

Blake watches from the sidelines, a pillar of strength with an expression that melts my fears into embers. He nods along, a silent reassurance that feeds my confidence. The culmination of emotions surges within me as I realize that I am not just presenting clothes; I am sharing pieces of myself. Each story, each memory, stitches me closer to the hearts of those who listen. The stage becomes a confessional, a space where vulnerability transforms into strength, and my heart beats in rhythm with theirs, a symphony of shared experiences resonating through the room.

As I unveil the final piece, a flowing gown that seems to dance with the air around it, I take a moment to pause. "This," I say, feeling the fabric slip through my fingers like silk ribbons, "is my dream—an embodiment of everything I aspire to be. It's a reminder that while we may feel fragile at times, we are all capable of brilliance." The words spill from my heart, raw and unfiltered, and the audience responds with a collective inhale, as if they too are grasping the weight of that truth.

In this kaleidoscope of emotions, I find liberation. I am not merely a designer showcasing fabric; I am a storyteller, weaving tales of hope, courage, and love. And as the final echoes of applause wash over me, I realize that I have not only shared my creations but have also stitched my heart into the very fabric of this evening, each thread binding us together in an unbreakable tapestry of dreams fulfilled and aspirations ignited.

The applause reverberates in my chest like the last notes of a symphony, wrapping around me in a comforting embrace. I stand on the stage, momentarily suspended in the warmth of the moment, a small grin breaking through the nervousness that had coiled in my stomach just moments before. My heart still races, each thump a reminder that I am alive, breathing, and, perhaps for the first time in a long while, exactly where I am meant to be. The café feels like a living entity, a collective heart that beats in sync with mine, swelling with pride and joy for what we have created together.

As the crowd begins to disperse, the air buzzes with animated chatter, and laughter spills like champagne bubbles over the wooden tables. Familiar faces are everywhere, their smiles brightening the dim café atmosphere. I catch snippets of conversations—words of encouragement, praises for my work, and the occasional burst of laughter that rings like a bell. My friends cluster together, their faces aglow with admiration as they recount their favorite pieces from the showcase. Becca's eyes twinkle as she talks about the ocean-blue gown, her hands flailing in excitement as she re-enacts the moment I spoke about summer nights and the scent of jasmine.

Blake strides over, weaving through the throng with an effortless grace that makes my heart flutter. He stops in front of me, his eyes warm and earnest, and I can see the sincerity written all over his face. "You were amazing," he says, his voice low and steady, pulling me closer to him. "You've poured your heart into every piece. I could feel it." I feel the weight of his words settle on my shoulders, a comforting cloak that lifts the lingering traces of anxiety.

"Thanks," I reply, trying to keep my voice steady while my cheeks flush with warmth. "It means a lot coming from you." The moment stretches between us, a silken thread that holds the weight of unspoken emotions. I want to tell him how much his support has meant to me throughout this journey, how his belief in my talent has been like sunlight filtering through the clouds, illuminating the path when I felt lost. Instead, I smile, allowing the unspoken connection to linger in the air, a tapestry woven from the threads of our shared experiences.

Just then, Eli bursts into the conversation, his laughter ringing like wind chimes on a breezy day. "If you keep this up, we're going to need to start calling you a fashion icon," he jokes, winking at me. "Seriously, though, when's your next show? I need to book a front-row seat."

I chuckle, feeling buoyed by the lightness of his jest. "I think I might need a breather before I take on another collection. This one nearly did me in!" The warmth of their camaraderie envelops me, and I realize how much I've missed moments like this—simple, unadulterated joy in the company of friends who see me for all that I am, imperfections included.

As the café slowly empties, I take a moment to absorb the atmosphere. The scent of coffee mingles with the lingering sweetness of pastries, and the low hum of conversation gradually gives way to the quiet chatter of closing staff. The soft glow of fairy lights reflects off the polished wood, and the remnants of the night's excitement linger like an enchanting spell.

I glance at Blake, who is speaking with Eli, their heads bent together in conspiratorial whispers. I watch him, fascinated by the way his smile crinkles the corners of his eyes, the way he leans in, completely engaged. I can't help but feel grateful for his presence in my life, like a lucky charm that has made this journey not just bearable but beautiful. He catches me watching and sends a wink my way, a playful spark igniting a flutter in my chest.

"Want to grab a drink?" he asks, his tone casual, but there's an undercurrent of something deeper—a question wrapped in a half-smile. I nod, my heart racing with the thrill of possibility.

We step outside into the cool night air, the world transformed beneath a canopy of stars twinkling like diamonds scattered across velvet. The café behind us buzzes with the afterglow of the evening, but here, in the quiet of the night, it feels like we are the only two people in the universe. I can hear the soft rustle of leaves in the trees and the distant hum of traffic, but they fade into insignificance compared to the warmth radiating from Blake.

"So," he starts, his gaze fixed on the stars above, "what's next for you?"

I take a moment to gather my thoughts, staring up at the constellation of dreams hanging overhead. "I think I need to reflect a bit, gather my ideas for what comes next. There's so much I want to explore, but I also want to ensure that whatever I create next feels true to me."

He nods thoughtfully, his eyes still locked on the night sky. "That's a good approach. It's easy to get caught up in the pressure, but at the end of the day, your heart has to be in it."

I smile, feeling an undeniable connection between us, one that transcends mere words. "You're right. It's just... sometimes I fear that if I don't keep pushing, I'll miss out on opportunities. It's like a never-ending cycle of wanting more."

Blake turns to me, his expression earnest. "You have the talent, that's undeniable. But you also have to give yourself grace. The world isn't going anywhere, and neither are your dreams. They'll be waiting for you when you're ready."

His words wash over me like a soothing balm, and I take a deep breath, feeling lighter. The night feels full of potential, a whisper of adventures yet to come. "Thank you," I say softly, meeting his gaze. "Your support means everything to me."

Blake steps a little closer, the space between us narrowing as he leans against the wall, a relaxed posture that speaks of ease and comfort. "Always," he replies, and in that simple word, I feel a promise—a promise of support, of understanding, and perhaps of something more.

The air thickens with unsaid possibilities, and I find myself leaning closer, drawn in by the magnetic pull between us. The night stretches out before us like an uncharted path, shimmering with all the potential that lies ahead. As laughter drifts from the café and the stars twinkle above, I realize that whatever comes next, I won't have to face it alone. Together, we'll navigate the fabric of our dreams, stitching new patterns into the tapestry of our lives, one thread at a time.

The crisp night air carries with it the faint scent of rain-soaked asphalt mingling with the rich aroma of coffee and fresh pastries. As Blake and I step away from the café, the world outside feels vibrant and alive, the streetlights flickering like fireflies caught in a moment of hesitation. I can still hear the echoes of applause reverberating in my chest, a sweet reminder of the warmth that filled the café just moments ago. The sidewalks shimmer under the soft glow of the streetlights, casting a golden hue that transforms the mundane into something magical.

We wander slowly, allowing the exhilaration of the night to settle around us like a soft blanket. I steal glances at Blake, who walks beside me, his hands tucked casually into the pockets of his jacket. There's an ease about him that is infectious, drawing me closer to the warmth radiating from him, a subtle dance of energy that threads us together. Each step we take feels like a leap into the unknown, the vibrant city surrounding us filled with potential stories just waiting to unfold.

As we stroll through the streets, I can't help but reminisce about the journey that has brought me to this moment. The late nights hunched over fabric swatches, the countless cups of coffee that fueled my creative fire, and the moments of self-doubt that crept in, whispering insidious thoughts of inadequacy. But tonight, those shadows recede, pushed back by the brilliant light of validation that has shone through every heartfelt conversation and every sincere compliment.

"Do you want to walk to the river?" Blake suggests, breaking the comfortable silence that had enveloped us. His voice is low and smooth, wrapping around me like a familiar tune. "I hear the view is amazing at night, and I could use a little more of this atmosphere."

I nod enthusiastically, thrilled at the idea of sharing this moment with him. The riverbank, with its winding paths and the soft lapping of water against the shore, has always felt like a sanctuary to me. The city's pulse seems to ebb and flow with the currents, and I crave the peace it brings.

As we approach the water, the distant lights reflecting on the surface create a canvas of shimmering colors—yellows, blues, and soft whites dancing together in a hypnotic display. It feels almost surreal, as though we've stepped into a painting, and the world around us fades into a gentle hum. The air is cooler here, carrying the soft sounds of laughter and music from a nearby outdoor café.

"Look at that," I say, pointing to the bridge that arches gracefully over the river, its structure a mix of steel and artistry. "It's like the city's heartbeat. Every time I stand here, I feel like I'm part of something bigger."

Blake follows my gaze, his eyes reflecting the soft light. "I get that," he replies thoughtfully. "It's like each moment connects to the next, like a thread in a tapestry."

The words resonate with me, weaving into the very fabric of my thoughts. I glance at him, the way the shadows play across his features, highlighting the intensity of his expression. "You're an artist too," I murmur, realizing just how profound his insight is. "You see the world in a way that makes everything feel significant."

He chuckles softly, the sound rich and comforting. "I just try to appreciate the small things—like tonight, watching you on that stage. You brought your dreams to life. It was incredible."

The compliment washes over me, a warm wave that leaves me breathless. I can't help but smile, feeling the rush of pride swell within me again. "Thank you," I reply, the sincerity in my tone surprising even myself. "It's terrifying to put myself out there, but tonight... I felt like I finally belonged."

A moment stretches between us, a golden thread woven through the stillness of the night. The world feels heavy with unspoken words, and for a heartbeat, I wonder if this is the moment where we step into something deeper. My heart quickens, and I glance at him, his gaze locked on mine, steady and inviting.

Just then, the distant sound of a musician strumming a guitar floats through the air, soft notes cascading like water. "Let's sit by the river," Blake suggests, breaking the spell. We find a bench, worn but inviting, and settle in. The sound of the water mingling with the music creates an intimate ambiance, and I lean back, letting my eyes drift to the stars above, sparkling like the glittering fabric I so love to work with.

"So, what's your next dream?" he asks, turning toward me with genuine curiosity, the light catching the glint in his eyes. "Now that you've showcased your work, what's next on your horizon?"

I ponder for a moment, the weight of his question stirring something within me. "I want to push the boundaries of my designs. I've been thinking of exploring sustainable materials, perhaps integrating elements of nature into my fashion. There's something poetic about clothing that honors the earth."

Blake nods, his expression thoughtful. "That sounds incredible. It's like you're creating a dialogue between your art and the world around you."

"Yes! Exactly!" I reply, feeling my excitement bubble over. "I want my designs to evoke feelings of connection, not just to the wearers but to the environment too. Fashion shouldn't be disposable; it should be a celebration."

"Imagine a collection that flows like water, using fabrics that mimic the textures of nature," he muses, his eyes sparkling with inspiration. "You could create pieces that tell a story—each garment a chapter of a journey."

His vision intertwines with mine, and suddenly the possibilities seem endless, blooming in my mind like the petals of a flower unfolding to meet the sun. We share ideas, bouncing thoughts off each other like playful sparks, igniting a fire of creativity that feels intoxicating.

As we delve deeper into the conversation, I find myself lost in the rhythm of our exchange, the laughter, the ideas flowing freely between us, unfiltered and raw. The connection feels electric, an undeniable current binding us together in this moment of shared dreams.

Hours slip away unnoticed, and the world around us fades into the background, leaving just the two of us suspended in this cocoon of possibilities. I lean closer, our shoulders brushing together, the intimacy of the moment igniting a warmth that spreads through me.

Eventually, we fall into a comfortable silence, the sound of the water soothing and the night wrapping around us like a cozy blanket. I turn to Blake, my heart swelling with gratitude for his unwavering support and the way he seems to understand me in ways I didn't know I needed.

"I'm really glad you were there tonight," I say softly, the weight of my sincerity tangible in the cool air. "You make this journey feel less daunting."

Blake meets my gaze, and for a moment, the world around us disappears entirely. "You're stronger than you know," he replies, his voice steady, yet tender. "And I'll always be here to remind you of that."

The promise lingers between us, a shimmering thread woven into the fabric of the night, binding our dreams and aspirations into something beautifully intricate. As I sit beside him, the stars twinkling overhead, I can't help but feel that the night is just the beginning. The path before us stretches infinitely, each step we take together a stitch in a new story, waiting to be crafted.

Chapter 25: The Fabric of Love

The sun dipped low on the horizon, casting a warm golden hue over the city as I stepped out of my little studio, the faint scent of freshly sewn fabric still lingering on my hands. My showcase had been a whirlwind, a tapestry of colors and textures, each piece a fragment of my heart laid bare for anyone willing to see. The applause still echoed in my mind, a melody that danced alongside the vibrant fabric swatches scattered across my table, remnants of my labor, my dreams, and now, my potential future.

As I settled into my favorite coffee shop, a cozy nook adorned with mismatched furniture and the lingering aroma of roasted beans, my phone vibrated incessantly, pulling me from my thoughts. Each buzz sent a thrill coursing through me—a new message, another inquiry from local boutiques eager to carry my creations. The unexpected attention felt surreal, like waking from a dream to find the world had transformed overnight. I glanced around, the eclectic decor vibrant with life: a faded mural of a jazz musician, the laughter of friends mingling with the soft strumming of an acoustic guitar in the corner. In this familiar chaos, I felt a growing sense of pride and disbelief.

But beneath the surface of my burgeoning success lay something deeper, an undercurrent of emotion that twisted and turned, refusing to be ignored. Blake had been my steadfast companion throughout this journey, his quiet confidence and gentle encouragement lifting me when my doubts threatened to pull me under. Our late-night conversations had transformed from lighthearted banter into something more substantial, a shared intimacy woven from laughter and moments of vulnerability. I could feel it deep within my bones; my feelings for him had grown into something more complex, more beautiful than I had anticipated.

The evening air was crisp as we made our way to the rooftop restaurant, the city sprawling beneath us like a living canvas splattered with twinkling lights. The sounds of laughter and clinking glasses drifted up from the streets below, mixing with the gentle rustle of leaves in the breeze. I took a moment to breathe in the scene, my heart racing not just from the height but from the anticipation of what this night could hold. It felt like the perfect setting for a confession—a place where the world could slip away, leaving only us.

Blake was beside me, his presence grounding yet exhilarating. He wore that well-loved navy blue sweater I adored, its sleeves slightly rolled, revealing forearms that were somehow both strong and gentle. He turned to me, his eyes bright with mischief as he teased about the evening's menu, but beneath his playful demeanor, I sensed an awareness, a shared understanding that thrummed between us like an electric current.

As we settled into our seats, the waitress brought us two glasses of wine, the rich, velvety liquid glinting in the candlelight. I swirled mine thoughtfully, the scent of ripe cherries filling the air, reminiscent of warm summer nights. Conversations flowed effortlessly; we discussed everything from the latest trends in fashion to the future of my burgeoning brand. Yet, as the night deepened and the stars blinked to life, I felt a weight in my chest that begged to be released.

"Blake," I began, my voice trembling slightly as I met his gaze, the intensity of it almost overwhelming. The city lights flickered like stars caught in a web of dreams. "There's something I need to tell you."

He leaned forward, curiosity sparking in his eyes, his usual playful demeanor replaced by a serious softness. The world around us blurred as I took a deep breath, the moment hanging delicately in the air like the finest silk thread, taut with anticipation. "I think... no, I know that what I feel for you goes beyond friendship. You've been there for me in ways I didn't think anyone could. You believe in me, Blake, and I—" My heart raced, each word a step further into the unknown.

A flicker of surprise crossed his features, quickly replaced by a warmth that spread across his face, illuminating the shadows of doubt that had lingered in my heart. "You have no idea how long I've waited to hear you say that," he replied, his voice low and sincere. The admission rolled off his tongue like a gentle wave, washing away my anxiety.

His honesty caught me off guard, and for a brief moment, time stood still. It was as if the city itself held its breath, the bustling noise of the world fading into a soft hush. I searched his eyes, looking for any hint of hesitation, but instead found a depth of feeling that matched my own, a shared vulnerability that was as liberating as it was terrifying.

"I thought it was just me," he confessed, a slight chuckle escaping him as he rubbed the back of his neck, a familiar gesture of his when he felt shy or uncertain. "I didn't know if I should say anything, afraid it might ruin what we have. But... I can't help it. You make me want to be better, to push boundaries."

His words resonated within me, echoing the very sentiments that had tangled my thoughts for weeks. I felt a warmth blossom in my chest, spreading like sunlight on a chilly morning. The city lights sparkled below us, and in that moment, the world shrank down to just the two of us, woven together in a moment that felt both fragile and fierce.

With the weight of unspoken feelings lifted, the night transformed into something breathtaking—a beautiful tapestry of shared hopes and dreams, entwined like the threads of my designs. I raised my glass, the clink of crystal a joyful affirmation, a promise of new beginnings. As we sipped our wine, I realized that this wasn't just a celebration of my success; it was the beginning of something wondrous, a venture into a shared future, one that shimmered with possibility under the stars above.

As the evening progressed, the vibrancy of the city below mirrored the exuberance swelling within me. Blake's laughter, rich and genuine, danced through the air, and it was a sound I wanted to bottle up and carry with me everywhere. I watched him as he animatedly recounted a story about a mishap at his last job—something involving a poorly timed coffee spill and a high-profile client. The way his eyes sparkled with mischief was intoxicating, and I found myself hanging on every word, captivated not only by the tale itself but by the man who spun it.

The rooftop was adorned with twinkling fairy lights that flickered like fireflies, casting a gentle glow over our table. The ambiance was intimate, cocooning us in our own world, separate from the bustling city that pulsed beneath. Each flicker of light mirrored the rhythm of my heart, each beat synchronized with the delightful energy between us. I leaned forward, eager to catch every detail of his expressions, the way his lips curled into a smile that seemed to reach his very core.

"Can you believe it?" he exclaimed, his eyes wide with a blend of disbelief and amusement. "I nearly ruined a multi-million dollar deal because I couldn't manage a cup of coffee!" He laughed, and I joined him, our voices intertwining in the cool night air, as effortless as the breeze that swept through the rooftop garden.

I savored this moment, this connection, realizing how much I cherished our playful banter. With Blake, even the simplest of conversations felt layered, rich with meaning. As I observed him, I noticed how the city lights caught the flecks of gold in his brown eyes, enhancing the warmth that radiated from him. He had an uncanny ability to make everything feel brighter, more vivid.

As dessert arrived—a decadent slice of chocolate cake adorned with a single raspberry—I was struck by a sudden urge to create a memory worth savoring. "Let's make a pact," I suggested, my voice playful yet earnest. "No more hiding behind coffee spills and awkward jokes. Let's be honest with each other, even when it feels scary."

Blake paused, the laughter fading from his eyes as he considered my words. "You mean... like right now?" he asked, his tone shifting slightly, a hint of seriousness coloring the air between us.

"Exactly," I replied, my heart racing. "What do you want to say? What are you really feeling?"

He took a moment, his gaze drifting past me, lost in thought. The city stretched out like a vast tapestry of dreams, and I could see the flicker of contemplation cross his face. "I want you to know that you inspire me. Your creativity, your passion—it's infectious. Sometimes I find myself questioning if I'm doing enough, if I'm living up to my potential. But when I'm with you, I feel like anything is possible."

The sincerity in his voice wrapped around me like a warm blanket. My heart swelled, filled with a mix of joy and vulnerability. "You're more than enough, Blake. You've always been. And you make me want to chase my dreams harder, too."

For a moment, we simply held each other's gaze, the space between us charged with unspoken understanding. The rooftop around us buzzed with life—clinking glasses, laughter echoing, and the soft strumming of the guitar in the corner—but in that instant, we were the only two people in the world.

Then, with a sudden burst of courage, I reached across the table, my fingers brushing against his. It was a small gesture, yet it ignited a spark that sent electricity through my veins. Blake's eyes flickered down to our hands, then back to me, a hint of surprise mixed with delight dancing in his expression.

"Do you think..." I hesitated, the weight of my thoughts hanging in the air. "Do you think we could be something more? I mean, we're already so connected. Why not explore what's beyond this?"

He studied me for a moment, the corners of his lips twitching upwards in a soft smile. "You know, I've thought about that a lot. And I think it's more than worth exploring. I've just been waiting for the right moment to say it."

"Maybe this is it, then," I suggested, my heart racing with the thrill of possibility.

A slow grin spread across his face, and he leaned in closer, his voice dropping to a whisper that felt like it was meant only for me. "I've wanted to kiss you since the first day I met you. I just didn't know how to approach the most talented woman I've ever met without sounding like a fool."

The heat rushed to my cheeks, a combination of embarrassment and excitement. "Well, I suppose you're going to have to figure that out now."

Blake chuckled, the sound rich and genuine, before his expression turned serious again. "Are you sure about this? I don't want to ruin what we have."

"I'm sure," I replied, my voice steady despite the whirlwind of emotions swirling inside me. "If anything, I think it'll strengthen it. I don't want to walk away from this feeling we have, even if it's risky."

He nodded slowly, his gaze searching mine for any flicker of doubt. Finding none, he leaned forward, his breath warm against my skin as he closed the distance between us. Our lips met softly, a tentative exploration that quickly blossomed into something deeper, more urgent. The world around us faded away, and all that mattered was the sweetness of that first kiss, the mingling of our hopes and fears, our dreams weaving into something beautiful.

As we pulled away, breathless and wide-eyed, I could hardly contain the joy that bubbled within me. The city continued its symphony below, but up here, in our little haven, everything felt timeless. The warmth of his hand still enveloped mine, and I reveled in the exhilarating uncertainty of what lay ahead.

"See? Not so scary, right?" I teased, the thrill of our new connection sparking laughter between us once more.

"No," Blake replied, his grin infectious. "It feels just right."

And in that moment, amidst the backdrop of the city lights and the hum of life swirling around us, I knew that this was just the beginning—a tapestry of love and dreams unfolding, each thread carefully woven into the fabric of our lives, promising an adventure far more exciting than either of us had dared to imagine.

The night air enveloped us like a gentle embrace as Blake and I lingered on the rooftop, our world narrowing to the flickering candlelight and the pulse of the city below. Each heartbeat echoed the thrill of our new connection, an exhilarating venture into uncharted territory that left me giddy with possibility. The skyline, a jagged silhouette against the velvet sky, twinkled with the promise of endless adventures waiting to unfold, each building a monument to dreams realized and hopes yet to be explored.

As we leaned into each other, the warmth of his presence felt intoxicating. I studied his features in the dim light, tracing the outline of his jaw and the way his hair caught the breeze, tousling slightly as he moved. It was a small gesture, but the intimacy of it made my heart flutter. I could hardly believe how quickly everything had shifted; just days ago, I was a bundle of nerves, fretting over the success of my showcase and the burgeoning attention that had caught me off guard. Now, here we were, both vulnerable and eager, entangled in something undeniably profound.

Blake broke the silence first, his voice a low murmur as he looked out over the city. "You know, I used to dream about living in a place like this," he said, a hint of nostalgia lacing his words. "Somewhere

where the skyline sparkles at night, and the air is thick with possibility. It's beautiful, isn't it?"

I nodded, caught off guard by the wistfulness in his tone. "It really is. It feels like we're at the center of the universe right now, doesn't it? Like anything could happen."

His gaze flicked back to mine, a playful glint in his eyes. "Anything? So, are we going to start planning our world domination or just figure out what to do with all those boutiques clamoring for your designs?"

I laughed, a lighthearted sound that felt freeing in the moment. "Well, world domination might take a bit longer. But the boutiques... that's a real opportunity. I can't believe how quickly everything has changed."

Blake's expression shifted to one of seriousness as he leaned closer. "And what about us? Where do we fit into this new chapter of your life?"

The question hung in the air, a beautiful tension that made my heart race. I felt the gravity of the moment and the weight of the possibilities stretching before us. "I think," I began, carefully choosing my words, "that you're an integral part of this journey. I don't want to imagine going through it without you."

His smile widened, transforming the earlier tension into a warmth that wrapped around us like a soft blanket. "Then let's see where this goes. Together. No more hiding behind coffee spills or jokes."

As the night unfolded, we shared dreams and aspirations over dessert, my heart swelling with each revelation. I learned that Blake harbored ambitions of his own—an artist's heart bound by the confines of practicality. He longed to showcase his photography, to capture the world through his lens, but he had always held back, uncertain of where to begin.

"I've always been afraid of putting myself out there," he confessed, glancing away, almost shyly. "What if no one cares? What if they don't see the beauty I see?"

"Blake, you have an incredible eye," I urged, my voice filled with sincerity. "If you see beauty, there's bound to be someone else out there who will too. You should pursue it. I believe in you."

The sincerity in my words hung between us, and I could see the flicker of hope igniting in his eyes. We spent hours talking, mapping out our dreams like a couple of architects laying the foundation for a shared future. The candor we shared, the laughter that erupted with each new idea, knitted us closer together, forging a connection that felt indestructible.

Eventually, as the evening drew to a close, we rose from the table, the city still alive with the chatter of night. Our fingers brushed together, an innocent touch that sent a shiver up my spine. We made our way to the edge of the rooftop, where a soft breeze tousled my hair. The city spread out below us like a tapestry of lights, each glowing dot a life, a story, a dream.

"What do you think is out there for us?" Blake mused, his voice barely above a whisper.

I turned to him, searching his face for any sign of doubt. Instead, I found a steadfast determination that mirrored my own. "I think there's so much ahead of us. New challenges, opportunities, moments that will take our breath away."

Blake stepped closer, his shoulder brushing against mine, a comforting warmth. "Are you ready to dive in? To face whatever comes next?"

With a deep breath, I nodded. "Absolutely. With you by my side, I feel like I can conquer anything."

As the stars twinkled above, I felt an undeniable sense of unity, as if we were standing at the threshold of something monumental. The world around us was a blur, but here, in this moment, we were perfectly aligned. I leaned into him, feeling the steady rhythm of his heartbeat against my side, and it was as if we were two pieces of a puzzle, perfectly fit together, ready to embark on this journey side by side.

In the following weeks, the excitement of my newfound opportunities blossomed like the spring flowers beginning to peek through the last remnants of winter. The boutiques, drawn by my showcase, began to place orders, their enthusiasm fueling my creative fire. I spent long nights in my studio, surrounded by vibrant fabrics and the hum of my sewing machine, pouring my heart into each piece. Every stitch felt like a declaration of my newfound confidence, a testament to my journey from uncertainty to ambition.

Blake became my anchor during this whirlwind, offering not just emotional support but also practical insights drawn from his own experiences. He'd often join me in the studio, his camera slung casually over his shoulder, capturing the process as I worked. I watched him lose himself in the art of photography, the way he framed each shot with a keen eye for detail, turning mundane moments into something extraordinary. It was inspiring, and it spurred me to push my creative boundaries further.

One evening, as I draped fabric over a dress form, Blake set up his camera nearby. "Do you mind if I take some shots?" he asked, his eyes sparkling with excitement.

"Of course not! Just don't distract me too much," I teased, a playful smile dancing on my lips.

As he captured the fluid movements of my hands, the concentrated furrow of my brow, I felt a sense of liberation wash over me. I was free to create, free to explore, and in that space, I felt empowered—not just by the recognition from the boutiques, but by Blake's unwavering belief in me.

His photography evolved, too, blossoming as he immersed himself in the work, and before long, he started sharing his images on social media, garnering interest from local galleries. I watched in awe as his passion took flight, mirroring my own journey of transformation.

We were two souls intertwined in a dance of creativity, pushing each other toward our dreams, no longer hiding in the shadows of doubt. Together, we began to envision a future that seemed not only possible but tantalizingly within reach. Each day brought with it a new opportunity, a new challenge, and through it all, we stood side by side, forging ahead into the unknown.

As the seasons changed, so did our relationship. The initial spark of attraction evolved into a rich tapestry of trust and understanding, our bond deepening with every shared experience. The city continued to thrive around us, but we remained cocooned in our world, a haven built on mutual respect and unwavering support.

With each passing moment, I felt a profound gratitude for everything—the showcase that had opened doors, the boutiques that had taken a chance on my designs, and most importantly, Blake, whose presence felt like a lifeline in this ever-shifting landscape. As I looked to the future, I knew one thing for certain: whatever challenges awaited us, we would face them together, our hearts woven together like the very fabric I cherished.

Chapter 26: The Thread Unravels

In the heart of Manhattan, where skyscrapers pierced the heavens and the streets pulsed with an unrelenting rhythm, I stood at the precipice of my dreams—an amalgamation of hope and dread, glimmering like the glass facades around me. The air was thick with the scent of roasted chestnuts, mingling with the faint undertone of fresh fabric from the nearby boutiques. Each day had unfolded like a beautifully crafted garment, thread by thread, but now, a gaping tear threatened to unravel it all. I had poured my soul into this collection, each stitch a whisper of my vision, my passion. Yet, as I scrolled through my phone, the cruel fingers of reality snapped me back, revealing headlines that glared like neon signs on the bleakest of nights: "Local Designer Accused of Plagiarism!"

The words clawed at my heart, leaving deep, jagged wounds. The buzzing of the city around me faded into a distant hum as I stumbled away from the glaring screens, seeking refuge in a small café tucked away on a side street. The cozy space smelled of freshly brewed coffee and sweet pastries, a sanctuary from the relentless onslaught of accusations that had rapidly spread across social media. The barista, a cheerful soul with bright pink hair, offered me a warm smile and a cinnamon roll that almost made me forget the storm raging outside. Almost.

Sinking into a corner booth, I absently picked at the flaky pastry, its sweetness clashing with the bitter taste of betrayal on my tongue. Nora, once a mentor and friend, had transformed into a phantom of malice, orchestrating a campaign that painted me as a thief in the night. Each post I saw twisted my gut further, the malicious intent oozing from every pixel. I had trusted her, admired her, and now, it felt as though I were drowning in quicksand, every attempt to rise met with new accusations that dragged me deeper.

The café, once a comforting cocoon, morphed into a cage of despair. I watched patrons chatting animatedly, oblivious to the war being waged just outside these walls. I wished for the power to shout my truth from the rooftops, to reclaim my narrative, but the weight of my plight made it hard to breathe. My designs weren't mere fabric stitched together; they were a reflection of my journey, of my very essence.

As the sun dipped below the horizon, casting long shadows across the tables, Blake slid into the booth across from me, his expression a mixture of concern and determination. He radiated warmth, a lighthouse amidst the stormy sea that my life had become. The soft light from the café illuminated his sharp features, and for a moment, I felt the ground beneath me stabilize. "We'll get through this," he assured me, his voice a gentle caress against the fraying edges of my spirit.

But the rallying cry of the industry rang in my ears, a constant reminder of how swiftly love could turn to venom. "How?" I whispered, my voice barely rising above the clattering of cups and laughter that surrounded us. "Everyone believes her. They've made their minds up."

Blake leaned forward, his hands clasped, the heat radiating from him grounding me. "We fight back. We show them who you are—what your work means. We'll reach out to your supporters, your loyal clients, and we'll create a narrative of your truth." His eyes sparkled with resolve, igniting a flicker of hope deep within me, a tiny ember fighting against the oppressive shadows.

His words felt like a lifeline, but the shadows lingered, clawing at my resolve. It felt surreal, like I was stuck in some cruel twist of fate where my passion had been turned against me. Each design I had so lovingly crafted now felt tainted, each stitch a reminder of the chaos that threatened to consume me.

The following days morphed into a blur of interviews, calls with my lawyer, and meetings with my dwindling team. The outside world was ablaze with gossip and speculation, while I was trapped in a storm of my own making. I could feel the weight of the industry pressing down on me, a thousand eyes scrutinizing my every move. But in the midst of this turmoil, I found solace in Blake's unwavering support. He organized meetups with fellow designers who had faced similar tribulations, each sharing their stories of resilience and recovery. With every encounter, I began to stitch together my own narrative, weaving it into the fabric of my identity, refusing to let it be dictated by others.

One afternoon, we found ourselves in a sun-drenched studio, the walls adorned with sketches and fabric swatches. A friend of Blake's, a seasoned designer, listened intently as I recounted my story, her eyes sparking with understanding. "You're not just fighting for yourself," she reminded me, her voice laced with passion. "You're fighting for all the artists who've faced this. You have to show them the heart behind your designs."

Her words ignited a fire within me. I was not merely defending my work; I was standing for every artist who dared to dream, who had bared their soul only to have it trampled. In that moment, I realized that I would no longer cower in the shadows cast by Nora's deceit. Instead, I would step into the light, my heart pounding in rhythm with the city outside, the familiar hum of life slowly returning to me.

Together with Blake, we crafted a plan. We reached out to my loyal clientele, orchestrating a small pop-up event in Brooklyn, inviting everyone to experience my designs firsthand. It was more than just an exhibition; it was a declaration. I was ready to unveil not just my creations but the very soul behind them, the passion and heart that had fueled every stitch.

As the day of the event approached, the city buzzed with anticipation. I could feel the energy coursing through me, the sweet perfume of determination mingling with the anxious flutter of doubt. This was my moment, a chance to reclaim not only my narrative but the very essence of who I was as a designer. And with Blake by my side, I felt the strength to face whatever storm awaited.

The day of the pop-up dawned crisp and clear, sunlight spilling over the rooftops of Brooklyn like a painter's brush. The air was laced with the tantalizing scent of fresh bagels from the corner shop, the kind that beckons you to indulge with its warm, yeasty promise. I stepped out of the subway, my heart thrumming in my chest as the vibrant neighborhood unfolded before me. Graffiti-clad walls whispered stories of artists past, while colorful cafes buzzed with conversations, each voice a thread woven into the tapestry of this eclectic community.

I arrived at the venue, an unassuming warehouse that had been transformed into a canvas of creativity. My team, though small, bustled around with a fervor that ignited my own spirits. They hung the garments with meticulous care, creating a visual narrative that mirrored the tumult of my journey. Fabrics danced in the gentle breeze from the open windows, each piece alive with the energy of dreams and aspirations. It felt surreal, almost as if I were standing on the brink of a new beginning, every moment steeped in both hope and trepidation.

Blake arrived, his presence a soothing balm against the frenetic energy that threatened to overwhelm me. He wore a simple white shirt, the sleeves rolled up, revealing forearms that looked ready to dive into any task. His eyes, however, sparkled with mischief, a glimmer of shared excitement that cut through the tension. "You ready for this?" he asked, a playful grin tugging at the corners of his mouth.

I inhaled deeply, the smell of paint and fabric filling my lungs. "As ready as I'll ever be," I replied, attempting to match his enthusiasm, though doubt still clung to me like an unwelcome shadow.

The clock ticked on, and soon the first guests began to trickle in. A mix of familiar faces and curious strangers filled the room, laughter and chatter intertwining with the soft strains of music drifting through the air. Each smile, each word of encouragement, wrapped around me like a comforting quilt, mending the frayed edges of my confidence. My heart raced as I greeted everyone, the warmth of their support igniting a fire within me.

I watched as they moved through the space, fingers brushing against the fabrics, eyes lighting up with recognition and delight. It was a surreal experience, seeing my creations worn not just as clothes but as pieces of my story—my struggles, my joys, my very essence woven into every thread. With each compliment, the weight of Nora's accusations felt just a bit lighter, the cruel tide of public opinion shifting, if only slightly, in my favor.

Blake floated around the room, charming guests and ensuring that everyone felt welcomed. His laughter echoed, a sound so genuine it was contagious. As I caught snippets of conversations—"I love the craftsmanship," "This design is so unique"—a warmth spread through me, wrapping around my heart like a snug embrace.

Yet, in the corners of my mind, the shadows of doubt lurked, whispering insidious thoughts that threatened to invade this moment of joy. What if this was merely a fleeting spark, snuffed out the moment the media circus returned to their next scandal? The world could be capricious, and fashion was a fickle mistress. Just as quickly as it had elevated me, it could just as easily cast me aside.

But as the event unfolded, I chose to focus on the present. I caught a glimpse of a familiar face in the crowd—a fellow designer who had faced her own trials. She approached me, her eyes filled with understanding, and we exchanged a knowing glance. "Your work speaks volumes, you know. The authenticity shines through," she said, her voice steady, bolstering my resolve.

"Thank you," I managed to reply, my voice barely above a whisper, overwhelmed by her kindness. It was moments like these that reminded me why I loved this industry: not the glitz and glamour, but the connection with fellow artists who understood the sacrifices behind every piece created.

As the night deepened, conversations flowed like the wine poured generously from the bar. Laughter punctuated the air, mingling with the rhythm of my heartbeat, the pulsating energy of the event feeding my spirit. It was as if we were all united by an invisible thread, woven together by the fabric of creativity and shared experiences.

But then came the twist, the unwelcome reminder that I was not yet free. A figure emerged at the entrance, a shadow against the light—a reporter, clipboard in hand, eyes scanning the room with a sharpness that cut through the jovial atmosphere. My stomach dropped, a knot forming as I recognized the familiar face from the articles that had stained my reputation. They had come to uncover dirt, to turn this joyous occasion into a spectacle of scandal.

Blake must have sensed my distress because he appeared at my side, his presence a fortress against the encroaching storm. "Focus on the moment," he whispered, his voice low and steady. "You've got this."

With a deep breath, I nodded, pushing aside the anxiety that threatened to unravel everything I had fought for. I was not a victim; I was a creator, an artist, and I would not allow anyone to steal this moment from me.

As the crowd swelled, I made my way to the center of the room, my heart pounding like a drum echoing through a silent valley. With a microphone in hand, I spoke, my voice steady despite the tremor of uncertainty beneath. I shared my journey, the love that infused each design, the struggles that had shaped my path, and the community that had rallied around me.

"I'm here not just to showcase my work," I declared, my gaze sweeping across the crowd, taking in their eager faces. "I'm here to celebrate the beauty of creativity, the stories that bind us together, and the resilience of every artist who has faced adversity."

Applause erupted, a wave of sound washing over me, lifting my spirit higher. The warmth of support enveloped me, drowning out the fears that had threatened to pull me under. For that moment, I was not defined by scandal or betrayal; I was simply an artist, basking in the glow of connection and authenticity.

As the evening drew to a close, the reporter lingered, their presence still a reminder of the battle that lay ahead. But as I exchanged farewells with my guests, each hug and word of encouragement solidified the foundation I was rebuilding. Blake's hand found mine, and together we stepped out into the cool night, the air crisp and invigorating against our skin.

The city pulsed around us, a living entity full of promise and possibility. My heart soared with renewed hope, a vibrant tapestry of dreams unfurling before me. Whatever storm awaited, I was ready to face it—stronger, braver, and more determined than ever. Together, we would weave a new story, one threaded with resilience and unyielding spirit, reclaiming my narrative, one stitch at a time.

As we stepped into the cool night, the cacophony of the city enveloped us, vibrant and alive, almost mocking the stillness I'd felt earlier. The sky, a rich indigo canvas, twinkled with stars like scattered diamonds, and for the first time in days, I felt a glimmer of hope flicker within me. Blake walked closely beside me, our fingers intertwined, and as we navigated the thrumming streets, the palpable energy of Brooklyn thrummed in my veins, igniting a spark of determination. I realized that the heart of this industry beat not in the grand halls of high fashion but right here among the passionate souls who lived and breathed creativity, who understood the struggle to stay afloat amid a tempest of doubt.

We found ourselves drawn to a nearby rooftop bar, the kind that overlooked the East River, where the skyline shimmered like a mirage against the backdrop of the moonlit water. It was a small space, festooned with twinkling fairy lights and scattered with eclectic furniture—mismatched chairs and rustic wooden tables that echoed the charm of a bohemian hideaway. A DJ spun mellow tunes that mingled with the gentle clinking of glasses, creating an ambiance that felt both intimate and liberating.

Blake ordered us drinks, his usual confidence spilling over as he bantered with the bartender, who wore a shirt plastered with a graphic of a disco ball. I took a moment to breathe deeply, the sweet, crisp air filling my lungs and pushing out the remnants of tension. The vibrancy around me was intoxicating, each laugh and cheer a reminder that life persisted, even when storms raged on.

As the drinks arrived—two vibrant cocktails garnished with slices of citrus and sprigs of mint—Blake raised his glass. "To new beginnings," he declared, his eyes shining with mischief. I clinked my glass against his, feeling the chill of the glass juxtaposed against the warmth radiating from him. "And to resilience," I added, my heart swelling with the weight of shared triumphs and struggles.

With every sip, I could feel the layers of the day peeling away, revealing the core of who I was beneath the accusations and turmoil. The city stretched out before us, a living entity teeming with dreams and desires, and I found myself wondering if this was how artists throughout history felt—on the cusp of something extraordinary, their passions ignited in the glow of camaraderie.

As we settled into a cozy corner, laughter bubbled between us, a melody that felt familiar yet new, reminding me of all the times we'd shared our hopes and fears. "You know," Blake said, leaning back in his chair, his eyes dancing with a mix of mischief and sincerity, "you could always start your own fashion movement. Something that challenges the status quo. Take the industry by storm."

The thought hung in the air, tantalizing and terrifying. My mind swirled with possibilities. Could I really create something so disruptive that it would shift the narrative? I envisioned a collection that championed authenticity, embracing imperfections as strengths, allowing every piece to tell a story—a tapestry of voices woven together in vibrant colors and textures.

"What would that even look like?" I mused aloud, leaning forward, excitement bubbling within me. "Fashion as a statement of resilience, of truth."

"Exactly," he encouraged, his enthusiasm igniting my imagination. "Let the garments speak for themselves. Each piece could carry a message, a history, a memory."

As we chatted, our conversation meandering through ideas and inspirations, the bar began to fill with familiar faces from the industry—designers, models, and stylists, all intertwined in a fabric of creativity. My heart raced; these were the very individuals who could influence the tides of public opinion, the ones I needed to connect with.

Determined, I stood up, squeezing Blake's hand before making my way to the group. "Excuse me!" I called out, my voice strong despite the fluttering in my stomach. They turned, intrigued, and I introduced myself, my passion spilling forth like an overfilled cup.

"I know things have been tumultuous lately," I began, the sincerity in my voice palpable. "But I believe in the power of fashion to tell stories, to spark conversations that matter. I want to share that with you all."

What followed was a lively exchange of ideas, a whirlwind of creativity that reminded me of why I had fallen in love with this industry in the first place. We talked about sustainability, about inclusivity, about celebrating individuality rather than conforming to a single mold. Each idea felt like a thread, weaving us closer together, forming connections that would withstand the pressures of external chaos.

Blake hovered nearby, a proud smile playing on his lips as he watched me flourish. The drinks continued to flow, laughter mingling with the soft beat of the music, and I felt the burdens I had carried begin to lift. My heart beat in sync with the vibrant energy around us, and I reveled in the warmth of acceptance and camaraderie.

As the evening wore on, we exchanged contact information, promises of collaboration, and plans to meet again. I returned to Blake, exhilarated and slightly dazed. "I can't believe I did that," I exclaimed, the thrill of connection surging through me.

"You did it effortlessly," he replied, his admiration evident. "You've always had this spark, but tonight, it ignited a fire. You can change the narrative, you know."

With the night drawing to a close, we stepped outside, the cool air refreshing against our flushed skin. The streets hummed with life, the city glowing like a beacon of endless possibilities. As we wandered hand in hand, I glanced up at the stars, their twinkling light a reminder of the dreams that lay ahead, still waiting to be captured.

Just as we reached the subway station, a flicker of movement caught my eye—a flash of a familiar silhouette slipping through the crowd. My heart sank as I recognized Nora, her presence a dark cloud that threatened to shadow the joy I'd just experienced. She turned, catching my gaze, and for a brief moment, time stood still. I could see the tension etched in her features, her expression unreadable.

"What do you want?" I asked, my voice steady despite the rush of emotions flooding my veins.

She hesitated, her composure wavering. "I came to apologize," she finally said, the words hanging heavy in the air. "Things got out of hand. I didn't think it would go this far."

I felt the weight of those words, the irony cutting deeper than I cared to admit. "You tried to ruin my career," I replied, unable to mask the hurt lacing my voice.

"I know," she said, her eyes darting away as if she couldn't bear to meet my gaze. "But I realized—no one owns creativity. We're all just trying to find our place in this chaotic world."

Her admission hung between us, and I searched for the right words, grappling with the storm of emotions churning inside me. Forgiveness seemed both an impossible leap and an essential step toward liberation. "Then let's create something together," I suggested, surprising myself as the words tumbled out. "Something that showcases authenticity, that celebrates us as artists, rather than tearing each other down."

Nora looked taken aback, the surprise in her eyes morphing into something softer. "You would really do that?"

"Why not?" I shrugged, the weight of animosity gradually lifting. "This industry is big enough for all of us."

As the subway doors slid open, I felt a wave of resolution wash over me. The darkness of betrayal no longer had a hold on me; I had the power to redefine the narrative. With Blake at my side and a newfound understanding between us, I was ready to embark on this journey of reinvention—armed not just with creativity, but with compassion. The city beckoned, its streets alive with the promise of new beginnings, and I was determined to weave my story into the ever-evolving tapestry of fashion, one vibrant thread at a time.

Chapter 27: The Burden of Choice

The sun dipped low on the horizon, casting long shadows across the sunbaked streets of Santa Fe. The vibrant adobe buildings, their stucco walls kissed by years of fading sun, seemed to hum with an energy all their own. I walked slowly, each footfall echoing against the cobblestones, an orchestra of uncertainty playing in my mind. My fingers brushed against the cool, worn surfaces of the buildings, each touch grounding me as the weight of my choices loomed overhead like the darkening clouds threatening rain.

At a glance, the landscape might have appeared serene, a picturesque blend of rusty reds and earthy browns. But I felt the tension swirling around me, thick and electric, crackling in the air like the promise of an impending storm. I had spent countless hours pouring my heart into my designs, each thread and stitch a reflection of my soul. And now, those very creations were under siege, caught in a scandal that threatened to unravel everything I had built. The vibrant colors of the sunset matched the vivid turmoil within me, hues of passion tinged with fear.

Blake's voice lingered in my ears, urging me to take a stand, to speak out against the accusations that had been hurled my way. He believed in me with a fierceness that made my heart swell and my insecurities bubble over. Yet, his fervor felt like a double-edged sword, sharpening my resolve while also igniting the fear deep within me. What if I fought back and lost? What if the backlash was too great? The thought sent a shiver down my spine, as if the wind had turned suddenly cold, wrapping around me in an icy embrace.

As I wandered, my mind drifted to the gallery where my work was showcased, each piece a fragment of my journey. I could almost hear the whispers of admiration, punctuated by the occasional gasp of surprise as someone discovered the intricate stories woven into each design. But now those voices seemed distant, muffled by the cloud of doubt that hovered over me. The city's charm—the twinkling lights of the shops, the enticing aroma of roasted green chilies wafting through the air—felt like a cruel reminder of what I stood to lose.

Seeking refuge, I made my way to a small café nestled in a quiet corner, its charm rooted in mismatched furniture and the sound of laughter spilling out from the open windows. The scent of freshly brewed coffee enveloped me like a warm hug, inviting me to forget the turmoil, if only for a moment. I chose a worn table outside, the wood weathered and painted in a kaleidoscope of colors. It was here that I often met Emma, my confidante and fierce supporter.

Emma arrived moments later, her presence a beacon of light amid the shadows swirling in my mind. She carried with her the warmth of friendship, her laughter infectious, a salve for the chaos brewing in my heart. We exchanged pleasantries, but her sharp gaze quickly zeroed in on my downturned expression. "You look like you've been through the wringer," she said, her voice laced with concern as she settled into her chair.

"I feel like I'm standing on the edge of a cliff, Emma," I confessed, my voice barely above a whisper. "One wrong move and I could tumble into oblivion."

She reached across the table, her hand enveloping mine with a comforting squeeze. "You're stronger than you think," she said, her eyes bright with conviction. "This is just a moment, not your entire story."

As I stared into her eyes, I felt a flicker of hope igniting within me. Emma had always been the one to see the light in dark places, to remind me that authenticity was the cornerstone of true strength. Her words wrapped around me like a comforting blanket, coaxing me back to the surface of my thoughts.

"What if I just let my designs speak for themselves?" I pondered aloud, my mind racing with the possibility. "What if I don't engage with the scandal at all?"

"Then let them!" Emma replied, her enthusiasm bubbling over. "Your work is stunning. It tells a story that no one else can replicate. People will see that; they will feel that."

The weight of her words settled into my chest, mixing with the bubbling cauldron of emotions swirling inside me. Perhaps there was merit in letting my art shine without the noise of controversy drowning it out. Each piece I had crafted was a chapter of my journey, a manifestation of my essence. But the fear of inaction clawed at my insides, a sinister whisper reminding me that silence could be misconstrued as complicity.

As the sun began its descent, painting the sky in vibrant oranges and soft pinks, I felt the tension begin to ease, if only slightly. The warmth of the day lingered in the air, wrapping around me like an embrace, offering a fleeting sense of comfort. I looked out at the bustling streets, at the families enjoying their evenings, and I wondered if they too carried burdens of their own, hidden beneath the surface of their laughter.

"Maybe I could find a way to express my truth through my art," I said thoughtfully, the words taking shape like the colors swirling together in the sky. "What if I used this moment as fuel instead of letting it extinguish my flame?"

Emma's face lit up, her eyes sparkling with inspiration. "Exactly! Channel that energy into your work. Let it be your voice in this chaos."

In that moment, surrounded by the cacophony of life in Santa Fe, I realized that I was not just an artist; I was a storyteller, and my canvas was not limited to fabric and thread. Perhaps the choice was not between fighting or retreating but finding a way to weave my narrative into the fabric of this unfolding drama.

With the café's charm wrapping around me, I allowed my thoughts to drift into a world of possibilities, each thread weaving itself into a tapestry of hope and defiance. The chatter around me created a symphony of life, punctuated by laughter and the clinking of ceramic cups, underscoring the pulse of Santa Fe, the place I called home. The sunlight cast a warm glow on the tables, and I could almost see the colors of my designs dancing in the air like the laughter of children playing nearby.

In that moment, clarity washed over me. The world of fashion was more than just a competitive arena; it was an intricate dance, a living entity. I envisioned the fabrics I had lovingly selected, each one telling a story, each seam stitching together pieces of my identity. As I gazed out at the bustling street, I felt a surge of determination coursing through my veins. Instead of shying away from the scandal, I would embrace it—transform it into something that would illuminate the authenticity of my artistry.

The flickering neon of a nearby sign caught my eye, its vibrancy a stark contrast against the soft pastels of the sky. I could feel the thrill of creative energy bubble within me, igniting a fire I thought had been doused by doubt. Perhaps this was my moment to break free from the constraints that had been tightening around me, a chance to stand tall amidst the chaos and declare that I would not be defined by someone else's narrative.

"Emma," I said, my voice steadying with resolve. "I want to create a collection that reflects everything I'm feeling right now. I want to channel this uncertainty, this fear, and make it beautiful. I want people to see my heart in my work, to feel the weight of my story in every piece."

Her eyes sparkled with excitement, a reflection of the creative spirit that ignited between us. "That's it! A collection that embodies not just the designs but your journey. You could create something raw and honest, something that resonates with everyone who's ever felt lost or unsure."

The weight of her words settled into my bones, each syllable like a brick being laid in the foundation of a new path I was determined to forge. I envisioned a vibrant showcase, the gallery walls alive with color, textures, and the palpable energy of authenticity. Each garment would serve as a testament to my resilience—a declaration of who I was, not just as an artist but as a woman navigating the storms of life.

As the sun dipped below the horizon, painting the sky in shades of deep indigo and fiery orange, I felt a kinship with the fading day. Just as the sun must surrender to the night, I too had to let go of the fear that had been suffocating me. With every inhale, I drew in inspiration from the world around me, and with each exhale, I released the suffocating grip of anxiety. The stars began to twinkle above, bright and unyielding, reminding me that even in darkness, there is beauty.

Over the next few days, I immersed myself in this new vision, pulling fabrics that whispered promises of hope and authenticity. My studio became a sanctuary, a kaleidoscope of colors and textures swirling around me as I sketched and draped fabric over mannequins, allowing my emotions to guide my hands. The chaos outside felt distant as I lost myself in the rhythm of creation. Each stitch I made was infused with purpose, every choice echoing my desire to speak my truth through my art.

I sought inspiration from the very streets of Santa Fe, where art collided with culture in an exquisite dance. The vibrant murals painted across the walls of the buildings felt like a conversation, telling stories of struggle and triumph. I began to incorporate elements of these stories into my designs, utilizing patterns that spoke of the land's history, the resilience of its people, and the vibrant spirit that thrived amidst adversity.

The day of the showcase arrived, and I stood before my creations, my heart racing with anticipation and a tinge of fear. The gallery felt electric, alive with the chatter of attendees as they mingled among the pieces I had poured my soul into. Each garment hung like a testament to my journey—some pieces flowing elegantly, while others bore the raw edges of life's struggles. I had deliberately chosen to leave some seams visible, an artistic decision that conveyed the beauty of imperfection.

Blake stood by my side, his presence a steady anchor in the sea of uncertainty. He was a comforting shadow, his unwavering support shining through the noise of the crowd. "You've done something incredible here," he murmured, his gaze sweeping over the gallery. "You've turned vulnerability into art."

As guests began to mingle and touch the fabric, I felt a surge of pride swell within me. They marveled at the stories woven into each piece, their fingers tracing the lines and patterns, connecting with the emotion I had so painstakingly infused into my work. I watched as people's faces shifted from curiosity to awe, the realization dawning that they were not merely viewing clothing but experiencing the essence of someone's journey.

In the midst of this whirlwind, Emma approached, her eyes sparkling with excitement. "You've created something magical," she said, her voice bubbling over with enthusiasm. "Look at how they're responding! They see you."

And in that moment, I understood. My fear had transformed into strength, each piece a bridge connecting my story to theirs. As the night unfolded, I could feel the weight of the scandal beginning to lift. I realized that my authenticity was more powerful than any words I could have spoken. I didn't need to defend myself against whispers; my art was my shield, speaking louder than any controversy ever could.

Under the twinkling lights of the gallery, surrounded by the warmth of friendship and the encouragement of those who believed in me, I felt a profound sense of belonging. I was more than an artist; I was a storyteller, and my narrative was alive, vibrant, and unapologetically mine. The future still held uncertainties, but now, instead of a daunting abyss, it seemed like a canvas waiting to be filled with new adventures and dreams, a promise of all that was yet to come.

The night blossomed into a symphony of light and sound, the gallery vibrating with energy. I found myself caught in a whirlwind of emotions, the air thick with laughter, whispers, and the occasional clink of wine glasses. Each face reflected a flicker of intrigue, their gazes lingering on the garments that had emerged from the depths of my soul. It was as though I had birthed a new life, each piece standing proudly, eager to share its story.

A soft jazz tune floated through the air, weaving through the conversations and melding into the ambiance, a backdrop to the unfolding drama of the evening. I stood in the midst of it all, my heart thrumming in time with the rhythm of the music. A few guests approached, their eyes wide with appreciation as they ran their fingers along the delicate fabrics, feeling the weight of the narratives hidden within the seams. I couldn't help but smile, a mixture of pride and disbelief washing over me as I watched their reactions.

"Tell me about this one," a woman in a vibrant red dress asked, her voice smooth as silk. She pointed to a gown that draped elegantly from a mannequin, the fabric shimmering under the soft lights, mirroring the vibrant hues of a sunset. The design was a chaotic blend of color and form, reminiscent of the tumultuous emotions that had inspired it.

"It's called 'Unraveled,'" I replied, my voice steady despite the fluttering in my chest. "It's a reflection of the moments when everything feels out of control, yet somehow beautiful. The chaos is part of the story."

She nodded, her expression thoughtful as she took in the cascading layers, the intertwining threads that symbolized the interconnectedness of life's complexities. As I spoke, I felt the words flowing from me, a river of passion and conviction. The scandal felt distant, a mere backdrop to the vibrant reality I was now inhabiting.

Blake caught my eye from across the room, his expression a mixture of pride and admiration. He was surrounded by a small group, engaged in animated conversation, but his gaze remained anchored on me. I felt a rush of warmth flood my chest, a silent acknowledgment that this journey was not mine alone. He had been my rock through the storm, always there with a steady hand and unwavering support.

"Your art is captivating," another guest chimed in, pulling my attention back to the conversation. "It feels like you're inviting us into your mind, letting us glimpse the depths of your creativity."

"Thank you," I replied, my heart swelling with gratitude. "Each piece is an exploration of vulnerability, an invitation to connect through shared experiences."

As the evening progressed, I found myself wandering between conversations, soaking in the laughter and compliments that surrounded me like a warm blanket. I chatted with artists, fashion enthusiasts, and even a few critics, each interaction a thread weaving into the fabric of my night. I was no longer just the girl standing at the precipice of uncertainty; I was an artist, a storyteller, and I was reclaiming my narrative.

The room swelled with life as guests shared their own stories, each anecdote a reminder that everyone carries their own burdens, their own struggles cloaked in the everyday facade. I listened intently, nodding along, recognizing pieces of my own journey within theirs. It was in these moments that I felt the deepest connections forming—an invisible thread binding us through shared vulnerability.

"Let's grab a drink," Emma suggested, her eyes alight with excitement as she navigated through the crowd toward the bar. I followed, laughter bubbling between us as we reminisced about our own struggles, the times we had fought through the noise to find our true voices. It felt invigorating to share our experiences, to remind one another of the strength we possessed beneath the layers of doubt and fear.

As we reached the bar, I ordered a glass of crisp white wine, the coolness of the glass offering a refreshing contrast to the warmth enveloping me. Emma clinked her glass against mine, a silent toast to resilience and friendship. "You've turned this chaos into beauty, and I couldn't be prouder," she said, her sincerity shining through her words.

We stood together, watching the night unfold like the petals of a blooming flower, revealing new facets and surprises with every passing moment. I felt grounded by Emma's presence, her unwavering belief in me a beacon of light as the shadows of uncertainty began to recede.

However, as the evening wore on, I couldn't shake the creeping anxiety that had settled in my chest. It was a nagging reminder that the scandal still loomed, its specter lurking just outside the gallery doors, waiting for an opportunity to pounce. But tonight, I resolved to focus on what was tangible—my art, the connections I was forming, and the opportunity to share my journey with the world.

"Let's take a picture," Emma suggested, her phone already poised, ready to capture the essence of the evening. We stood in front of one of my pieces, the colors behind us a vivid backdrop. As she snapped the photo, I felt a sense of release, as if the click of the camera was sealing away the worries and fears that had plagued me for so long.

"Smile like you mean it!" she encouraged, and I couldn't help but laugh. As I flashed a genuine grin, I felt the weight of the world begin to lift, if only momentarily. Perhaps this was the beginning of something new—a rebirth of sorts, where I could emerge from the shadows of doubt and uncertainty, ready to embrace the future.

The evening drew to a close, guests lingering to discuss my work, their enthusiasm buoying my spirit. With each passing moment, I felt more empowered, more in control of my narrative. I had transformed my fears into art, woven them into the very fabric of my designs. The voices that had once threatened to drown me out were now nothing more than echoes in the background, faint and easily ignored.

As the last of the guests departed, Blake joined me, his hand finding mine, a silent promise of support. "You were incredible tonight," he said, his voice low and sincere, as we stepped outside into the cool evening air. The stars twinkled overhead, a million tiny lights illuminating the night sky, mirroring the hope igniting within me.

"Thank you for believing in me," I replied, squeezing his hand tighter. "This wouldn't have been possible without you."

He smiled, his eyes crinkling at the corners, and I knew then that whatever lay ahead, I wouldn't have to face it alone. Together, we would navigate the challenges that awaited us. The weight of the scandal felt less burdensome in that moment, as if the stars above were whispering promises of brighter days.

In that swirling tapestry of art, friendship, and newfound resilience, I found the strength to forge ahead. My designs were not just fabric; they were declarations of who I was, who I had become, and who I would continue to be. Each stitch, each color, held a piece of my journey, a reminder that I was more than the challenges I faced. I was an artist, a storyteller, and the narrative was mine to shape.

Chapter 28: Threads of Redemption

The afternoon sun spilled through the towering windows of my studio, casting a warm glow over the sea of fabric swatches strewn across the cutting table. Each bolt of material, ranging from the softest silks to rugged denims, told a story of its own, waiting to be woven into something extraordinary. I loved this chaotic sanctuary, where creativity danced in the air, mingling with the heady scent of jasmine from the potted plant perched precariously on the windowsill. Yet, the joy that usually accompanied my work had recently been dulled by a heavy cloud of doubt.

New York City hummed beneath me, a living, breathing organism that thrived on ambition and passion. I watched from my perch, a loft that teetered between art and disorder, as people spilled onto the streets like paint splashes across a canvas. The bustling crowd below was a constant reminder of the world outside, a world that felt increasingly hostile after the scandal had erupted. My heart raced with each headline that screamed betrayal and deceit, words I never thought would be used to describe me. I could almost hear the whispers of judgment wafting through the streets, wrapping around me like an invisible shroud.

Yet, amidst the turmoil, I clung to a flicker of hope. It was Blake's steady presence that grounded me, his unwavering belief in my vision a balm to my frayed nerves. He would often arrive with coffee in hand, his face a mix of concern and determination. "You can't let them take this away from you," he would say, his voice rich with conviction, as he leaned against the doorway, arms crossed, surveying the disarray of my sanctuary. There was something about his faith that felt like a lifeline, pulling me from the depths of despair.

It was on one such sun-drenched afternoon, with the sounds of the city filtering in through the windows, that the clarity I had been waiting for washed over me. I glanced at the chaos around me—dresses in various stages of completion, sketches scattered like fallen leaves—and I realized this was my voice, my truth. My designs were born from late-night musings and early-morning inspirations, each stitch a testament to my struggles and triumphs. I had to share that truth.

My fingers trembled slightly as I picked up my phone, the sleek device feeling foreign in my palm. With a deep breath, I began crafting a message to the media, baring my soul in a way I had never done before. I wrote about the emotions behind my work, the passion that drove each creation, and the deep-seated fears that had pushed me to the brink of despair. I revealed how the designs were not merely fabric and thread but threads of my very identity. The more I wrote, the lighter I felt, as if I were shedding layers of doubt with each keystroke.

When I hit send, a strange mix of exhilaration and terror coursed through me. I watched the clock on the wall, its ticking a constant reminder of the time slipping away. I could feel the anticipation thrumming in my veins, an electric buzz that urged me to step outside my comfort zone. Soon after, the responses began to trickle in—fellow designers, friends, and even strangers reached out, sharing words of encouragement that enveloped me like a warm embrace. Their support ignited a fire within, rekindling the passion that had felt stifled for too long.

Fueled by this newfound energy, Blake and I devised a counter-campaign. We would celebrate creativity, resilience, and the unyielding spirit of those who dared to dream. We plastered the walls of our studio with colorful posters proclaiming messages of hope and self-expression. Each corner transformed into a vivid tapestry of inspiration, with snippets of my journey and images of my designs interwoven into a cohesive narrative. I was not merely a victim of circumstance; I was a warrior, ready to reclaim my narrative.

On the day of our launch, the city felt alive with possibility. I stood in front of a crowd gathered outside my studio, the golden rays of the setting sun casting a halo around me. It was a moment suspended in time, the energy palpable as I prepared to share my truth. With Blake by my side, I took a deep breath and stepped forward, my voice steady as I recounted the tale of my creations—the late nights spent stitching away in solitude, the moments of vulnerability that had birthed each design, and the fear that had nearly consumed me.

As I spoke, I could see the faces in the crowd, their eyes glistening with understanding and empathy. It was a reminder that we are all woven together by our shared experiences—the struggles and triumphs that shape who we are. The applause that followed felt like an anthem, a celebration of resilience that surged through my veins.

For the first time in what felt like ages, I felt whole. I had transformed my pain into something beautiful, reclaiming my narrative with each word, each heartfelt sentiment. The journey was not merely about fashion anymore; it had evolved into something far greater—a testament to the power of truth and the strength that blooms from vulnerability. As the sun dipped below the horizon, casting a vibrant glow over the city, I knew I was ready to embrace whatever came next, armed with my truth and the unwavering support of those who believed in me.

The evening air was heavy with anticipation, each breath tinged with the promise of something remarkable. The crowd gathered around my studio, their faces illuminated by the soft glow of string lights overhead. It felt as if the entire city had turned out to bear witness, a patchwork of souls woven together by shared stories and unspoken dreams. I stood on the steps of my studio, heart racing like a wild stallion, ready to unfurl my truth into the world.

The applause that erupted felt like a tidal wave, sweeping over me, carrying me along on a current of hope and solidarity. I was no longer merely a designer; I had become a symbol of resilience, a living testament to the beauty that emerges from chaos. My hands shook slightly as I held the microphone, and I couldn't help but feel a rush of gratitude for everyone who had shown up to support me. It was a potent reminder of why I had poured my soul into my creations—each dress, each pattern was a piece of my heart, a fragment of my journey laid bare.

With Blake standing just behind me, radiating strength and encouragement, I began to speak. My voice, though initially quivering, grew steadier with each word. I talked about my earliest inspirations—the bright colors of my childhood home, the way the light filtered through the trees in Central Park, creating dapples of warmth and shadow on the ground. I described how every sketch was born from a moment of vulnerability, a glimpse into my insecurities, and my deepest desires to connect with others through the fabric I created.

As I spoke, I noticed familiar faces in the crowd—friends I had known for years, fellow designers who had once been competitors but had now become allies. They nodded along, their expressions a mirror of understanding, as if each of them was recalling their own struggles and triumphs. I could see the emotion reflected in their eyes, a gentle reminder that we all shared this vast tapestry of human experience, woven together by threads of joy, pain, and an unyielding desire to create.

The more I shared, the more liberated I felt. The burdens I had carried were beginning to lift, making room for the exhilarating freedom that came from owning my narrative. It was a bizarre contrast—the earlier weeks of despair had morphed into this incandescent moment of revelation, where every shadow I had faced became a stepping stone toward the light. With every story I recounted, I felt the atmosphere shift, charged with the electricity of authenticity and hope.

I could see a few journalists capturing every word, their cameras clicking like the heartbeat of the crowd, but instead of feeling the familiar tightening in my chest, I embraced the attention. This was my moment to reclaim not just my career but my spirit. As I glanced at Blake, a swell of gratitude washed over me. He had been my rock, my shield against the storm, and now he stood beside me, a steadfast reminder that vulnerability could be a strength rather than a weakness.

As the last echoes of my voice faded into the twilight, I opened the floor for questions. A woman in the front raised her hand, her eyes bright with curiosity. "How do you overcome self-doubt?" she asked, her voice steady yet tender. The question hung in the air like a delicate thread, and I could feel the weight of it settle upon my shoulders. It was one I had grappled with more times than I cared to admit.

"I remind myself that doubt is just part of the process," I replied, my heart racing as I searched for the right words. "Every creative journey is fraught with challenges. It's in those moments of uncertainty that we find our true voice. I learned that allowing myself to be vulnerable is actually a superpower." The crowd erupted in applause, and I realized the catharsis wasn't just mine; it was shared.

The evening continued to unfold like the pages of a long-awaited novel. Conversations sparked around me, a lively exchange of ideas and support. Designers began to connect, exchanging business cards and stories, and I felt the warmth of a community rising from the ashes of previous rivalries. This was what I had yearned for—a sense of belonging, a tribe that celebrated not just success but the struggles that paved the way for it.

As night draped its velvet cloak over the city, I caught a glimpse of myself in the glass reflection of the studio window. I looked different; the shadows that had once clouded my spirit were replaced by a radiant glow, a flicker of determination dancing in my eyes. The person staring back was a woman transformed—a designer who had reclaimed her voice and her vision.

The studio became a sanctuary of creativity that evening. Artists began brainstorming ideas for collaborative projects, their enthusiasm infectious. We shared laughter and exchanged stories about our journeys, discovering common threads in our experiences. I could feel the energy humming around us, a collective heartbeat of inspiration that was intoxicating.

Blake leaned closer, his voice low and conspiratorial. "We should plan a showcase—an event that highlights the power of community and creativity." His eyes sparkled with excitement, and I couldn't help but grin at the prospect. The idea felt like a natural progression, a chance to celebrate not just my journey but the journeys of others who had fought their battles, each of us unique yet united by our passion for design.

"Absolutely," I replied, my heart swelling with anticipation. "Let's bring everyone together and create something magical." As we exchanged ideas and sketched plans for the showcase, I realized this was just the beginning. I had stepped into a new chapter, one where my vulnerabilities transformed into strengths, illuminating the path forward.

The crowd began to disperse, but the night lingered, a tapestry woven with connections and revelations. I felt a profound sense of gratitude for the journey, every twist and turn leading me to this vibrant moment. As I turned off the studio lights, the glow of the city outside seemed to pulse with promise. Tomorrow would bring new challenges, but I was ready to face them, not as a solitary figure but as part of a larger narrative that celebrated resilience, creativity, and the undeniable power of truth.

The aftermath of our event unfurled like a masterpiece being unveiled. The city seemed to breathe a collective sigh of relief, its pulse quickening with the warmth of newfound connections. A sense of community enveloped me, and I reveled in the idea that I wasn't just a designer anymore—I was part of a vibrant tapestry woven with countless stories, each thread representing the struggles and triumphs of those around me. The exhilarating hum of collaboration crackled in the air, a symphony of creativity that filled every corner of my studio.

As days morphed into weeks, the preparations for our showcase began in earnest. Blake and I, fueled by the adrenaline of success and a shared vision, dove into the logistics. We transformed my once-chaotic workspace into a hub of activity, filled with laughter, sketches, and a myriad of materials—shimmering silks, bold prints, and textures that beckoned to be touched. Each piece was a testament to the journey that had led me here, a celebration not just of my own story but of the voices that echoed within my newfound community.

Amidst this whirlwind, I found solace in my rituals. Mornings were spent in quiet reflection, with steaming cups of herbal tea cradled in my hands, allowing the aromatic notes to seep into my very being. I would sit by the window, watching the city awaken beneath the soft glow of dawn. The streets transformed as sunlight spilled across the pavement, casting long shadows that danced with the first stirrings of life. This serenity was a stark contrast to the vibrant chaos that would soon engulf my day, yet it nourished the creative fire within me, grounding me as I prepared to take on the world.

Blake often joined me, bringing a sense of calm to my frenetic energy. He had an uncanny ability to coax out the beauty in the mundane, reminding me to breathe and appreciate the little things—like the way the light caught the edges of the fabric or how the sound of a street musician could lift even the heaviest of spirits. Together, we explored the city, seeking inspiration in the places where our dreams intersected with reality. From the bustling markets of Chelsea to the quaint corners of Greenwich Village, each encounter filled our minds with possibilities, sparking ideas that flowed effortlessly onto the pages of our sketchbooks.

With the date of our showcase fast approaching, a palpable excitement thrummed in the air. Our small team—an eclectic mix of artists and designers—worked tirelessly, each person infusing their unique flair into the collaborative pieces. I watched in awe as creativity unfolded before my eyes, each stitch and seam a reflection of the diverse backgrounds that came together in that sacred space. We became a family, bound not by blood but by the shared understanding of our struggles and the beauty that emerged from them.

The showcase itself blossomed into an event that transcended fashion, transforming into a celebration of resilience and connection. We adorned the walls with photographs, not just of the designs but of the people behind them, their smiles radiant against the backdrop of their stories. Each outfit walked the runway not just as a piece of clothing but as a chapter in the lives of those who wore them, tales of hope and perseverance that echoed through the fabric.

On the night of the showcase, the atmosphere pulsed with electricity. A kaleidoscope of emotions mingled in the air—nervous anticipation, joyful celebration, and a fierce sense of pride. As the lights dimmed and the first model stepped onto the runway, I felt my heart leap into my throat. The applause erupted like thunder, a wave of sound crashing over me, reverberating with every heartbeat.

As the designs twirled and flowed down the catwalk, I couldn't help but reflect on the journey that had brought me to this moment. The gowns, the textures, the colors—all spoke of the struggles I had faced, each stitch holding the weight of doubt and fear. Yet, here they were, transformed into art that shimmered under the stage lights, a vivid testament to my evolution. I stood backstage, my heart swelling with gratitude as I watched my creations come to life.

When the final model took her turn, draped in a breathtaking gown that cascaded like liquid gold, the crowd erupted into cheers, their applause echoing like a heartbeat through the venue. I could feel the warmth of their support wrap around me like a comforting embrace, and in that moment, I realized I was no longer alone in my journey. The applause was not just for my designs; it was for every person in that room who had faced their own battles and emerged stronger on the other side.

The afterparty unfolded like a scene from a fairytale. Laughter filled the air, conversations flowed easily, and every corner of the venue glimmered with joy. Friends, family, and even strangers mingled, sharing their own stories of resilience and creativity. I wandered through the crowd, soaking in the vibrant energy that pulsed through the space, every smile a reminder of the connections we had forged.

Blake found me in the midst of the celebration, his eyes alight with pride. "You did it," he said, his voice filled with a mix of awe and admiration. "You turned your pain into something beautiful." His words struck a chord deep within me, and I realized how far I had come. The shadows that had once loomed over me were now merely echoes of a past I had transformed into strength.

As the night wore on, I took a moment to step outside, needing to breathe in the crisp night air. The city sparkled beneath the stars, a tapestry of lights twinkling in rhythm with the heartbeat of dreams. I leaned against the cool brick of the building, allowing the energy of the evening to wash over me like a warm tide. It was in this moment of stillness that I fully embraced the enormity of what had happened—the transformation that had taken place not only in my career but within my soul.

I felt a hand on my shoulder, and when I turned, it was one of the models from the showcase, a young woman whose journey mirrored my own. "Thank you for believing in us," she said, her voice laced with emotion. "You've shown us that vulnerability is our greatest strength."

Her words resonated deeply, echoing the very essence of what I had learned. I realized then that the showcase was not just about me; it was a celebration of every story, every struggle, every victory shared within that room. We were all threads in a greater tapestry, and together we were weaving a narrative of resilience and creativity that would inspire others.

As I reentered the warmth of the venue, I was met with smiles and embraces, a sense of belonging that enveloped me like a favorite blanket. I was no longer defined by the shadows of doubt; I was illuminated by the light of possibility and connection. The future stretched out before me, a canvas waiting to be painted with new dreams and adventures, and I was ready to step boldly into it, armed with the lessons of the past and the unyielding support of my newfound family.

The journey was far from over, but with every step I took, I felt the threads of my story intertwining with those around me, a testament to the power of truth and the unbreakable bonds that had formed along the way. Together, we would continue to create, inspire, and celebrate the beauty of vulnerability—a legacy that would echo through the fabric of our lives for years to come.

Chapter 29: The Final Stitch

The warm glow of the late afternoon sun streamed through the expansive windows of my studio, casting a golden hue over the swathes of fabric draped across my workspace. Each piece whispered stories of their own—silks that fluttered like the gentle breeze on a summer day, cottons sturdy yet soft like an embrace from a long-lost friend, and bold prints that shouted defiance against the mundane. This was my sanctuary, a little universe nestled within the bustling heart of Chicago, where the noise of the city faded into a distant hum, and the only sounds that filled the air were the rhythmic snip of scissors and the soft thud of fabric hitting the floor.

Blake stood across from me, a dapper figure in his tailored shirt, sleeves rolled up to reveal forearms that bore the marks of our creative struggles. He was the perfect blend of patience and passion, always ready to share an idea or offer a critique that stung just enough to ignite a fire in my belly. As I adjusted the pattern of a flowing dress, I caught his eye, and a spark of encouragement flickered between us. He had a way of making me believe in myself even when the weight of self-doubt threatened to suffocate my spirit.

"Can you imagine the look on their faces?" he mused, a grin spreading across his face like sunshine breaking through a clouded sky. "When they see the colors—vivid reds, soft pastels—each piece telling a part of your story."

I paused, fingers hovering over the fabric, contemplating his words. The collection wasn't just about showcasing my skills as a designer; it was a canvas for my heart, painted with the vibrant strokes of love, loss, and renewal. The memories of last winter still haunted me, like shadows lurking at the edges of a sunlit room, but now those shadows had begun to dissolve, giving way to a brightness I had almost forgotten existed.

With renewed vigor, I pulled the fabric tighter, imagining it billowing in the wind, a testament to the resilience I had cultivated through each sleepless night and tear-streaked day. The runway was no longer just a platform; it was a stage where I would finally reveal not only my work but the essence of who I had become.

As the days bled into each other, our studio transformed into a whirlwind of activity, every corner cluttered with sketches, fabrics, and an array of design tools. I became a creature of habit, pouring over every detail with relentless determination, guided by the intoxicating blend of excitement and anxiety that fluttered in my stomach. Each piece evolved under my hands, stitched together with threads of hope, anticipation, and a healthy dash of fear.

Amid the chaos, Blake became my anchor. He was there through the late nights, providing snacks and coffee that often turned cold before I could take a sip. He would play music that filled the room with a pulsating energy, each beat syncing with my heartbeat as I lost myself in the creative process. In those moments, when we worked side by side, I felt an unspoken connection growing between us, a tether woven from shared dreams and late-night confessions.

"Do you ever wonder what it would be like to see your designs on someone walking down Michigan Avenue?" he asked one afternoon, as we took a rare break from our relentless work. The studio was filled with sunlight, casting playful shadows that danced across the floor.

I leaned back, allowing myself to dream. "I do," I replied, my voice barely above a whisper. "To see someone wear something I created... it would be surreal."

Blake nodded, his expression contemplative. "It's not just about the clothes. It's about the person wearing them, how they feel in that moment." His gaze met mine, and in that fleeting moment, I understood the depth of his passion.

As the showcase approached, our bond deepened, forged in the fires of creativity and camaraderie. We spent hours discussing color palettes, shapes, and fabrics, each conversation peeling back layers of our personalities. I learned about his family, his struggles, and his aspirations beyond the world of fashion. He spoke of his dreams with a fervor that ignited something within me. I, in turn, shared my insecurities and the moments that had led me to this crossroads in my life.

The night of the Spring Fashion Showcase arrived like a thunderstorm rolling in, charged with electricity and a hint of uncertainty. Backstage was a cacophony of laughter, shouts, and hurried movements as models slipped into garments that I had painstakingly crafted. I could feel the adrenaline coursing through my veins, propelling me forward as I flitted between fittings and last-minute adjustments.

As I stood in the shadows, watching the first model step onto the runway, a rush of emotion swept over me. Each step she took echoed the heartbeat of my journey—the struggles, the victories, and the unyielding desire to rise above it all. The audience gasped, their faces illuminated by the flashing lights of the cameras, and I felt a swell of pride, mingled with vulnerability.

This was my moment, the culmination of my efforts, and as the models continued to walk, each showcasing a piece that reflected a fragment of my heart, I realized I was no longer just a designer. I was a storyteller, weaving tales of resilience and hope through fabric and thread, each stitch binding my past with my present.

And as Blake's proud smile met my gaze from across the chaos, I knew I wasn't alone in this. Together, we had crafted something beautiful, not just for the world to see, but for us to cherish, a testament to the journey we had embarked on together. The lights dimmed, the applause swelled, and I felt the tide turning, not just for my career, but for my heart, finally ready to embrace the next chapter.

The atmosphere backstage was electric, charged with a symphony of laughter and the scuttling of heels on polished floors, punctuated by the occasional shout of encouragement. I found myself caught in a whirlwind of activity, watching as models flitted about, their skin aglow under the harsh lights. The air smelled of hairspray and fresh linen, a heady mix that made me dizzy with anticipation. Each model, adorned in the pieces that had been birthed from sleepless nights and countless revisions, was like a canvas waiting to be unveiled to the world.

Blake stood beside me, his eyes sparkling with excitement, like a child on the cusp of Christmas morning. He adjusted the collar of a delicate blouse, ensuring it framed the model's neck perfectly. I admired his attention to detail; it was a quality I often wished I possessed. As he tucked a stray strand of hair behind his ear, I couldn't help but smile at the familiar gesture that had become a sweet, unspoken rhythm between us. It was in these little moments, shared amidst the chaos, that I felt a warmth blossom in my chest, a feeling that had grown from mere admiration into something deeper, richer.

As the first model stepped onto the runway, my breath caught in my throat. She wore a flowing dress of soft lavender, the fabric catching the light like a morning dew. Each step was a heartbeat, pulsing with the energy of the audience, who leaned forward in their seats, mesmerized. My heart raced alongside her, each movement of the fabric a testament to the countless hours spent perfecting the silhouette, the drape, and the delicate stitching that held it all together. The applause that followed felt like an electric wave, crashing against my chest, filling me with a heady mixture of pride and disbelief.

In those moments, time stood still. I watched as the models graced the runway, each piece unfolding like a chapter of a book I had long yearned to share. There was a deep emerald gown that hugged the body like a lover's embrace, the fabric whispering promises of elegance and allure. A fiery red ensemble burst forth next, radiating confidence, each seam a declaration of strength. I felt like a painter standing before a canvas, witnessing the strokes of my brush come to life, each color resonating with emotions I had poured into every design.

As the show progressed, I caught glimpses of familiar faces in the audience—friends, mentors, and a few who had doubted my talent. Their expressions shifted from curiosity to awe, and I couldn't help but revel in the feeling of vindication. I had poured not just my skill but my soul into this collection, transforming pain into beauty, loss into triumph. Each garment was imbued with a spirit that told my story, a narrative of resilience woven through the seams.

With each model that stepped onto the stage, the audience grew more animated, their applause morphing into a chorus of appreciation that filled the grand hall. I exchanged glances with Blake, whose eyes shone with pride, as if we were sharing a secret language only we understood. It was in these fleeting moments of connection that I felt the unmistakable bond between us deepen. He had become my partner in every sense, supporting me through the darkest storms, and now celebrating with me in the light.

As the final model glided down the runway, draped in a cascading gown of midnight blue, I could feel my heart swell. The fabric shimmered as if it were woven from stars, the perfect metaphor for the journey that had led me to this moment. The audience erupted into applause, their cheers a rapturous tidal wave that washed over me, drowning out my insecurities and fears. I glanced at Blake, who was beaming with uncontainable joy, and in that instant, I felt a sense of belonging that anchored me amidst the whirlwind.

When the last model took her final turn, she raised her arms in triumph, as if embracing the world, and the audience rose to their feet, a standing ovation that reverberated through the hall like a heartbeat. I stood in the shadows, overwhelmed by the sheer magnitude of it all. My vision blurred, and I blinked back tears, my heart soaring with gratitude. It wasn't just about the clothes; it was the stories they carried—the pain transformed into art, the struggles woven into the very fabric of each piece.

Blake caught my eye again, his expression a mixture of admiration and something deeper—an understanding that transcended words. As the applause continued to echo, I knew this moment was just the beginning. I stepped into the spotlight, feeling the warmth of the lights envelop me like a long-lost hug. The audience's faces were a blur, but their energy wrapped around me like a soft cocoon, granting me the strength to embrace the moment fully.

With a deep breath, I raised my arms in acknowledgment, letting the audience see the pride I felt not just for my designs but for everything I had endured to get here. Each clap resonated with the weight of my journey, and I wanted to savor it.

When I finally descended from the runway, Blake was waiting for me, his arms open wide, ready to catch me as if he knew I might collapse under the weight of my emotions. I fell into his embrace, the warmth of his body grounding me. "You did it," he whispered, and I could hear the smile in his voice, the unyielding support that had been my compass throughout this whirlwind.

"I couldn't have done it without you," I replied, my voice muffled against his shoulder.

The world around us faded away, leaving only the two of us, enveloped in the aftermath of triumph and the soft glow of a new beginning. As the lights dimmed and the crowd began to disperse, I knew this moment would be etched into my memory forever. This was not just a showcase; it was a declaration of who I was becoming. A designer, a storyteller, and, perhaps most importantly, a woman ready to embrace the vast, beautiful, and unpredictable journey ahead.

The backstage atmosphere buzzed with an electric energy that felt palpable, almost like a living entity dancing around us. The sounds of laughter mingled with the rhythmic pulse of music that seeped through the walls, each beat reverberating in time with my own racing heart. As the last of the models made their way off the runway, the room erupted into jubilant chaos, an explosion of color and sound, as people celebrated the culmination of what had felt like a marathon of creative expression.

With the euphoria of the showcase still coursing through my veins, I slipped away from the crowds, seeking a moment of quiet reflection. The hallway leading to the outside terrace was dimly lit, adorned with heavy velvet drapes and mirrored walls that seemed to whisper the secrets of the night. I leaned against the cool surface of the glass railing, my eyes wandering over the cityscape spread before me—Chicago, with its towering skyscrapers glinting like gemstones against the deepening twilight, felt alive and vast, a tapestry of dreams and ambitions unfurling beneath my feet.

"Are you ready for the next step?" Blake's voice broke through my reverie, a melodic sound that resonated with both warmth and sincerity. He joined me at the railing, the soft breeze tousling his hair. The mingled scent of the city—street food, fresh rain, and a hint of gasoline—washed over us, grounding me in the reality of the moment.

"I think so," I replied, feeling the weight of those words settle comfortably in my chest. "This is just the beginning, isn't it?"

His gaze held mine, steady and reassuring. "It is. We've created something beautiful together. Now it's time to let it breathe, to see where it leads us."

The way he spoke about our work felt as if he were referencing a living entity, one that we had nurtured from a fragile seed into something vibrant and real. I was no longer just a designer but a curator of experiences, crafting pieces that resonated with the stories we all carry—struggles, joys, and everything in between.

The night felt ripe with potential, a canvas waiting for the brushstrokes of our dreams. It was then that I realized this collection was not merely a reflection of my journey but a roadmap, a testament to the resilience that had become my lifeblood. It was a collection woven with threads of love and heartache, every piece a silent scream of liberation.

As we stepped back inside, the atmosphere had transformed, the initial frenzy settling into a jubilant celebration. Friends and family mingled, their laughter like a soundtrack to the evening. I spotted my parents across the room, their faces glowing with pride, a sight that filled my heart to the brim. I navigated through the throng of bodies, finally reaching them.

"Mom, Dad!" I exclaimed, embracing them both tightly. Their warmth enveloped me, and I felt anchored by their unconditional support.

"Your designs were breathtaking," my mother said, her eyes shimmering with unshed tears. "You've truly outdone yourself."

"Thank you," I murmured, feeling the flush of gratitude wash over me. "I couldn't have done it without all the love and encouragement you've always given me."

Dad clapped me on the back, his presence a comforting pillar. "You've always had it in you, sweetheart. We knew you'd shine."

With every shared laugh and word of affirmation, I felt the threads of my past weaving into the fabric of my present, solidifying the foundation upon which I would build my future. The joy of the night swelled within me, filling the empty spaces that had once felt so cavernous.

As the evening wore on, I found myself drawn back to Blake, who had been mingling with guests, his charm and charisma effortlessly drawing people in. He was in his element, animatedly discussing the intricacies of fabric and design with a group of aspiring designers, their eyes wide with admiration.

I admired him from afar, his passion palpable, and a surge of affection flooded through me. It was more than admiration; it was a recognition of the journey we had undertaken together, the late nights and endless brainstorming sessions, the laughter and the occasional frustration. I had grown not just as a designer but as a person alongside him, learning the importance of vulnerability, creativity, and trust.

When he noticed me standing by, a smile broke across his face, illuminating the room more than the overhead lights ever could. "Hey there, runway star! Come join us," he beckoned, his voice laced with warmth.

As I approached, the energy shifted. The group welcomed me into their circle, and soon we were swept into a lively discussion about fashion, the industry's trends, and where it might be heading. I realized how far I had come; the girl who had once hesitated to voice her opinions now stood confidently among others, her voice steady and sure.

"Your collection has such a story behind it," a young designer said, her enthusiasm infectious. "I could feel it in every piece. How did you come up with the concepts?"

I opened my mouth to share my journey—the inspiration drawn from personal experiences, the trials that had forged my creativity into a weapon of empowerment. But as I spoke, I felt a deeper truth bubbling beneath the surface. "It's more than just fashion. It's about connection, about sharing a part of yourself with the world," I said, my heart racing with each word. "In every stitch, there's a piece of my story, my heart. And I believe that resonates with people."

Their faces lit up, a collective understanding passing among them, a silent acknowledgment that we were all part of this intricate web of shared experiences. As we exchanged ideas and visions, I felt a camaraderie forming, one that celebrated our individuality while recognizing the collective journey we all undertook as artists.

As the evening reached its zenith, laughter rang out like bells, the clinking of glasses creating a rhythm that punctuated our conversations. I glanced around the room, taking in the joyful faces, the bright lights, and the tapestry of colors. It was a celebration of creativity, resilience, and above all, love—the love for our craft, for the people who had supported us, and for the stories that would continue to unfold.

Eventually, as the night began to wane, I found myself stepping outside onto the terrace once more, breathing in the crisp night air. The stars twinkled above like scattered diamonds, a stark contrast to the chaotic beauty of the city below. I felt a soft presence beside me, and it was Blake, his gaze following mine as we both took in the breathtaking view.

"Tonight was incredible," he said softly, his voice barely above a whisper, as if afraid to disturb the magic of the moment.

"It truly was," I replied, feeling a rush of emotion swell within me. "I can't believe how far we've come."

Blake turned to face me, the light of the moon casting gentle shadows across his face. "And this is just the beginning. We have so much more to create, to explore. Are you ready for that?"

I nodded, an unshakeable sense of resolve blossoming within me. "More than ever. I want to continue telling stories—our stories—through fashion."

With those words, I felt a weight lift, replaced by a buoyancy that filled my spirit. The future stretched out before us, an unwritten page, and I was eager to pick up the pen, ready to craft the narrative of my heart. Together, we would embark on this journey, hand in hand, weaving the fabric of our lives into something breathtakingly beautiful, one design at a time.

Milton Keynes UK
Ingram Content Group UK Ltd.
UKHW041822201024
449814UK00001B/49